An Angel's Touch

STOLEN KISSES

Caitlan swallowed and found her voice. "What are you doing?"

"More like what are you doing in my bedroom?" J.T. countered in a low, husky voice. "A woman usually comes to a man's bed uninvited for one reason only. Are you looking to finish what we started this morning in the line shack?"

"No." She tried to move away, but his body was hard and solid as a rock. The hand that had so deftly grabbed her now secured her wrist at the side of her head. The other hand cupped the back of her head, his long fingers tangled in her hair, his thumb grazing the shell of her ear. She shivered.

Releasing her wrist, he picked up a strand of her hair and absently rubbed it between his fingers. "Then what are you doing in here?"

"I only wanted to check on you and make sure you were okay."

Slowly, he trailed a finger down her cheek, his gaze warm and sensual. He looked into her eyes, a lazy, sexy smile curving his mouth. "I want to kiss you while I'm wide awake. I want to see if you taste as good as in my dreams."

"No—"

"Yes. You came in here, Caitlan," he reminded her. "If you want to leave, it'll cost you." J.T. nuzzled her neck. "I think a kiss is just punishment for sneaking around like a thief in the night."

Heaven's Gift

JANELLE DENISON

LOVE SPELL ✦ NEW YORK CITY

LOVE SPELL®

October 1995

Published by

Dorchester Publishing Co., Inc.
276 Fifth Avenue
New York, NY 10001

Printed in the United States of America.

To Jamie Ann Denton, who was heaven-sent to keep me from giving up when the going gets tough. Thank you, friend, for everything.

To Laura Hardy and Pam Scheibe, for your support and encouragement; to Mica Kelch, for keeping me updated on all the latest gossip and for being such a great long-distance friend.

And, as always, to my husband and soul mate, Don, for your unending patience, support, and understanding. I love you.

Prologue

Amanda Hamilton slipped into the viewing room and smiled at her angel Superior. "I'm ready to be sent back to earth for my next mission, Mary."

"Good." Mary motioned Amanda to the viewing portal, which enabled the Superiors to observe occurrences on earth. "We seem to be short on guardian angels today, and of course nothing is going as planned. It seems He has made some adjustments in our schedule."

"Where will I go?" Amanda asked.

"You're to become a guardian angel to that little boy."

Before the crisp images could materialize in the portal, Christopher, another Superior, barged into the viewing room. "Excuse me,

Mary," he cut in breathlessly, "but an emergency has arisen."

Mary frowned at the interruption. "What is it, Christopher?"

"It's John Thomas Rafferty. His life is in jeopardy."

The familiar name caught Amanda's attention, and she listened to their conversation with sudden interest.

"J.T.? Oh, my, that does present a problem." Mary's delicate brows furrowed in dismay. "Things are progressing with him faster than we expected."

"Yes, and we need to get a guardian to him immediately. Look." With a wave of his hand, a scene appeared in the viewing portal.

A man sat atop his horse, working to extract a bulky pine tree blocking the flow of water down a creek. The rope running between the horn of the man's saddle and the trunk of the tree stretched taut. Grabbing the rope with gloved hands, he spoke a soft command to the horse, urging him forward. The horse snorted and labored against the heavy weight of the timber, dragging the tree parallel to the shore with the help of his rider. The rush of trapped water quickly filled the creek and surged toward the pasture.

Glancing toward the dismal sky, the man scowled at the gray, bloated clouds heading his way, a sure warning of an oncoming storm.

Amanda's breath caught in her throat as she glimpsed the face of her eternal soulmate. Mesmerized, she stepped closer to the portal, cataloguing Johnny's rough-hewn features beneath the brim of his hat. Before he returned his gaze to his chore, she caught the cold remoteness in his green eyes, a loneliness that made her ache for him.

She hadn't seen him in years—sixteen to be exact—but the rapid span of heavenly time made the tragic car accident that had claimed her life seem like only yesterday. He'd been a boy of nineteen then, working on his father's ranch, with the hard-edged promise of becoming a lean and muscular man. They'd been childhood sweethearts, deeply in love and so full of dreams and promises—until fate had interfered and sent her on to the next plateau to wait for him.

Sliding off the horse, he deftly untied the rope from the saddle, then made his way to the base of the tree, half hidden beneath the heavy underbrush lining the creek. Squatting, he loosened the knot he'd made around the trunk.

A gust of wind whipped the hat off his head, sending it tumbling across the meadow. He spared the battered Stetson a quick glance but didn't give chase. Instead, he flipped the collar of his wool coat up around his ears and continued with his task. The breeze tugged through his sable hair, rumpling it around his head.

Behind Johnny, a figure dressed in a large,

bulky jacket approached, his face obscured by the hood covering his head. He held a two-by-four in his left hand. At first Amanda thought he was there to help, until he raised the board and slammed it into the back of Johnny's skull with one savage strike.

Amanda sucked in a breath as Johnny crumpled to the ground, his head falling precariously close to the rapidly rising water in the creek. "Johnny!" she gasped, unable to keep the panic from her voice. She looked up at her Superiors. "What's going on?"

"Nothing for you to worry about," Mary assured her, placing a comforting hand on her shoulder. "Christopher, send Jay to protect J.T."

Christopher shifted on his feet. "That's the problem. Jay hasn't returned from his last mission yet."

"Then send Corey."

"He, too, is unavailable."

Mary sighed tiredly and rubbed her forehead. "And I suppose Tanner is indisposed as well?"

"Yes. We can always send Jeff, but you know how he tends to get on one's nerves with his knowledge of chemistry. He's hardly fit for this mission."

As her Superiors argued over who they should send, Amanda stepped closer to the portal, her heart thudding with uncharacteristic heaviness in her chest. She watched the unidentified man administer a sharp slap to the rump of the untethered horse with the board, spooking the animal into galloping away. Then he hoisted himself up on his own chestnut, and with a vicious kick to the horse's sides he bolted away.

The cruel man intended to leave Johnny, she realized—leave him to die in the sleet storm just beginning to break. Icy rain swirled in the wind and settled over his limp body, blanketing him in a deep chill that would eventually kill him, if the water from the creek didn't rise over his head and drown him first. A weak puff of condensation from his parted lips indicated the swift drop in temperature. His breathing slowed to an alarming, comatose state. The urgent need to save Johnny swelled within Amanda.

Making a split-second decision, she whirled to face her Superiors. "Send me."

They both stared at her incredulously. Then Mary smiled softly. "That's impossible."

"You know I'll protect him well."

"Amanda," Mary said slowly, "sending you to protect your childhood sweetheart, the man you're waiting to be joined with, is a conflict of interest."

Christopher leaned close to Mary and whispered out of the corner of his mouth, "We have no one else to send and this *is* an emergency."

Amanda knew Mary was right. She had no business meddling in her soulmate's life, but she couldn't help wanting to be with Johnny again, if only for a little while. She'd left her mortal life so suddenly, there had been no opportunity to say good-bye to him, and it would be years yet before they were joined again. The thought of being with him, touching him, overwhelmed her. "Please assign me this mission," she pleaded.

Mary's lips pursed in disapproval. "It's too risky," she said to Christopher. "J.T. is still deeply in love with Amanda. You know his soul and Amanda's are matched for eternity and that they will be reunited after he passes from earth." She gave him a pointed look. "He's not due to join us for another fifty-two years. If Amanda botched this mission because of her feelings for J.T., we'd have to answer to *our* Superior. I don't think He'd be too happy to find out we've broken the heavenly law."

"In this case I would think He'd understand," Christopher countered, exasperated. "J.T. Rafferty *must not* die, and without a guardian angel he will surely do just that, lying in freezing temperatures with a bleeding head wound and a concussion!"

Mary hesitated, glancing from J.T. to Amanda.

"We can suppress her memory of everything she knows of her past with him," Christopher suggested.

"I don't like this one bit. Suppressing her memory is too risky."

"We don't have a choice. We must act immediately, and Amanda is the only one available."

"Very well," Mary said on a reluctant sigh. "But

14

she must remember nothing about her past with J.T., only that she must protect him."

Amanda listened to her Superiors, holding back the urge to object to their plan to suppress her memory. The thought of the treasured memories she'd shared with J.T. being erased, even if only for a short time, alarmed her.

"It's only temporary, Amanda, until the mission is complete," Mary said, as if reading her thoughts. "Come here so we can block your memory and properly equip you for this assignment."

Amanda took a deep breath, reassuring herself that even without the recollection of her time on earth with J.T., in her heart she would always love him. He was, after all, her soulmate.

Obeying her Superior, she stood in front of Mary and closed her eyes.

The heavy weight of Mary's hand settled on her shoulder and her body tingled from head to toe, as she was supplied with the background and identity of Caitlan Daniels for her new mission.

"Hurry along," Mary said after the moment had passed. "J.T. doesn't have much time. Oh, and here is your medallion." She produced a gold chain with a shiny gold piece attached and dropped it onto Caitlan's palm. "Use it sparingly. Only in dire emergencies. You know the rules."

Caitlan nodded and slipped the chain around her neck, the warmth of the medallion nestling

Janelle Denison

just above her breasts. In the next instant she was gone.

Mary looked at Christopher. "I hope we don't come to regret this decision."

"We really had no choice."

"What if she remembers him?"

Christopher gave Mary a confident look. "As long as she wears the medallion her memory will be protected. She knows better than to take off the medallion."

Mary nodded but wasn't totally convinced. A second later she let out a soft gasp, her eyes widening. "Oh, my goodness. We forgot to tell her who is trying to harm J.T.!"

Christopher smiled. "She's a smart angel. She'll figure it out."

Chapter One

"Can I take this silly blindfold off yet?"

"In a minute." Grinning at Amanda's impatience, J.T. Rafferty guided her into the line shack situated on the west end of his father's ranch property, three miles from the Circle R's main house. Wanting complete privacy for this once-in-a-lifetime occasion, he'd waited until he knew for certain the ranch hands had retired for the evening before bringing Amanda here.

She fidgeted anxiously on her sandaled feet and pleated her fingers in the pink dress she wore. Pearl buttons down the bodice added a simple elegance to the plain country dress. "Where are we, Johnny?"

"Hold your horses, Mandy," he drawled, lighting

17

the oil lamp by the door. Leaving her for a moment, he walked to the scarred wooden table in the middle of the small room. Holding back a chuckle at the sight of the lopsided birthday cake he'd conned his sister into making for him, he set it in the center of the table. "I know the ride out was bumpy, and this place is musty, but it'll be worth it."

"You're worth anything I have to endure," she said softly.

God, he loved her, he thought, glancing over his shoulder. His chest expanded with a sense of awe. Beautiful, spirited Amanda Hamilton was all his. From her crown of long glorious blond hair to the tips of her pink-painted toenails. From the dimple in her right cheek to the birthmark behind her left knee.

He stared at the delicate features of her face, her soft skin, and those full lips he loved to kiss. Desire stirred within him, warming his blood, and he returned his attention to the cake before he forgot the real purpose for bringing her here. Striking a match, he lit all eighteen candles, casting a soft glow about the cabin.

Stepping behind her, he slipped off the blindfold. "Happy birthday, Amanda," he whispered into her ear.

Unable to miss the blazing cake on the table, she let out a sentimental sigh. "Oh, Johnny, this is so sweet."

Turning her in his arms, he swept his hands down her back to rest at the base of her spine. "I wanted tonight to be special."

Her deep blue eyes sparkled with adoration, and a sweet smile brushed her mouth. "It is. I have you."

He grinned. "That you do." After dropping a light kiss on her lips, he ushered her toward the table. "Make a wish, sweetheart."

She laughed, the sound light and melodious. "What do I have to wish for when I have everything I could ever want?"

Not yet, but soon, he thought. "I'm sure you can think of something."

She closed her eyes, a frown of concentration creasing her brow. A moment later a brilliant smile lit her face, dimpling her cheek. She released a deep breath of air, her lashes fluttering open. The candles sputtered and went out. "I hope my wish comes true."

"I hope so too." He placed a small square velvet box in her palm. "This is for you, Amanda. May all your dreams come true."

She looked up at him, her gaze curious.

"Go on," he urged, wishing he could calm the anxiety clenching his belly. What if this wasn't what Amanda wanted?

His heart thundered in anticipation as tentatively she opened the box and peeked inside. A diamond engagement ring, nestled within the folds of black satin, winked up at her. Her breath caught and she glanced at him, her eyes shimmering. "It's beautiful," she breathed.

Bending on one knee, he grasped her left hand. Taking the modest ring from the box and bringing it to her finger, he met her bluer-than-blue gaze and asked, "Will you marry me, Amanda Hamilton?"

Her hand trembled in his. "Are you sure?" she whispered.

"Absolutely." He knew what she was asking. They were young, had never dated anyone except each other. Lately his friends had been badgering him to break things off with Amanda so he could sow his oats before he shackled himself to just one woman. But J.T. didn't want anyone but Amanda.

"You've always been mine, Amanda, ever since you were seven and fell into the creek and I saved you from drowning."

She smiled at the memory, but he still saw the doubts lingering in her eyes. "Your cousin Randal told me you weren't ready to settle down yet."

Anger gripped him in a cold, hard fist. He hated that the rivalry between himself and Randal had touched Amanda. "He lied, Mandy. I want my future with you," he continued, his hold on her hand tightening. "I'm not rich, you know that, but Dad gave me a raise, so you won't have to get a job. We can live at the ranch house until we can afford a place of our own. I want babies with you, and the whole works. Amanda, please," he implored. "I love you."

She touched the tips of her fingers to his jaw and slowly nodded. "Yes, John Thomas Rafferty, I'll marry you. I've loved you forever. . . . "

His body shuddered with relief and he secured the ring on her left hand before she could change her mind. Standing, he dropped his mouth over hers, officially sealing their engagement with a deep kiss that quickly turned hot and urgent.

Lips fused, tongues mating, his hands sought the curves of her waist and hips, then moved upward, cupping the weight of her breasts. Moaning softly, she moved closer, pressing her petite form to his tall, muscular frame. The top of her head barely reached his shoulder, but what she lacked in height she more than made up for in feminine contours. And his mouth and hands knew every one of them intimately, knew just how to touch and caress her to make her melt in his arms.

J.T. grew hard against her belly, his body tingling in a familiar way that told him he wasn't far from losing his sanity and embarrassing himself. Tearing his mouth from hers, he drew in a steadying breath. "Amanda, we have to stop."

She gave him a seductive smile that did nothing to ease his predicament. "No, Johnny."

Gritting his teeth, he caught the hand skimming down his chest to the leather belt cinching his waist. "I don't know if I'll be able to hold back tonight."

"What if I don't want you to?"

He stared at her, smoothing the silky strands of hair away from her face with his free hand. Her words inflamed and aroused him; the sultry look in her eyes caused havoc with his libido. They'd fondled and petted and knew every creative approach to foreplay, but they'd never made love.

They were both virgins.

He swallowed the thickness gathering in his throat. "Mandy, we've both waited so long. Are you sure?"

She nodded, and with a shy innocence more provocative than that of a more experienced woman, she slowly slipped the pearl buttons on her bodice through their holes. Fascinated, he watched the ever-widening gap of material reveal a cotton bra and the smooth, apricot-hued flesh of her stomach. Blood surged to his groin, straining his arousal against the fly of his jeans.

"Amanda—"

"If I'm going to marry you, there's no reason why we can't make love now," she said, her voice husky. "I've wanted you for so long. I want more than caresses and kisses." Giving her shoulders a delicate shrug, the dress slipped down her arms, over her hips, and down her legs to pool at her feet. She unhooked her bra and added it to the pile. She stood before him in nothing more than wispy panties and the moonlight from the window streaming across her skin. "I want to feel you inside me. Please, Johnny."

His mouth went dry as dust and a shudder ran the length of his body. Any good intentions he might have had to discourage her from this seduction vanished, along with his self-control. He'd seen her naked before, but the perfection of her lithe and supple body, the fullness of her breasts, the gentle flare of her hips, and the shadowed secrets between her thighs, never ceased to take his breath away.

Lifting her into his arms, he carried her to the twin bed in the corner of the shack. He took off her sandals and removed her panties. She reached for the buttons on his shirt, but he pushed her hands away, too impatient to feel skin against skin, softness against hardness, to let her help. A minute later he was as naked as she, and so powerfully aroused, he thought he'd burst before he had the luxury of being sheathed inside her.

He didn't want to hurt her, and even though his body demanded he ease his smoldering need, he took the time to prime her for his entry. Pushing her to the absolute brink of pleasure, he widened her thighs and settled his hips in that natural cove. He met immediate resistance, a blunt pressure, and she gasped, her fingers gripping his arms. Through the hazy fog enveloping his mind and the thundering pulse in his veins, he managed to murmur, "Sorry."

He shook with the effort to go slow and be gentle. Then male instinct took over and he thrust forward, pushing deeper and deeper inside her, until he passed that maiden barrier.

She arched against him and cried out, a sharp sound of pain and uncertainty. He groaned, awed by the incredible feeling of finally being one with her, of taking her innocence and giving her his in return. She was tight and hot, and as he slipped even deeper, she melted around him like liquid satin. As his hips began a slow rhythm, he watched her pained expression change to wonder, heard that soft, sweet moan that told him she was close, so close. The wave of tiny tremors tensing the muscles deep inside her triggered his release.

Sensations unlike any he'd ever experienced closed in on him: tingles, tremors, a building, roaring heaviness, and most pronounced was the desperate need to bind her to him forever. If he let go, if he succumbed to the pleasure whispering to his senses, he would lose her. . . .

No!

The screeching sound of steel grinding into steel echoed in his head. Shattering glass. Shrill, agonizing screams that ripped into his soul. Then spine-chilling, absolute silence that would haunt him for the rest of his life.

"Amanda," J.T. groaned. She started to slip away and he tightened his hold. A crushing emptiness enveloped him, a loneliness so bleak he couldn't breath. *Please don't leave me, Amanda. Please!*

"Hey, wake up," a soft, feminine voice called.

She wiggled beneath him, soft and pliant, a vague reassurance that Amanda was still with him. He cupped a breast in his palm, confused by the feel of soft cotton and the restraint of a bra. She squirmed a little more, her jeans-clad legs tangling with his. In a fragmented part of his mind he realized she was fully clothed. How could that be when she'd just undressed for him?

"Amanda," he murmured, valiantly trying to pull himself from the murky depths of sleep.

"Wake up!"

Something hard shoved against his chest, and he grunted as a shaft of pain ricocheted in his skull. Groggy and slightly disoriented, he managed to open his eyes to mere slits. Blue eyes, so dark and velvety they reminded him of lush violets, met his. He smiled lazily. "Amanda," he whispered, relieved that her dying had been a bad, awful dream. Lowering his head, he pressed his damp open mouth to the warm skin of her neck. "Amanda."

"I'm not Amanda," the woman beneath him said, struggling to push his weight off her. "Please, you're crushing me."

Frowning, he forced the thick cobwebs from his mind and pulled back enough to get a clear look at the woman. The sunshine streaming through the window sharpened his blurry vision, and he found himself staring not at his blue-eyed, blond-haired Amanda in the throes of passion, but a blue-eyed, brunette stranger determined to fend off his advances.

"What the hell?" Lightning quick, he rolled off her, and the bed, to his bare feet. A sharp, brutal pain lanced through his head, and for a moment the room dipped and whirled. He sucked in a harsh breath.

Grabbing the back of the chair by the bed, he regained his balance and focused on the woman he'd left sprawled on the bed. She looked embarrassed and flustered by their encounter. Disheveled, chin-length, glossy brown hair rumpled around a face set with delicate features, and a slight flush painted her cheeks a rosy hue. Her lips were damp and a little bit swollen. He couldn't deny that he'd kissed her; he still had the honeyed taste of her in his mouth.

He closed his eyes and swore. For the sweetest moment he'd believed Amanda was still alive, that a drunk driver had never hit them head on, killing her, when he'd driven her home that night after they'd made love. It had been so long since he'd dreamed of her, and everything had seemed so real.

"Are you okay?" came the woman's worried voice.

He looked at her and suddenly realized he was completely naked and painfully aroused from his dream—and from having her pressed beneath him. Swearing again, he snatched the pillow from the bed and covered himself.

A half smile of amusement brushed her lips as she sat up and swung her legs off the side of the mattress. Self-consciously, she straightened her flannel shirt and ran her fingers through her hair. "No need to get modest on me. I saw everything there was to see last night."

"No kidding?" J.T. searched his mind for a

memory, anything to explain why he was in the ranch's line shack with a woman he didn't know and a splitting headache threatening to explode his brain. He didn't drink, so he knew he didn't have a hangover. And he didn't pick up strange women. And even if he did, he wouldn't bring them to a one-room shack, the only accommodations being a twin bed, a woodstove, a table, and a few blankets and rations.

Whos, whats, and whys tumbled through his head faster than he could log them. He settled for the most basic question. "What's going on?"

Standing, she walked past him to the wood stove and added a few more logs to the fire. "You don't remember what happened?" She placed a metal coffeepot over a burner.

Another wave of dizziness assaulted him and he sat back down on the bed before he toppled over. Keeping the pillow strategically in his lap, he rubbed his aching forehead and replied with a bit of sarcasm, "Sweetheart, you can bet if I remembered bringing you here you'd be as naked as I am. I don't remember a damn thing."

She turned around, her brow furrowed with distress. "I hope you aren't suffering from amnesia."

"Amnesia?" He watched her approach, his gaze drawn to the subtle sway of her hips in form-fitting blue jeans. Lifting his eyes to her face, he suppressed the stirring of awareness and the sense of familiarity nudging him. "I know who *I* am; I just don't know who the hell *you* are and what you were doing pinned beneath me on the bed, fully clothed and obviously struggling to get away."

"I'm Caitlan Daniels." She knelt in front of him and pressed a palm to his forehead, her voice soft. "I think your fever is gone."

"Depends on what kind of fever you're referring to," he replied irritably, pushing her hand away. The care and tenderness in her touch unnerved him, aroused him even. He found he wanted to kiss those full lips of hers again, a dangerous thought. "What about the part of you and me on the bed?"

She sat back on her heels. Another sweep of dusky rose stained her cheeks, as if she was remembering in detail his attempt at seduction. "You were tossing in your sleep; a bad dream, I suppose," she said in a voice gone a little husky. "You were calling for Amanda. Is she your wife?"

"I'm not married," he said flatly. "Go on."

She shrugged. "You were thrashing around. I tried to wake you, and you pulled me down on the bed. You were . . . very determined. Must have been some dream."

"Yeah, one I wish I'd never wake up from." He shivered from the frigid draft in the room—or was it the memory of that fateful night when he'd lost Amanda that had shaken him so?

Leaning toward him, she grabbed the wool blanket from the bed and settled it over his wide shoulders. The smell of fresh, rain-scented skin curled around him like some kind of narcotic, a natural, feminine fragrance that enticed him more than any expensive perfume might have.

"Well, I'm glad you did wake up," she said, fussing over him. "You've been out cold for about fifteen hours and I need to check that nasty bump on your head."

"Bump?" His eyes narrowed. "Why do I feel like Alice in Wonderland? Absolutely nothing is making any sense." Plowing his fingers through his hair, he found a huge knot on the back of his head. He winced and cursed as a dull ache throbbed in his temples.

Images flashed before him. The blocked water in the creek. Pulling the tree to the shore. Untying the rope from the trunk. Realizing the tree had been cut deliberately. Sleet, rain, cold numbing wind. Then a loud thud, a fierce paralyzing jolt, and blackness.

Apprehension coiled in his belly. "I'm starting to remember. Someone knocked me out," he said slowly, suspiciously. "You wouldn't have anything to do with that, would you?"

"Of course not!" she said, her chin rising indignantly.

His gut instinct told him she was innocent of the crime. "I believe you, but that doesn't explain how we both came to be holed up in this line shack."

She didn't reply. Averting her gaze, she adjusted the blanket around his legs. Her slim, warm fingers brushed over his knee, and a startling heat spread up his thigh, pooling in a place that didn't need any more encouragement.

He drew in a deep breath and caught her busy hands. "Excuse me," he said tightly, "but I feel at a distinct disadvantage here. Why don't I have any clothes on?"

She looked from her bound wrists to his face, and he could have sworn her pulse quickened beneath his fingers. Her expression, however, betrayed nothing. "I had to take them off you. You were soaking wet and freezing when I found you, and I didn't want hypothermia to set in."

"*You* found *me?*"

"Yes."

"This scenario is getting more intriguing by the second." Letting go of her, he rubbed his palm over the stubble on his jaw. The prickly beard confirmed that a night had passed without him realizing it. "Why don't I put some clothes on and we can discuss everything from the beginning? I'm grateful *you* found *me,* but I have to admit I'm a little curious what you were doing trespassing on private property that's at least fifteen miles from the main road. You mind getting me my jeans and shirt, please?"

Standing, she cast a glance at the table, where she'd spread out his clothes. "They're still damp."

His gaze skipped down the length of her, taking in her neat and tidy long-sleeved shirt and crisp, very dry jeans. Her boots looked brand spankin' new. If his clothes hadn't dried in the time they'd been in the shack, hers should be at least a little soggy, he thought. "Why are you nice and dry?"

She shifted on her feet. "I had a jacket on."

"So did I." He nodded to where the jacket hung on a hook by the door. "By the looks of it, it's still pretty soaked." She opened her mouth to reply, but he held up a hand to cut her off. "No, don't tell me; you had an umbrella with you, right? You were wearing a wide-brimmed hat? Your clothes are waterproof?" His tone was sardonic.

Her lips were pursed, and sparks of annoyance brightened her eyes. Too bad. He wanted to know exactly what was going on. Something didn't add up.

She turned away to check the percolating coffee, and when she glanced back at him a moment later his heart stopped for a fraction of a second. Her dark violet-blue eyes hit him like a bolt of lightning, sending a rush of memories of another woman tumbling through him. Her eyes beckoned to him. . . .

He scrubbed an agitated hand down his face. *Get a grip, man! That dream about Amanda is putting silly notions in your head—or the whack to your skull has made you a little crazy!*

"I saw an extra set of workclothes in that cupboard," she offered, and started toward a floor-to-ceiling pantry about three feet wide, stocked with a variety of staples and basic necessities to survive a few weeks secluded in the shack.

He removed the pillow from his lap but kept the blanket around him. "Yeah, for emergencies like this."

She stood on the toes of her boots and grabbed the neatly folded clothes on a high shelf. "Let's hope they fit."

"They should. They're mine." He watched her inventory a pair of jeans, a flannel shirt, socks, and briefs. "I put the extra clothes there a few years ago after getting caught in a rain storm and didn't have anything to change into. It gets damn cold in here soaking wet. That woodstove is pretty useless when it comes to heating anything beyond the table."

She arched a brow, approaching with strident steps that echoed off the floorboards. "Ah, so this isn't the first time you've been in this predicament."

"As a matter of fact, it is." He met her gaze. Very softly, with an undercurrent of challenge, he said, "I've never been rescued by a woman who seemingly appeared out of thin air."

A private smile touching her lips, she placed the clothes on the bed next to him. "I suppose an unexpected sleet storm in the middle of a beautiful spring day is a normal occurrence in Idaho?"

He sighed at her attempt to keep the conversation steered away from important questions.

"Yes, especially up against the mountains. You're not from around here, then?"

She shook her head and looked away, but not before he caught a glimpse of mystery in her eyes. "Go ahead and get dressed and I'll pour you some coffee and make you something to eat."

He wanted the answers she was avoiding but figured he'd at least have an upper hand in the interrogation if he had some clothes on. He straightened to his full height slowly, careful to keep from aggravating his head. The blanket dropped to the floor and cool air brushed over his skin. The muscles across his belly and chest tensed in response to the shocking caress.

"Don't turn around," he warned, reaching for his briefs, "unless you care to get another eyeful."

"No, thanks."

While J.T. changed Caitlan fetched a can of stew from the pantry, casting a surreptitious glance his way, even though she'd just declined his invitation to look. She wanted to make sure he was okay, *really* okay, and could dress himself on his own. Reassured that he seemed to be steady on his feet, she told herself to get back to preparing his meal, but a strange feminine instinct kept her gaze riveted to his backside.

She caught a glimpse of firm, muscled buttocks before he pulled on his briefs, and a feathery warmth settled in her stomach. True, last night she'd seen every bare inch of him, but she'd been too concerned about his health to truly appreciate the magnificence of his body. In the light of day, with the late-morning sun streaming through the only window in the shack, his nudity took on a different perspective. He was power-fully built, the muscles across his shoulders, down his back, and in his legs honed to athletic perfection. He picked up his shirt and pushed his arms through the sleeves, and she finally forced her attention back to her task.

Grabbing the stew, a can of peaches, and a manual can opener, she set the items on the table and began opening the cans. She didn't normally respond to mortals so strongly—her emotions were calculated and doled out in accordance to the given situation—but from the first moment she'd landed on earth and rescued him, she'd felt an odd connection to him that perplexed her. Ig-noring the feeling for more pressing matters, she'd quickly transported him to the line shack with the help of Christopher's powers and had begun the process to save his life, starting with healing his massive head injury, then warming him and keeping his body from slipping into a dangerous state of shock.

However, with the crises over and him awake, she noticed things about him that had nothing whatsoever to do with her mission, a curiosity she was certain her Superiors wouldn't encour-age. And when he'd kissed her and touched her and called her another woman's name she'd felt a surreal harmony with this man that transcended anything in her station as a guardian angel.

Retrieving two metal cups and plates from the pantry, she sneaked another peek at him. He was sitting on the bed, head bent, as he pulled wool socks on his feet. His sable hair was a tousled mess from rain, wind, and general abuse from his hands. Dark stubble shadowed his jaw. The disheveled, morning-after look only made him appear more masculine and sexy.

He was a pleasant enough assignment, she mused, dishing out the peaches and stew onto their plates. But a part of her feared the forces of evil she was up against would be hard to dissuade, not to mention making J.T. believe the outrageous excuses the Superiors had seen fit to give her for this mission. She had the medallion for assistance, but as a guardian angel her powers were limited, to be used only in extreme situations. As a rule, she didn't contact the Superiors unless an emergency occurred.

She poured the steaming coffee into each of their tin cups. "Lunch is ready. It's nothing fancy, but you need to eat something to keep up your strength."

He sauntered toward the table, dragging the bedside chair with him. His stomach grumbled. "It looks like a feast to me," he commented, seating himself in front of a plate heaped with food.

She pushed aside the damp clothes on the table to make more room for them. "You must have gotten knocked harder on the head than I thought."

"No. Considering I haven't eaten since . . ." He frowned as he thought about it, "I guess it would be breakfast yesterday morning, I'm hungry enough to devour a whole cow."

"It's a good sign that you have a healthy appetite."

He nodded, observing her intently as she sat in the chair across from him. "I'm sorry for what happened earlier, Caitlan."

The way he said her name, his voice warm and husky, made her fully, femininely aware of him. "It's okay."

He slowly ran his index finger around the rim of his cup. "I didn't mean to get rough with you on the bed. I obviously didn't know what I was doing."

She lowered her lashes and stabbed a wedge of peach with her fork, trying to forget the warm, silky feelings he'd evoked in her when she'd been pinned beneath his lean body. Reminding herself that he'd thought her another woman in his delirious state, she replied, "I understand, really."

"Weren't you afraid of what I might do to you?"

"You were dreaming," she said, distinctly uneasy with his bold speculation.

He leaned toward her, his green-gold gaze lowering to her mouth as her lips closed around the peach on her fork. "Still, I could have made love to you."

She nearly choked on the fruit. Images of his hands sliding over her body sent a frisson of heat spiraling to her belly. Good Lord, what was wrong with her that she was entertaining such shameless thoughts about this man? Shifting in her chair, she forced the peach down her throat with a deliberate swallow. She concentrated on her food, clearing her plate in record time. Standing, she took her plate and utensils to a bucket of soapy water she'd filled earlier with some bottled water.

She washed and rinsed her dishes, then began drying them with a terry towel. She turned to him with every intention of getting back to business. "I think I should check your head injury."

"I'm fine." He ate the last of his stew and pushed his plate away.

"You can't even see it," she reasoned, cleaning up his dishes as well.

He reached for the coffeepot she'd set on the table and poured himself another cup, then filled hers too. "I can *feel* it, and even though it hurts like the devil, it doesn't appear to be an open wound."

That's because I mended the deep laceration, she thought. Wiping her hands on the towel, she circled the table to stand next to him. "You just sit there and drink your coffee. It'll only take a minute to check it."

"Who appointed you my guardian?" he growled, batting her hands away from the back of his head. "I'm a grown man—"

"With a thick head?" she interrupted, jamming her hands on her hips and giving him a fierce look.

He had the grace to look a little contrite for his impolite behavior. "Yeah, that's probably why the blow didn't split my head wide open."

Her lips tightened in disgust. "Yes, well, someone definitely wanted to do away with you." But who had been the culprit? she wondered with a little frown. Moving closer, she wove her fingers gently through his hair, searching for the site of his injury.

"How do you know?" He took a swallow of coffee, then balanced the cup on his thigh.

"What? That someone wanted to kill you?" she asked, luxuriating in the velvety feel of his hair sifting over her hand.

"Yes." He finished off his coffee and put the cup on the table. "A bullet would have been more effective."

"You're right, of course," she countered, trying to concentrate on her task and not the peculiar sensations swirling deep inside her. "But what if someone wanted this to look like an accident?"

"I would have come around eventually."

She pulled away to look into his eyes, remembering how close to dying he'd been when she'd reached him. Without the aid of her Superiors, he wouldn't be sitting in front of her, looking so strong and healthy. "It wasn't likely you would have 'come around.' Not only were you unconscious from the blow, and your body freezing, but your head was near the creek. By the time I found you the water had risen to your forehead."

The implications of her statement registered in his eyes, then was replaced by something more watchful and searching. "Which brings me around to an intriguing question I'd like answered," he said, his gaze laser-intense. "How, exactly, did you stumble upon me? I hate to be skeptical, but I don't believe in miracles."

Chapter Two

J.T. crossed his arms over his chest and waited for Caitlan's answer. After a hesitant second she broke eye contact and once again resumed checking the bump on his head. Except this time her fingers worked tensely, pressing over his skull without the gentleness she'd used before.

"You remember the sleet storm, right?" she asked.

"Yeah. I got hit in the head just as the sky split wide open." Her fingers probed an especially sensitive area and he winced and sucked in a harsh breath. "Hey, watch it!"

"Sorry," she mumbled, and continued on with a bit more care. "I was on my horse, Daisy, when I saw your body by the creek."

"Whoa, back up," he interrupted. "How about telling me where you came from and what you were doing trespassing on private property?"

"Turn your head toward me just a bit, would you please?"

As a stall tactic, he had to admit her approach was original and quite effective. He turned his head slightly and found himself eye level with her breasts. He tried focusing on the nondescript material of her shirt, but his gaze kept straying to the collar, where the first three buttons were undone, granting him a more enticing view of creamy flesh and wisps of satin and lace.

She shifted from one foot to the other. A gold pendant nestled between her breasts caught his attention. The piece of gold looked ancient, with a swirled design that was neither unique nor spectacular, yet he had the strangest urge to reach out and touch the medallion.

Troubled by the lure of something so insignificant, he frowned and averted his gaze back to the slope of her breast, which only served to prompt fantasies in which he had no right to indulge. He closed his eyes, a low moan escaping him. Hell, what was it about this woman that made him want her so badly?

"I'm sorry," she said, obviously misinterpreting his aches and pains. "I wish we had some ice for your head. It sure would help ease the pain and take down the swelling."

"You're absolutely right," he said through

41

clenched teeth. Except he needed the ice in his lap, not on his head! "Stop trying to distract me and quit avoiding my questions," he growled, turning his head forward once again.

"I'm not," she replied, her fingers still touching and exploring.

"You are."

"Don't be such a grouch. I'm only concerned about you."

"Leave me alone. There's nothing you can do about my head anyway." She ignored him and pressed the swollen perimeter of his bump. Brilliant sparks of pain exploded in his head. He grimaced. "Dammit, Caitlan! Enough!" Grabbing her wrists, he jerked her away, pinning her with a scowl he hoped she'd interpret as intimidating. "Sit down."

Any woman with lick of sense would have heeded his tone and expression and done as he ordered, but she only tossed him an indulgent look that made him feel like a small boy. "Are you always this bossy?"

"I *am* the boss."

"Of this ranch?"

"Yes." He let go of her hands, enjoying too much the feel of her soft, warm skin and wanting even more to pull her onto his lap and kiss some compliance into her. A long, deep, lazy kiss ought to do the trick, he thought, then immediately chastised himself for entertaining the notion. He didn't want involvements and entanglements with this woman, or any woman, for that matter. The tragic loss of Amanda and a bitter, loveless marriage had taught him that he had no emotion left to give. As soon as they arrived at his ranch house, she'd be back on her way to wherever she'd come from, and that's exactly how he wanted things.

She rubbed her wrists, as if branded by his touch. He saw the awareness in her eyes, a hint of confusion, and knew she felt the same sizzle of attraction he did. Looking away, she walked to the other side of the table and sat down in her chair.

"I don't even know your name," she said softly.

"J.T. Rafferty, and you're doing it again," he said, unable to keep his exasperation from his voice.

"I'm just curious about you," came her innocent reply.

"Then we have something in common, because I'm more than a little curious about you. Answer my question, Caitlan."

"Which was?"

A broken laugh escaped him, a cross between irritation and mild amusement. He rubbed the taut muscles at the back of his neck and sighed. If any other woman had dared to provoke him like this, he would have been gruff and demanding in response. He didn't want to analyze his reaction to Caitlan too deeply, and instead strove for a stern tone of voice. "You're trying my patience, Caitlan Daniels. Listen up: Where did you come from and what were you doing trespassing on private property?"

She hesitated for a moment, as if thinking up a plausible excuse. "I'm a guest at Parson's Dude Ranch," she began, folding her hands primly on the table before her. "It was an absolutely gorgeous day yesterday. At least in the morning it was sunny and pleasant." The direct look she gave him made him feel as though the temperamental change in weather had been his fault. "I was out on a trail ride doing a little sightseeing on my own, except I have a lousy sense of direction. I got lost." She cast a dubious look heavenward and gave a slight shake of her head, as if even *she* couldn't quite believe her tale.

He had his doubts as well. "Parson's Dude Ranch is well over eight miles away, most of which is rugged terrain."

She shrugged delicately. "See how lousy my sense of direction is? I *thought* I was headed back *toward* the dude ranch."

Her story had a loophole, and he zeroed in on it. There was only one way to and from Parson's that separated the dude ranch's property from Rafferty land. "Didn't you wonder where you were going when you crossed the bridge over the American River?"

"I wanted to explore the other side of the river." An impish expression etched her features, and he found himself totally charmed by the mischief sparkling in her eyes. "I never thought I wouldn't be able to find my way back. How can you miss a body of water as big as the American River?"

"*You* obviously did."

Her spine straightened defensively. "If it wasn't for the sleet storm, I would have found it again eventually."

"Sure." He settled back as comfortably as the unyielding wooden chair would allow. Stretching his legs out under the table, he laced his fingers over his stomach. "Go on, please," he said in a lazy drawl.

"I started to panic when the storm rolled in. When I found the creek I followed it, hoping it would lead back to the river, a main road, or another ranch."

"Creeks don't necessarily lead to roads or ranches, and they can take miles to reach the river, depending on which direction you're heading."

"Well, excuse my ignorance," she said haughtily. "I didn't know what else to do."

Feeling appropriately reproved for making light of a situation that could have been perilous, he murmured, "I'm sorry." He could well imagine her fear of being stranded in a strange place and softened a bit. After all, she wasn't here in his line shack of her own choice, and she *had* saved his life.

Seemingly satisfied with his apology, she continued. "I was following the creek when a bolt of

45

lightning struck nearby. Daisy didn't take too well to the thunder and lightning and took off like a bat out of—" She stopped abruptly, her cheeks pinkening.

"Hell?" he supplied, holding back a chuckle at her chagrin over a simple swear word.

"Uh, yeah, I guess that's the term." She cleared her throat and fiddled with a napkin on the table. "Anyway, I shouldn't have asked for such a spirited horse. I could barely control her. We passed this shack, and when I tried to stop her she just got more skittish. By the time I got her back under control, we were only feet away from where you lay by the creek. I jumped off Daisy to see if you were still alive and she took off before I could tether her to a tree."

He stared at her for the longest time, past those deep blue eyes and beyond. Finally, he shook his head. "That's the damnedest story I think I've ever heard. It's so unbelievable, I actually believe it."

"It's what happened," she said, brushing a swath of hair from her cheek, the movement artless and feminine. "How else would I have found you?"

"Hell if I know." Leaning forward, he braced his forearms on the table. His humor fled when he thought of another important fact. "If I was unconscious when you found me, how did you manage to get me to the shack?"

"I dragged you," she replied without missing a

beat, then gave another one of those heavenward glances he would have found endearing if her answer hadn't been so preposterous.

His eyes narrowed perceptively. "You couldn't even push me off you when we were on the bed and you expect me to believe you *dragged* me over a hundred yards?"

"You're here, aren't you?" she shot back.

"I guess I am." If she was lying, J.T. decided she had it down to a science. He searched her gaze, seeing nothing but a delicate pureness that reached deep into his soul and tugged. Startled by the warmth unfurling in him, he glanced away.

Her chair scraped against the wood floor as she scooted back and stood. "I'm sure you've heard that people do incredible things when they find themselves in a panicked situation. Adrenaline and all that," she said, gesturing with her hands.

"Yeah, adrenaline," he agreed, suddenly tired of doubting her every word. What other explanation could there be? And if she meant him harm, she'd had plenty of opportunity to do so while he'd been unconscious. As outrageous as her story sounded, everything she'd told him was possible.

Rubbing a hand over his jaw, he watched her flit about the shack. She put away their dishes and washed up the coffee pot, then stored everything where she'd found it in the pantry. She worked quickly, efficiently, and he marveled at how at home she seemed with none of the normal everyday conveniences one usually takes for granted.

"Let me help," he offered, pushing back his own chair. Before he could stand she shook her head and sent him an adamant look.

"Absolutely not." Folding the blanket on the bed, she set it at the foot of the mattress. "You sit and relax. I'll take care of this. You need to save your strength."

He didn't like feeling like an invalid. "I'm fi—"

A firm hand on his shoulder pushed him back into his seat. "Stay put." Her tone rivaled a drill sergeant's.

He resisted the urge to click his heels, salute her, and say, "Yes, sir." "Are you always so bossy?" he asked, repeating her earlier question to him.

"Only when I'm in charge," she replied over her shoulder.

She bent over to dig something out of a tin can in the pantry, and his gaze slid over her bottom, admiring and appreciating her curves. "I'm not going to win this one, am I?"

"Nope. Have a snack and relax." Turning, she tossed him a sealed package of dried apricots, and he caught the bag.

Using his teeth, he tore open a corner of the plastic bag. Pinching a dried apricot between his fingers, he examined the shriveled piece of fruit for a second before deeming it edible. "Relaxing isn't one of my strong suits."

Caitlan picked up the damp pair of jeans draped on the far side of the table and shook them out before folding the denim into a tidy square. "You might want to get used to it, at least for a few days. You really should give your head, and your body, time to recuperate from your accident." She added a folded shirt to his pile of soggy clothes.

He looked up, intending to tell her he wasn't about to sit around for a couple of days. Even the nastiest of flus couldn't keep him down, and he wouldn't let this mishap keep him from overseeing the ranch and cattle, either. Especially if someone was bent on sabotaging his livelihood.

Ultimately, he popped another apricot into his mouth and kept his protest to himself. He didn't owe this woman an explanation, and he didn't need her permission to do anything. As protective and concerned as she seemed to be, he considered himself lucky she'd be gone once they reached the ranch house.

"I'm surprised no one has found us by now," he commented, reaching for his cowboy boots, sitting under the table. "My horse should have wandered back to the ranch without a rider. Unless whoever hit me over the head killed Quinn, he should have gotten there last night, which should've alerted someone that I'm out in the pasture alone." He glanced out the window, trying to gauge the hour. "How long ago did it stop raining?"

"Sometime last night."

He watched her with his briefs, her fingers tucking and creasing the cotton easily, as if she'd been folding his underwear for years. The intimacy of the simple task started a slow burn in his veins and made him too aware of how her hands might have felt against his flesh as she'd stripped those same briefs off him last night.

Jamming his right foot into his boot, he scowled in disgust as a cold dampness seeped into his thick sock. Since he lacked an extra pair of boots in the shack, and he didn't relish walking the three miles back to the ranch house in bare feet, he put the other boot on and arranged his jeans over the tops.

"What time is it anyway?" he asked, realizing his watch was no longer strapped to his wrist. "And what did you do with my watch?"

"It's right here." She glanced at the timepiece before handing it to him. "Ten A.M. Your watch, at least, *is* waterproof," she said, an unrestrained grin canting the corners of her mouth.

"I don't think—" J.T.'s hand froze as he reached for his watch, and his heart stopped midbeat. Every thought flew from his head and the room seemed to shrink as he stared at the dimple creasing Caitlan's right cheek, a single dimple identical to the one Amanda had when she grinned. The same violet-blue eyes, the same dimple . . .

Sweet, haunting memories crowded in on him, suffocating him with their poignancy. Then, like a cloud of smoke, the recollections dispersed, and it was Caitlan he wanted to touch, Caitlan's feminine scent that wrapped around him, seducing him, tempting him, making him long for something that was just beyond his grasp and always would be.

He squeezed his eyes shut, hating the vulnerable way he felt, despising even more that this woman made him remember and feel things he thought he'd permanently locked away. Dammit, *why her?*

"J.T., are you okay?"

She placed a caring hand on his arm, and he flinched as her fingers seared him through the thin material of his shirt. Swearing at his reaction, he put distance between them the only way he knew how, shoving up a wall in front of his emotions before he made a fool of himself. "I need to take care of some personal matters, if you know what I mean. Outside. *Alone.*"

She nodded and backed away. "I understand."

The hurt look in her eyes grabbed at him, but he kept his tone deliberately brusque. "As soon as the shack is cleaned up, we'll start toward the ranch."

"Are you sure you're up to it?"

He wasn't about to spend the afternoon in the

shack with her; too small a room with too many possibilities. He strode to the door and opened it, welcoming the slap of brisk morning air.

"We'll get to the house even if I have to crawl," he said, then glanced back at her with purpose, his harshness fading. "*Or* you could always drag me." Before she could offer a retort, he stepped outside and closed the door.

Caitlan looked out the window and watched as J.T. strode toward a copse of trees, wondering at the light flutters in her belly as she admired the leashed power and strength of his body. An altogether strange sensation, she thought, like none other she'd experienced as a guardian angel. Something about J.T. Rafferty elevated her nerves to a level of consciousness and made her feel things that were dark and surely forbidden to her. Yet she couldn't seem to stem the desire and longing sweeping through her. She was even more ashamed because the feeling wasn't at all unpleasant to her.

Once J.T. disappeared from view and she knew she'd have a few moments to herself, she cleared her mind of those disconcerting thoughts and closed her fingers around her medallion.

"*Yes?*"

"You guys gave me a real doozy of an excuse to convince J.T. how I found him unconscious," she said, remembering his doubts. "He probably thinks I'm a real ditz."

"*It was the best we could do at such short*

notice. He believes you, which is all that matters. Your expressions and emotions flowed naturally. Now, please, you mustn't summon us unless it's an absolute emergency. We've been swamped since you left."

Sighing, Caitlan let the medallion drop back between her breasts. Time to get back to work, she told herself. She had a very obstinate man to protect.

J.T. took care of nature's call and, instead of returning to the shack, he walked along the edge of the creek, heading toward the spot where he'd been ambushed the day before so he could investigate the area. The sun warmed his back and a clean, chilly breeze blew. Up above, a blue sky greeted him, stretching on for as far as the eye could see. Except for the damp soil beneath his boots there wasn't any evidence of the tempestuous sleet storm that had hit yesterday.

The water in the creek was higher than normal, a good indication that the storm had dropped a couple of inches of rain, which he always welcomed. The water flowed from the mountains down to the pasture for his cattle. From the looks of the rapidly cascading water, he surmised there were no more blockages up-river.

Finding the severed tree resting by the side of the creek, he squatted at the base of the trunk and examined the cuts in the bark indicating an ax had been used to fell the tree.

Someone had intentionally sabotaged the creek so the water supply to the cattle would be cut off. Had that same someone intended for him to find the blockage? He had proof the whole scene had been a setup of some kind—an aching head and a woman who'd saved him from a sure departure from earth.

He shivered at how close he'd come to meeting his death, and the thought of never seeing his daughter again. Laura was his life, a twelve-year-old pixie whom he adored and would do anything for. Knowing too well the devastation of losing someone you loved, J.T. was grateful God had seen fit to spare Laura from losing him. Especially at such a tender age.

"The shack is cleaned—"

Startled, J.T. stood, spun around, and crouched, ready to face his adversary. His heart pounded wildly in his chest and a shaft of pain detonated in his head. He hadn't heard Caitlan approach—no crunch of boots over the soil and brush, no rustle of clothing, nothing.

"Damn! Don't sneak up on me like that." Straightening, he speared his fingers through his hair and took a breath to calm the pitching in his stomach. "After what happened yesterday I'm strung as tight as a bow."

"I'm sorry," she said softly. "I only wanted to tell you the fire in the wood stove is out and the shack is straightened. We can start back to the ranch." She held up a bulky knapsack for him to see. "I packed some beef jerky and filled a canteen with bottled water." She thrust her other hand toward him. "And I found a jacket in the cupboard for you."

The vise of pain in his head eased and his pulse returned to normal. He took the jacket, staring down at Caitlan's upturned face. "Thanks," he murmured, shrugging into the jacket and zipping it. He noticed she'd put on her own jacket. "I'm beginning to think you're a regular girl scout."

"I just like to make the best of a situation."

"So do I," he agreed, wondering if taking advantage of her damp, parted lips would be considered making the best of a situation. Her hair looked soft and inviting with the sun dancing upon it. The strands ruffled about her head like a curtain of silk, enhancing those bluer-than-blue eyes of hers.

Looking away, he absently kicked a small rock with the toe of his boot. "I wanted to check out the area before we left. I was hoping to find something to give me a clue as to who might have done this. All I know is that the tree was purposely cut and situated across the creek to stop the flow of water to the main pasture."

Frowning, she glanced at the crystal-clear water rippling downstream. "Why would someone do that?"

"Hell if I know." Frustration gnawed at him.

"The only thing I can figure, if this was a deliberate sabotage attempt, is that the water would back up and flood the pasture, making it too marshy for grazing. But that doesn't explain why I got clubbed."

She transferred her gaze back to him. "Why would someone want to harm you?"

"I don't know."

Her brows creased, and J.T. found he wanted to reach out and smooth the wrinkle with his thumb. Thrusting his fingers into the front pockets of his jeans, he stared out across his land. "Maybe a transient hit me over the head." Even to his own ears, the explanation sounded like a last-ditch effort to convince himself he wasn't on someone's hit list. "Maybe he wanted my horse, and that's why no one has come looking for me yet. If Quinn never made it back to the Circle R, Frank, my foreman, probably thinks I spent the night in the line shack and am out assessing any damage done by the storm."

"Maybe, but you said the tree was cut deliberately. Why would a drifter go to that much trouble—?"

"Yeah, I know," he interrupted, anger coiling inside him. "Maybe I'm just making excuses because I don't want to believe I have an enemy nearby, or that I'll have to watch my back twenty-four hours a day." He glanced at her. "At any rate, when we do get back I'm going to tell everyone I had an accident, that I slipped and fell and knocked myself out and you found me."

"Why not tell the truth? That someone tried to kill you?"

"I don't want whoever is behind this stunt to panic because everyone is searching for him. I want this person to feel confident so he'll try something else. I plan to get this son of a bitch, Caitlan."

She worried her bottom lip, her eyes clouding with concern. "I don't think that's such a good idea."

J.T. resented being disputed by a woman, especially one he didn't really know. He leaned close, making sure she saw how dead serious he was. "It doesn't matter much what you think, Caitlan. This is my ranch. While you're at the Circle R you'll follow my rules. Got that?"

Her chin thrust out and she met his gaze steadily. "Yes, sir."

Why did he get the feeling she was mocking him? "I owe you a great deal," he conceded softly. "You did save my life."

One of those secret smiles curved her mouth and she shrugged off his gratitude, as if saving lives was a regular habit of hers. "I just happened to be at the right place at the right time."

"Lucky me, huh?"

"I'd like to think so."

Something inside J.T. shifted at her softly spoken words. A sharp pang of emotion he vaguely recognized as longing pierced him. Rolling his shoulders to shrug off the sensation, he grasped her elbow and guided her around the tree. "Come on; let's get moving. Once the sun goes down it gets damn cold. No offense to the stew and peaches you made, but I have to admit I'm looking forward to Paula's chili and cornbread."

"No offense taken." Caitlan fell into step beside him as he started away from the creek through an open pasture. He let go of her arm and she lost that delicious warmth he seemed to generate within her. Curious to know more about him, and wanting to fill the silence between them, she asked, "Who's Paula?"

His stride was steady yet reserved, to save his energy for the long trek ahead. "My foreman's wife. She keeps an eye on my daughter, Laura, while I'm working. She cooks for us and takes care of the main house."

Caitlan slung the knapsack over her shoulder. "You have a daughter, but you're not married?"

"No."

The word was spoken with such finality, Caitlan automatically thought the worst. "Did your wife die?"

His gaze cut to hers, a sardonic smile on his lips. "No, she left me for something better and more exciting."

Caitlan's cheeks grew warm. "Oh, I'm sorry."

"Don't be," he replied, bitterness seeping into his deep voice. "It was for the best. She's been gone almost ten years."

His tone was cold and harsh and didn't welcome further scrutiny of his ex-wife. Casting a glance at the chiseled lines of his profile, she noticed the grim set of his mouth and the deep furrow of his brow. Both belied his attempt to remain unconcerned about the topic. "Don't you ever get . . . lonely? I mean, not having a wife and all?"

"No. I have Laura."

His pace picked up, forcing Caitlan to quicken hers to stay by his side. "That's not what I meant."

"The only thing I miss is a warm body to share my nights with. *Sex*, Caitlan." His jaw hardened and he shot her a scathing look. "Other than that, I don't have any use for a wife. And my personal life is really none of your business."

She glanced away. He was right, of course. Meddling in his affairs wasn't on her heavenly agenda, yet she found it odd he didn't want the intimacy and love that flowed between a man and a woman. Such emotion seemed to be the ultimate aspiration of most mortals.

An arctic gust kicked up, slicing through the warm sunshine to maliciously steal the warmth from their bodies. She shivered and watched J.T. flip the collar of his jacket around his neck to ward off the brisk breeze. Shoulders hunched, he tucked his hands into the lined pockets. The wind tugged at his hair, tousling the thick strands around his bent head. He seemed so much the loner, suddenly distant and remote, yet the glimpses of sincerity she'd seen told her he was a compassionate man who deserved the love of a good woman.

"I've never met anyone who didn't want to share his life with someone," she said quietly, more to herself than to him.

He heard her and met her gaze. "The person I wanted to share my life with died, Caitlan. I've never wanted anyone but her." The desolation in his eyes made his words that much more profound.

Instinctively, Caitlan knew the woman he spoke of was his eternal soulmate. But didn't J.T. realize he could find another to love while waiting for the woman of his heart? He only needed to allow himself the emotion to live out his years happily. "You could still be happy with someone else—"

Slicing a hand through the air, he cut her off, slanting her a look of disgust. "Don't tell me you're one of those females who believes in fairy tales and happily-ever-after."

"Well, yes, I believe everyone has a soulmate, and what's more—"

He interrupted her again. "I hate to be the one to burst the bubble you've been living in, little girl, but Cinderella and Prince Charming only exist in books. And 'soulmates' went out with the seventies."

His subtle insult made her bristle. "I'm hardly a little girl."

Stride slowing to a leisurely pace, he slid his gaze over her, lazily, thoroughly, making her feel as though he'd physically caressed the length of her with his hands. Heat suffused her body, making it difficult to put one foot in front of the other without wondering if her legs would hold out or turn to mush. She felt as if she was melting, which was ridiculous, considering the windchill factor. By the time he finished his inspection and had the good manners to lift his gaze from the vicinity of her breasts, she knew she was in big trouble.

"Pardon me, Ms. Daniels," he replied in a silky drawl that stroked over her senses and tickled her belly. "You're absolutely right. I take that back. You're *very* much a woman. Built quite nicely, I might add." A wicked, unrepentant grin curved his lips. "However, your philosophy on love is right along the mentality of my daughter's. She thinks everything is hearts and flowers. She's just discovering boys, so I can understand *her* romantic notions."

What could she say to top that? Nothing, so she didn't try. Once her mission with J.T. was over, she was going to discuss his single status with her Superiors. Surely there was *someone* for him.

They walked into a channel between two grassy knolls. The sun struggled to break through the canopy of trees surrounding them and failed.

A shiver chased down her spine. "It's getting cold. Where are we?"

"We're still on Rafferty land. I'm taking a short cut to the main ranch road." He rubbed his forehead, frowning. "Just keep walking. It'll keep you warm and your blood pumping."

"Don't you want to stop and rest?" He looked tired, and she wouldn't be surprised if his head was throbbing. "Maybe have a drink of water and some beef jerky?"

He briefly glanced at the knapsack. "No. I want to get back to the house as soon as possible."

"Your head—"

"Is fine. I'll let you know if I need a break."

How am I suppose to take care of him and protect him when he won't let me? "Fine," she replied, deciding to play the game by his rules. "Just don't pass out on me, because I refuse to drag you back to the shack."

He chuckled softly, and Caitlan decided she loved the deep, rumbly sound. "I promise," he said.

The path they followed narrowed, the grass tapering to dirt and rocks. Unexpectedly, he grabbed her hand, enveloping her fingers in his. "Be careful; it's a little rough through here."

Caitlan stumbled over a cluster of small rocks, unsure if her balance had been knocked off kilter by the terrain or by the man whose hand held hers with such gentleness and care. As she careened toward him, his other hand shot out to steady her, landing on the swell of her hip. Shocked to the tips of her toes by the current of heat spreading where his fingers pressed into her flesh, she dropped the knapsack. The bag fell to the ground at her feet with a muted *thump*. Catching her breath, she stared into his eyes, watching as the orbs darkened in slow, tempered degrees.

The unusual connection she'd felt to this man earlier stirred within her, a bond so deep it shook her to the core of her being. A warm ripple of excitement teased her body. *What is happening to me?* she wondered. *Why do I feel this way?*

"Hey, you okay?"

Snapped from her daze by his concern, she pushed the disturbing thoughts aside for another time. "Um, yes. I should have paid more attention to where I was going." Then, ensnared by his gaze, she said the silliest thing. "Your eyes remind me of fresh moss dusted with gold."

"Like the moss that grows on the rocks in the stream?" His palm slowly slid from her hip to the indentation of her waist beneath the jacket she wore.

She managed a nod, her throat too dry to speak.

"How flattering." His voice was low and husky and full of a playful charm Caitlan suspected he didn't use very often. He stared at her as if seeing someone else, and the hard edge of his jaw softened. "And your eyes remind me of . . ." He caught what he'd been about to say and gave his head a slight shake, as if dislodging the thoughts in his mind.

Sorrow flickered in his eyes and, strangely, Caitlan felt his sadness as if it were her own. She didn't understand its source, and as she reached out to touch his face and offer what comfort she could, he saw her intent. Abruptly, he let her go and stepped away. Wrapping her arms around her stomach, she tried to sort through the upheaval of rampant emotions in her. But how did she begin to understand something so powerful and foreign in her experience as a guardian angel?

J.T. bent down and picked up the knapsack, still unable to believe he'd almost told Caitlan her eyes reminded him of lush violets. How incredibly stupid and sappy. Damn. He'd wanted her to touch him in the worst way, but he knew if she did, he'd go up in smoke and take her with him.

Scowling at everything in general, he grasped her hand in a businesslike manner and practically dragged her behind him. "Let's get the hell out of here," he muttered, forging a path up over the final crest of the ravine. A couple of times her boots slid from under her, but he had a firm enough grip on her to keep her on her feet. Once they were on flat land he let go of her hand.

Another pasture stretched out ahead, and beyond that was the main ranch road. A sweet, clean breeze curled around them.

"Oh, J.T.," Caitlan breathed, gesturing to the group of elk grazing near the tree line. "This is so beautiful."

Seeing the wild beauty of his land through someone else's eyes gave J.T. a new appreciation for it. "I guess I see them so often, I take everything for granted."

"I could watch them for hours," she said in a soft voice. The animals maintained a guarded wariness and wouldn't need much provocation to bolt.

"We don't have hours," he reminded her, and started forward. Several of the elk backed away; others sprinted into the grove of trees lining the far side of the pasture. When she caught up to him he said, "You never did say where you were from or what you do."

Caitlan looked surprised at the switch in conversation. "Chicago. I'm an illustrator for a children's magazine."

"You're a long way from home, city girl."

"Yes." One of those secret smiles brushed her lips. "But I get a hankering for the country and horses every once in a while."

And she'd no doubt get bored after a week or two, he thought, knowing from experience that city women didn't adapt well to life in the country. "Did you grow up in the country and around horses?"

"My uncle owned a ranch in Montana and I spent my summers there."

"So what brings you to such a rural place as an Idaho dude ranch?"

She shrugged and scuffed her boots over the grass. "A vacation. I just wanted to get away for a while."

"Are you staying at Parson's by yourself, or is there someone waiting and worrying about you?" And why did he even care? His only concern should be getting her safely back to Parson's, regardless of who might be waiting for her there.

She shook her head, and the sun painted golden highlights in her hair. "No, I came by myself."

"Well, you can call Parson's as soon as we get back to the main house and let them know you're okay."

She gave him her dimpled grin, and this time J.T. only felt a minimal shock at seeing it. "Look!" she exclaimed, pointing. "Someone's coming."

J.T. glanced up. Sure enough, three figures appeared on the horizon: two men on horses and a horse with no rider. J.T. whistled loud and shrill, garnering their attention. The riders spurred the horses into a gallop. Minutes later, J.T. recognized his ranch foreman, Frank, and his brother-in-law Kirk. J.T.'s faithful chestnut, Quinn, tagged behind on a lead rope.

Kirk reined to a stop a few feet away, a sly grin on his handsome face. "Sorry, boss," he said, thumbing back his Stetson on his head, his light blue eyes appraising Caitlan. "We didn't consider you might not want to be found, or realize you'd have company with you."

Frank, chuckling at his partner's comment, halted his horse and Quinn beside Kirk. He grinned good-naturedly, adding more wrinkles to his well-weathered face. "And here we were, worrying you'd got stranded out in the open and froze to death last night," he said, his voice a raspy drawl.

J.T. watched a blush rise on Caitlan's cheeks from the men's innuendos. A rush of protective-ness gripped him. Assuring himself that the feel-ing was nothing more than paternal instinct kicking in, he pinned both men with a shrewd look. "Can it, guys. This is Caitlan Daniels and, quite frankly, she saved my life."

Frank and Kirk exchanged incredulous glances.

"Say again?" Kirk asked. "I could have sworn you said she saved your life."

Quinn stepped forward, seeking his owner's fa-miliar hand. J.T. obliged the horse, stroking his palm down the side of Quinn's neck. "You heard me correctly," J.T. said, irritated for a reason he couldn't pinpoint. "I had an accident in the west pasture." He met Caitlan's gaze, telling her with-out words to go along with his story and not to dare refute him. "A tree was blocking the creek. After I pulled it out and untied the rope I slipped and fell and must've hit my head on a rock. I was out cold, and when I woke up I was in the line shack."

Frank leaned into his saddle, eyeing Caitlan curiously. "And where does this pretty lady fit into all this?"

J.T. summarized the story Caitlan had relayed to him, about her being a guest at Parson's Dude Ranch and stumbling upon his body by accident. By his men's dubious expressions, J.T. knew they were having a little trouble digesting the tale, just as he had. Yet he asked himself again, what other explanation could there be?

"By the way, Caitlan," J.T. began, nodding to Frank, "this ancient cowpoke is my foreman Frank, and Kirk here is my sister's husband and one of my best hands."

"Nice to meet you," she replied, looking from one man to the other.

"Same here, Ms. Daniels," Frank said politely.

Kirk tipped his Stetson at her, a broad smile on his lips. "Any friend of J.T.'s is a friend of ours. Welcome to the Circle R."

J.T. tied the knapsack on the saddle, annoyed with the way both men, *married* men at that, were so totally captivated by Caitlan's smile. "So, what the hell took you so long to find me?"

Kirk spared him a glance. "Randal said you'd been working on the north side of the ranch and insisted we search for you there. When nothing turned up Frank and I decided to give this end a try."

"I was working on the north side of the ranch in the morning, until I found the blockage in the creek and followed it west."

"Well, no matter," Frank cut in. "At least we found you. Quinn made it back to the corral late last night and was acting spooked."

"Probably from the storm," J.T. said, even though he knew it would take more than a little thunder and rain to terrify Quinn. The horse had never deserted him before in bad weather.

"Yeah," Kirk agreed. "Let's get moving so we can tell the other guys the search is off."

J.T. nodded, checking the saddle and the girth before he helped Caitlan mount Quinn. "As soon as we get back to the main house I'll be driving Caitlan back to Parson's."

Kirk's horse danced impatiently, chomping at the bit to go. "Uh, that's not going to be possible," he said uneasily.

A sense of foreboding settled on J.T. "Excuse me?"

Kirk took an audible breath, clearly uncomfortable being the one to impart bad news. "She won't be going back to Parson's anytime soon—at least another week or two. The bridge over the American River was heavily damaged in the storm. It isn't safe for crossing."

Chapter Three

"What the hell do you mean, the bridge was damaged in the storm?" J.T. bellowed, unable to believe this newest turn of events. Quinn, startled by his master's sudden rage, flattened back his ears and shied away. "That's impossible," he said in a softer tone, soothing the horse with a gentle caress. "That bridge is built like a fortress!"

"Was," Kirk corrected, then shrugged. "It's one of those freak things that happens, I guess. From what we hear, even Hugh Parson and the county engineers can't figure it out. With ordering all the materials and getting a crew out this way, they're figuring a couple of weeks to reconstruct it."

J.T. glanced at Caitlan, scowling at her expression. She was actually smiling! Didn't she understand the implications of what was being said? *Two weeks,* echoed through his mind, taunting him with the realization that she'd be underfoot on his ranch. Fourteen days of seeing her and trying to curb this overwhelming attraction to her. Hell.

"You realize, don't you," he began succinctly, impaling her with a steady gaze, "that you won't be going back to Parson's Dude Ranch anytime soon."

She had the grace to look a little worried. "You did say the bridge is the only way over."

"Exactly. The bridge or eight miles of rough, rocky, *vertical* terrain, and I'm not about to endanger one of my valuable horses, or myself, to take you back." For a moment she seemed almost glad, relieved even, that the bridge had collapsed. Irritation coiled in him, bunching the muscles across his shoulders. "You're stuck here, Caitlan." And that was the very last thing he wanted or needed.

"I guess it's my own fault," she said softly, moving toward him and Quinn. She stroked the horse's nose and received a gentle, appreciative nuzzling in return. "I'll just have to make the best of things, won't I?"

J.T. was grateful his men had started ahead and were far enough away so they couldn't hear his conversation with Caitlan. "This is a working ranch, Caitlan. Don't expect guided tours. In fact, I'd prefer you stay off my horses. I don't want to be responsible if you should get lost again."

"I won't go off on my own, I promise." She gave him an upswept glance that had his gut tightening. "In fact, I'd love to go out with you sometime, just to see how a working ranch operates."

"Absolutely not. I don't have time to baby-sit."

Exasperation sparkled in her eyes. "You won't even know I'm there."

Oh, he'd know. He'd *feel* her presence, *smell* her light feminine scent that did crazy things to his body. "No."

J.T. watched Quinn brush his nose against Caitlan's cheek affectionately, wanting more of her attention. What a pushover his horse was, he thought. What was it about her that so totally captivated everyone, himself included?

"This isn't a private retreat," he went on, before he gave in to the temptation in those violet eyes. "It's dangerous out here, and I won't have you distracting my men or disrupting their work because you want to tag along."

Caitlan wisely kept quiet, even though she wanted to argue. Her job was to stay near him, but how could she accomplish that when he was so adamant about keeping her at a distance? He didn't seem to care that his life was in jeopardy. Well, she could be just as stubborn as he, and even if she had to face his wrath, she'd be by his side, or close to it, until her mission was accomplished.

J.T. knew he couldn't put the inevitable off any longer. Time to get the show on the road. "Mount up, Caitlan." He moved out of the way so she could use the stirrups.

She shook her head. "Oh, no, really, J.T., you should ride Quinn. I'll walk."

He rocked back on his heels. "Don't worry about me; I'll be sitting right behind you."

She glanced from the saddle to him. Shock enveloped her face and her eyes widened in comprehension. "We can't both ride on him—"

"We can and we will." She opened her mouth to say something, and he grabbed her arm and pulled her toward the saddle, cutting off her words. "You really know how to try my patience, Caitlan. This is an order, not a polite request. Now get up on Quinn or I'll put you there myself." Letting go of her, he crossed his arms over his chest and waited.

She shot him a disgruntled look. "Mount up," she mimicked in a huff. Shoving her boot into the stirrup, she hoisted herself up into the leather saddle. "I've never met anyone so bossy as you!" she said, glaring down at him.

There was something infinitely sexy about this woman in a temper, her eyes snapping with anger. "Get used to it," he replied, and in one smooth, fluid motion settled himself in the saddle behind her.

She gasped softly as he shifted into a more comfortable position—if one was possible under the circumstances. Her bottom nestled into the crux of his hard, tense thighs. She leaned forward—to keep her back from pressing into his chest, he guessed—but it only caused her to become more intimate with the fly of his jeans and the growing arousal that would be more pain than pleasure in a matter of seconds, when he spurred Quinn into a gallop.

"Be still," he said roughly into her ear. Doubts about this brilliant idea of his settled over him. He swore under his breath. *Two weeks*. He'd die from sexual frustration before *one* week was out.

With a barely perceptible tug on the reins he urged Quinn forward, eager to be on their way. The swaying motion of the horse's first few steps rocked Caitlan closer to him, tighter, until not even a whisper could slip between their wedged bodies. Until he knew she felt the proof of his desire for her.

Her breath caught again, a soft intake of air that was more provocative than anything J.T. had heard in a long time. Like one of those delicate sounds a woman makes when she's on the precipice of pleasure . . .

"I don't think this is a very good idea," she said.

He didn't think so, either, but he wasn't about to admit it to her. "We don't have a choice. I'm not walking, and I sure as hell am not going to saunter along on Quinn while you do. Just hang on and we'll be at the house soon."

Before she could protest his actions, he anchored a strong arm around her waist, bent forward, and deliberately pressed into Caitlan so they leaned low over Quinn. At the same instant he spurred the horse out of a canter and into a heavy gallop. A moment later he gave Quinn his head, and the stalwart animal practically took flight across the pasture.

Caitlan tensed, her fingers gripping the saddle horn. She locked her knees against Quinn's sides since she didn't have the security of having her feet in stirrups, and hung on for dear life. J.T. urged Quinn faster, and the horse complied, his hooves pounding on the soil. Fear pumped through Caitlan's veins. The wind whipped through her hair, tangling the strands around her face.

"J.T., are you crazy?" she yelled.

He chuckled, and since his face was next to hers she heard the wickedly sensual sound clearly, felt the warmth of his breath on her cheek. "Don't worry. I've got you." For emphasis, he tightened the arm banded around her waist.

Don't worry? A hysterical laugh escaped her. She was riding a horse that raced so fast that if he happened to stumble over the uneven terrain they'd be catapulted a hundred feet ahead, not to mention the danger of being embraced by a man whose hard body was draped all over her. He was so close, the stubble on his jaw grazed her cheek, a delicious friction that brought an involuntary flutter to her stomach. The heat of his thighs

Janelle Denison

bracketed hers, his chest a slab of muscular heat along her spine. And then there was the forearm around her waist, and the large hand splayed just beneath her right breast, his thumb nudging the soft underside through her jacket. Her nipple bloomed into a tight bud, aching for something more.

Quinn no longer provided the biggest threat; J.T. did. She thought of using the medallion to slow Quinn, and to take the edge off her quivering response to J.T., but she didn't want to risk the Superior's suspicions. How could she explain that she felt things for this man, physical, shameless things, that would surely shock them? *She* was shocked by her quickening pulse and the electrifying tempest pounding through her.

J.T. slowed Quinn slightly to accommodate for the ravine they were approaching at a rapid rate. Caitlan automatically stiffened.

"Relax, Caitlan," J.T. murmured, his tone gentle. "I won't let you fall."

Willing herself to do as he commanded, she drew in a deep breath of cold, biting air and loosened her hold on the pommel. Allowing J.T. to support her, she marveled at the sleek strength and power of the animal beneath her, and of the man holding her. Funny, but she felt safe and secure with him, an exceptionally odd feeling considering *she* was *his* protector.

The trail dipped into the ravine, and Quinn took the change in grade with ease. Caitlan, however, leaned to one side of the saddle and clutched once again to the pommel.

"We're almost there," J.T. said, holding her upright. "About another mile. Can you hang in there?"

She nodded.

J.T. wondered if *he'd* survive the short distance left. The soft feel of Caitlan, and the rain-scented smell of her hair and skin, would be his undoing, he was sure. Pure, 100 percent woman, a temptation more intoxicating than a shot of liquor. He had the compulsive urge to press his mouth to the sensitive flesh beneath her earlobe and flick his tongue out to taste her skin. The way her slim body moved with his and Quinn's stride was nothing short of fluid and graceful, evoking images of a more rhythmic sliding, of bodies joined so inseparably there'd be no tomorrow, only molten heat and sheer paradise. J.T. couldn't remember the last time he'd desired a woman so fiercely, and wondered if taking her once would quench the unrelenting need he seemed to have for her.

He shook his head free of those dangerous thoughts. From what he'd learned so far about Caitlan Daniels he didn't think she'd agree to a brief, mutually pleasurable fling for the two weeks she was at his ranch. Yet that's all he had to offer any woman. Good, hot, satisfying sex. Nothing more. Nothing less.

In the distance a large red barn and a two-story

ranch house came into view. Home never looked so good, he thought, spurring Quinn the last quarter mile. They passed the ranch hands' bunk house and a few cabins nestled off to the side. Frank and Kirk had arrived and were speaking to a group of his ranch hands by the corral, no doubt relaying the tale he'd told them about his accident and Caitlan's part in it all. His newest ranch hand, Mike, a drifter hired for a few months' work, stood alone by the barn, smoking a cigarette. With a brooding expression, he eyed the other hands but made no move to join them.

In order to give him and Caitlan a minute before they were bombarded with questions, J.T. halted Quinn by the corral, some fifty yards away from his men. J.T. dismounted, then stepped back to give Caitlan room to do the same. Moving slowly, stiffly, she swung her leg over Quinn's rump and lowered herself to the ground, grimacing. Still holding on to the saddle, she groaned.

A deep chuckle escaped him. He didn't have to ask to know that, not being a seasoned rider, Caitlan would be sore from the rough ride and cramped quarters of the saddle, her legs probably the consistency of cooked spaghetti.

She attempted to glare at him for laughing at her expense, but he saw the sparkle of humor in her eyes. "Thanks a bunch, Rafferty. This is your fault, you know."

Hooking his thumbs in his belt loops, he lifted a brow. "Really?"

She straighten moderately and gave another moan for the effort it cost her. "I'm not used to riding so hard. I hurt in places I didn't know I could hurt."

"Then maybe you ought to ride more often, city girl," he drawled. "You're too soft." He knew that much for a fact.

His playful goad backfired on him. "Well, maybe I'll take you up on your offer, considering I'll be here for a while."

The group of men started toward them, headed by his cousin Randal, preventing J.T. from responding to her comment. By the looks of collective interest and speculation cast Caitlan's way, J.T. knew he'd have to set some ground rules for the men living in the bunk house—Caitlan was off limits and he wouldn't tolerate any advances made toward her during her stay at the ranch.

Ever the womanizer, Randal chased anything with breasts and long legs, and Caitlan definitely fit that bill. However, Randal looked more intent on throttling Caitlan than trying to flirt with her, which surprised J.T. Curiosity over the ominous looks Randal cast Caitlan mingled with a sense of relief J.T. didn't want to analyze too deeply. At least he wouldn't have to battle with Randal for making a move on Caitlan, and cause more discord between himself and his cousin.

"Who is this?" Randal demanded.

J.T. stared at Randal's matted blond hair and

bloodshot brown eyes and guessed his cousin was suffering from one helluva hangover, which explained, not excused, his surly attitude. Glancing over Randal's shoulder to the other hands, he gave them a brisk nod of acknowledgment. "Would you mind excusing us for a few minutes?"

The men dispersed without question, one of them taking Quinn to cool the horse down for the boss. Beside him, Caitlan shifted on her feet, and when he looked at her he wondered at the intent way she studied Randal. Once the hands were out of earshot J.T. turned back to his cousin, whose face was now flushed.

"This is Caitlan Daniels," J.T. explained. "She's from Parson's Dude Ranch and happened to get lost on Rafferty property."

"All the way from the dude ranch?" Randal's scowl deepened. "Parson's is eight miles away. That's impossible!"

A wry smile tugged at J.T.'s mouth. "About as impossible as the bridge over the American River collapsing, but it happened."

"I was sightseeing on my own and lost my way," Caitlan interrupted, striving to substantiate her presence.

"Stupid female," Randal said, his gaze slurring over her as insolently as his words. "Didn't you see the private property signs posted on the main road and fence posts? Maybe charges of trespassing would make you think twice before you wandered off on your own again."

"Randal, cool it," J.T. said in a deceptively mild voice that warned most people they were treading on very thin ice. J.T. was used to Randal's explosive temper—worse since Randal's father had died two months ago—but J.T. saw no justification in Randal's hostility toward Caitlan for an incident that had resulted in more good than bad.

Randal's fists clenched and unclenched at his sides, as if battling to contain the fury brewing in him. "Don't you think it odd that she showed up out of nowhere—"

Lightning-fast, J.T. grabbed a fistful of Randal's shirt, jarring the other man into submission. He heard Caitlan's soft gasp at the aggressive move, but his only thought was to shut Randal up. "Good God, man! Who the hell cares where she came from?" He gave Randal a slight shake, then let go of the wad of material in his hand. Randal stumbled back, eyes wide. "Caitlan saved my life. Didn't Kirk and Frank tell you about my accident and how she found me?"

Caitlan watched Randal transform from raging madman to subdued composure in the blink of an eye. The abrupt change made her wary and cautious.

"Yeah. Sorry." Discreetly straightening his shirt, he shoved his fingers into his hair, which did nothing to tame the thick, unwashed strands. "I don't know what came over me. We've all been so worried about you. I'm glad to see you're okay." He glanced at Caitlan and smiled, but she saw the resentment and bitterness banked in the depths of his eyes. "I guess you're lucky this woman came along when she did. No telling what would have happened to you if she hadn't."

Caitlan didn't miss the flash of challenge in his eyes, and gave him a demure smile in return. A muscle in his cheek twitched, and she saw the beginnings of that madman surface again.

Unaware of the turmoil between his cousin and Caitlan, J.T. sighed tiredly. "I suggest you lay off the bottle, Randal. You know I'll do whatever I can to help you with your father's debts, but I won't put up with your mood swings."

The fire in Randal's gaze blazed an infuriated molten gold, but J.T. didn't see it. He'd glanced beyond Randal, a warm smile teasing his mouth. Caitlan followed his line of vision to a willowy young girl running down a path from the main house toward them, her long mahogany hair streaming down her back in wild abandon. In her wake, a woman with shoulder-length blond hair followed at a more leisurely pace, and tagging along were two tow-headed girls bundled in jeans and jackets.

"Dad, you're home!" the young girl squealed, launching herself into J.T.'s arms. The expression on her pretty face brimmed with unconditional love.

J.T. laughed, a deep, rumbling chuckle, and

swung her around in a big bear hug. "Of course I am, Smidget." He set her down, grinning as he chucked her affectionately under the chin.

She looked up at him, green eyes crowded with concern. "I was so worried when Quinn came back last night without you. Uncle Kirk said you had an accident."

"I'm fine, Laura," he assured her gently. "Just a little bump on my head, but it'll take more than that to get rid of your old man."

Caitlan watched the reunion, a feeling of rightness ribboning through her. Out of the corner of her eye she caught a stiff movement from Randal, a slight bristling as he straightened his lanky frame. Randal watched J.T. with Laura, his eyes narrowing to menacing slits before he turned and stormed away. No one but Caitlan seemed to notice Randal's malevolence—or if they did, no one made mention of it.

A shiver of apprehension passed through Caitlan. J.T. seemed to treat Randal's animosity as a common occurrence, which made her wonder what kind of relationship the cousins shared. She knew without summoning her Superior that Randal was the man she had to protect J.T. from. The vibrations of evil and hatred emanating from Randal were so strong and gripping, Caitlan shuddered to think such a person was free to come and go at will. And why didn't J.T. see the threat Randal posed?

There was nothing she could do about Randal,

except make sure he didn't harm her ward. One of the first lessons she'd learned as a guardian angel was that she was to interfere as little as possible with destiny—less for the Superiors to cover up or repair once the mission was complete. Her job was to protect and nothing more. J.T. had to learn for himself who stalked him.

"Uncle J.T.!" the two little blue-eyed girls chorused as they neared. A moment later they clamored around him, and J.T. obligingly squatted so they could smother him with hugs and wet, smacking kisses.

He grinned, receiving his penance for his absence with obvious relish. "How are my favorite nieces?"

"Uncle J.T.," one of the sprites chided, eyes sparkling. "We're your only nieces!"

He tapped her on the nose and received a girlish giggle in response. "You're getting too smart for me."

Standing, he approached the other woman and placed a chaste kiss on her cheek. "Hi, Deb."

"Hi yourself." Tilting her head to the side, she shoved her fingers into the back pockets of her jeans. "You really had everyone worried. When Kirk left at dawn to search for you I knew it was serious."

His quick, devilish smile was meant to reassure. "Your brother wouldn't dare leave you with a ranch to run and an extra hellion to raise." He punctuated that statement with a wink to his daughter.

Debbie's mouth curved with sibling fondness. "He'd better not."

Caitlan marveled at how at ease J.T. was with his family, so openly caring and warm, a direct contrast to the temperamental man who'd just accompanied her from the line shack—the man with a melange of emotions churning within him.

"Who's that, Dad?" Laura asked, nodding toward Caitlan, her eyes shimmering with questions and blatant interest.

"This is Caitlan Daniels, and I'll explain the details once we get up to the main house," he said, then began a round of introductions. "Caitlan, I'd like you to meet my daughter Laura, my sister Debbie, and my two nieces, Brittany, who is eight, and Alisha, who just turned seven," he added, pointing to the girls peeking at her curiously from his side.

Caitlan accepted each of their greetings of hello with a smile. "It's nice to meet all of you."

"You have pretty eyes," Alisha said shyly, moving closer to her mother.

"Thank you," Caitlan replied softly, too aware of J.T.'s eyes on her.

Brittany swept Caitlan with a head-to-toe inspection. "Were you with my uncle last night?"

"Honey," Debbie interrupted, trying not to grin

at her young daughter's impudence, "that's not a polite question to ask."

Brittany frowned at her mother. "Why not?"

"It's okay," Caitlan said before Debbie could dredge up an appropriate answer to appease her daughter's innocent query. Addressing Brittany, she replied, "Yes, I was with your uncle last night, but only because he needed my help."

"Oh. Are you and my uncle getting married?" Brittany's delicate features were etched with solemn seriousness. "Mom is always saying that Uncle J.T. needs a wife."

Caitlan glanced at J.T. and found him staring at his niece as if he couldn't quite believe what he'd heard. Then he glanced at his sister, speculation glittering in the depths of those striking eyes. Laura giggled, and Debbie looked decidedly uncomfortable.

Brittany waited patiently for Caitlan's response, childishly ignorant of the discomfort she'd cast among the adults. "Uh, no, we're not getting married. We're just friends," she told the little girl.

J.T. cleared his throat and lifted an inquiring brow at Debbie.

"What?" she said defensively, an embarrassed flush sweeping across her cheeks. "I only mentioned it once or twice to Kirk in casual conversation. You know how the girls repeat everything they hear."

J.T. gave her a pointed look, but an amiable

smile teased his mouth. "Then watch what you say," he said, his tone a gentle rebuke.

"Oh, Dad, it's not a big deal," Laura cut in, slipping her arm through his. "I'm just so glad you're home. I missed you last night." She glanced at Caitlan with a sly smile, then looked back at her father. Standing on tiptoe, she whispered into his ear, loud enough for everyone to hear, "But I understand why you stayed out, and I want to let you know that I don't mind at all. Next time, just make sure you let us know so we don't worry."

J.T.'s groan of defeat rolled into a deserving chuckle. Shaking his head, he looked at Debbie. "What happened to that angelic little girl of mine?"

"I grew up," Laura replied with a self-important smile.

"It does happen," Debbie agreed with a sigh, then offered Caitlan a friendly smile. "You two must be exhausted and hungry. Why don't we go on up to the house where it's warm?"

"Uncle Kirk said you saved my father's life. I want to hear all about it," Laura said eagerly, eyes shining.

Caitlan didn't have to see J.T.'s warning look to know he wanted her to tell his family the story he'd fabricated. As they followed the paved walkway to the house, she relayed the same story J.T. had told Kirk and Frank, with J.T. adding in the "accident" that had happened before she'd found him. Debbie and Laura expressed their gratitude that J.T. had been so fortunate, and his life had been spared.

The group clamored into the entryway of the ranch house. A cozy warmth greeted them, mingled with the thick, fragrant smell of spicy chili, heavy yeast, and a sweeter scent of pastries.

"God, that smells good," J.T. said, shrugging out of his jacket. Hanging it in the coat closet, he helped Caitlan out of hers and added it to the rest.

"Paula's been so nervous since they started searching for you this morning that she's been cooking all your favorites," Debbie told him.

J.T. grinned, the skin around his eyes crinkling with humor. "I was hoping she would." Then, to Caitlan, he explained, "Paula cooks like there's no tomorrow when she's nervous or worried."

A woman in her mid-forties with soft blue eyes and short brown hair bustled out of a doorway, the worry on her brow vanishing when she spotted J.T. Frank followed close behind. "I thought I heard J.T. talking about me," Paula said, wiping her hands on the apron tied around her waist.

"I sure was," he admitted unabashedly, accepting her light, caring embrace. "I was just telling Caitlan here what a wonderful cook you are. Couldn't manage without you, Paula."

She looked him over, as if to reassure herself that he really was fine. "I'm relieved to see a black bear didn't get your onery hide."

He grinned. "Nope. They wouldn't dare mess with me."

"And this must be Caitlan." Paula grabbed Caitlan's hand and gave it a congenial squeeze, bonding an instant friendship. "Frank told me the exciting story of how you saved J.T.'s life. I'll tell you, J.T. must have had a guardian angel sitting on his shoulder!"

"I believe he did," Caitlan replied with a smile.

"Caitlan will be staying with us for a while," J.T. said brusquely, his tone suddenly business-like.

Caitlan noticed she wasn't the only one who'd caught J.T.'s abrupt shifting of mood, as if she was stepping too close to his territory and he didn't like it and wanted distance.

Giving J.T. a purposeful look, Caitlan transferred her gaze back to Paula. "I'll try and keep out of your way while I'm here."

"Nonsense!" Paula waved a chiding hand through the air. "It'll be nice having another woman around the house."

J.T.'s lips thinned at that remark, but he remained silent.

"Hey, what about me?" Laura jumped in indignantly.

"Excuse me." Paula's gentle smile placated Laura. "I sometimes forget you're not a little girl anymore. Come on, everyone, there's plenty of food to eat."

The group started toward the kitchen. Caitlan

grabbed J.T.'s shirtsleeve. He stopped, his gaze traveling from the hand on his arm to her eyes.

"Yes?" he asked tightly, moving his arm so her fingers fell away.

Caitlan ignored the tingles on her palm and the odd yet deliciously exciting shivers racing down her spine. "I need to call Parson's. May I use your phone, please?"

"Laura," J.T. called, and his daughter stopped at the doorway connecting the foyer to the dining room to look back at him. "Would you show Caitlan my office so she can use the phone?"

"Sure, Dad." Smiling, Laura nodded her head down the connecting hall. "Right this way, Caitlan."

Caitlan followed Laura, recognizing J.T.'s strategy for the ploy it was—to avoid being alone with her any more than he had to. She felt his gaze on her back, and the tiny hairs at the nape of her neck tingled in acute awareness. With a soft curse, he turned and strode into the kitchen.

Laura glanced over her shoulder as J.T. disappeared from view, then leaned close to Caitlan. "So, tell me what *really* happened between you and my father."

Caitlan eyed Laura, seeing the wistfulness in her gaze and a glimmer of hope. Not wanting to disillusion the young girl in any way, she strove to keep her answer simple and to the point. "Like your father said, I found him."

"Oh, how romantic," Laura said on a dreamy sigh.

A wry smile found its way to Caitlan's lips. "Your father has been anything *but* romantic."

Laura stopped before a closed door at the end of the hall. Grasping Caitlan's hand, Laura met her gaze. "You'll have to excuse my dad. It's been a long time since he's really dated someone—"

"Laura, this isn't what you think," Caitlan said gently, not wanting to hurt her feelings. "Your father and I aren't romantically involved."

"Not yet," she replied, her tone holding more insight than Caitlan would have liked.

"How old are you?" Caitlan asked, knowing the wisdom reflected in Laura's eyes didn't come close to matching her young years.

"Twelve." Laura's chin lifted haughtily. "Old enough to know that my father is interested in you."

Shaking her head at the absurdity of that statement, Caitlan smoothed a strand of silky hair from Laura's cheek. "Honey, the only thing your father is interested in is getting me off this ranch as soon as possible."

Laura's lips pursed. Eyes identical to her dad's flashed knowingly. "It's the way he watches you when he thinks no one is watching him," she said in a low voice, glancing covertly around them to make sure they were still alone. "I've never seen such a soft look in his eyes. It's the kind of look Aunt Debbie gives Uncle Kirk sometimes, and then they'll sneak off somewhere to kiss and do other things. . . . " Her words trailed off when she realized her slip, her face turning crimson.

Caitlan understood Laura's compulsion to find someone for her father, but matchmaking her and J.T. was strictly out of the question. Nothing good would come from it, and the interference would only make things more difficult and awkward while she protected J.T. "Laura, don't get your hopes up for something that's not there. The only reason I'm here is because of my own stupidity and the fact that the bridge is out."

"Do you believe in fate?" Laura asked, looking deeply into Caitlan's eyes.

Caitlan felt cornered and didn't care for the knowledge in this young girl's luminous gaze. "Well, yes," she said slowly, cautiously. Fate was part of her occupation.

Laura pressed closer. "Do you believe fate can bring two people who belong with each other together?"

Goosebumps raised on the surface of Caitlan's flesh. *Do you believe fate can bring two people who belong with each other together?* Yes, she believed in fate and destiny, but she would know if J.T. was her eternal soulmate. Caitlan frowned. Who was her soulmate? She knew she had one. She was employed as a guardian angel while she waited to be joined with him. But who was he? Fragments formed in her mind, a shadowy face with rugged features she couldn't quite identify.

Struggling to grasp the recollection, she received a sharp piercing pain to her memory for her efforts. Mentally, she drew back. The gold medallion between her breasts grew warm, then startling hot.

"Caitlan?"

Caitlan's gaze cleared and she stared at Laura, a little rattled by what she'd just experienced. "Can you excuse me for a moment while I make this phone call?"

"Sure." Laura hooked her thumb back toward where they'd just come from. "We'll be in the kitchen when you're done. Down the hall, the third door on your right."

Caitlan forced a smile. "Thanks." Slipping inside J.T.'s office, Caitlan leaned against the heavy door and let out a deep breath to steady her out-of-control pulse. The heat in the medallion subsided, and the ache in her head slowly faded away.

Even though Caitlan wasn't registered as a guest at Parson's Dude Ranch, she went through the ritual of calling them, without actually dialing the number and connecting, just in case someone was at the door and overheard her. She felt foolish speaking to the dial tone but accomplished the task within a few minutes, then headed for the kitchen.

The family sat around a massive wooden table ladened with a smorgasbord of aromatic food: chili, cornbread, chicken fried steak, green beans, mashed potatoes and gravy, corn on the cob, and biscuits with honey and butter. Long bench seats flanked either side of the table, making dining in the kitchen an informal affair. She noticed Kirk had joined the group, and assumed this was a daily supper ritual.

"Sit down and help yourself, Caitlan," Paula said cheerfully, obviously happiest in her element as cook. "Would you like lemonade or iced tea?"

"Iced tea, please." Caitlan sat down in the only available spot at the far end of the table, which happened to put her directly across from J.T. He spared her a brief glance, his eyes shadowed and distant, then went back to finishing his bowl of chili. His remoteness didn't invite casual conversation.

"What did Parson's have to say about your escapade?" Frank asked, helping himself to a second serving of chicken fried steak and potatoes.

Startled for a moment, Caitlan stared at the older man. She felt all eyes on her as she groped for a feasible answer, then an explanation flowed easily into her mind, as if her Superior had anticipated the question.

She filled her bowl with chili and grabbed a warm biscuit. "They're relieved I'm okay and that I have a place to stay until the bridge is repaired." Slathering butter on her biscuit, she reached for the honey jar and drizzled some on top. "Sounds like things are real hectic around there with the bridge out."

"I'll bet." Kirk gave his head a rueful shake. "I wonder how they're going to transport people and food in and out."

Caitlan swallowed a mouthful of the best chili she'd ever tasted. "I don't know. They didn't say. The clerk sounded a little frazzled, so I made the conversation as brief as possible."

"Well, you're welcome to stay as long as it takes to repair the bridge," Paula offered, as if she had complete authority over the Rafferty ranch and its occupants.

J.T.'s spoon clattered in his empty earthenware bowl. He sent Paula a look of annoyance, his jaw clenched, but the housekeeper, busy taking an apple pie out of the oven, didn't see it.

Debbie glanced from her brother to Caitlan, an intuitive smile canting the corner of her mouth. "I'd be more than happy to loan you some clothes, Caitlan. You're a bit shorter than I am, but I think we can find something that will fit you comfortably."

"Thank you," Caitlan said, overwhelmed by their graciousness. If only her real host would be so congenial and cooperative, her mission would be a breeze.

J.T. abruptly stood, the legs of his chair scraping on the wooden floor. Eight pairs of eyes darted his way. "Excuse me," he said, surprised at the gruffness of his own voice. "There's a few things I need to take care of." He turned and strode from the kitchen, down the hall, and out the front door.

Ignoring the chill in the evening air, and the fact that he should have grabbed his jacket, he headed for the barn. He just wanted to get away from Caitlan. She was getting under his skin in a way he couldn't shrug off, with those violet eyes and that flashing dimple. The feeling irritated the hell out of him, because he'd vowed never to let another woman get that close.

Unbidden, thoughts of his ex-wife Stacey filtered through his mind; of her unrelenting pursuit of him while he'd been at the No Bull Bar and Grill one evening three years after Amanda's death. Still grieving over the loss of Amanda, he'd followed Stacey's come-ons in an attempt to forget memories of another woman. Their affair had been tempestuous and steamy—a calculated ploy on Stacey's part to land herself a wealthy husband. She got her wish when she turned up pregnant.

J.T. shoved his thumbs into the front pockets of his jeans and scuffed his boots over the gravel walkway, remembering how he'd wanted things to work with Stacey, how he'd hoped she'd be the one to make him forget Amanda. What a fool he'd been. Once married, Stacey had realized her mistake. Although J.T. lived comfortably, he led a simple life that didn't include fancy clothes and expensive jewels and nights on the town. The novelty of living on a remote ranch and being Mrs. John Rafferty lost its appeal shortly after Laura was born, and from there things only went from bad to worse, until Stacey's indiscreet affairs with the seasonal ranch hands lost their excitement and she left him and two-year-old Laura. He had given her the divorce she wanted with the stipulation that he received full custody of their daughter. The last he'd heard, she'd married a rich oil baron from Texas.

That had been ten years ago, and since then he'd had a few flings. Hell, he wasn't a monk, but neither did he want strings or commitments—he was not good with either. The women he'd seen knew the rules, and he always ended the affairs before they got emotionally messy. Like he'd told Caitlan, he didn't have any use for a wife, except maybe for the physical pleasure and convenience a wife would afford.

So why, then, did he look into Caitlan's eyes and feel not just desire but a need that tangled his emotions into one big knot? Emotions he had sworn he wasn't capable of feeling any longer.

Lost in his thoughts, a red glow by the corral finally snagged J.T.'s attention: the tip of a burning cigarette. J.T. strained in the darkness to see who it was, and as he walked closer, he recognized the man as his newest hand, Mike.

"Evening," J.T. said, nodding his head in the man's direction.

Mike muttered something—could've been a

greeting or a curse, for all J.T. knew—then he flicked his cigarette to the ground and crushed the butt with the toe of his boot. With a dark frown, Mike turned and headed toward the bunkhouse.

J.T. didn't know a thing about Mike except that he was a Vietnam veteran. Definitely a loner. No one seemed to like him much, but he worked hard and earned his pay, and that was all J.T. cared about. So far, he hadn't caused any trouble.

Entering the barn, J.T. inhaled the sweet scent of fresh hay and the sharp, natural tang of livestock, tack, and ointments. Walking down the wide corridor, he stopped at King's Ransom's stall. The prized stallion glared at him with suspicious black eyes, daring J.T. to enter his pen. King stomped his hoof defiantly and whinnied.

"King's Ransom, hell." J.T. shook his head, regreting his impulse to purchase the animal he'd thought merely spirited, not downright mean. "More like Fool's Gold, you wretched animal."

The pitch-black stallion tossed its glorious head and snorted. The horse was more trouble than he was worth, J.T. thought. No one could even get near the wild beast without the threat of being trampled.

J.T. didn't know how long he stayed in the barn. The cold seeped into his bones, stiffening his joints and aggravating his head. Breaking the stare-off with King, J.T. shoved off the stall and headed back inside the house to get some neglected paperwork done, hoping to keep his mind occupied so he wouldn't think about a certain violet-eyed woman.

Caitlan met J.T. in the foyer just as he stepped inside the house. He saw her and scowled, then shouldered past her without a word. His office door slammed shut a moment later.

Sighing at J.T.'s bristly attitude, Caitlan decided to take a quick tour of the ranch to familiarize herself with the spread. Donning her jacket, she went outside and followed the gravel walkway leading to the barn. Overhead, a blanket of stars twinkled in the clear sky, and a three-quarter moon illuminated the path.

Caitlan sensed more than heard Randal behind her. And she knew it was him. An unmistakable sinister aura surrounded him, an evil that alerted her and made her cautious. She kept on walking, and it didn't take long for Randal to make his presence known.

"Well . . . if it isn't Ms. Caitlan Daniels," Randal drawled insolently from behind her. "You managed to con my cousin, but you can't fool me."

Caitlan didn't relish having a confrontation with Randal, but she knew there'd be no getting around it. Stopping, she turned to face him, and he nearly bumped into her. Glaring at her as if she was to blame for his clumsiness, he straightened.

"I don't know what you're talking about, Randal," she replied, keeping one eye on the ranch house to be sure no one saw or heard them.

His eyes glittered savagely. "Don't play stupid with me! Who the hell are you?"

She recoiled from the sour odor of onions and liquor on his breath. Although he'd been drinking, he seemed to be in complete control of his senses. "You know who I am."

His gaze narrowed. The moonlight highlighted his face, giving his features a diabolic slant. "What are you doing here?" he demanded.

She knew what he was asking and chose to avoid the obvious. "You heard what happened." Her voice was calm and well-modulated. She felt no real fear or threat from him. Yet.

"Oh, yes," he said disdainfully. "The story of how you're a guest at Parson's and how you just *happened* to get lost on Rafferty property."

Crossing her arms over her chest, she affected a pose of casualness, refusing to take his bait. "That's correct."

"Funny how Parson's doesn't have a Caitlan Daniels registered."

"Pardon?" A frisson of panic raced down Caitlan's spine. How could he have known?

"I called Parson's." A smug smile lifted his mouth and challenge lit his eyes. "They've never heard of you."

Careful to keep her composure intact while her mind raced with explanations, she replied in a mild tone, "There's obviously been a mistake."

He leaned close, and his noxious breath nearly made her gag. "I don't think so," he said in a low, menacing voice. "I'll ask you again: Who are you and what are you doing here?"

"I think you're getting a little paranoid, Randal." She turned to go, but he grabbed her arm, whirling her around.

"Bitch!" he hissed. "I don't know what you're up to, but by the time I'm done with you you'll be off this ranch and wearing handcuffs for trespassing—"

"J.T. won't allow it." Caitlan knew that even though J.T. had been gruff at times today, he wasn't a cruel man.

He gripped her arm tighter, pinching the flesh so fiercely she winced. "We'll just see what J.T. has to say about your lies," he sneered, jerking her around and shoving her back toward the house. "He doesn't take lightly to women lying. All it will take is a phone call to Parson's to verify who's telling the truth and who's an imposter."

Chapter Four

Randal barged into J.T.'s office without knocking and thrust Caitlan into the middle of the room with such force that she stumbled. Catching her balance by grabbing one of the two chairs in front of J.T.'s desk, she shot Randal a vexed look, briefly wondering how she was going to explain herself out of this predicament.

J.T. glanced up from the open ledger on his desk to the unexpected intrusion, a deep frown pulling at his brows. Casting a sharp glance from Randal to Caitlan, he closed the ledger and pushed it aside. "What's going on?"

Taking up guard next to Caitlan, Randal crossed his arms over his chest, a look of belligerence about him. "We have a liar on our hands."

"Randal, what the hell are you talking about?" J.T. asked irritably. Standing, he rubbed at the muscles in his neck.

Randal glanced at Caitlan, a cocksure smile curling his lips. "Would you like to tell him or should I?"

"It's your story," she replied sweetly. "By all means, go right ahead."

His eyes darkened to a turbulent shade of brown at the sarcasm threading her words; then he turned to J.T. again. "I called Parson's to check up on our *guest*. They've never heard of her," he said, his voice dripping with accusation.

Something flickered in the depths of J.T.'s eyes, a blending of wariness and his own growing suspicion. "Caitlan?" His tone indicated that he wanted an explanation.

She shrugged negligently, belying the nervousness settling within her. "I told him they must have made a mistake."

Their eyes held for an eternity, his gaze searching and probing for the truth. Finally he released a long breath of air. "She's probably right, Randal."

"She's a fraud, J.T.!" Randal stepped up to the desk and planted his palms on the surface, leaning across. "She shows up out of nowhere, has free access to the ranch and house, and she isn't registered at Parson's. She's probably a gold digger of some sort, no better than Stacey—"

A muscle in J.T.'s jaw twitched. "Randal—"

"I was very thorough when I called Parson's," he continued determinedly. "The registration clerk, Jason, assured me that there's no Caitlan Daniels listed as a guest. If you don't believe me, then call yourself. Or does she have you too ensnared?" His eyes glinted with challenge. Digging into his jacket pocket, he tossed a piece of paper with a phone number on it to J.T. "Go ahead, and then I'll be more than happy to call the sheriff to come pick her up."

Indecision played across J.T.'s face, and his cousin's influence won the battle. With a sigh, he reached for the phone.

Caitlan honestly didn't expect J.T. to side with her after all the evidence Randal had just given him, but she couldn't understand why J.T. wasn't suspicious of Randal's overzealousness. With a sense of dread, she watched J.T. punch out the phone number for Parson's, identify himself to the person on the other end of the phone, then ask to speak with Hugh Parson.

J.T. glanced at Caitlan as he waited on hold for his call to connect to Hugh. She was chewing on her bottom lip, her face shadowed with an emotion similiar to worry. This whole confrontation in his office was bizarre: Randal's fanatical conduct, Caitlan's sudden anxiousness, and his own need to confirm that Randal was wrong about Caitlan. He didn't want to think that everything had been a lie with her, a setup of some kind.

Dammit, he didn't want to think she might be as cunning as Stacey.

"Rafferty, what can I do for you?" boomed the voice of the sixty-four-year-old Hugh Parson. "You callin' to offer some of that brawn of yours to help repair the bridge?"

J.T. grinned his fondness for the old family friend. "Sorry, Hugh. I've got my hands full here at the Circle R."

"Yeah, well, those damn county engineers don't know their heads from a hat rack!" Hugh grumbled. "At the rate they're going, I'll be bankrupt before they're through! Can't get people in, can't send them out. Can you believe this has happened? I'd of sworn that bridge was indestructible. It's been around since your father and I were boys. We watched them build the dangblasted thing!"

J.T. gave a low whistle. "That long ago, huh? Maybe that's why it collapsed."

"Hey, watch yourself, boy!" Hugh's gruff retort held only affection. "Now, what can I do for you?"

J.T. met Caitlan's gaze, and she offered him a slight smile more tentative than confident. Clearing his throat, he addressed the older man, "I believe I have one of your guests here on my ranch."

"You do?"

"Yes," J.T. said, uneasy with Hugh's perplexed tone. "I need to know if you have a Caitlan Daniels registered at the dude ranch."

"Caitlan Daniels?" Hugh repeated the name slowly, as if running a mental index on all his customers. "Can't say the name sounds familiar, but then, I've got over fifty people registered right now. Unfortunately, I don't know everyone by name, but that doesn't mean she's not a guest here."

"Could you check her out for me?"

"I could, but the storm did a number on my computers and they're down," Hugh said with a regretful sigh. "Don't know when they'll be up and runnin' again. I can check with the guides and see what I come up with."

"I'd appreciate that."

"I'm sure if she says she's one of our guests, she is. Where else could she have come from?"

Exactly, J.T. thought. How many times had he speculated on that very same question?

"I'm just glad she wasn't harmed in that nasty storm," Hugh said, concern evident in his voice.

"She's just fine," J.T. reassured him. "So don't worry about her."

There was a pause on Hugh's end of the line, then, "If the bridge is out, how the hell did she get on Rafferty property?"

"She crossed the bridge before it was damaged."

Hugh swore. "No kidding?"

"That's what she claims."

Hugh released an abrupt laugh. "Stranger things have happened. In this business you learn to expect the unexpected."

Randal moved toward J.T.'s desk, fury contorting his features. "I called and they confirmed that she's not a guest!" he said in a burst of anger. "She's a fraud, I'm telling you."

J.T. stared at Randal. The injustice and rage in Randal's gaze spurred him to follow up on his cousin's accusation, if only to appease Randal. Caitlan's chin had lifted indignantly at Randal's slur, which gave J.T. a slight reassurance that her claim was fact, not fiction. Still, a sense of suspicion lingered.

"Hugh, Randal called earlier and talked to the registration clerk. Jason told him there wasn't a Caitlan Daniels registered there."

"With the computers being down, there's no way to know that for certain," Hugh replied. "Jason's a new guy, and everything's been so hectic around here. One little sleet storm and everything falls to sh—"

"Thanks for your help, Hugh," J.T. interrupted the man's tirade, more concerned with Randal's increasing temper.

"It won't be a problem if she stays at the ranch until everything gets halfway back to normal, will it?" Hugh asked hopefully. "We're looking into chartering a helicopter to transport food and supplies in and out, but until the bridge is repaired, the fewer people I have here to get in the way, the better."

"It's not a problem, Hugh. We'll keep in touch."

J.T. hung up the phone and looked at Randal. "The computers at Parson's are down, but Hugh seems to think she's more than likely a guest there." What other explanation could there be?

"She's lying!" Randal said through gritted teeth.

J.T. glanced at Caitlan, searching for the perfidious woman Randal claimed her to be. All he saw was the caring woman who'd saved him from death. He rubbed the back of his neck, suddenly tired of doubting her motives. "Caitlan's given me no reason to believe she's lying."

Randal's nostrils flared; then he spun around and glared at Caitlan. Without a word he stormed out of the office, slamming the door behind him. J.T. winced as the sharp sound reverberated through his aching head like a cannon shot.

"I'm sorry." Caitlan's soft voice drifted over J.T. like a balm. "I didn't mean to cause trouble."

J.T. released a long, controlled breath. "No, I should be the one apologizing. I don't know what Randal's problem is." Letting loose a dry laugh, he plowed his fingers through his hair in an agitated movement. "Hell, who am I foolin'? I know exactly what his problem is. Too much booze and too many obligations and debts dumped on him by his old man. I guess I'd be pretty strung out if I were in his shoes."

"He's had a rough life?"

"Yeah, you could say that."

"Want to talk about it?" Her silky voice could have coaxed a confession from the devil himself.

Dropping into his leather chair, J.T. scrubbed a hand over his stubbled jaw. He figured he owed Caitlan the truth after everything Randal had put her through in the short time she'd been at the ranch. Maybe if he explained, she'd better understand his cousin's resentment and bitterness. And maybe if he talked to Caitlan he could work out some of his own frustration over the situation. "You sure you wanna hear this?"

An encouraging smile on her lips, she lowered herself into the chair in front of his desk. "I've been told I'm a good listener."

And that's exactly what he needed right now, besides an aspirin for the splitting headache spawned by Randal's abuse with the door. J.T. leaned back in his chair. "My Uncle Boyd, Randal's father, never did care for ranching life. He was always looking for an easy investment. When some guy from town offered him a copper mine sure to produce millions, Uncle Boyd sold his portion of this ranch to my father, Jared."

"How long ago was that?"

J.T. thought for a moment, a little surprised to realize just how long ago the trouble had actually started. "About fourteen years ago." He pressed his index finger to the throb in his temple and the pain eased.

"So what happened?" she asked, genuine interest in her voice.

"Uncle Boyd sank every penny he had into his mine, but he couldn't produce enough copper to stay afloat. The mine played out after a few years, and Uncle Boyd lost everything."

"Everything?"

"Yep. His house, his truck, his wife—"

"His wife?" She frowned, her smooth brows furrowing over violet eyes. "Did she die?"

"No. Aunt Gina left Uncle Boyd after he went bankrupt."

Caitlan straightened in her chair, contempt flaring in her gaze. "She should have stayed by his side—"

"She probably would have if Uncle Boyd hadn't been abusing her."

Caitlan sucked in an audible breath. The spark in her eyes mellowed to sympathy. "That's horrible. Why would he do such a thing?"

"My best guess would be so he'd feel like a man. After Uncle Boyd lost everything he had no choice but to tuck his tail between his legs, swallow his pride, and come to work for my father on a ranch that had once been half his. He was hard to get along with, always drunk and taking his anger out on the livestock and anything and anyone who'd take it."

"And your father allowed him to continue working on the ranch?"

J.T. picked up a gold-plated letter opener from his desk and slid his fingers along the smooth surface, remembering all the tension and arguments between his father and Uncle Boyd, and his dad's answer when J.T. had asked him a question similar to Caitlan's. Jared had slapped him on the back and looked him straight in the eye, saying, "You never turn your back on family, son. Someday it might be you who needs a helping hand."

Tossing the letter opener back onto the blotter, he met Caitlan's inquisitive gaze. "Uncle Boyd was family, Caitlan. My father's brother. He had no one and nowhere to go. The Raffertys are a loyal bunch. We take care of our own. I guess that's why I put up with Randal."

Caitlan rubbed her thumb along the leather arm of her chair, head tilted curiously to the side. "But what does Randal have to be so angry about?"

J.T. smiled sadly. "When my father died two years ago I inherited the ranch. Rightfully, half should have belonged to Randal, but since Uncle Boyd sold his half to my father, Randal got nothing. Two months ago my uncle committed suicide and left Randal a mountain of debts as his inheritance. I really can't blame Randal for being resentful. Uncle Boyd wasn't the easiest man to live with, and he never should have sold his portion of the ranch to invest in something as chancy as a copper mine.

"The least I can do is try and help Randal out. I pay him well as a hand, he has his own cabin to live in, and I'm helping to pay off his father's debts. I'm hoping in time he'll come around. Things have been difficult for Randal since Uncle Boyd died."

A hint of a smile touched the corners of Caitlan's mouth. "You mean Randal used to be a nice guy?"

J.T. chuckled, unable to miss the dry humor in Caitlan's tone. "Not in the traditional sense. He's always been short-tempered and extremely competitive, especially with me." He shrugged. "I've grown used to it."

"He's lucky to have you for a cousin. I don't think anyone else would put up with his temper."

"Like I said, he's family. I'll do what I can to help him." J.T. sat up, deciding he'd revealed enough family secrets for one evening. Putting away the ledger, he shuffled some papers on his desk into a neat pile. He hadn't meant to go on and on, but Caitlan had been so easy to talk to. He couldn't remember the last time he'd had such an unreserved conversation with a woman, without the pretense of something more.

He glanced up and found her studying him intently. Growing increasingly uncomfortable under her scrutiny, he asked, "What's the matter?"

Speculation simmered in her eyes. "I was just wondering . . . do you think Randal would try to harm you?"

Something in her gaze made him decidedly restless, a perceptiveness that went as deep as he could see. He knew exactly what Caitlan was getting at, pinpointing Randal as a suspect for his accident, and quickly shook his head. "No. Randal's hotheaded, but he's pretty harmless. All talk and no action, I've learned. He's just bitter over his father's mistake, and the debts he's responsible for, which is understandable." But his cousin's drinking habit was another matter, J.T. thought, especially since it was starting to affect his work.

The ache in his temples had worked its way up to where he'd been hit in the head. He needed rest, he decided, watching as Caitlan stood and walked to the floor-to-ceiling shelves filled with books. Clasping her hands behind her back, she casually examined the titles. Now that the crisis with Randal was over, and an explanation given for his cousin's odd behavior, J.T. couldn't help but consider the intimacy of Caitlan alone with him in his office, and the endless possibilities of such a confinement. Shifting restlessly in his chair, he tried to shake off the provocative thoughts invading his mind.

"I see you're a fan of Stephen King and John Grisham," she commented. Glancing over her shoulder, she smiled at him, and in the next instant an incredible awareness, as vital and hot as flame, settled between them. Fast as lightning, the easy friendship they'd established altered to a sexually charged energy that arced the distance between them.

J.T. saw the awakening glint in her eyes, felt

the sensuality of new discovery cloak the room. Her hair feathered softly around her face, and as he dropped his gaze to her mouth, lips moist and slightly parted, an achy emptiness settled deep inside him.

Abruptly, he stood, determined to send her on her way before he took full advantage of the soft invitation and curiosity in her gaze. "It's been a long day and my head is killing me," he said, which wasn't a total lie. His head *was* killing him, the throb unmerciful. "If you'll excuse me, I think I'm going to turn in."

Caitlan started toward him, concern dissolving the desire of moments before. "Are you going to be okay? Maybe I should check the bump on your head."

His thoughts took an inappropriate turn as she neared. Damn, the last thing he wanted from her was mothering. He wanted something hot and basic, her warm, soft feminine body to lose himself in. And something more. He longed for the temptation of tenderness and care in Caitlan's violet eyes. But he'd be no better than a thief if he gave into his greed, because he'd give her absolutely nothing in return. At least not what a woman with her capacity to care truly deserved: love and affection, laughter and joy. And promises.

She skirted the desk, and before she could touch him he stepped away so his chair separated them. He ignored her perplexed look. "I'm sure this is just a backlash of all the excitement of today. All I need is some sleep. Did Laura show you the guest room?"

Caitlan nodded. "Yes." *It's the room beside yours.* "And your sister loaned me some clothes. Your family is wonderful. Everyone has been so nice about me being here."

"Everyone except Randal," he stated.

She shrugged. "I'll just stay out of his way and I'll be fine."

J.T. jammed his hands on his hips and held her gaze steadily. "Stay out of everyone's way, Caitlan," he ordered, a hard edge to his voice. "Like I told you before, I don't want my men distracted."

His commanding tone made her bristle defensively, and her chin shot up a notch. "Fine."

There was something in his look, something very explicit and very male. A challenge of sorts with a sexual undertone. The heated message in his gaze said he wanted her, in the simplest, most primitive way. Her pulse quickened and she struggled for breath, drawing in the scent of musk and man. A familiarity in those darkening green-gold eyes of his reached deep inside her and tugged, demanding her attention. Yet she couldn't quite focus on the images, and when she tried her medallion scorched her skin.

J.T. swore under his breath and shoved his fingers through his hair in a frustrated gesture. "If you'll excuse me, I'm going up to bed."

Caitlan watched him start for the door, wishing for the easy truce they'd shared before this startling awareness had intruded. In an effort to make amends she quickly asked, "Would you happen to have a pencil and pad of paper I could borrow?"

Turning, he frowned at her request. "Somewhere in one of those drawers I do." He made his way back to the side of the desk. "Mind me asking what you need it for?"

Noticing that the harsh lines between his brows were no longer present, she smiled. "I'm not really tired and I like to sketch. It helps me to relax."

"Sketch?" He lifted a brow. "That's right. You're an illustrator." Opening a drawer, he rummaged through the contents and withdrew a pad of unlined paper. He began setting supplies on the desk. "Here you go. Paper, a pencil . . . and a sharpener." He placed the red heart-shaped sharpener on the blotter, then glanced at Caitlan, a boyish smile curving his lips. "A Valentine's Day gift from Laura," he explained.

"I'll be sure to return it." She picked up the novelty item, relieved that he wouldn't be going to bed angry at her. No sense complicating her job any more than necessary. She headed for the door and turned just before leaving. "Well, good night, J.T. I'll see you in the morning."

"No, you won't." He rubbed his forehead and winced, then opened another drawer and pulled out a bottle of aspirin. "I'll be out of the house before you get up."

She watched him toss back two aspirins and swallow them dry. He closed his eyes, his face pale. Faint lines of pain bracketed the corners of his eyes. He wasn't in any shape to work tomorrow, but she knew her suggestion to stay indoors would only anger him.

Drawing a deep breath, he opened his eyes, grimacing at being caught in a moment of weakness. "Good night, Caitlan," he said, an obvious dismissal.

"Good night." Hugging the pad of paper to her chest, she slipped from the room.

The old grandfather clock in the living room chimed one o'clock, intruding on the quiet stillness of the house. Everyone had retired hours before. Unable to sleep, Caitlan sat on the padded cushion in the window seat next to the couch, sketching by the light of the full moon streaming through the curtainless window. She didn't need the light; the force of the visions she saw in her mind were so powerful and overwhelming, she could have reproduced them blindfolded.

Legs drawn up and the extra-large University of Idaho jersey she'd borrowed from Laura to sleep in covering her knees, she rested her pad against her thighs and let the strong images guide the strokes of her pencil across the paper.

The scratch of lead against paper soothed Caitlan in a way nothing else could.

The face of a young boy haunted her, and she duplicated every feature with precision, right down to the stubborn tilt to his chin and the rebel stance. A thick, untamable crop of hair rumpled around his head, a swath falling over his high forehead. His mouth, even in youth, was cut sensually, with the firm upper lip and the bottom full and lush.

She'd always had a natural talent for drawing and enjoyed using the skill while on a mission to pass idle time. Tonight, however, she was *compelled* to draw, and the pictures she created confused her. The boy she'd drawn was familiar to her, but where and how did she know him? Had she been his guardian angel at one time? And why, when she closed her eyes, did she see flashes of him and a blond-haired girl running across a pasture together, laughing and smiling at one another? The two were in love, she realized. Even at their young age the emotion shone in their gaze.

Caitlan blinked her eyes open, erasing the images. A pang of longing swept through her, a wave so strong it left her breathless. Staring at the sketch of the boy, she concentrated, digging deep into her mind for the mysterious connection tugging at her. A man's features materialized, but before she could bring them into sharper focus, a pain seized her temples. Gasping at the assault, she mentally recoiled, abandoning the thin, wispy vision. Beneath her jersey the medallion heated, tingling like fire upon her flesh. Grabbing the pendant in her shirt, she waited until the gold cooled before letting it rest against her skin again. For a reason she didn't understand her subconscious wasn't allowing her to trespass into certain regions of her memory.

Drawing in a slow, steadying breath, Caitlan willed herself to relax. Glancing out the window to the shadowed darkness beyond, she thought about her mission. She was glad J.T. had confided in her earlier about Randal. Now she understood Randal's motivation for trying to harm J.T.: greed and resentment. This wouldn't be the first time she'd played guardian to those evil elements.

However, her response to J.T. was another matter altogether. This was the first time she'd ever felt desire for a mortal as a guardian. A shameless wanting that whispered provocatively to her senses. What would it be like to kiss him again, this time without him thinking her another woman? Realizing how selfish her thoughts were, she silently chastised herself. Nothing could come of them being together. Soon she would be gone, and she'd be nothing more than a faded memory to J.T. She didn't need the added complication of their attraction while she protected him.

Janelle Denison

The old ranch house creaked and settled and Caitlan glanced toward the staircase leading to the second floor. She wondered if J.T. slept well, or if his head was still giving him problems. She'd healed the worst of the wound, but a tortuous headache wouldn't be uncommon as a repercussion to the deep gash he'd actually suffered.

Before she could analyze her true intent, she stood and padded across the floor and up the stairs, telling herself the whole way that the urge to check on J.T. was purely maternal. Turning the knob, she slowly opened his door, grimacing when the hinges gave a small squeak of protest. She waited and watched the form on the bed, illuminated by the beam of moonlight filtering through the window. No movement. Soundlessly, she crossed to the bed, careful not to trip over the jeans and briefs heaped on the floor.

J.T. lay on his back, gloriously naked, limbs sprawled, the blanket tangled at the foot of the bed. The only thing affording him a measure of modesty was the thin cotton sheet draped over one leg and the juncture of his thighs. Searching his face, she found his features relaxed and softened by slumber. He looked peaceful. His breathing was steady and deep. Even after she reassured herself he was fine, she didn't leave.

The muscular contours of his body fascinated her even though she'd seen him naked before. She followed the light sprinkling of hair covering his wide chest down to a stomach washboard lean. She wanted to touch him there, feel the strength of work-toughened muscles flex beneath her fingertips. His hip was bare, tapering to a hard, muscular thigh. Even his calf was defined and lean.

A slow heat flowed through Caitlan, that curious desire coiling like a tight spring inside her. Leisurely, she journeyed back up the length of his body—until her gaze collided with his wide-eyed stare. She froze, her heart slamming against her ribs. She made a move to turn, but he was faster. Lunging at her, his hand manacled her wrist and jerked her toward the bed. With a soft gasp of surprise, she stumbled and fell on him. Still holding her wrist, he rolled, pinning her beneath the heavy weight of his body. It all happened so fast, Caitlan's head spun.

The unexpected attack was like the one in the line shack while he'd been delirious, but this time he wasn't sleeping or dreaming. His eyes were wide open, hot and fierce—predatory and a little savage, like a hunter gone too long without capturing his prey.

In the fray, her shirt had worked its way up to her hips. He'd wedged a thigh between hers. The sheet no longer providing a barrier between them, she couldn't miss the hard, heated length of him pressing against her thigh. Their position was compromising, thrilling, and arousing in a way that should have shocked her but instead sent uninhibited quivers racing through her body.

She swallowed hard and found her voice. "What are you doing?"

"More like what are *you* doing in *my* bedroom?" he countered in a low, husky voice. "A woman usually comes to a man's bed uninvited for one reason only. Are you looking to finish what we started this morning in the line shack?"

"No." She tried to move away, but his body was hard and solid as a rock. She wouldn't be able to escape until he allowed her to. The hand that had so deftly grabbed her now secured her wrist at the side of her head. The other hand cupped the back of her head, his long fingers tangled in her hair, his thumb grazing the shell of her ear. She shivered.

Releasing her wrist, he picked up a strand of her hair and absently rubbed it between his fingers. "Then what are you doing in here?"

Her free hand came between them as a safety precaution, her palm flattening on his chest. Upon contact, warm, firm muscles bunched and rippled, but he didn't move. "I only wanted to check on you and make sure you were okay."

Frowning slightly, he gazed into her eyes. "Why do you care?"

"I don't know why, but I do." And that was the truth. She cared more than was appropriate, but she didn't understand why. She needed and wanted him in ways that frightened her. He felt like a missing part of her soul.

Slowly, he trailed a finger down her cheek, his gaze warm and sensual as his eyes tracked the path of his touch. His thumb stroked over her bottom lip, then tugged so his finger could slide along the edge of her teeth. A sensation laboring between fever and chill swept down Caitlan's spine. Feeling frantic and trapped, she pushed at his chest and tried twisting away. "Please, let me up."

"No." He grabbed her hip to still her, his strong fingers biting into her flesh. His other hand tightened at the back of her head, holding her hostage.

Spears of fire shot along her nerve endings. Continuous waves of heat and sensation found their destination in the tips of her breasts and that secret place where his thigh fit so snugly. Eyes darkening, he lowered his head, skimming his lips over her jaw to her ear. He gently bit the sensitive skin just below her lobe, then soothed the nip with his soft, damp tongue.

Caitlan gasped, her breath caught between her lungs and throat. A delicious pressure contracted in her belly, spreading lower like liquid heat spilling through her veins. "J.T." The feeble protest sounded more like a breathy plea for more.

Lifting his head, he looked into her eyes, a lazy, sexy smile curving his mouth. "I want to kiss you while I'm wide awake. I want to see if you taste as good as you did in my dreams."

"No—"

"Yes. You came in here, Caitlan," he reminded her. "If you want to leave, it'll cost you." J.T. nuzzled her neck, intoxicating himself with her soft, feminine scent. "I think a kiss is just punishment for sneaking around like a thief in the night," he murmured, hoping one kiss would be enough to get her out of his system.

"We can't," she whispered.

He kissed her mouth softly, ran his tongue playfully across her bottom lip, melting her resolve. "You're not in a position to argue."

The hand on his chest slackened considerably, but her taut body had yet to fully warm to the idea. "One kiss and you'll let me go?"

"Unless you want more." Before she could utter another word, he dropped his mouth over hers, parted her lips with his, and slid his tongue inside that warm, wet cavern. Every male instinct urged him to be greedy, to give her a hot, carnal kiss that would warn her of the possibility of him possessing her body in the same way, but something held him back. He wanted to savor the sweet taste of her, the way she gave so freely and responded so openly. So trustingly.

Deliberately, he made the kiss slow and long and lazy. His tongue coaxed hers to join the sensual foray, and after a timid minute she did. The silken glide of tongues tangling sent a shaft of heat to J.T.'s groin and hardened every muscle in his body.

A deep-throated, arousing moan escaped her, and she grew pliant beneath him, relaxing. Her thighs moved restlessly against his, and she arched sinuously, seeking more contact.

The plan to drive her from his mind with one kiss backfired. Needing more from her than he knew he had the right to take, he ignored the little voice in his head telling him to stop, before it was too late. Letting go of her hip, he reached down and slid his fingers around the back of her left knee, stroking the soft, sensitive flesh there.

Her breath caught at the electric caress, and he swallowed another one of her sexy moans. For a moment he wondered if Caitlan had a birthmark in the bend of her knee, just like Amanda, then decided he didn't really want to know. He didn't really care, because the only woman he wanted right now was Caitlan. He wanted her to fill the loneliness that was more profound when he was near her. He wanted to take her, over and over again, in every way, until she no longer threatened the barricades he'd built around his heart.

Keeping her mouth occupied with his languid kiss, he drew her leg tight over his hip, brought her as close as her silky panties would allow, and slowly slid his palm up the back of her thigh. Cupping her bottom, he squeezed the flesh gently, appreciatively, then continued on, slipping his hand beneath her shirt and over her quivering belly. Her bare skin was soft and fine as gossamer. God, had he ever touched anything so exquisite before?

The tiny, mindless sounds she made inflamed him. He broke the kiss and stared at her face, taking in her swollen lips and the desire and confusion blending in her eyes. And probing questions he wasn't prepared to answer, like, what was happening between them?

Raw need tore a shudder from him, and he argued with his conscience, telling himself he only wanted sex from Caitlan, not the tender promises of forever shimmering in her eyes. He hated this weakness and vulnerability he felt with her, this gut-wrenching need, and the way she made him feel so alive, as if he'd been dead inside until her.

Dammit, no! Attempting to convince himself this was nothing more than a physical encounter, he boldly swept his hand upward, swallowing her breast in his large palm. His fingers kneaded the flesh, making the mound swell and peak at his command.

Shock registered in her eyes, and she stiffened, her hands gripping his arms. Before she could object, he moved down and bent his head, taking the pebbled tip of her breast into his mouth, suckling her through the cotton of her shirt.

A gasp of stunned pleasure passed her lips, and her fingers sank into his hair, pulling him closer, her back arching. Then, suddenly, she was pushing him away, as if he was taking her to the point of no return and she wasn't sure she wanted to go.

"We can't," she said, squirming desperately to stop him. "Please, J.T., let me go."

The fear and panic lacing her voice stopped him cold. He was moving too fast, scaring her, scaring himself with the intense intimacy luring him deeper into her clutches. He withdrew his hand from her shirt. Anger coiled in him. Dammit, when had things gotten so out of control?

"I'll let you go," he said evenly, raising those walls up around him again so she couldn't get too close, "but the next time you come in here in the middle of the night, I'll assume you want to share my bed, and not to sleep. And let me warn you up front, if we do make love, I don't make promises. I'm not looking for a woman in my life or a commitment, so keep that in mind." Her gaze clouded with hurt at his callous words, but he knew this would be for the best—for both of them. These were rules he lived by, no exceptions. "I want you, Caitlan, more than I've wanted any woman in a long, long time. But it's sex. Nothing more, nothing less."

She stared at him for long seconds, then reached up and touched his jaw, her brows drawn in a contemplative frown. "Your heart is bruised," she said so softly he almost didn't hear her.

Her see-through-him gaze seared his soul. Hardening himself against the tug-of-war with his emotions, he forced a harshness to his voice. "It's completely shattered, Caitlan. I lost any softness or tenderness long ago. If you let me, I'll take and take and give nothing in return. I have *nothing* to give, so don't get it into your foolish head that you're just the woman to repair my heart. And don't make the mistake of thinking my desire for you is something more; you'll only get yourself hurt. I have nothing left to give a woman, Caitlan. Any woman."

She shook her head, wisdom lighting her eyes. "I don't believe that."

"Believe what you want, but consider yourself warned." He rolled completely off her and let his gaze take in the disheveled length of her, then noticed she was looking at that traitorous part of him still eager to consummate what they'd started.

Leaning close, he made sure she didn't miss the warning in his tone. "I'm about two seconds from stripping you naked and easing this ache of mine, so I suggest you leave while I'll still let you." He ran his fingers purposely up her thigh, and she jackknifed into a sitting position. Grimly, he said, "Go, Caitlan. Now!"

He watched as she slid from the bed and bolted from the room as if the devil was on her heels.

Caitlan closed the door to the guest bedroom and leaned against the slab of wood for support, her legs trembling in a series of gentle aftershocks. Heaven help her, she could still feel the imprint of J.T.'s hard body pressing into hers, could still taste the sleepy warmth and male earthiness of him in her mouth. Flattening her palms to her burning cheeks, she tried to calm the fine tremors running the length of her body.

In the darkness, she felt the damp material of her shirt where he'd suckled her nipple to an aching peak. The pleasure he'd given her at that moment had been so intense, her desire for him nearly overwhelming, she'd wanted to drown in the exquisite sensations. A dart of heat shot to her abdomen when she thought how his mouth and hands brought a part of her to life, *real* life, and how she'd craved more contact and deeper, more intimate touches. As her body blossomed with each kiss and bold caress, a deeper need had settled in, pulling her under and opening herself to him, physically and emotionally. Powerfully. Her soul felt the rightness of the connection, yearned for a joining that tugged at her heart. She'd almost given in. . . .

And then the purpose for being at J.T.'s ranch wove through her mind, jolting her past the passion clouding her judgment and thrusting her back to her responsibilities as a guardian angel— none of which included making love with her ward. Thank goodness J.T. had let her go. But not until after a lecture from him, a warning she'd be smart to heed. For his sake as well as her own.

Feeling more stable, Caitlan walked across the room and pulled back the covers on the bed and slipped between the sheets. Lying there, she stared at the ceiling, replaying J.T.'s words in her mind. *I have nothing left to give* echoed in her head and brushed across the surface of her heart. And why did she want to be the one to give him joy again?

"Oh, Caitlan, your thoughts are futile," she whispered to herself. "You know you can't allow this attraction to interfere with your mission. How would you explain that mess to the Superiors?"

Rolling to her side, she tucked her hands beneath her pillow, deciding the best course of action would be to act as if tonight had never happened when she next saw J.T. A dry laugh escaped her. *Wish for a mortal life while you're at it, Caitlan.* There was no way in heaven she could forget the shameless way her body had responded to his, that a look from him could make her breathless with sensual anticipation.

Her groan of dismay broke the silence in the room. She was here to protect J.T., but who would protect *her* from this forbidden desire she had for him?

Chapter Five

Blinking irritably at the heavy, burning sensation in his eyes, compliments of a sleepless night invaded with erotic dreams of Caitlan, J.T. headed toward the kitchen for breakfast the following morning. The heavy scent of bacon and coffee, mingled with the sweeter aroma of Paula's delicious pancakes, provoked a rumble of hunger from his stomach. He needed food and coffee, then a fast run on Quinn to take the edge off his strung-out nerves.

J.T. stopped short when he walked across the threshold, his gaze riveted to the one woman he'd thought to avoid by getting up this early. Caitlan.

He felt like hell, knew he *looked* like hell, and to compound his ire, she sat at the end of the table looking as refreshed as a daisy after a spring rain—as if she had had a good eight hours of sleep under her belt. At five in the morning, for chrissakes! She should have looked a *little* wilted!

Her silky hair swung about her shoulders as she glanced at him. A slight smile curved her mouth. "Good morning," she said cheerfully.

Despite her attempt to be amiable, he detected the guardedness in her eyes. A look of uncertainty that said she wasn't sure she wanted to get too close to him. Good. After last night he wanted her to stay the hell away from him. The further, the better.

"Morning," he muttered. Crossing to the coffeepot, he poured himself a cup of the brew, then carried it to his regular seat at the table, across from Caitlan. Settling himself on the bench, he glanced around. "Where's Paula?"

"In the pantry," Caitlan replied, concentrating on the task of slathering strawberry jam on her toast.

"Breakfast will be on the table in a sec," Paula called. The sound of canned goods being shuffled from the shelves drifted out of the walk-in pantry. "Frank and Kirk are on their way up."

"That's fine." Taking a long swallow of coffee, J.T. studied Caitlan. She wouldn't look at him, acted as though he wasn't there. Her indifference annoyed him because he was all too aware of her.

She stood and went to refill her mug with coffee, offering him an unobstructed head-to-toe view. He recognized the thigh-length beige cable-knit sweater she wore over her jeans as Debbie's, and was grateful for the concealing and bulky top. He knew she had curves, had felt every one of them last night, and wanted no visual reminder of how lush her body really was.

She returned, and he took another drink of his coffee, parading his thoughts in a different direction. "What are you doing up so early?"

Grabbing the sugar container, she poured a long stream into her coffee, added a splash of cream, and stirred. "I couldn't sleep."

"Join the club." He watched her take a bite of her toast and lick a smudge of jam from her thumb, unaffected by his dry comment. *Dammit, look up at me!* After a reassuring glance to confirm that Paula was still busy in the pantry, he said in a low voice only Caitlan could hear, "*I* couldn't sleep probably because I'm not in the habit of receiving late-night visitors."

Her gaze flew to his, the violet depths smoky with awareness. He smiled, a measure of wicked satisfaction rushing through him at the telltale flush sweeping across her cheeks. He waited in anticipation for her rebuttal, but before she could reply they were interrupted.

"Don't mind J.T.," Paula said, bustling back into the kitchen, her arms full holding a container of dried noodles and a sack of potatoes. "A cup of strong coffee usually takes the grizzly out

of him. Our J.T. isn't much of a morning person."
She cast him a fond smile over her shoulder before unloading her staples onto the counter.

No, he wasn't much of a morning person, J.T. thought, staring at Caitlan's amused expression. Especially since wakening with an arousal so painfully hard it had taken a cold shower in order for him to zip up his jeans. And it was *her* fault. Even after she'd left his bed last night the scent and warmth of her lingered, haunting him and his dreams.

Frank and Kirk ambled in the back door, hanging their hats and coats on the rack situated there. Their discussion about the day's plans abruptly ended when they saw Caitlan sitting at the table.

"Morning," they greeted at the same time, both wearing congenial grins.

"Good morning," Caitlan replied with a bright smile.

J.T. gave them a brief nod of acknowledgment, refusing to wish them a good morning when his was as lousy as it got.

"Morning," Paula said, and began scrambling the eggs sitting in the frying pan, as was her regular routine once all her "boys" arrived.

"You're up mighty early, Ms. Daniels," Frank commented, taking a seat next to J.T.

Kirk poured two cups of coffee and carried them back to the table. Setting a mug before Frank, he lowered himself beside Caitlan. "Only fools like us get up this early," he added to Frank's observation, then slanted J.T. a goading look from across the expanse of wood. "You plan on making her work the range, or what, J.T.?"

Only from his brother-in-law would J.T. take such blatant ribbing. "No, and I don't want Caitlan to leave the general area without someone with her. Considering her bad sense of direction, I don't want to chance her getting lost."

Caitlan gathered up her dishes and stood. "You won't have to worry about entertaining me." A serious expression etched her features, but J.T. saw the sassy twinkle in her eyes as she repeated the order he'd given her last night in his office. "I'll do my best to stay out of everyone's way."

He watched her take her dishes to the sink, expecting her to leave the kitchen on that parting remark. To his surprise, she picked up a dish of bacon and a stack of clean plates and brought them to the table.

"Honey," Paula said, a little flustered with Caitlan's assistance. "You're a guest here. You don't have to do that." She scooped the fluffy scrambled eggs into a bowl.

"It's not a problem." Caitlan grabbed the entree before Paula could put the skillet back down and delivered the dish and the platter of pancakes to the hungry men. "Four hands are better than two. Besides, I've got nothing but time to kill. The least I can do for everyone's generosity is help out around here."

J.T. forked a couple of pancakes onto his plate, wondering how long Caitlan's enthusiasm would last. Today a novelty, tomorrow a chore, he thought in private, wry amusement. As soon as those soft hands of hers became chapped, dry, and sore, he was sure she'd be singing a different tune.

Turning his attention away from Caitlan, he glanced at Frank. "Do you have all the hands lined out for today?"

Frank nodded and took a gulp of coffee to wash down a bite of scrambled egg. "Gotta get that fence on the east end repaired, and I've got a group rounding up the cattle in the north pasture."

"Good." J.T. bit off a chunk of bacon and chewed. "If you don't need the extra body, I need to spend the day in the office." Out of the corner of his eye J.T. saw Caitlan look his way. He glanced at her just as she smiled and cast a long look upward. He frowned, wondering what she found so fascinating about the kitchen ceiling.

"I think we can manage without you today, boss," Kirk cut in while Frank nodded his agreement, since his mouth was full. "Wouldn't hurt us any if you took it easy for a few days, considering your accident."

"I'm fine," J.T. insisted, refusing to admit even to himself that he was exhausted and could use a few days to recuperate. Sticking around the house doing paperwork would have to do as far as rest and relaxation was concerned. "With Graham out because of his slipped disc, our feed order is falling short. I need to take inventory of our supplies and get everything back up to date again."

"Not a problem, boss." Frank wiped his mouth with a napkin and tossed it on his empty plate. "We've got the work covered."

"Great." With that settled, J.T. thanked Paula for breakfast and went to his office to immerse himself in bookkeeping and order-filling for the day.

"Caitlan, do you want to see the new kittens we have in the barn?" Laura asked, shoveling a spoonful of Frosted Flakes into her mouth.

At the kitchen sink, Caitlan glanced over her shoulder and smiled at Laura's excitement. "I'd love to. Just let me finish peeling this last potato for Paula." Finishing the task quickly and with ease, she placed the skinned potato with the others on a paper napkin.

Paula filled a huge pot with water to boil the potatoes. "The bus is going to be here in thirty minutes, Laura," she reminded her.

"Do I have to go to school today?" Laura complained, finishing off her bowl of cereal. She brought her empty juice glass and dishes to the sink. "Can't I stay home and show Caitlan around?"

Paula sent her a gently reproving look. "I don't

think your father would be too pleased if you did that."

Laura let out a long sigh. "Why do I have to go to school while everyone else gets to stay home and have all the fun?" she grumbled.

Caitlan and Paula exchanged amused glances.

"I promise not to have any fun while you're at school," Caitlan vowed in a serious tone, drying her hands on a dishtowel. "Besides, today's Friday and you'll have all weekend to spend with me. We'll have all kinds of fun together. I promise."

Laura brightened marginally. "Sundays we usually go to Aunt Debbie's for dinner. Will you come with us?"

If the invitation had been issued by J.T., Caitlan would have accepted without hesitation. She needed to stay close to him, but how would he feel about her intruding on something as personal as a Sunday supper ritual? "I don't know—"

"Of course she'll go, Laura," Paula interrupted, lighting the burner beneath the pot of potatoes. "Your father wouldn't leave Caitlan all alone."

Don't bet on it, Caitlan thought.

"Good." Laura hooked her arm through Caitlan's, beaming a grin up at her. "Come on; let's go see the kittens."

"I'll be back to help with those cherry tarts, Paula," Caitlan called as Laura tugged her out of the kitchen. "Don't start without me!"

Instead of heading for the front door, Laura made a detour down the hall toward J.T.'s office. Realizing her intent, Caitlan pulled back and stopped just as Laura grabbed the doorknob. "What are you doing?"

Laura tilted her head to the side, grinning. "I just want to say good morning to Dad. It'll only take a second."

Before Caitlan could bow out gracefully, Laura opened the door and, arm still linked in Caitlan's, dragged her into the room with her. "Morning, Dad!" Laura announced, her bubbly mood nearly infectious.

J.T. glanced up from the papers and ledgers spread out on the wide desk in front of him. "Hi, Smidget." His gaze flickered from his exuberant daughter, bounding across the room, to Caitlan.

Caitlan gave him an apologetic look for interrupting his business, but he truly didn't seem to mind the intrusion. Standing by one of the chairs in front of J.T.'s desk, she watched as he accepted Laura's hug and quick kiss on the cheek. The closeness between father and daughter was evident, and Caitlan fleetingly wondered about Laura's mother, and how any woman could walk out on her own child. The young girl seemed well adjusted, her Aunt Debbie and Paula doted on her, but what about that constant mothering attention and guidance a girl Laura's age needed?

J.T. glanced at his watch, then chucked Laura lightly under the chin. "The bus is going to be here in twenty minutes. Don't miss it."

"I won't. I just want to show Caitlan the kittens, and then I'll go to the bus stop." Laura crossed back to Caitlan, then turned to her father with an impish grin. "Oh, and I just wanted to tell you so you don't worry about it; Caitlan is going to Aunt Debbie's with us on Sunday. Aunt Debbie really likes Caitlan, so I'm sure she won't mind having her over."

J.T.'s gaze slid to Caitlan, a half grin turning up the corners of his mouth. "I'm sure Debbie won't," he murmured.

Caitlan shifted on her feet, suddenly uncomfortable with his lazy observation. "If this is a family thing, I don't really need to go—"

"Debbie would skin me alive if I left you at home." He leaned back in his chair, his countenance relaxed. "We go over to her place every Sunday. I think she feels sorry for me, because it's the only day Paula doesn't cook supper."

"Dad can't cook," Laura said out of the side of her mouth.

"Hey, I thought you liked my grilled cheese sandwiches." J.T. feigned a hurt look. "I'm kind of partial to them myself."

Laura rolled her eyes dramatically. "Dad, you can't live on grilled cheese sandwiches alone. You need a wife; that way you wouldn't have to depend on Paula or Aunt Debbie."

J.T. shook a finger Laura's way. "And you need a swat to your bottom."

The words were tossed teasingly, but Caitlan noted the barely perceptible shift in J.T.'s easy mood. His jaw hardened, and the sparkle in his eyes faded. He kept his emotions tightly leashed, careful not to take his own personal grudge about a wife out on his daughter.

Sitting up, J.T. picked up his pencil and flipped open a folder. "Now get going before I make good on my threat."

"You're too much of a softy, Dad. I'll see ya after school." Laura blew her father a kiss from across the room, then headed for the door. "Come on, Caitlan; time's a wastin'."

Caitlan couldn't help delivering a parting remark to J.T., sugar-coating it with a grin. "Considering I have a *full* schedule ahead of me today, I'd better get a move on, huh?"

As she slipped out the door behind Laura, she heard J.T. say, "I ought to swat *your* butt."

Smiling to herself, Caitlan walked beside Laura as they cut across to the barn. The day promised to be beautiful. A slight, chilled breeze blew, but the sky was clear for as far as the eye could see. The ranch hands had long since gone, leaving the area peaceful and serene for the time being.

Laura looked at Caitlan, concern creasing her delicate brows. "Dad doesn't usually stick around the house. I hope he's feeling okay."

"I'm sure he's fine." Caitlan rubbed Laura's back in a gesture meant to soothe her worries.

141

"He mentioned this morning at breakfast that he had some paperwork to catch up on." Caitlan was grateful J.T. had decided to stay indoors. Having him so close made her job easier. She knew where he was and didn't have to worry about defying him, and angering him even more, by following him around the ranch while he worked. How would she explain the need to be by his side all day long? The longer he stayed around the house, the better.

Laura grabbed Caitlan's arm. "Will you keep an eye on him while I'm at school, just to be sure he's *really* okay?" she asked, her tone a shade away from a plea.

Caitlan patted her hand reassuringly. "Consider it done."

"Good." Laura smiled, her step suddenly light and buoyant. "You might want to have lunch with him, just to be sure he takes a break."

Caitlan lifted a brow, seeing through Laura's scheme. "Don't push your luck, sweetie. Your father barely puts up with me as it is. He knows where the kitchen is if he gets hungry."

"He likes you."

Caitlan shook her head. "Trust me. We've been over this before, Laura. Your father just tolerates me, and I don't think he'd appreciate you trying to play cupid." He'd made his feelings about relationships and involvements crystal clear last night.

"Someone has to do it." Laura tossed her head,

her mahogany mane of hair tumbling around her shoulders. "Give my dad a chance; he'll come around. I know he's a little stubborn and grouchy sometimes, but he can be really sweet, too."

Sweet wasn't a word she'd use to describe J.T. Sexy, tough, arrogant, and *maybe* a little humorous sometimes. Sweet? Never. "I'm all wrong for your father, and nothing good could come out of this. I'll be gone in a few days."

"You might find you like it here." Laura flashed her a smile and skipped ahead.

Caitlan liked it here—too much. She liked J.T., way too much, despite his resolve to keep her at arm's length and his sometimes gruff manner. There had been glimpses of a tender man, but he'd never allowed that side of his personality to fully develop with her. He always withdrew just in time, leaving her grasping for the promise of something more.

Shaking those thoughts from her mind, she followed Laura into the large red structure. Inside, the barn was cool and dim. Dust motes danced in a beam of sunlight filtering through a window in the loft.

"They're over here," Laura said, motioning to the far end of the barn.

At Laura's outburst, a huge black horse snorted and kicked the side of his stall. Caitlan stopped and peered through the pen's slats at the spooked animal as he tossed his head and bared his teeth. Caitlan moved closer, trying to make eye contact with the horse.

"Stay away from him," Laura said, a bit of fear in her voice.

"He's a beautiful stallion," Caitlan said in a soft voice, so as not to scare the horse any more than he already was. "What's his name?"

"King's Ransom, and he's mean and dangerous." Laura glanced at King warily and shuddered. "Dad would freak if he knew we were even this close to his stall."

"King," Caitlan whispered, and the stallion immediately settled down. Ears twitching, he searched for the source of the gently coaxing voice.

"Caitlan, leave him alone. He's worthless." Laura tugged on her sweater. "Come on, I only have a few minutes before I've gotta catch the bus and I want you to see the kittens."

Reluctantly, Caitlan left King, promising to return when she could be alone with him for a few minutes. The vibrations of terror she'd sensed from the horse concerned her.

In the corner of the barn, in a large box lined with shredded newspaper, five kittens stumbled about on shaky legs and mewled for their mother, their cries sharp and insistent.

Laughing at the expressive kittens, Caitlan knelt by the box. "They must be hungry." She reached in and picked up a smoky gray striped one.

Laura knelt beside Caitlan, looking over the

kittens with pride. "The momma kitty, Missy, will be here any minute. She's very protective of her kittens."

Rubbing noses with the gray, Caitlan chuckled as he licked the tip of her nose. "They're adorable."

"The one you're holding I named Brutus."

The kitten squirmed and twisted in Caitlan's grasp, trying to escape. "He's a strong one, isn't he?" She put him back with the rest of the litter and stroked the head of another kitten.

"That one I named Sunshine, and that's Pumpkin, and this one is Bandit," Laura said, pointing to each one in turn.

"What about this one?" Caitlan picked up the little feline getting trampled by its rambunctious siblings.

"I haven't figured out a name for her yet." Laura frowned as she thought. "She's the runt. Why don't you name her?"

Caitlan held the kitten up for inspection, her heart giving a little tug at the sweet, furry face with deep blue eyes staring back at her. The kitten let out a howl of protest and Caitlan laughed, placing her back in the box. "How about Sassy?"

"Yeah, I like that." Laura nodded. "Sassy it is."

Missy, the mother cat, nudged her way past Caitlan and jumped into her domain. After finding all five of her kittens safe, she cast a baleful look Caitlan's way, then promptly stretched out.

Each kitten clamored greedily for a nipple, sucking noisily.

Laura sighed. "I guess I'd better get going."

Straightening, Caitlan brushed the hay off her knees. "Yes. I don't want to be the one responsible for making you miss the school bus. Your father would just love that."

Once Laura was gone Caitlan went back inside the house and helped Paula make cherry tarts for that evening's dessert. They talked and joked, and Caitlan found she enjoyed the older woman's company immensely.

The day progressed slowly, even though there was plenty to do to help Paula with household chores. Every time Caitlan passed J.T.'s study she debated whether to stop and talk to him. But what would she say? Knowing he probably wouldn't appreciate being disturbed, she decided against the idea. He didn't even emerge for lunch. Paula took him a sandwich, a side of freshly made potato salad, and a glass of iced tea.

By early afternoon boredom set in. Caitlan thought about sketching, but after the disturbing vision she'd drawn the night before she wasn't all that eager to put pencil to paper. At least not in the light of day. She wanted the privacy of secluded night hours to delve deeper into her mind for the source of those images.

Sitting on the window seat in the living room, Caitlan gazed out the window, thinking of King's Ransom's peculiar behavior. Within five minutes

Caitlan stood by the stallion's stall, sugar cubes in her hand.

As soon as King saw her, he went wild, kicking and rearing like an animal possessed. "King," she called softly, and quietly unlatched the door to his stall.

The horse whinnied, a sound so mournful and hurting Caitlan ached deep inside for him. Slowly opening the door, she whispered his name again and again, a soothing litany that eventually calmed the stallion enough so he wasn't thrashing any longer. He stood at the far end of the stall, breathing hard, watching her warily.

Holding his gaze, she silently urged the horse to relax, giving him no reason to fear her. Heart pounding, she stepped inside his pen. King backed up anxiously, terror flashing in his gaze. She willed him to trust her, and gradually the trust came in the form of a soulful nicker. And then Caitlan knew, the perception so strong her animal sense tapped into the source of the stallion's anguish.

"Oh, you sweet, sweet thing. You're not dangerous, are you, boy?" she said, her throat thick with sorrow. "Someone's been abusing you. I'll make it better, I promise, but you've got to let me get close so I can help you."

After a long, tense minute King's Ransom took a tentative step forward.

*   *   *

J.T. pushed his chair back, stood, and stretched his stiff muscles. His body ached more from sitting in one position for hours, bending over a desk and pushing a pencil, than it would have if he'd ridden out with the boys today. He'd accomplished a lot, but he still needed to take inventory of supplies, and that would take a good day or two, considering the task had been neglected for far too long.

Right now, though, he needed a break.

Leaving the office, he found the house quiet and Paula gone, as was her daily routine. She'd be back to prepare dinner for the family later that afternoon, when Laura returned from school.

Walking through the kitchen and living room and finding them empty, J.T. wondered where Caitlan was. As much as he tried to convince himself he didn't want to have anything to do with her, he couldn't stop thinking about her warm, sweet response to him last night before he'd pushed her further than she'd been ready to go. He'd wanted her badly, but he wasn't such a brute that he'd take her by force or without setting down his ground rules first. And she'd clearly made her decision when she'd bolted from his room. He told himself it was for the best, but that didn't stop him from desiring her in a way that made him restless and edgy.

Rolling his shoulders to relieve the taut muscles there, he headed for the barn, deciding to take Quinn out for a run. The door to the structure was open, and he frowned as he stepped inside. His men knew better than to leave the barn door unsecured.

Caitlan's voice drifted to him from down the corridor. Soft. Gentle. Cajoling. Curious, he silently followed the sound of her murmured words and froze when he saw exactly where she was. In King's Ransom's stall. His heart hammered in his chest. Thinking of what the powerful, schizophrenic stallion was capable of doing when spooked, stark fear congealed the blood in his veins. His mind raced with ways to get Caitlan safely out of the pen without alarming King. Any sudden moves would put Caitlan in danger. And if he didn't get her out of there soon, chances were King would snap out of the trance she seemed to have him in and turn wild and possibly harm her.

Caitlan inched subtly forward, deeper into the stall. King's ears flattened back and he whinnied, the sound laced with uncertainty. His hoof pawed the ground, yet something in the beast's eyes softened as he watched Caitlan, as if he wanted to trust her.

"You know I won't hurt you, don't you, pretty boy?" Slowly stretching her hand toward King, Caitlan uncurled her fingers and revealed the treat in her palm. "Look. I've got some sugar cubes for you. You only need to come get them."

Hell, the fool woman was trying to sweet-talk the animal into submission. And if J.T. didn't know better, he'd think King was considering the offering in Caitlan's hand. But J.T. did know better, and despite how calm the stallion seemed, it would only take a movement to trigger a tantrum that could kill Caitlan if she didn't get out of the stall in time.

Shoving his apprehension aside, J.T. moved stealthily into the doorway. King's gaze darted in his direction and he snorted. Caitlan, absorbed in her task, didn't glance back.

"Come on, King," she coaxed in a low purr. "Come get the sugar cubes."

Praying Caitlan wouldn't resist his efforts, and King wouldn't charge at them, J.T. moved fast. Lunging into the stall, he grabbed Caitlan's arm in an iron grip and jerked her out through the doorway. Caitlan gasped in surprise just as King reared back on his hind legs and pawed at the air.

Shutting the door, J.T. turned and backed a wide-eyed Caitlan into the wall, pinning her there with his hands on either side of her head. His initial fear for her safety dissolved into anger that she'd been so careless as to approach an animal like King without thinking of the repercussions.

"What the hell do you think you're doing in King's stall?" he demanded, his tone smoldering with fury.

Now that his surprise attack was over, her chin

lifted a notch and she shot him a look of annoyance. "Relax."

"Relax?" Pushing off the wall, J.T. raked a hand through his hair, unable to believe *she* was perturbed at *him* for taking her out of a potentially deadly situation. "King could tear you apart, stomp all over you and kill you, and *you* want *me* to relax? *I* don't even go into his stall. It would be like committing suicide. Look at him." He waved a hand toward King, who punctuated J.T.'s words by kicking fiercely at the stall with his hind legs.

Pacing away from her, he dragged in a deep breath and forced himself to calm down. The clenching in his stomach subsided, and his pulse returned to normal. But deep, deep inside, past all the superficial stuff, he still felt jittery and a little provoked.

Damn! Face it, Rafferty. You aren't so angry at Caitlan as you are with your reaction to seeing her in King's stall. Fear. Helplessness. He cared too much, and caring was an emotion he didn't want to have anything to do with.

He whirled to face her. She hadn't moved, her eyes watching him as if he were a snake getting ready to strike. "I'm sorry," he said, the words sounding rusty, but he felt he owed her an apology for his rough handling of moments before. "You didn't know any better, but dammit, he's unpredictable and dangerous and my only thought was to get you out of his stall in one piece." Scrubbing a hand over his jaw, he resumed his agitated pacing. "Feeding him sugar cubes, of all things! You could have been seriously hurt."

Caitlan pushed off the wall and passed him. At first he thought she was going to walk out on him, but then she stopped in front of King's stall, staring through the slats at the stallion until he quieted.

Her ability to reach the stallion without words unnerved J.T. She crossed her arms over her chest and glanced back at him, her brows drawn over her eyes in consternation. "If he's so dangerous, why did you buy him?"

Sighing, J.T. came to her side. "Because I'd hoped I could break him."

"He's a beautiful animal," she said softly.

Caitlan's gentle serenity whispered to J.T., filling a void in him. He wondered if that was how King felt when she was near. Maybe that was why the animal responded so well to her. "Quite honestly, King wasn't this wild when I first bought him. He was a little spirited, which I liked, but he's gotten progressively worse over the months." He glanced down at Caitlan, looking into her upturned face. "I'm surprised you got as close as you did without him taking a chunk out of you."

She chewed on her lower lip, and he read the hesitation swirling in her violet eyes. Finally, she said, "Someone's been spooking him."

He lifted a brow, her declaration making him uneasy. "After five minutes in King's stall you came to that conclusion?" He forced an amused note to his voice. "I suppose King told you that while you were in his stall? Whispered it in your ear, maybe?"

She glanced away, but not before he saw her annoyance at his teasing remark. "I have . . . a way with animals," she explained, her attention drawn to the sugar cubes that were beginning to crystalize in her palm. "Your stallion is very spirited by nature, but he has some symptoms of being mistreated."

Her words were spoken with such conviction, he wondered if he should be insulted. "You're not insinuating I mistreat my animals, are you?"

Her gaze flew to his, her lips pursed. "Of course not. You're far too gentle and caring to abuse anything or anyone."

He jammed his hands on his hips, impatient and unsettled by all her observations. "Is my stallion marked?"

"No, not physically."

The woman was a witch, J.T. thought. Or an animal psychologist, if there was even such a thing. In so many words she was telling him that King was scarred emotionally. What a crock! He shook his head, retaining the urge to laugh off this whole verbal exchange. "You're crazy, you know that, lady? I'm going to just forget we ever had this weird conversation." He turned and started for the door. At the last minute he stopped and glanced back at her. "And stay out of his stall, Caitlan."

Caitlan watched J.T. slip out of the barn; then she moved to King's stall. She knew her comments about King's emotional abuse sounded strange to J.T., but she had no concrete evidence with which to back up her claim; only this strong sense she shared with the stallion.

Looking through the slats, she met King's gaze and knew in that moment that the stallion trusted her. "Good boy," she murmured, smiling. "I have a feeling you and I are going to become good friends."

Chapter Six

At three in the morning, after two hours spent with King, forming a fragile trust, Caitlan slipped quietly into the ranch house and up the stairs to the guest bedroom. Everyone had been asleep for hours, and she was careful not to make any loud noises as she shrugged out of her jacket and pulled off her boots.

Caitlan was pleased with the open way King had responded to her. With time and care J.T. would be able to fully enjoy the stallion's spirit, without the threat of the horse being dangerous. She couldn't help but wonder who was spooking King, and why.

More exhilarated than tired, Caitlan changed into her nightshirt, grabbed her sketch pad and pencil from the dresser drawer, and went back downstairs to cozy up in her spot in the living-room window seat. Drawing up her knees slightly for a table, she rested the pad on her thighs. Tonight she was too keyed up to lay down.

Thumbing past the disturbing sketch of the young boy she'd drawn last night, Caitlan started on a clean sheet of paper, consciously sketching a picture of J.T. astride King to keep herself oc-cupied. The contours of J.T.'s handsome face came easily to her, and as the image came to life, each feature at a time, a warm, shimmering sen-sation settled in her belly. Familiar images once again touched the edges of her memory. She closed her eyes to probe deeper, searching val-iantly for the link to these visions.

Strangely, the fragrance of a spring afternoon surrounded Caitlan, and the sensation of a warm breeze wafted across her skin. The sky above the beautiful meadow was cloudless. She heard the chirp of birds, and two orange butterflies flut-tered past. The sound of giggles and boyish laughter reached Caitlan's ears; then she saw them in her mind. The boy she'd drawn last night was playfully chasing the blond-haired girl, de-liberately allowing her to take the lead. Caitlan realized with sudden clarity that the boy was J.T., at about the age of fifteen. Why hadn't she no-ticed the resemblance in her drawing? And what significance did the girl hold to her visions?

J.T. chased the girl, closing in on her as they neared a stream and a large shady tree. The girl taunted him over her shoulder, daring him to catch her. One last long stride and he tackled her gently to the soft carpet of grass, her squeal of surprise rending the air.

"I gotcha!" he said, smiling down at her.

She gave him an upswept look, much too sultry for a girl so young. "So what're you gonna do about it?"

"This."

Caitlan watched in her mind as J.T.'s fingers fluttered over every ticklish spot on the girl's body. Impossible as it seemed, Caitlan's body began to tingle, as if she was being tickled, and she had the strangest urge to laugh along with J.T. and the girl. The young girl's gales of laughter filled the meadow and she gasped for breath, begging him to stop the torture.

"Say the magic words," J.T. coaxed, all the while his fingers were finding every vulnerable area—her neck, under her arm, her waist, just above the knee.

"I love you," she said breathlessly, then grew serious when J.T. stopped tickling her. She stared up at him, eyes shining with adoration. "I love you, Johnny."

"Much better," he murmured, a grin of satisfaction curving his mouth. All play vanished, replaced by a sensual hunger. "Now kiss me, Mandy." Lowering his head, he dropped his mouth over hers.

The kiss the young lovers shared was passionate, like the one she'd shared with J.T. last night. Caitlan's breath caught as ripples of silky heat rushed along her nerve endings, and the sensation of being deeply, thoroughly kissed stole through her. She was being swept away, into her vision, taking the place of the blond-haired girl.

J.T.'s feelings poured into her soul, an aching tenderness, an eternal love that twined around her heart, seducing her in the sweetest way. . . .

The creak and soft thud of someone coming down the stairs penetrated Caitlan's mind, banishing the images, but leaving the soft hum of awareness in her veins. Startled out of her thoughts, the pencil fell from her fingers and hit the wooden floor at the same instant that J.T. rounded the corner into the living room. He stopped abruptly, and even in the dim moonlight she could see his whole body go rigid and alert. Then a hiss of breath escaped him when he saw her form silhouetted in the window seat.

"Jesus, Caitlan, you scared the hell out of me." He dragged his fingers through his disheveled hair. "What are you doing up at this hour?"

Willing her pulse to subside, she watched him approach in slow, lazy strides, his bare feet padding on the floor. The only article of clothing he wore were his jeans, and Caitlan's mouth went a little dry when she remembered the hard warmth of his chest beneath her fingers last night. She swallowed and answered his question. "I, uh, I'm drawing." Flipping the pad closed, she concealed her private thoughts and images. "I couldn't sleep."

He sat down on the other end of the seat, his thigh touching her toes. His smile was sleepy, warm and sensual, and did intimate things to her already aroused body. Somewhere along the way last evening, through a pleasant dinner and afterward, watching a video with Laura, a truce had been called silently between them. She liked being comfortable with him and hoped it would last.

"Do you *ever* sleep?" he asked, moonlight glinting off the humor in his eyes.

"Yes." Considering two nights in a row he'd caught her up in the early morning hours, his question was a valid one. "I function fine on a few hours."

"I wish I could say the same." He leaned closer, looking over her jersey-covered knees to the sketch pad she held against her chest. "What are you drawing?"

"Nothing." Her chest tightened with apprehension. Now that she knew the boy she'd drawn was him, she wasn't sharing her sketches with anyone. If she didn't understand all the crazy things happening to her, how could she begin to explain them to him?

"Can I have a look at your nothing?" he persisted.

He touched a finger to her ankle—just a but-

terfly touch, really—but after the vision she'd
seen and experienced, her reaction was anything
but mild. Pleasurable waves of heat lapped up
her leg, making her conscious of a growing heaviness in secret places. He didn't seem aware of
the turmoil he caused in her, and she wasn't
about to let on to it by jerking her foot away.

"I'm just sketching a picture of King, nothing
spectacular." She surprised herself with the casualness of her voice.

"Don't tell me you're self-conscious about your
work." He smiled, that lazy, sexy smile that lit up
his eyes.

She shrugged. "I guess I am."

His finger fell away from her ankle and he
stared thoughtfully out the window. "I knew
someone who was the same way with her drawings. She had this natural gift, yet she was so
modest about it, like you." He glanced back at
her, and the distant pain in his eyes gripped her
heart. "Maybe someday you'll show me your
sketches?"

Someday. The future. There wouldn't be one for
them. Why did that thought make her ache deep
inside? "Maybe," she said, knowing it was a
promise she didn't have half a chance of keeping.

He stood and nodded toward the kitchen. "I
was just going to get a glass of orange juice. Since
both of us seem to have insomnia, care to join
me?"

J.T.'s invitation was one Caitlan couldn't resist.

She wanted to be near him, for reasons beyond protecting him. For selfish reasons that could never really amount to anything. He made her feel reckless and bold, and she went with the moment before it was lost to both of them.

"I'd love a glass of orange juice." Sliding off the window seat, she followed his form through the darkened living room.

J.T. flipped on the light when they walked into the kitchen. Caitlan sat down at the table. Setting her sketch pad and pencil aside, she watched as he strolled to the refrigerator, opened the door, and peered at the contents. The smooth muscles across his back flexed as he bent over and reached inside.

"I'm gonna wring her neck," J.T. grumbled irritably.

"Whose? Paula's?"

"No. Laura's." He brought out a glass pitcher with a ring of orange juice staining the bottom. "She always puts the pitcher back with only a few drops left in it. Does that look like enough to fill a glass to you?" He held the container up for her inspection.

Caitlan laughed softly, suspecting he asked the same question, and used the same patronizing tone, when reprimanding Laura herself. " 'Fess up. I'm sure you did it when you were a boy."

His fierce frown dissolved into a guilty grimace. "Actually, I was worse. I drank the juice directly out of the pitcher, then put it back in the fridge empty. Now I know why my mother used to get so upset, because it annoys the hell out of me when Laura does it." He set the pitcher in the sink, went back to the refrigerator, and grabbed the container of milk. "How about a cup of hot cocoa instead?"

"Sounds good." Standing, she walked to the counter where Paula had left the tarts. She pulled the plastic wrap off the plate, and the sweet yet tangy aroma of cherries drifted up to her. "Would you like one?" she offered. "I made them. You didn't have one after dinner, and if I do say so myself, for a first attempt they aren't half bad."

Filling the pan on the stove with milk, he glanced at her, his eyes glittering with a teasing light. "I'll risk eating one. Warmed, please."

She smiled. Setting two on a plate, she popped them into the small microwave, set the timer, and let them warm. Leaning her hip against the counter, she watched as he scooped sweetened cocoa into two mugs and then stirred the milk so it didn't scald.

Interested to know more about his family, and him, she asked softly, "Has your mother been gone for long?"

The surprise her question triggered was quickly replaced by a distant sadness in the depths of his gaze. "She died from cancer when I was eight."

His long-ago grief touched her. "You were so young." The microwave buzzed. Removing the plate, she took it to the table and sat back down.

"Yeah." He sighed, pouring the milk into each of their mugs. Bringing them to the table, he sat in his usual spot across from her. "It was tough when Mom died. Debbie and I were both close to her."

"Your father never remarried?"

"Nope. He loved Mom so much, he said he didn't even want to try and find someone as sweet as her." He grabbed one of the pastries and took a huge bite.

Caitlan smiled to herself, instinctively knowing that, with a love as binding as the one his parents had shared, they were joined in heaven. "So you grew up without a mother around," she went on, taking the other pastry and nibbling on the corner of it.

"Yeah." He stared thoughtfully at the filling oozing from his pastry. "I missed her, but I still had Dad for guidance. Mom's death was hardest on Debbie." He transferred his gaze to her, distant emotions shading his eyes. "Dad wasn't all that comfortable explaining 'female' things, and even though Paula was around, Debbie got cheated out of that closeness mothers and daughters seem to share. That's probably why Deb is so protective and extra loving with her own girls. She wants to give them everything she missed out on."

Caitlan swirled the cocoa in her mug, deciding

to take a gamble with her next question. "What about Laura's mom?"

Glancing at her sharply, he swallowed the last of his tart, chasing it down with a drink of his cocoa. "What about her?"

His tone and expression didn't encourage further questions, but Caitlan was too curious about this mystery woman. "Will you tell me about her?"

"What are you more interested in hearing?" he began, bitterness deepening the timbre of his voice. "That Stacey was a gold digger? That she deliberately got pregnant so I would marry her? Or maybe you'd like to hear about how she got bored with ranch life right after Laura was born and started sleeping with the hands before she divorced me to marry some rich guy from Texas?" His mouth stretched into a grim line, and there was a challenge in his gaze. "Not a pretty story, is it?"

Caitlan didn't allow his bluntness to dissuade her from wanting to know more. "Did you love her?" For some reason his answer was important to her.

He stared at her for a long moment, the air charged with turbulent emotions. Dragging his palm down the side of his face, he released a long breath burdened with regrets. "I tried, Caitlan. I really did. I wanted so badly to forget Aman—" He stopped abruptly, as if catching himself revealing too much. Then his jaw hardened. "It's difficult to love a woman who traps you into marriage for her own selfish means. I cared for Stacey. She gave me Laura, and for that I'll always be grateful."

"But you never loved her," she stated softly.

He shook his head. "No. I've already told you, I've only loved one woman and she's dead."

Caitlan understood his loneliness and pain so much better. What she didn't understand, however, was why her own heart felt exposed as a result of his lost love. Crazy. Unexplainable. Staring at the dregs of cocoa in the bottom of her mug, she channeled her thoughts down a different avenue. "Does Stacey ever see Laura?"

"Not since the day she left the ranch ten years ago. She had visitation rights, but she never exercised them. She didn't want the complications of a kid messing up her life with her rich Texan." He shrugged. "Actually, I'm grateful, because Laura doesn't need to be in the middle of a tug-of-war between Stacey and me. I know it has to be difficult for Laura without a mother around, but I try and do the best I can."

Caitlan heard the doubt threading through his voice, and without really considering her actions, she reached across and placed her hand on his arm and gave him a light squeeze. The contact of his warm flesh against her palm radiated up her arm like a ray of sunshine. "She's a wonderful girl. You should be proud."

He smiled, a genuinely proud grin that reached

his eyes. "Yes, she is, and yes, I am."

Caitlan grinned back and reluctantly withdrew her hand from the solid strength of his arm. He stared at her, his smile slowly fading into something more curious. His gaze gradually lowered to her mouth, making her suddenly conscious of her lips, and the way his had felt moving over hers. Like heated silk and, deeper, the taste of man and earthy desire. A light, fluttery sensation settled within her.

"What about you, Caitlan?" he asked, turning the tables on her. "Ever been married?"

"No."

He studied her closer, a scrutiny that made her uneasy. "How old are you?"

"Thirty-four."

"An old maid." He grinned, humor creasing the skin around his eyes. "That clock of yours is ticking."

"Yeah," she agreed for his benefit. She pressed her hand to her stomach, an unexpected, vast emptiness consuming her. For the first time since passing on, she resented not having had the chance to have children, the love of a good man, and a full life. Why did that bother her so much now?

"Ever been close to getting married?"

She glanced at J.T., his question evoking all kinds of feelings in her. Elusive sensations, and even more distant, wispy emotions. "Yes," she automatically answered. "Once. A very long time ago. Things didn't work out." She frowned, wondering how she knew she'd been close to getting married at one time, but unable to fully grasp the answers she sought. Vague images danced in her mind, and she closed her eyes to bring them into focus, ignoring the sudden heat of the medallion against her skin.

J.T. as a young man knelt in front of the blond-haired girl. His eyes openly displayed his love for her as he slipped a ring on her finger. "Will you marry me, Amanda Hamilton?"

"Are you sure?" the girl whispered in a voice mingled with happiness and insecurity.

"Absolutely. You've always been mine, Amanda. . . . "

Caitlan sucked in a sharp breath as a brutal pain seized her head and the images dispersed. Pressing her fingers to her temples, a distressed moan rolled from her throat. Heaven help her, what was her connection to these strange visions?

J.T. watched Caitlan squeeze her eyes shut, her face pale. She drew in a deep, steady breath as she rubbed her temples, as if warding off a sudden headache. "Caitlan, you okay?"

"No," she said on a low moan, blinking her lashes open. Confusion and pain glazed her eyes; then they cleared. "I mean yes, yes, I'm fine," she quickly amended, avoiding his gaze. "Just tired, I think."

Nodding his agreement, he gathered up their

plates and stood. "Considering it's nearly five in the morning, you should be." He rinsed their dishes, wondering at how easily she'd pried personal confessions from him, how easily he'd whiled away over an hour with her. What surprised him the most, though, was that he'd enjoyed every minute of being in her company.

He turned back toward her, noting that the color in her cheeks had returned, and she looked more in control of her senses. "Come on; I'll walk with you upstairs."

Grabbing her sketch pad and pencil, she slid from the bench. She passed him on the way to the door, giving him a facsimile of her normal bright smile. He shut off the light, throwing them into shadowed darkness. Quietly, side by side, they ascended the stairs. At the landing he grabbed her elbow and stopped her when she would have veered off toward her room.

She glanced at him, and he saw the questions in her eyes. Her tongue slid along her bottom lip, a nervous gesture he found endearing, and arousing. His gut tightened and heat flared like wildfire inside him.

For a reason he couldn't explain he didn't want to let her go, even though he knew he should. What he wanted was to lead her into his bedroom, lay her down on the bed, ease deep inside her, and stay in that paradise forever. He wanted to fill her up the same way she filled him when he was near her. Completely. Unequivocally.

Looking into her eyes, he wanted to drown in their endless depths that promised everything he'd lost faith in so long ago. Things he had no right expecting or taking from her.

He slid his fingers from her elbow and down her arm. Picking up her hand, he rubbed his callused thumb across the soft skin of her knuckles. "Thanks for listening to the sordid details of my life," he said, his voice low, a wry grin curving his mouth.

Caitlan got the distinct impression that J.T. didn't discuss his private life freely, yet he'd been so open with her. "They say confession is good for the soul." She resisted the urge to pull back the hand he caressed so softly. The way he stroked the sensitive skin in between each of her fingers made her knees weak and heat shimmer up her arm. Clutching her sketch pad to her breasts in an effort to stop the tingling in the sensitive tips, she forced a smile. "At least I'm good for something, huh?"

"You're good for a lot of things, I'm sure," he said, his suggestive tone adding to Caitlan's already overloaded senses. Leaning close, he grinned. "Don't tell Paula, but those cherry tarts were better than hers."

He looked so much like the young boy she'd drawn, so carefree and full of mischief, that she allowed an unrestrained grin to grace her lips. "I'm glad you liked them."

"Oh, I did," he murmured. "Very much." Suddenly growing serious, he let go of her hand and caressed the dimple creasing her right cheek with his finger, his touch feather-soft and reverent.

A shiver swept down Caitlan's spine. His gaze darkened hungrily, and deeper, she saw the desire and need that matched the building tension in her. Her breath caught, and a delicious anticipation sped up her pulse. *Leave before it's too late*, she told herself, but she ignored the warning, too caught up in the essence of J.T. A powerful force kept her rooted to the spot.

J.T. moved closer, his bare toes touching the tips of hers. Sliding his hands along her jaw, he cupped her face in his warm palms and lifted her mouth to his. Slowly lowering his head, his lips whispered over her cheek. Then his tongue darted out to stroke her dimple, a warm, damp caress that electrified her.

His assault was so gentle, so sensual, her lips parted on a soft moan.

J.T. glided his thumb across Caitlan's bottom lip, his mouth hovering inches above hers. "I'm gonna kiss you, Caitlan," he said, his voice husky with barely leashed restraint. "If you want me to stop, tell me now."

Even if she had wanted him to stop, she couldn't have found her voice to say so. The only sound she could manage was a whimper when his mouth skimmed over hers, then pressed more intimately. His fingers slid into her hair, and he cupped the back of her head in his hand, angling her mouth just so for his heated invasion.

Before Caitlan could catch her breath his tongue surged into her mouth, taking possession and stealing what little sanity she had left. His other hand wrapped around her waist and pulled her so close, the only thing separating them was their scant clothes and the tenacious hold she had on her sketch pad. Automatically, she splayed her free hand on his chest. The moment she touched his warm, firm flesh, her body swelled with awareness and an intense heat flooded her. Her connection to J.T. was stronger, more powerful than ever.

A groan of surrender rumbled up from his chest, and his kiss gentled. He made love to her mouth like a man who had all the time in the world. Like he couldn't get enough of her. Like she was water and he was dying of thirst.

She yearned to give him any sustenance he craved.

He broke the kiss and rested his forehead against hers, both of them struggling to regain a normal breathing pattern. Caitlan ran her tongue over her swollen lips, tasting the unique flavor of J.T., cherries, and chocolate.

Eyes closed, smiling, she whispered, "I like the way you taste."

He brushed his mouth over her lips again, his tongue following suit. Fingers still tangled in the hair at the back of her head, he gently pulled her away, waiting until she blinked her eyes open to look at him. "And I want to taste more of you. Everywhere, Caitlan. In every way possible. That kiss wasn't nearly enough."

She shivered at the wicked promises glittering in his eyes, wanting everything as much as he. Somehow, a semblance of reason stole through the desire making her lethargic, and she stepped from his embrace. She hated the chill that replaced the heat of moments before. "We can't. We shouldn't."

"Yeah, I know." His voice was rough, like sandpaper. "But it doesn't stop me from wanting you." Shoving his fingers through his hair, he glanced away, as if he'd revealed too much.

Finally he released a heavy sigh. "Go to bed, Caitlan."

The following day at noon, restless and unable to concentrate on the columns of figures in front of him, J.T. left his office. Strolling into the kitchen, hoping to catch a glimpse of Caitlan, he instead found Paula and Laura making sandwiches for lunch. His guest was nowhere to be seen.

"Hi, Dad." Laura greeted him with a huge smile, eyes sparkling. Abandoning her chore of shredding chicken, she gave him a kiss on the cheek. "Nice to see you've come out of hibernation. Are you going to stay in the office all day today?"

J.T. couldn't suppress a grin at his daughter's impudence. He was feeling pretty good, despite his lack of sleep last night. Refusing to admit Caitlan was responsible for his pleasant mood, he replied, "I thought I'd check the creek for blockages."

Laura shot him a disproving glance. "What about your head?"

"My head is fine, Smidget. I only want to check and make sure the creek is clear." Leaning his hip against the counter, he nabbed a piece of chicken and tossed it into his mouth.

Frowning, she spread mayonnaise on a slice of bread, then heaped it with chicken and a slice of cheese. "Why can't the other guys do that?"

"They can, but I want to get out for a bit. I won't do anything strenuous, I promise." To prove his point, he added, "Want to go with me?"

She looked at him, and he caught a flicker of pleasure in her eyes before it was quickly replaced by something much more mischievous. "No, but I'd bet Caitlan would like to go with you. She's been cooped up for two whole days. You can show her how beautiful it is here."

J.T. glanced at Paula, who gave him a light shrug and a I-had-nothing-to-do-with-Laura's-scheme kind of look before she continued slicing the loaf of fresh bread she'd made that morning. Paula might not have anything directly to do with Laura's ploy, J.T. thought, but she definitely wasn't against the idea.

Neither was he, which should have been enough to warn him he was getting too damned close to her. After their hot kiss last night, and the truce they'd established, taking things a couple of steps farther would be so easy. . . .

Reminding himself of the complications of getting involved with Caitlan, he shored up his resolve. "We haven't had much time together lately, Laura. I'd really enjoy if you came with me."

She waved a hand between them. "I've got things I want to do around here today. And Karen might come over this afternoon. Caitlan was saying just yesterday how she'd love to see the ranch." A sudden smile lit up her features, her eyes dancing with excitement. "You know, I just thought of something."

"Really?" he said dryly. "I can hardly wait to hear this one."

"Dad, stop being so stuffy!" she huffed in exasperation.

He raised his brows. "Me? Stuffy?"

"Yes, you." Laura poked him playfully in the chest, then gave him her best impression of an angelic look. "I was thinking, why don't I make you a couple of sandwiches, and after you and Caitlan check the ranch you can take her on a picnic?" Satisfied with the merit of her plan, she began wrapping sandwiches in plastic wrap.

"Laura, I don't think that's a good idea—"

She gave him a pointed look. "If you're going to be out checking the ranch, then you're both bound to get hungry." Grabbing a knapsack from a kitchen drawer, she put three sandwiches inside. "Here, I'll pack you a few sandwiches, some potato salad, and apples."

Paula chuckled, and J.T. glared at her, somehow knowing he'd lost this round.

"The girl's right, you know," Paula said, handing over two shiny apples to Laura. "You need to get out of the house, and Caitlan would love to see the place. You both just might get hungry, too."

J.T. didn't mention that he could just as easily eat lunch before he went out. He'd always used ranching as an excuse to forget everything and clear his head. Now, cooped up in his office, he found he constantly wondered where Caitlan was and what she was up to. What harm could there be in taking her with him? And a picnic was an innocent enough gesture, considering they *were* bound to get hungry.

"Where is Caitlan, anyway?" He watched as Paula filled a thermos with lemonade and added it to the sack.

Laura handed J.T. the care package with an encouraging smile. "She went to take Missy some milk and scraps. She's probably still down in the barn. Why don't you go get her?"

"I guess I will." J.T. grabbed one of his old Stetsons off the coat rack and jammed it on his head. "We won't be gone long."

"Don't worry about hurrying back." Laura practically pushed him out the kitchen door. "Oh, and have a good time!"

J.T. shook his head at his daughter's matchmaking. In the back of his mind he knew he should at least be annoyed by Laura's meddling, but he found it difficult to get mad at her for something he wanted just as much.

"Hello, Missy," Caitlan said in a soft voice as she approached the momma cat and her kittens. "I brought you some milk and chicken." As soon as she placed the bowl and plate next to the cardboard box housing Missy's family, the feline abandoned her nursing kittens for the food. Caitlan laughed softly at the loud mews of protest coming from the box.

Missy feasted on her meal, and Caitlan stroked the cat's back and scratched her behind the ears. Missy purred deep in her throat and let out an appreciative meow.

Smiling, Caitlan turned her attention to the mewling kittens. Murmuring sweet words to them, she reassured each of them with a touch and a caress that their mother would be returning soon. She heard steps behind her and assumed it was one of the hands working around the ranch today. From what Laura had told her, on weekends the hands rotated days off, and most of the men spent their time lazing around the bunkhouse and barn area.

Then the fine hairs at the nape of her neck tingled with apprehension.

"Well, if this isn't a tender scene."

The familiar, insolent voice sent a shiver racing up Caitlan's spine. Standing, she turned and gave her nemesis a tolerant look. "What do you want, Randal?"

He pushed off the stall he'd been leaning against and approached her with slow, stalking steps that made Caitlan uneasy. "You know what I want." Bloodshot eyes raked her from head to toe. "I want some answers."

Caitlan didn't care for the heinous glint in his gaze. "I don't know what you're talking about." She started past him, determined not to get into another confrontation.

Blocking her path, he shoved his hands hard against her shoulders, and she stumbled back into the wall. Missy, eating by Caitlan's foot, hunkered down and glared at Randal, her tail swishing in warning.

Gaining her composure, Caitlan made an attempt to dodge Randal, but the quarters were cramped and his hands shot out and slammed against the wall on either side of her head before she could make a clean getaway.

His eyes glittered with malevolence. "You're not going anywhere."

She turned her head slightly as his breath, hot

and fetid with the odor of liquor, slipped up her nose. Knowing better than to provoke someone who'd been tipping the bottle, she remained calm. "Let me go, Randal."

"I want to know what the hell is going on!" he said in a low voice infused with fury. "You being here is just too damned convenient."

Lifting a brow, she looked him square in the eye, hoping to intimidate him. "Do you have something to hide, Randal?"

Panic flashed in his glassy eyes, then was quickly replaced by a challenge of his own. "You tell me."

If she informed him she knew he was behind J.T.'s attack, she'd put J.T., and this mission, in jeopardy. She couldn't say anything; J.T. had to discover Randal's intentions on his own. So, instead, she gave Randal a noncommittal shrug.

He looked at her long and hard, the uncertainty in his gaze shifting to an outright leer. Slowly, a crude grin curved his mouth. "I don't know how you've managed it, but you've got J.T. wrapped around your finger." He pressed his body to hers, grinding his hips obscenely against hers. "You must really be something in the sack."

A thread of panic stole through Caitlan. Randal was a solidly built man, and she was no match for his strength. She pressed her hands against his chest and pushed, but he didn't budge. "Let me go, Randal." Her voice was even, in control. "You don't want to do this."

"Oh, I think I do." He laughed, the sound full of malice. "The perfect retribution. I think I'd like a piece of J.T.'s woman for myself. J.T. always gets everything, and since he's taken everything from me, I can show him what it feels like to be betrayed."

Caitlan shook her head, seeing a chance to reason with Randal. "J.T. has never betrayed you. He wants to help you, Randal—"

"What do you know about it?" His hostility lashed out at her like a whip.

God, there had to be some good in Randal, she thought desperately. A shred of decency somewhere. She tried to tap into some virtuous part of him, wanting so badly to convert him. *It's not your job to redeem Randal,* she reminded herself, but she wanted to at least try. For J.T.'s sake. "J.T. is a good man. It doesn't have to be like this."

"Yeah, but it'll be worth it just to see the look on J.T.'s face when I tell him I've had you." That thought alone seemed to give him great satisfaction, brightening his leering face.

Ignoring the panic tightening her chest, she thrust up her chin a notch. "You touch me and I'll scream. There're quite a few people around."

He laughed again, seemingly enjoying the game. "And when they come runnin' I'll tell them you came on to me. Wouldn't be the first time J.T. got himself involved with a slut." He lowered his mouth to her ear. "Besides, you might find you like bein' with me better than J.T."

She shivered in revulsion. Drawing a deep breath, she shoved at Randal with all her might. He grunted at the unexpected move, and as she fought against him, he tried to grab her hands. In the shuffle he kicked the box of kittens, and Missy retaliated.

With a low-throated growl, Missy clawed at Randal's leg as if it were a scratching post. Randal let out a howl of pain, then cursed, backing away from Caitlan. Even as Randal shook his leg to dislodge the feline, Missy hung on to his pants, her sharp claws ruthless.

Blessing Missy's interference, Caitlan feinted around Randal and ran to the entrance. Slipping outside, she glanced back to make sure Randal wasn't in pursuit . . . and slammed into a solid wall of flannel-covered muscle.

J.T. caught her arm before she would have bounced back and fallen on her bottom in the dirt. "Damn, Caitlan. Watch where you're going."

Caitlan had never been so relieved to see anyone in all her guardian days. Pressing a hand to her galloping heart, she caught her breath and glanced up into J.T.'s face, shadowed by his hat. "I'm sorry."

"What's the matter with you?" His lips compressed into a thin line and his eyes narrowed. "You weren't with King again, were you?"

She groped for the truth, unsure if she wanted to tell J.T. about her run-in with Randal, and risk a potentially explosive confrontation between cousins. In Randal's state of mind, which was precarious at best, Caitlan feared for J.T.'s safety. "No, I, uh, was with Missy and her kittens." She smiled up at him as if she didn't have a care in the world. "Did you need me for something?"

Frowning, he stared at her for a long moment, suspicion coloring his eyes. Finally he let go of her arm. "I was just going to do some spot-checking around the ranch." Glancing over her shoulder, he shifted restlessly on his feet. He cleared his throat. "Laura mentioned you might like to see the spread."

Despite the underhanded way he'd delivered his invitation, Caitlan couldn't stem the thrill of pleasure racing through her. "I'd love to."

"Go on up to the house and get a jacket," he said, nodding in that general direction. "I'll saddle up the horses."

J.T. stared after Caitlan as she made her way to the main house, wondering why he felt like a gawky adolescent again, like the first awkward time he'd asked Amanda to go riding with him with the intentions of stealing a kiss from her. He'd been thirteen, and J.T. could still remember the rapid hormonal awakening that had made him see Amanda for more than just a "buddy," had made him want to kiss her and touch her in more than a brotherly manner.

The first time he'd attempted to kiss Amanda she'd socked him in the arm. She'd been spitting mad, and confused. He'd seen the conflicting emotions in her eyes, and when he'd tried to apologize, she'd charged after him, knocking him to the ground. A skirmish ensued, but he came out the victor. He had kissed her again, gently, softly, and when her lips parted on a gasp, he'd introduced them both to their first deep kiss. Seconds later she had melted beneath him, warm and receptive to his exploration. And J.T. knew he was in love.

The sweet memory drifted through J.T., leaving him achy and empty inside. Why had he thought of that now? Shaking off the sensation of loss, he walked inside the barn, searching for a clue as to what Caitlan had been running from. And she had been running from something; he'd felt her tremble when he'd caught her arm, like she'd been spooked.

The horses in their stalls seemed calm, King included. He passed Missy, who shot him a disgruntled look before tending to her kittens. J.T. was on the verge of dismissing his concern when he saw his newest hand, Mike, in the tack room. Had the man said or done something to frighten Caitlan? Mike was moody, but he didn't seem the surly type.

Mike turned, a curry comb in his hand and a cigarette dangling from his lips. He gave J.T. a curt nod, but before he could escape out the back door to the adjoining paddock, J.T. stopped him.

"You know the rules, Mike: No smoking in or around the barn."

Mike squinted as plumes of smoke curled from the tip of his cigarette. "I was just getting a comb for—"

"No exceptions," he said, watching as the other man's jaw hardened.

"Sorry, boss," Mike murmured, pulling the cigarette from his mouth. "It won't happen again."

"Make sure that it doesn't." With a curt nod J.T. dismissed the hand, then went to saddle up the horses.

Chapter Seven

An hour and a half later, after checking the west fences and the creek for any problems and finding none, J.T. reined Quinn to a stop in a meadow brimming with wildflowers. Caitlan's mare, Blaze, automatically halted beside him. The creek cut a path through the meadow, and a huge apple tree, veiled with green leaves and white blossoms, dominated the area, its branches extending to form a shady canopy. Two elk sprinted into a nearby copse of brush and trees, followed by a scampering ground squirrel.

Caitlan's gaze encompassed the daisies, primrose, and wild yellow plum blooming in riots of color around them. "This place is beautiful," she said softly.

"Yeah." J.T. didn't know what, exactly, had drawn him here, especially since it had been years since he'd come to this spot. So many memories of Amanda lived here, of their childhood together, that he reconsidered the wisdom of bringing Caitlan to a place he almost thought of as sacred.

Strangely, the grief and pain he used to feel when visiting this meadow was now only a dull, distant sorrow. Maybe coming here was a good thing, he decided. Maybe it was time to face old memories, then pack them away for good.

J.T. dismounted Quinn in a fluid motion. "Ready for lunch?"

Smiling, Caitlan slid off Blaze and removed her jacket, hooking it on the saddle. "Sounds great. I'm starved."

He grinned back. "Good. Laura packed plenty of food." He handed her the knapsack and blanket he'd brought along. Taking her mare's reins, and Quinn's, he led the horses to the creek and left them there to graze.

"Will they be okay like that?" Squinting against the sunshine, Caitlan watched J.T. approach her again.

"Unless something spooks them they'll be content to graze on the grass." Grabbing the blanket from her, he snapped it out under the tree. Tossing his hat to the corner of the blanket, he ran his fingers through his hair and gestured with his other hand for Caitlan to sit down. He joined her and divvied up the food.

They ate in companionable silence, punctuated by an occasional comment about the ranch and its operation, or something equally mundane. The light scent of apple blossoms curled around them, and the faint hum of bees in the trees served as a relaxing symphony.

Caitlan finished her sandwich and potato salad and put away the remnants of her lunch. She licked a smear of mayonnaise from her thumb. "I do have to say, Laura puts together a terrific meal."

"It wasn't half bad." J.T. reclined lazily on the blanket. "Apple?" he offered, then crunched into his own.

She shook her head. "Maybe later. I think I'll go rinse my hands in the creek."

Away from J.T., Caitlan absorbed her surroundings, searching beyond the beauty of the land to tap into something more profound. Since the moment they'd arrived at this meadow, peculiar sensations had taken up residence in her. As if she'd been here before with J.T. But how could that be?

Dipping her hands into the creek, the water sparkled from the sun as it rippled away from her and over the smooth rocks. Glancing downstream, she saw places where the creek was shallow, where a person could easily walk across, and other areas too deep to detect anything but a bottomless, black pit. A chill swept through her, despite the pleasant warmth of the spring day, and she straightened, backing away from the swirling water. In her mind's eyes she saw the water churning and a little girl struggling to keep her head above the surface and slowly losing the battle.

Heart pounding, Caitlan turned away from the creek and banished the oppressive image. Where had that vision come from? she wondered, still a little shaken, as if *she'd* been the little girl on the verge of drowning.

Dismissing her unease, she started back toward J.T., smiling at his relaxed pose. He lay on his back, hands stacked beneath his head, eyes closed. His chest rose and fell in slow, even breaths. She stole a few moments to admire his lean form, and the way denim and flannel fit his muscular build to perfection.

Not wanting to disturb him, she strolled to the base of the tree, compelled by forces she didn't understand. A familiarity ribboned around her, like invisible strings pulling her closer to a precipice. A deeply etched carving in the trunk of the tree caught Caitlan's attention: a heart with an inscription of some sort, she noticed. She smiled at the sweet sentiment, until she stood close enough to recognize the names engraved in the center of the heart. *J.T. loves Amanda.*

Tentatively touching her finger to the smooth engraving, Caitlan traced the letters, feeling as though this was somehow a part of her. Deeply and widely sculpted, the declaration would remain for decades in the tree. Warmth rushed through her veins, and images flashed in her mind.

Young J.T. held the blond-haired girl's hand, pulling her toward the large tree by the creek.

"I've got a surprise for you, Mandy. Look."

The girl's breath caught when she saw the heart carved in the tree; then her face reflected the love he'd inscribed for her there.

"I did it so everyone will know how much I love you," he said.

"Amanda," Caitlan whispered, the name thick in her throat. *Amanda,* the girl in her visions with J.T. Caitlan frowned. Why did she share such a strong and powerful link to these two people, that she could tap into their past and see it so clearly? Heaven help her, what was the significance of these visions?

She glanced over her shoulder at J.T. Eyes open, he regarded her pensively, as if he too was remembering the day he'd shown Amanda the carved heart.

"Is she the one who died?" Caitlan knew before he answered that Amanda was the woman he'd loved and lost: his eternal soulmate.

"Yes." A sad smile brushed his mouth. "This was our special place. I think we christened it our meadow the day she fell into the creek."

"What happened?"

He hesitated, as if debating whether or not to share the memories with her. After a moment he propped himself up on his side, a reminiscent smile curving his mouth. "Amanda was seven, and she and my sister had come here to play with their dolls. I just happened to ride by on my mare, with the intention of antagonizing them, as all good brothers do to their little sisters and their friends. I saw Amanda slip and fall into one of the deepest parts of the creek. She couldn't swim, so I dove in and saved her from drowning."

That explained her earlier vision of the little girl struggling in the creek, Caitlan thought, but it didn't unravel the mystery of why she had experienced those momentary flashes of fear, as if *she* was the one drowning.

She went back to the blanket and sat cross-legged a few feet away from J.T. "I take it you became her hero?" she prompted, wanting to know more about this illusive child-woman who'd captured his heart.

"Yeah. After that day she was a complete nuisance, always following me around like a devoted puppy. We played together, but I remember wondering if Amanda would always be my shadow." Shaking his head, he chuckled softly. His eyes sparkled with a mischievous light. "Then I grew up and discovered why boys like girls so much. I started looking at Amanda differently, started noticing she had nice breasts and long legs. And whenever I got too close to her or she'd accidentally brush up against me, I'd feel warm and anxious . . . and aroused. Typical male hormones running rampant," he said with a grin. Then his humor fled, his expression touched with melancholy. "It only took a kiss, a very reluctant kiss from her," he admitted, "to know we were made for each other."

"Childhood sweethearts." Caitlan pulled up her knees and wrapped her arms around her legs.

"Yeah." His finger drew lazy patterns on the red-and-black-checkered squares on the blanket. "We grew up together. Our families had been neighbors all our lives, so it seemed only natural that the two of us get together. I don't think either of our parents expected it to last, but I knew Amanda was the only one for me. I knew we'd get married someday. . . . " His voice trailed off, his eyes filling with a tangible pain.

Caitlan watched him struggle with an internal anguish, his torment becoming her own. His loss and pain weighed heavily on her, making her heart ache. Unexplainable emotions crowded her throat, and she resisted the urge to touch him and chase away his misery.

He took a deep breath and forged on, as if wanting to purge himself of all his haunting memories. "Remember in the line shack when I was dreaming?"

"Yes."

"I was dreaming of Amanda, and when I started to wake up I thought you were her." An abrupt, harsh laugh escaped him. "I actually thought Amanda hadn't died, and I was so disappointed to find it was all just a dream. She was my life, Caitlan."

He stared at her for long moments, then reached up and ran the back of his knuckles down Caitlan's cheek, a feather touch so gentle it made her breath catch. A distinct tingle shot through her as their gazes locked. Very softly he said, "You remind me a lot of her."

An illusion of intimacy shimmered around Caitlan, and something else, a nagging familiarity that tugged at the edges of her consciousness. *You remind me a lot of her.* Could that explain the bond to him, and Amanda? And what, exactly, was her resemblance to Amanda?

"Do I . . . look like her?" Caitlan asked, needing to find answers to all the confusing emotions and visions plaguing her on this mission.

A lazy smile eased up the corner of his mouth. "She had eyes like yours, the same deep violet color. And she had a dimple too, like yours." His finger brushed over the crease in her cheek before falling away. "But that's where the physical similarities end. She had blond hair."

She had eyes like yours, the same deep violet color. And she had a dimple too, like yours. A pressure clamped around Caitlan's chest, suffocating her. Something taunted her conscience, like an itch she couldn't quite reach to scratch. Mentally, she searched her own background, desperate for answers, but found that section of her memory locked from her, as if she suffered from amnesia.

Frustration coiled through her. Why couldn't she remember any of her own memories of her past? Determined to learn more about this woman who seemed such an integral part of her visions, Caitlan asked, "What happened to Amanda?" When J.T. glanced at her questioningly she clarified, "I mean, how and when did she die?"

His mouth tightened with grief, and his eyes flashed with old, harbored anger. Immediately Caitlan knew she'd barged past the boundaries J.T. had constructed around his heart and those painful memories. "I'm sorry, J.T. I didn't mean—"

"No, it's okay." Heaving a heavy sigh, he pulled a blade of grass from the edge of the blanket and began shredding it. "I've never really talked about that night, but . . . I want to now."

Caitlan propped her chin on her knees and listened attentively as J.T. recited the events of his last night with Amanda: how he'd taken her to the line shack and proposed to her for her eighteenth birthday. He told Caitlan of their hopes and dreams for the future, painting a beautiful picture of two people so deeply in love that their devotion and passion for one another wove through Caitlan like intrinsic ribbons to her soul.

Then the darker side of the story came, the

ending to the beginning of J.T. and Amanda's life together.

"We were on our way to tell her parents about our engagement when a drunk driver hit us head on." J.T.'s voice vibrated with gut-wrenching loss. "Amanda was killed instantly."

At that moment Caitlan was thrust into a maelstrom of visions and emotions that echoed through her body and brought on a splitting headache that made her gasp.

The screech of brakes. The grind of metal against metal. Screams that seemed to rip from her soul. Shattering glass. Horrible, awful pain. Darkness. Then a burst of light at the end of a black corridor, accompanied by a peacefulness as she drifted up and away, toward the sky.

The medallion burned like fire between Caitlan's breasts, and she pulled the gold pendant out of her blouse, wanting more than ever to summon her Superiors and ask them what was going on and why she was experiencing such intense recollections that made no sense to her. And why, heaven help her, had she experienced Amanda's terror and anguish during the car crash?

"Caitlan? Are you okay?" J.T.'s hand was on her knee, shaking her back into the present.

Caitlan blinked, and the tears gathered in her eyes rolled down her cheeks. She dropped the hot medallion, deliberately setting it on the outside of her blouse until it completely cooled.

Hand trembling, she wiped away the moisture on her cheeks, still stunned by her reaction to his tale. Sniffling, she offered J.T. a wobbly smile. "That's such a sad story."

"Don't cry, Caitlan. It happened sixteen years ago." J.T. sat up. Caitlan's tears affected him deeply, because he knew they were genuine and offered in compassion. God, she was so sweet and pure, so unpretentious and giving—the same qualities he'd loved in Amanda and had thought no other woman possessed.

He thumbed another tear from her cheek, loving the silky texture of her skin. "I've learned to live with the loss, but I'd be a liar if I said I've never wondered what my life would be like if Amanda hadn't died. I still think about it. And sometimes I've even wished I would have died instead of her."

Caitlan's eyes widened slightly. "No!"

Her heated protest made him smile. "Yeah, you're right. Then I never would have had Laura." *Then I never would have met you.* Unable to define where that had come from, he mentally shook the thought right out of his head.

And just as easily another thought took its place. He wanted to kiss her, and the soft, sensual look in her violet eyes said she wanted it too. But he'd tasted her before, and he knew better than to think he'd be able to put her aside after one kiss. No, if his mouth so much as touched hers, he wouldn't stop until they'd made love—

and it would be a long, slow, lazy process because he'd want to taste and explore every inch of her. Even then he couldn't guarantee that would be enough to satisfy him. Not with her.

His eyes slid from her parted lips to the pendant around her neck: the pendant she'd clutched so desperately only minutes before. The gold glowed as if it held a life of its own, just like the first time he'd seen it in the line shack while she'd checked his head injury. This time, he gave into temptation and picked up the medallion. The warm gold tingled in his palm as he examined the swirled design.

He glanced up at her. A banked wariness lit her eyes, and he noticed she watched him closely. "Where did you get this?" he asked easily.

J.T. heard the reluctance in her voice when she replied, "Its been in the family for years."

"It's . . . different." The medallion *did* look like a family heirloom, but there was something else about it that lured and fascinated him. He rubbed his thumb over the surface, and a heat radiated up his arm, tingling along his nerve endings. Then, incredibly, he felt a pull on his senses, like a huge magnet drawing the very life out of him. He was powerless to stop it from happening. In the next instant a part of him seemed to merge with Caitlan, in her mind, in her soul, a union so extraordinary in its power and beauty, he felt intimately joined with her, heart, body and soul. The pendant blazed like fire in his hand

and he let it drop back to her blouse.

The whole exchange had happened so fast, he wondered if he'd only imagined the odd experience. The startled look in Caitlan's eyes confirmed that something had passed between them, but he couldn't bring himself to ask and possibly look like a fool for suggesting a psychic encounter had momentarily linked them. The incident had been too weird for his peace of mind, like a quick out-of-body experience.

Maybe he *was* losing his mind, he thought.

Deciding it was time to get back on the trail and put things into proper perspective, he grabbed his hat and jammed it on his head. He stood and extended his hand to her. "It's getting late. We'd better head back."

She nodded her agreement and put her hand in his, allowing him to help her up. "Thank you," she said softly, her fingers flexing in his palm.

They stood there, neither one moving, gazes locked. Caitlan's eyes darkened and her cheeks flushed with awareness. Her tongue darted out to touch her lower lip, as though the lingering effects of their encounter had aroused her. J.T. swore under his breath as a surge of heat sped through his veins. Hell, his own traitorous body throbbed with sexual excitement, demanding satisfaction. For a reckless second J.T. thought about damning consequences and lowering his mouth to hers and letting things proceed from there. Lord knew they both wanted each other, the sexual tension between them so palpable nothing but a physical joining could ease it.

Knowing nothing could come of them making love, despite the closeness they'd established this afternoon, J.T. summoned every source of will-power he possessed. He tried to convince himself that Caitlan would be grateful he hadn't taken advantage of the situation once she was back in the city, where she belonged, heart intact.

Distance, Rafferty; you need to put distance between you. Letting go of her hand, he stepped away. "You fold the blanket and I'll get the horses," he said in a rough voice. He headed toward Quinn and Blaze, hating the glimpse of hurt he'd seen in Caitlan's gaze. He swore again. Didn't she know how difficult it was to walk away from the sweet promise in her eyes?

Once they were packed up and mounted, J.T. spurred Quinn into a heavy gallop, as much to work off his frustration as to get back to the house and around people so Caitlan wouldn't be such a temptation. He made sure Blaze kept up, but left enough distance between himself and Caitlan so that conversation was impossible.

Coming up the last hundred yards, J.T. slowed Quinn. Looking ahead, he noticed a cluster of people standing around the barn—a few hands, Frank, Kirk, and Randal. Off to the side, Paula embraced Laura in a hug, his daughter's face buried in the woman's shoulder. Laura's friend,

Karen, stood beside them, looking as though she'd been crying.

A sense of foreboding twisted in J.T.'s gut. Bringing Quinn to an abrupt halt, he jumped off the horse, tossed the reins to a nearby hand, and strode toward Frank, Kirk, and Randal.

Just as he reached the trio, Laura broke away from Paula and ran toward him. "Dad!" she wailed, tears streaming down her face.

J.T. caught his daughter in his arms. She bawled against his chest, her body trembling violently as she clung to him. Momentarily stunned, he tried to console and calm her with words and gentle caresses, but she only cried harder. The words she spoke were unintelligible, garbled by her sobs and tears.

Fearing something had happened to jeopardize his daughter's life, he glanced up at his men, vaguely aware that Caitlan had come up beside him and was attempting to pacify Laura.

"What's going on?" he demanded.

The three men looked at him uneasily. Kirk spoke, his tone as grim as his expression. "Someone put Missy's kittens into King's stall."

Caitlan gasped audibly, and Laura's sobs increased.

"What?" J.T.'s fear of seconds before liquified to white-hot outrage.

"It's true." Frank shifted on his feet, glancing from Caitlan to Laura, and then back to J.T. again. "King, uh, trampled them to death."

J.T. let out a string of swear words he'd *never* used in the presence of ladies before, but anger overruled his manners. "Who the hell would do such a thing?"

"That's what we're trying to figure out," Randal said, averting his gaze to the entrance of the barn.

J.T. glanced around for Mike. Just before leaving with Caitlan today he'd issued the man a slight reprimand. Would he be spiteful enough to kill innocent kittens? And was this incident at all related to what had happened to him at the creek? Or was this a warning of some sort from the sick person stalking him? Damn, he didn't like not being able to trust his own hands.

"Who found the kittens?" he asked.

Kirk cast a sympathetic look at Laura. "Laura and Karen found them about fifteen minutes ago."

"Ah, Smidget," J.T. murmured, rocking her gently, his heart breaking for her. "I'm so sorry."

Laura looked up at him, her eyes puffy from the tears she'd shed, misery in their depths. "They're . . . they're all dead." She gulped in a breath, then another sob broke from her.

"Shhh." J.T. comforted Laura for a moment longer, then gently extricated her from his arms, anxious to do some investigating. Wanting to separate Laura from the situation, he glanced at Caitlan beside him, grateful for her presence.

Except she seemed preoccupied. A troubling

frown marred her brow and suspicion colored her eyes as she glared at Randal. Hell, was the woman still holding a grudge against Randal for his behavior the other night?

Might as well kill two birds with one stone, he thought. "Caitlan, would you please take Laura up to the house?"

She pulled her gaze from Randal and glanced at Laura, her features softening with concern and compassion. "Of course."

Laura shook her head wildly at J.T., on the verge of hysterics. "Who's gonna get the kittens?" she asked around a fresh wave of tears, sobs, and convulsive shudders.

"I'll take care of it," he promised, handing her over to Caitlan. "Go with Caitlan. I'll be up in a bit."

"Come on, honey." Caitlan wrapped her arm around Laura's shoulder and guided her toward the walkway leading to the main house. As Paula and Karen joined her, Caitlan glanced over her shoulder at Randal.

Randal met her gaze, a self-satisfied smirk curling the corners of his mouth. Then he turned and followed the other men into the barn.

The import of Randal's silent goad made Caitlan so physically ill, she thought she'd lose her lunch.

Paula shook her head, her lips pursed in disgust as she looked off into the distance. "I just don't understand who would do such a thing to those poor, helpless kittens."

The answer came all too easily to Caitlan: Randal.

Traumatized by what she'd witnessed, Laura lay on the couch in the living room, hugging a throw pillow to her chest, her body curled into a fetal position. Her head rested in Caitlan's lap, and Caitlan offered whatever comfort she could to the young girl while Paula called Karen's mother to pick up her daughter.

After all Laura's tears had been shed she stared into space, her body shuddering with an occasional sigh or hiccup. Caitlan rubbed Laura's back and played with her hair, granting the girl time to grieve for her precious kittens.

Laura refused to eat dinner. A little after seven, weary and exhausted, Laura fought her body's natural reaction to fall into slumber. Caitlan, seeing Laura's struggle with the inevitable, accompanied her upstairs to her room, helped her into a fresh nightgown, and pulled down the bedcovers.

Laura looked from the bed to Caitlan, her bottom lip trembling. "I don't want to be alone, Caitlan. Will you stay with me until I fall asleep?"

Caitlan realized she'd do anything for this sweet girl. Keeping her company, and keeping the terrible memories of what she'd experienced at bay, was so little to ask. "Sure, honey. Come on; get into bed."

Laura climbed up on the frilly canopied bed and snuggled under the covers. Caitlan turned off the light and joined her, lying on top of the bedspread. Within minutes of Caitlan stroking Laura's hair, the young girl had fallen asleep, her breathing deep and even. Still, Caitlan threaded the silky strands of Laura's hair though her fingers, reluctant to leave her.

A shaft of light from the hallway illuminated the room in a soft glow and enabled her to see Laura's puffy eyes, red nose, and swollen lips. Her features, although softened in repose, still held traces of the tragedy she'd suffered. And what about the emotional scars that would remain forever?

Fierce anger and protectiveness welled in Caitlan. Laura was an innocent person in this whole ordeal, and Caitlan resented that the ugliness had touched her. How far would Randal go in his quest for vengeance?

The sound of someone climbing the stairs brought Caitlan out of her musings. Recognizing J.T.'s lazy, booted stride, anticipation fluttered in her stomach. A moment later he filled Laura's doorway. Tiredly, he leaned his shoulder against the jamb, hip cocked, and crossed his arms over his chest. Silently, he stared toward the bed, his gaze drifting over Laura's prone form.

The hallway light silhouetted his large build, accentuating the width of his shoulders and the leanness of his waist and hips. There was a quiet strength about him that made Caitlan want to slip into his embrace for warmth and comfort. At the same time she had the undeniable urge to touch her mouth to his and soften the hardness there, wanted to caress her thumb over the frown creasing his brow.

His eyes moved from his daughter to her. Their gazes connected in the dimness. An incredible awareness, as hot and vital as flame, replaced the worry she'd detected moments before. Boldly, his smoky gaze traveled the length of her, undressing her with his eyes. Seeing the sensual heat in his gaze, the sudden carnal desire, she knew he was imagining her lying in *his* bed, naked, waiting for him. She shamelessly wished she were.

Desire danced through her, a wanting so explicit and urgent it should have shocked her but no longer did. This smoldering hunger was a remnant of the heat he'd generated during their picnic but hadn't had the courtesy to extinguish. Desire and need mingled as one, a yearning so powerful that a delicious warmth cascaded through her veins.

She searched for something appropriate to say to break the spell and managed a whispery, "Hi."

"Hi." Wrapped in the shadows of the room, his voice was rough, gravelly, and sexy, sliding over all those warm, secret places that responded so effortlessly to him.

Pushing off the doorjamb, he slowly crossed to

the bed and ran his knuckles down Laura's cheek, then smoothed his large hand gently over her head. A shuddering sigh escaped Laura, and she snuggled deeper into her pillow, murmuring incoherent words. Straightening, he glanced at Caitlan, and she saw the true weariness in his eyes.

J.T. jammed his hands on his hips, his expression taking on a protective edge. "How is she?"

"Emotionally exhausted, but I think she'll be fine." Caitlan came up on her elbow, a little self-conscious about being with Laura, as if J.T. might think she was trying to horn in where she really didn't belong. "She didn't want to be alone. I hope you don't mind."

"Mind what?" A wry, private smile touched his lips. "You being a surrogate mom?"

"If that's what you want to call it." She shrugged lightly and glanced at Laura's pretty face, knowing once her mission ended that this child would still be special to her. "She needed someone to be with her. I'm just glad I was around to help."

J.T. rubbed the muscles at the back of his neck. "I should have been with her," he said in a low voice filled with self-recrimination. "But I needed to get to the bottom of this incident with the kittens."

"I understand," she reassured him softly. "And I think Laura understands too."

Their eyes met and held for endless seconds.

Then J.T. expelled a deep, resigned breath. "Thank you, Caitlan. For everything."

"You're welcome." She couldn't help the smile lifting her lips, inordinately pleased that he actually appreciated her and had swallowed his pride enough to admit it. Then her thoughts detoured to more important matters. "Did you find out who's responsible for killing the kittens?"

Laura stirred, shifting onto her back, mumbling something about Tommy pulling on her hair.

J.T. lifted a brow at his daughter's comment, then whispered to Caitlan, "Why don't we finish this discussion down in the kitchen?"

Nodding, Caitlan slid off the bed. She adjusted the covers over Laura and placed a light kiss on the girl's soft cheek. "Sweet dreams, honey." Glancing at J.T., she found him watching her with a caring and warm glimmer in his eyes.

Shaking off the bout of awareness shimmering over her, she passed him as she moved through the doorway. "Let's go," she said, too aware of how quiet the house was, now that Paula had left a half hour ago.

He caught up to her on the stairs. "Who in the hell is Tommy?" he growled like an overly provoked papa bear.

Caitlan grinned at J.T.'s prickly attitude in relation to boys and his little girl. "Probably a boyfriend at school who pulls her hair to get her attention." She shot him a pointed look. "Don't embarrass Laura by asking her about it."

"A boyfriend?" he said incredulously, dogging her steps through the living room. "She's only twelve years old, for crying out loud!"

Caitlan laughed softly, amused. "A very *pretty* twelve-year-old," she stated emphatically, then gave him a sidelong look. "How old was Amanda the first time you kissed her?" She flicked on the kitchen light and turned to face him.

"Uh, twelve. Damn!" He scowled. "If this Tommy kid so much as touches Laura, I'll break his legs."

For a moment Caitlan wished she could be around when Laura started dating, just to be a buffer between an overprotective father and his daughter. "I sure pity Laura when she starts dating. Are you going to be the kind of father who greets Laura's dates with shotgun in hand?"

His brows lifted a fraction, considering her suggestion. "Not a bad idea."

Caitlan shook her head and dropped the subject, not wanting to be held accountable for planting these wild ideas in J.T.'s head. Laura would never forgive her. Opening the refrigerator, she retrieved the Sloppy Joe mix Paula had prepared for supper, but no one had eaten because of all the earlier chaos. Under the circumstances Frank and Kirk had gone home for supper.

Turning on a burner, she scooped enough

meat for J.T.'s meal into a saucepan. "What did you find out about the kittens?"

"Not much as far as who actually threw them into King's stall." He sat down on the bench, legs spread, elbows braced on his knees. Plowing all ten fingers through his hair in a frustrated gesture, he stared at the floor between his booted feet. "Everyone seems to be accounted for when it happened."

While the meat simmered, Caitlan pulled three hamburger buns from the bread box and put them on a plate. Placing a slice of cheese on each, she glanced back at J.T. "Where was Randal?" She strove to keep her tone neutral.

J.T.'s head shot up, his eyes narrowed. "Randal? You think he had something to do with this?"

Caitlan didn't *think*, she knew for certain Randal had thrown the kittens into King's stall as an act of revenge—toward her and possibly toward Missy for attacking him. Yet she had no concrete evidence beside her gut instinct, and Randal's awful smirk, that he'd actually done the deed.

Heaping the meat onto the buns and cheese, she gave a casual shrug. "I'm just curious where he was when this happened."

"He was with Hank and Sam down at the cookhouse when Laura started screaming."

Great alibi, Caitlan thought, but how long had the kittens been dead before Laura found them?

Caitlan set J.T.'s dinner on the table, along

with a tall glass of iced tea.

J.T. turned around toward the table, glancing from his plate of Sloppy Joe's to Caitlan, who'd taken a seat across from him. "Thanks. You didn't have to make my dinner." A smile tipped the corners of his mouth. "I'm not such a lousy cook that I couldn't have warmed the meat myself."

She smiled. "I'm sure you could have, but you look exhausted and I really don't mind."

He picked up a sandwich, then looked back at her. "Aren't you going to eat?"

"I'm not hungry. Go ahead."

He devoured the first Sloppy Joe with gusto and gulped down half his iced tea. After swiping his mouth with a napkin he said, "I'm still trying to figure out if this incident with the kittens has anything to do with what happened to me at the creek. I'll be damned if I can think of any reason why someone would want me killed, or what killing those kittens would accomplish. It all seems like someone's demented idea of fun." He picked up another sandwich, a ruthless look entering his eyes. "I especially don't like the thought that my daughter's life could be in danger."

His concern was a very realistic one, Caitlan thought, considering the fact that Randal showed no remorse for the acts of violence he'd already committed. "Are you sure there's no one around here holding a grudge of some sort against you?" she prompted.

J.T. washed a bite of sandwich down with a long drink of iced tea. "The only person who's held a grudge against me has been Randal, but it's a personal grudge that has been ongoing since our childhood." He waved a hand in the air, dismissing Randal as a possible suspect.

Caitlan ignored the subtle hint to let the subject drop. "Does Randal stand to gain anything if you should die?"

"You mean the ranch?"

"Yes."

He shook his head. "No. If anything should happen to me, everything, right down to the last head of cattle, will go to Laura when she turns twenty-one. Until then Kirk and Debbie would have control of the estate and her trust."

He finished off his last sandwich, stood, and took his dish to the sink and rinsed it. Wiping his hands on a dishtowel, he stared out the kitchen window to the darkened night beyond. Caitlan thought this was his way of ending their discussion until he turned around and propped his hip against the counter, looking at her intently.

Indecision warred in his gaze, then finally he said, "There's one person I'm getting increasingly suspicious of."

Startled by the possibility that she'd somehow been wrong about Randal, she sat up straighter. "Who?"

"Mike Peterson, a hand I hired a few months back."

Janelle Denison

"What has he done?"

"Nothing, really." Releasing a tight breath, he scrubbed a hand down the stubble shadowing his jaw. "At least nothing that I've actually caught him doing, but it's the way he slinks around the place that annoys me. If *anyone* had a reason to throw those kittens into King's stall, he did."

"Why?" Caitlan found it hard to believe that someone else had as much motivation as Randal for killing those kittens.

"Remember when you came running out of the barn and bumped into me?"

"Yes," she answered cautiously, trying to guess what he was getting at.

"Did you see Mike in there before you came out? He's a lanky guy with dark hair, kind of brooding."

Caitlan hadn't seen anyone but Randal, but that didn't mean Mike hadn't been there, witnessing the argument between herself and Randal. If Mike had, wouldn't he have said or done something to help her? "No, I didn't see him. Why?"

"Because after I sent you up to the house for a jacket I went into the barn and ran into him. He was smoking a cigarette in the tack room and I got on his case about smoking in the barn. He knows better. One little spark and the place would go up like an inferno. He apologized and promised it wouldn't happen again, but there's just something about him I don't trust. I'm thinking about letting him go, but I can't prove he's done anything." He shifted on his feet, frustration rippling through him. "Hell, I don't know anymore, Caitlan. I hate looking at my men, men I've trusted, and wondering if any of them are involved in these incidents."

He whirled around and braced his hands on the counter, his gaze trained out the window again. The muscles across his shoulders bunched with tension, and it took deliberate restraint on Caitlan's part not to jump up and go to him, to put her arms around his waist and offer quiet reassurance and support.

After an eternity of seconds had passed J.T. swore harshly, his words bitter and succinct to match his mood, and pushed away from the counter. Mumbling something about going into his office, he disappeared from the kitchen, leaving Caitlan feeling alone, emotionally drained, and empty inside.

Somehow she knew J.T. felt the same.

Chapter Eight

Carrying a plate of fresh sliced bananas and a piece of toast, Caitlan knocked softly on Laura's bedroom door, wanting to reassure herself that the girl was okay, since she hadn't come down for breakfast.

"Come in," Laura answered, her quiet voice barely reaching Caitlan's ears.

Opening the door, Caitlan peeked inside. Laura stood in front of her dresser mirror, methodically running a brush through her long hair. Her face looked freshly scrubbed, and although sadness lingered in her eyes, the puffiness around them had diminished. In accordance with the unusually warm spring day, she'd dressed in pink shorts, a white shirt, and sandals.

Stepping inside the room, Caitlan smiled. "I brought you something to eat before we leave for your Aunt Debbie's. How are you feeling?"

Laura put the brush down and shrugged. "Okay, I guess. Dad's already been up here three times to check on me."

"He's just worried about you. We all are."

"I know." Tears welled in Laura's eyes, and her bottom lip trembled slightly. "Is it okay if we don't talk about what happened yesterday?"

"Absolutely." Caitlan understood. The memory was still fresh and raw. Laura needed her own time to heal. "But when and if you do want to talk about it, I'd be happy to listen."

Laura nodded, sniffling.

Caitlan gave her the plate of food, attempting to keep Laura's mind occupied with other things. "How would you like me to French braid your hair before we leave?"

Laura's eyes widened. "You know how?"

"Yep."

Laura grinned. "That'll be so cool!"

Pleased that her tactic had worked, Caitlan motioned for her to sit down on the bed while she retrieved a comb and an elastic band from the dresser. Coming up behind Laura, Caitlan sectioned off her hair and began the braiding and layering process.

"Tell me what to expect when we get to your Aunt Debbie's today," Caitlan said, purposely making her request sound more like interest, rather than a diversion.

For the next fifteen minutes, while Laura ate her snack and entertained Caitlan with tales of many Sunday afternoons past, Caitlan finished the French braid and secured the end with the elastic band.

Caitlan was so in tune with J.T., she felt his presence before she actually saw or heard him. Heat tingled along her nerve endings and a light flutter tickled her belly. While Laura chatted on, Caitlan glanced surreptitiously toward the doorway, already knowing what she would find.

Her gaze collided with J.T.'s. This was the first time she'd seen him since he'd walked out on her in the kitchen the night before and she had to admit he looked much better, the tension and frustration seemingly gone for the time being. He wasn't wearing his hat, and she decided she preferred him without it.

Darker threads of gold warmed his green eyes, and the corner of his mouth curved in a smile so sexy and intimate, Caitlan's body flushed with a startling excitement that robbed her of breath. Before she could find her voice to acknowledge him, his gaze drifted over the blue chambray shirt Debbie had loaned her, and down the length of her jeans-clad legs to her beige leather boots. When he looked back up approval and something much more primitive flickered in the depths of his eyes.

Casually, he strode into the room, as if he hadn't just put her body in a state of nuclear meltdown. "You girls ready to go?"

Laura's head whipped around to J.T., and she smiled up at him. "Oh, hi, Dad. Do you like my hair?" she asked, turning her head so he could check out Caitlan's handiwork.

"Umm. I love it," he commented, playfully tugging the tail of the braid.

Casting her father a tolerant look, Laura smoothed her hand over the intricate weaving "I want to get a bow for the end of my braid. Wait here, Caitlan," she said, then rushed out of the room. Seconds later the sound of drawers being open and closed echoed from the bathroom.

The smile on J.T.'s lips belied the accusatory arch of his brow. "What did you do to my daughter? I've been in here three times this morning trying to cheer her up, and each time I could barely coax a smile out of her."

Caitlan gave him an upswept look injected with teasing charm. "It's a woman thing."

"Well, whatever it is, I like it." He grew serious, his gaze warming with gratitude. "Sometimes I don't know the right things to say or do to make it better for Laura."

Caitlan heard the hint of insecurity in his voice. "I don't think she's all better, J.T., but at least the day at Debbie's will give her a temporary diversion from what happened."

"Yeah," he agreed, just as Laura bounded back

into the room and presented Caitlan with a pretty pink bow for her to clip on the end of her braid. Once that had been accomplished J.T. locked up the house and escorted them to his Ford Ranger.

He opened the passenger door for them and motioned toward the bench seat. "Slide on in."

"Go ahead, Caitlan," Laura said, smiling innocently. "I like to sit by the window."

What difference did that make when windows encased all four sides of the truck? The difference, Caitlan presumed, was that she'd be sitting next to J.T.—very close to him, by the looks of the small cab. The mischievous sparkle in Laura's eyes confirmed the girl's intent.

"I promise I won't bite," J.T. murmured from behind Caitlan, his low voice sliding over her like heated honey. "At least not much."

A shiver rippled down Caitlan's spine, settling low in her belly. Mentally shaking off her foolishness—she was only going to sit next to him, for heaven's sake!—she climbed into the truck and settled herself in the middle—and realized what a compromising situation Laura had actually put her in.

The small cab had been built to seat two comfortably, three if the middle person put one leg on either side of the stick shift, which Caitlan did, trying her best to keep her legs modestly together. She refused to let this situation affect her!

Her resolve liquified when J.T. slid into the driver's side next to her. Her knee bumped his and the hard length of his thigh pressed against hers, the heat so intense Caitlan scooted subtly closer to Laura, giving her and J.T. an inch reprieve that lasted all of five seconds, when his hand brushed her hip—deliberately?—as he buckled his seat belt. A slow kind of fever found its way to the tips of her breasts, tightening her nipples.

The torture wasn't over yet. J.T. reached between her legs to grab the stick shift, his forearm draping over her thigh. He attempted to put the stick into reverse but came up against her knee before he could shove the gear into the appointed slot.

Her breath caught, not so much from any pain he might have inflicted, but from the way his thumb caressed the inside of her knee, a slow circular pressure that quickened her pulse.

"Sorry," he murmured, his tone more a husky purr than contrite. "You're gonna have to spread your legs a little more."

Heat scored Caitlan's cheeks, and when she risked a glance at him she saw the silent laughter in his eyes. While she squirmed, he found her discomfort and embarrassment amusing, the cad! Doing as he requested, she widened her legs, giving him more access to shift freely, but leaving herself feeling too self-conscious, too aware of hands and fingers . . . *Oh, just stop it, Caitlan!*

"Much better," he said, grinning wickedly.

The man might not bite, Caitlan thought, but

Janelle Denison

the heat wave that killer smile radiated proved just as dangerous.

Laura, grinning and singing along to a tune on the radio, looked out the window, oblivious to the charged energy between the adults.

Thankfully, the drive to Kirk and Debbie's neighboring house took less than five minutes, but for every one of those three hundred seconds she concentrated on the passing scenery and *not* the musky, masculine smell of him, the way denim stretched taut over his muscular thighs, or the way he'd cuffed back his shirtsleeves, exposing strong, tanned forearms dusted with dark hair.

Caitlan grit her teeth to stop the onslaught. Who was she trying to fool? The man was too masculine, too sexy, too . . . everything, for her not to notice.

J.T. wheeled into his sister's driveway and brought the truck to a stop next to a barn. He pulled the emergency brake, and before he could shut off the engine and unclasp his seat belt, Caitlan had scrambled out of the cab behind Laura.

Shutting the truck door, Caitlan glanced up and froze. Laura skipped up the walkway, calling for Caitlan and J.T. to hurry, but Caitlan barely heard her past the sudden roar in her ears. A peculiar sensation cloaked her, one she couldn't clearly define or pinpoint. This house, this place, seemed so familiar, like she'd been here before.

Searching her memory for any recollection, Caitlan scanned the area. The house looked recently painted, a beige color with dark brown trim, and the front yard was well manicured. Planters of blooming flowers bordered the porch. To the side of the house three horses grazed in a small fenced-in pasture. Fuzzy, wispy images teased her mind, and she concentrated to bring them into focus.

"Earth to Caitlan." J.T. waved a hand in front of her face.

J.T.'s voice snapped Caitlan back into the present before the vision had a chance to focus. Frowning, she looked up at him, wishing she could shake the images rushing through her mind.

J.T. snapped his fingers in front of her. "Hey, Caitlan. Are you with me?"

"I'm here," she said, then continued cautiously, "I know this is going to sound weird, but I feel like I've been here before." Yet when she sifted through her memory she found nothing.

"Déjà vu, huh?" He grinned at her.

"Yeah, something like that."

He chucked her lightly under the chin, an amused glint in his eyes. "If you've ever been here before, then it must've been in another lifetime. Come on; I smell chicken being barbecued, and I'm starved."

He said the last on a playful growl that made Caitlan laugh and forget her worries. Grabbing her hand, J.T. guided her up the walkway and through a side gate, which led to a landscaped backyard and a covered porch, where the family had gathered.

Determined to enjoy the day, and J.T., Caitlan did her best to forget the strange feelings, although she couldn't completely diminish her awareness or her sense of familiarity.

Greetings went around, and Caitlan found herself being embraced by Debbie. "I'm so glad you came. I have to agree with Paula; it *is* nice having another woman around to talk to."

Caitlan held back the urge to remind Debbie that her "visit" was only temporary. "Need any help?"

"Sure, come on in the house." Debbie shooed at J.T. with her hand. "You go on and help Kirk barbecue the chicken and ribs."

"Yes, ma'am," he drawled, and, after giving Caitlan a look she could only describe as bone-melting, he turned and strolled to a paved area at the end of the yard.

Caitlan spent the next half hour with Debbie, helping her put the baked beans in a dish, wrapping the corn on the cob in tinfoil, warming the bread and taking those covered dishes to the picnic table on the porch.

They ate an early afternoon supper. Caitlan found herself seated between Brittany and J.T., compliments of Laura's sly maneuvering. Ignoring the heat of J.T., and the heady scent of his aftershave, she contributed her share of input to the lively conversation at the table.

Caitlan loved the closeness this family shared, the way everyone laughed and teased and generally had a good time. Throughout the meal she'd caught J.T. casting subtle glances at her in a way that made her breath catch; then he'd brush up against her reaching for a dish of food on the table, eliciting a wave of heat lapping along her nerves. All gestures were innocently executed, but her reaction was shockingly arousing.

She was getting used to her instantaneous response to J.T., and the way he felt like a significant part of her she hadn't realized was missing until she'd rescued him. The hum of desire invading her body when he touched her was a delicious sensation, and she was becoming increasingly curious to see where it might lead but knew better than to pursue such a brazen impulse. And woven into all these intricate sensations sprang a deeper emotion of caring, that strange link to J.T. nudging gently at her heart and soul, demanding entrance.

At the end of the meal, Brittany reached across the table for another napkin to wipe her sticky fingers, and as she pulled back, her elbow connected with Caitlan's full glass of lemonade. The plastic cup tumbled over, the juice splashing onto Caitlan's lap. With a startled gasp, she stood, but the cold liquid had already seeped into her jeans.

"Oh, Caitlan, I'm sorry," Brittany said, pressing the napkin she'd just grabbed to Caitlan's soaked jeans.

"It's okay, sweetie," Caitlan reassured the stricken little girl, dabbing at her thigh with her own napkin. "It was just an accident."

"Need some help?" J.T. offered in a low voice laced with a sexy challenge.

Caitlan shot him a look and couldn't help but smile when she saw the amusement flickering in his gaze. "I think I can handle this one myself."

"Just checking."

"Girls," Debbie began, spurring into action, "clear the table for me, please. Come on, Caitlan; let's go find something dry for you to wear."

Caitlan followed Debbie into the house. "I shouldn't have had my glass of lemonade so close to the edge of the table."

Turning down the hallway to the back rooms, Debbie waved away Caitlan's concern. "Spills are pretty common in this household. I remember once when Laura accidentally dropped a platter of pork chops onto Kirk's lap. . . . "

While Debbie recited the tale, the sense of familiarity Caitlan had held at bay since first arriving came rushing back to her, stunning in its force. They arrived in Debbie's bedroom and the sensation grew. Prickles of awareness danced across her skin.

Debbie opened her closet and searched through her things. "Since the lemonade only spilled on your jeans, I have the skirt that goes with that blouse." Smiling in satisfaction, she handed Caitlan a blue chambray skirt with a ruffled hem. "It'll be nice and cool, and I even have a matching petticoat."

Caitlan caught on to the woman's ploy. "Debbie, I don't need a petticoat—"

"Oh, come on, Caitlan," she chided her gently. "All us women like to wear pretty things under our clothes." Debbie lifted the skirt of her simple green pastel dress to show off the petticoat she wore, a cotton slip edged in a row of lacy feminine ruffles. An impish grin creased Debbie's mouth. "Kirk thinks they're sexy."

Caitlan truly didn't need the frilly undergarment, but Debbie was a woman on a mission, and by the gleam in her eyes Caitlan knew this was one argument she would lose. *Be honest with yourself, Caitlan. You want to look pretty for J.T. You like the thought that he might find you sexy.*

Goodness, when had she become such a brazen angel? And did she have the right to play with the flames J.T. created between them, and possibly kindle an out-of-control bonfire? The emotions stirring within her for J.T. went beyond anything in her experience as a guardian angel, and the urge to follow those intimate feelings overruled her usually good judgment.

Just for today she'd indulge herself and wear

the skirt and petticoat. What harm could there be in that?

"I know it's in here somewhere," Debbie mumbled, pushing past hangers of clothes on the wooden rod.

As Caitlan watched Debbie, another premonition swept through her, so commanding in its force, she couldn't ignore the awareness demanding her immediate attention. Surreptitiously, she glanced around the room, searching for a clue to explain her apprehension.

Her gaze drifted from the king-sized bed covered in a patchwork quilt and then onto an old mahogany armoire against the far wall. A matching vanity and stool occupied the other side of the room. Typical bedroom furnishings.

A vision whispered at the edge of Caitlan's consciousness, a pull so undeniable she automatically closed her eyes to bring it into focus. After a few seconds of intense concentration the backside of a young girl appeared, her short height giving the illusion of a six or seven year old. Long blond hair streamed from an elaborate straw hat, and at first Caitlan thought it was Brittany or Alisha. The girl was in this room, playing dress-up in front of a large oval standing mirror, admiring the sophisticated dress overflowing on her tiny body and the too large, wobbly high heels on her feet.

"Amanda Marie, are you into my things again?" a woman chastised gently, coming into the room.

The little girl whirled around, smiling sweetly, "Momma, I only want to look as pretty as you when we go to church today."

A maelstrom of emotions swelled within Caitlan, strangely enough, for the woman who seemed to be Amanda's mother. The woman took Amanda into her arms in a loving hug, and the tenderness of the embrace wrapped around Caitlan like a soft, warm blanket.

"Amanda," Caitlan murmured, confused by her latest vision.

The medallion tingled hotly between Caitlan's breasts, bringing her back to reality. When she opened her eyes she found Debbie looking at her oddly, the petticoat folded over her arm. Oh, goodness, Caitlan thought, how long had Debbie been watching her?

Debbie tilted her head to the side, scrutinizing her. "J.T. told you about Amanda?"

The tinge of disbelief Caitlan heard in Debbie's tone made her wary. "Yes. Why?"

Debbie gave Caitlan a speculative glance. "I'm just surprised, is all. He hasn't talked about Amanda since the night she died."

Yet he'd told *her*, a stranger, the whole story. Caitlan shivered slightly when she remembered experiencing the tragic car accident that had claimed Amanda's life. She still didn't understand the significance of that vision, or any of the others. She seemed to hold a key to J.T.'s past, but why did she have access to J.T.'s history with

225

Amanda? She'd never been able to tap into a ward's memories before.

Debbie handed Caitlan the petticoat, her gaze probing and full of questions. "Did J.T. tell you this used to be Amanda's parents' house?"

"No." *Amanda's house.* Another shiver cascaded down Caitlan's spine. Holding the two skirts close to her chest, she forgot about the dampness of her jeans and that she needed to change. "Why do you and Kirk live here?"

Debbie sat down on the edge of the bed. "About a year and a half after Amanda's death her father died of a heart attack, leaving Amanda's mother all alone. Mrs. Hamilton was so devastated by the loss of Amanda and her husband that she put the place up for sale. She told me the memories were too painful for her to stay, and she wanted to live with her sister in Connecticut."

Shaking her head, Debbie smoothed her hand over the quilt, a reminiscent smile curving her mouth. "J.T. went a little crazy when he found out Mrs. Hamilton was going to sell the place, since this property adjoins Rafferty land. J.T. said he didn't want strangers living in *Amanda's* house. He was only twenty-one at the time, but he worked out a deal with Mrs. Hamilton, and my father co-signed a loan for him. J.T. bought the place.

"Funny thing is, J.T. couldn't bring himself to live here. Even when he married Stacey he still stayed at the main house. When Kirk and I got married he let us take over the payments, and he signed the deed over to us as a wedding gift."

The depth of J.T.'s love for Amanda astounded Caitlan. "It doesn't seem to bother J.T. to come here."

"No, it doesn't," Debbie agreed. "I think he just wanted the house to stay in the family, because Amanda was like a part of our family. We were neighbors all our lives. She was J.T.'s girlfriend for years, and my best friend since we were toddlers." Debbie's gaze skimmed over the clothes she'd just given Caitlan, then lifted back up to Caitlan's face. "We used to wear each other's clothes all the time, except Amanda was a little shorter and had a cuter shape, much like yourself," she reflected thoughtfully.

Caitlan fingered the soft chambray material in her arms. "Well, I appreciate you lending me your clothes."

"I'm happy to do it." Hesitating briefly, Debbie glanced covertly at Caitlan, as if sizing her up. Her speculative smile reached her eyes. "I think you're good for J.T., Caitlan. I know this is presumptuous of me, considering you've only been here a few days, but have you and J.T. . . . I mean, are you and J.T. . . . ." She flushed and pressed her hands to her cheeks. "Oh, never mind!"

Caitlan laughed softly at Debbie's apparent embarrassment. "Are you trying to ask if J.T. and I are involved?"

"I know it's none of my business," Debbie rushed on, the color from her cheeks fading. "And you don't have to answer, but J.T. has changed in the short time you've been here."

Caitlan couldn't help wondering about that, even though she had to admit she'd seen a softening in him the last day or so, since the incident at the creek. "In what way?"

"I noticed the biggest change today." Debbie shrugged and picked at a piece of lint on the quilt. "It's the way he watches you. He seems so relaxed and at ease." She struggled for the right words. "There isn't that loneliness in his eyes that always makes me ache for him, an emptiness like he's lost a part of himself he can't find. Today, his eyes are clear and his smiles are genuine. You're good for him, Caitlan," she said softly, earnestly. "I knew that the first time I saw you and him together."

Caitlan lifted a brow at Debbie. What was it with his family conspiring to matchmake her and J.T.? "I care for your brother, but I'll be leaving Idaho soon." Why did the thought make her feel so forlorn?

"You can always visit, and you might find you like it here."

Not two days ago she'd heard the same lecture from J.T.'s daughter. "Have you been talking to Laura?" she teased.

Debbie smiled. "No. I just know it takes a special kind of woman to adapt to life in the country, and you fit in well. You seem happy here."

"I am happy here." And content. Caitlan sensed she belonged here in a way she couldn't fully define; she only knew J.T. was the reason. Then reality put things back into perspective. "But that doesn't mean I belong here."

"I wouldn't be so sure about that." Debbie shook her head, an apologetic look crossing her features. Standing, she grabbed Caitlan's hand and squeezed it affectionately. "I'm sorry, this is really none of my business, but I know J.T. better than anyone, and it's good to see him so carefree and happy."

Caitlan backed away subtly, knowing it was best if they let the subject drop. "Well, I guess I'd better change."

"Yeah." Debbie grinned ruefully. "Sorry; I didn't mean to go on and on. You're very easy to talk to, just like Amanda was. She's been gone sixteen years, but I still miss her friendship."

Caitlan managed a smile for Debbie's compliment, but couldn't shake off the sensation of being suffocated. Disturbing impressions of Amanda crowded in on her until she wanted to run from this room and out of this house. She needed to change and get outside so she could breath in fresh air and clear her head. "Where can I change?" she asked, startled by the strangled sound of her voice.

"Go ahead and use my bathroom." Debbie waved a hand toward a connecting door. "I'll meet you outside. I'm sure the guys are wondering what happened to us. Maybe if we're real lucky they cleaned up the kitchen, but I won't pin my hopes on that too much."

Caitlan forced a light laugh and agreed, even though everything in her coiled up as tight as a spring, ready to snap at any given moment. Once Caitlan stepped inside the bathroom, she closed the door and leaned against it, willing her taut body to relax and the images taunting her mind to cease. Gradually, with each slow breath she drew, her throbbing head began to ease.

Pushing off her damp jeans, Caitlan slipped on first the petticoat, and then the matching chambray skirt, vowing that this niggling feeling of hers wouldn't ruin her day.

For the tenth time in the past twenty minutes J.T. glanced toward the slider leading into the house, looking for a sign of Caitlan. Shifting in his plastic lawn chair, he spared a brief look at his watch, then glanced back at the door. He perked up when Debbie passed the window, waved, and mouthed, "I'll be out in a sec," then moved on to the kitchen. J.T. waited for a glimpse of Caitlan . . . and waited and waited. Had he missed her when she'd walked by?

"You lookin' for someone?" Kirk asked from the chair beside him, his tone filled with goading humor.

J.T. pinned him with a quelling look, then

turned his attention to the girls playing jump rope over on the slab of pavement. "Just wondering where the women are."

Kirk grinned. " 'Fraid they're talking about you?"

"I'm sure Debbie is. We all know how she loves to gab about my lack of a love life. It's her favorite pastime for anyone who'll listen."

Kirk stretched lazily and clasped his hands behind his head. "Well, I do believe they've spent enough time together for Debbie to convince Caitlan she's the perfect woman for you. They should be planning a wedding right about now."

J.T. scowled, declining to comment.

"So, what *is* going on between you and Caitlan?"

J.T. wanted to ask his brother-in-law to define "going on." Physically, nothing was happening between him and Caitlan—at least not what he'd like to be doing: making slow, deep love to her, losing himself in her gentleness and warmth. Emotionally? Well, that was something he'd rather not discuss. Even *he* didn't understand the feelings Caitlan evoked in him. He wrote off the chaotic emotions to lust, because wanting Caitlan, naked and in his bed, was becoming a consuming need, blending in with passion and desire.

"Nothing's going on," J.T. replied, slouching in his chair and squaring an ankle over the opposite knee. "She'll be going back to Parson's soon.

From what I hear, the bridge should be fully repaired by the end of the week."

Kirk slanted a look J.T.'s way. "You know, you could always drive her to the airport and put her on the first flight back to Chicago. She'd be out of your hair within three hours."

"And ruin her lovely vacation in paradise?" J.T. said dryly.

Kirk laughed, a deep masculine chuckle. Standing, he slapped J.T. on the back. "Man, you've got it bad for her."

Watching Kirk walk toward the slider, J.T. searched for a retort to his comment but couldn't come up with anything appropriate. What could he say to something that held too much truth? Caitlan was becoming a fever in his blood.

J.T. mused over Kirk's comment about taking Caitlan to the airport. He'd thought about doing exactly that the first night she'd stayed at the ranch, but something had held him back. He'd told himself this was her vacation, and as long as she stayed out of his way he'd let her remain. Thinking back, he realized she hadn't been any trouble, but everywhere he turned she'd been there, with her violet eyes and soft smiles. Hell, he'd even spent the day with her yesterday, pouring out all his secrets and heartaches—to a woman he barely knew.

Maybe he should've given Caitlan the option of flying back to Chicago; maybe she would have wanted to go home rather than wait at his ranch for the bridge to be repaired. He hadn't asked, and she hadn't mentioned it. For the most part she seemed perfectly satisfied at the Circle R.

"Maybe she hasn't asked you to take her to the airport because you were such a bastard about the whole situation her first day at the ranch," he mumbled to himself, remembering how abrupt and harsh he'd been with her, how he'd wanted nothing more than to send her on her way to wherever she belonged.

Now he wasn't sure he wanted her to go, which was ridiculous considering the havoc she played with his body, and the delicate way she threatened the barriers he'd built around his heart. But eventually she'd go back to Chicago, and ultimately that thought kept his emotions locked up, safe and secure.

J.T. glanced toward the slider again and did a double take. He hadn't known what to expect when he saw Caitlan again, but the sight that greeted him tied his insides in knots. Desire surfaced, hot and swift, nearly overwhelming him.

His gaze slid over Caitlan's shirt, the long sleeves rolled to just below her elbow. The first three buttons down the front were undone, the tails tied into a knot around her tiny waist. The skirt she wore aroused more than just his interest. She had nice legs—he remembered that from the night he'd nearly seduced her in his bed— long, graceful limbs that conjured up images of them wrapped around his hips, hugging him tight as he made love to her.

She smiled shyly and started his way. The muscles in his belly tightened as she neared, and he briefly wondered how much longer he'd be able to keep his hands off her. She tempted him to the brink of insanity.

"Caitlan!" Laura grabbed Caitlan's hand and tugged her toward where her and Brittany and Alisha were playing. "I need a partner for double jump rope."

Caitlan glanced doubtfully at the two lines of rope arching in a large loop, engineered by Laura's cousins. "Are you looking to lose?"

Laura laughed. "It's not that hard, really. It'll take you a few times to get the hang of it, but you'll have fun. Aunt Debbie loves to do this."

Caitlan shrugged, pulling off her beige boots and socks and tossing them aside. "I'm game."

J.T. wasn't sure if he should have been annoyed or relieved with Laura's interruption, then decided he'd just sit back and enjoy Caitlan from a *safe* distance, where touching her wouldn't be such a temptation.

Caitlan attempted to jump in cadence with the two ropes, but only succeeded in tangling up the line. Chuckling at her clumsiness, J.T. teased her, watching in delight as sparks of determination lit up her incredible eyes. After a few more botched attempts she finally got the rythym of the rope coordinated with the flow of her jumping and managed to execute the game beautifully, like a pro.

Caitlan shot him a triumphant look over her shoulder as she kept up the rhythm. J.T. grinned. Despite her accomplishment, he couldn't help but feel like the victor, because at his vantage point she presented him with a winning view.

Holding her skirt to her thighs, she clutched the material tightly in her fists so it wouldn't get tangled in the rope, giving him an unobstructed view of her endlessly long, shapely legs and bare feet. Ruffles from her slip spilled from beneath her skirt, a soft, feminine contrast that served to give her a countenance of childlike innocence. She even had cute knees, he mused, enjoying himself thoroughly.

She laughed breathlessly, tilting her head back as the sweet sound escaped her. The setting sun sparkled threads of gold off her dark bouncing hair and kissed her cheeks with a natural blush.

She looked wild and radiant. Incredibly beautiful. Vibrant and warm. The slow burn of desire for her ignited into a scorching flame of pure need.

Twilight settled in, bringing with it a slight evening chill. The group moved indoors for peach cobbler and to watch a Sunday evening program. J.T. deliberately kept his distance from Caitlan, not trusting himself to give in to the urge to touch her in ways that went beyond a friendly manner. However, sitting a couch away didn't stop him from watching her every move, listening to her every word. The wanting and hunger in him grew with each passing look between them.

At ten-thirty they said their good-byes and headed home. Except for Caitlan thanking him for a nice day, the short drive was made in silence.

Laura yawned as they walked in the front door. "I'm going to bed." She turned to J.T. and gave him a hug, then embraced Caitlan. "Good night, Dad, Caitlan."

"Good night, Smidget," J.T. replied.

"Sweet dreams," Caitlan added as Laura bounded up the stairs.

Caitlan was the type of woman who would say sweet dreams, J.T. thought with a smile. Gentle. Caring. She glanced up at him, her eyes luminous pools of violet that reached deep inside him and gripped him in unrelenting desire. He'd turned on the hallway light, and the soft glow illuminated the nervousness in her gaze now that they were totally alone. He found her anxiousness endearing.

She stepped back, her tongue running over her bottom lip. "I, uh, think I'll go to bed, too. I'm exhausted."

"Yeah, me too." Maybe a good night's rest would cool his attraction to her. *Don't count on it, buddy. This ache isn't going to leave until she does.*

That silent taunt rerouted his thoughts to his

earlier conversation with Kirk. "Caitlan, there's something I'd like to ask you."

"Yes?" A curious expression etched her features.

He forced out the words before he had a chance to consider what he might be giving up. "Would you like me to take you to the airport so you can fly back to Chicago? It's about a three-hour drive from here."

Dismay flashed in her eyes. "Do you want me to leave?"

No. Glancing over her shoulder so she wouldn't see the truth in his eyes, he absently rubbed at the back of his neck. "I just don't want you to feel like you're stuck here. I know I should have asked you sooner, but, well, I guess I haven't been such a gracious host, have I?" His gaze slid back to hers, and he offered her an apologetic smile. "Anyway, the bridge should be repaired by the end of the week. You're welcome to stay until then, or if you'd like, I'll take you to the airport."

She didn't hesitate. "I'd really like to stay, if you don't mind. I'm having a nice time, and I'm not due back home for a while."

"No, I don't mind."

"Great." A smile touched the corner of her mouth as she backed away again to leave. "Good night, J.T."

" 'Night." He watched her climb the stairs, eyes riveted to the gentle sway of her hips. He wished he had the right to follow her up to her bedroom, or take her to his, and make love to her until the sun came up.

Frustrated with his sensual thoughts and his anatomy's natural response, he started up the stairs to his bedroom, knowing it was going to be a long tossing-and-turning kind of night.

Chapter Nine

Three hours later, hot, restless, and still aroused, J.T. lay in bed, cursing the woman down the hall for the sensual effect she had on him. He couldn't remember the last time he'd been so hungry for the feel of a woman pressed beneath him. Not just any woman, but Caitlan.

The sound of the guest bedroom's door creaking open broke the night's silence. J.T. listened, unmoving but alert. Recognizing Caitlan's tentative booted steps on the wooden floor, he frowned. Seconds later he heard the latch on the front door unlock, and the squeak of the hinges when she opened the door.

He bolted upright in bed. Where in the hell was she going at one-thirty in the morning? Damn!

Caitlan of all people should've known better than to roam around the ranch alone, especially at night, when an "accident" could easily befall her.

Fearful for her safety, J.T. threw the covers off his naked body and jumped out of bed. Hastily, he pulled on his jeans and donned the shirt he'd shucked only hours before. Within minutes he was dressed, boots on, and out the front door, his fear congealing into anger at her foolishness. The emotion ran parallel with the tense, aroused state of his body.

Caitlan wasn't on the porch, or anywhere around the close perimeter of the house, from what he could see. Pure instinct had him heading for the barn, the glow from the full moon guiding the way. The cold night air wrapped around him, yet the welcoming chill did nothing to temper the heated blood running through his veins. Only one woman had the cure for that.

She'd left the barn door open and he slipped in quietly. Her soft voice drifted to him. Was she with someone, he wondered, unable to stop thoughts of another woman's infidelity. He had no ties to Caitlan, but he found himself silently praying she was alone, that she wasn't out here to meet one of his men. Jealousy, an unfamiliar emotion, coiled tightly inside him.

Stopping in the shadows of the last stall, he saw her, standing by King's Ransom. Alone. She was talking to the stallion, sweet, encouraging words and praise. The tension cramping the muscles across his shoulders slackened, and he released a long, slow breath.

Curbing the impulse to make himself known and chastise Caitlan for going against his orders to stay away from King, he watched her cajole the animal into accepting whatever she extended in her hand through the slats. Sugar cubes, J.T. guessed, mesmerized by the gentle way the normally crazed stallion nuzzled the treat from her palm, then allowed her to stroke his nose before sidestepping away. How in the hell did she manage to calm the beast?

She laughed softly, the sound curling around J.T. like a narcotic. "See, that wasn't so bad, was it, King?" Pulling back her hand, she brushed her palm on her skirt. "You know I won't hurt you, don't you, boy?"

The horse gave a soft snort as his reply but didn't venture back to her.

The moonlight filtering into the barn from the loft window gave Caitlan an ethereal appearance, shimmering off her hair like a halo. Taking in the view of her profile, J.T. put to memory every delicate feature of her face. God, she was beautiful. Not in an elegant sense, but in a way that went deeper than the surface. Much, much deeper.

Suddenly she straightened, glancing over her shoulder toward where he stood cloaked in the shadows. "J.T.?"

How did she know it was him? Or had she just guessed? Not wanting to scare her, he stepped into the beam of moonlight so she could see him, feeling a little guilty that she'd caught him spying on her.

"It's late, Caitlan." He tried to summon some authority, but his tone lacked conviction, so he gave up the pretense for something more basic and honest: concern. "You shouldn't be out here alone."

She didn't seem all that surprised to see him. A beguiling smile curved her mouth. "Then come keep me company."

Had he only imagined the sultry invitation in her voice? Probably so, considering everything she said and did took on a provocative aspect. "It's past one-thirty." Hooking his thumbs through his belt loops, he moved toward her slowly, lazily. "You should be in bed."

She lifted a brow, playfully flitting to the back of the barn. "Are you *ordering* me to bed?"

Damn. That time he hadn't mistaken the huskiness and desire in her voice. Suddenly, subtly, the game changed, and he wanted to play by whatever rules she set down. "Would you go if I am?" he challenged, following her.

She shrugged, giving him an upswept look that held an arousing combination of innocence and temptation. "I suppose not. I'm not tired."

In a lithe move he backed her against a nearby wall and propped a hand on one side of her head, leaving the other side open so she could escape if she wanted to. Surprise flared in her eyes, then simmered to a sensual heat that matched the flame licking along his body.

Caressing his knuckles down her soft cheek, he slipped his hand inside the collar of her shirt, resting his palm on the warm curve where her neck and shoulder joined. Drawing his thumb along her jaw, he said very deliberately, "I've got the perfect cure for insomnia."

Her luminous gaze darkened and she swallowed. He followed the movement down her throat with his thumb, stopping at the quickening pulse at the base of her neck. Beneath the touch of his fingers on her shoulder, a delicate shiver stole through her.

"You're cold." He shifted closer to share his body heat. His thighs rubbed provocatively against hers. "You should've put on your jacket."

Another tremor ran the length of her. "I'll be fine." Her voice was a breathy whisper of sound.

Pushing her chin up with his thumb, he lowered his head to meet her lips. "I can make you warm," he promised huskily. Brushing his mouth over hers, softly, tenderly, something unraveled deep inside him, a yearning and a hunger he could no longer deny.

He nibbled on her full bottom lip and ran his tongue over her smooth teeth, needing to taste her deep inside. "I want you, Caitlan," he growled.

She gave a slight shake of her head. "We can't do this," she said, even as her lips parted to allow him access to the moist, sweet recesses of her mouth.

Hearing the wistful catch to her voice that contradicted her objection, he pulled back just enough to capture her gaze. Feminine awareness flickered in her eyes, another contradiction. "Why not, Caitlan? We've both been fighting this from the first day we met."

Confusion and uncertainty creased her brow. Reaching up, she touched her fingers to his stubbled jaw. "When you touch me I feel things I know I shouldn't."

He chuckled softly. "Are you that innocent?" Leaning close, he nuzzled the sensitive flesh just below her ear with his lips and damp tongue, giving her plenty to feel and experience. "It's called lust, Caitlan," he whispered in her ear just before his tongue traced the delicate orifice.

She moaned and shuddered at the sensual onslaught, then shook her head. Grabbing his face between her palms, she made him look at her. "No, it's more than that. It's an . . . emotional link." She caught her lower lip between her teeth, her eyes smoldering with passion and apprehension. "I can't fight it any longer, J.T. You feel too perfect for me, yet I know I shouldn't give in. . . ."

An emotional link. J.T.'s first instinct was to scoff at the idea, but damn if he didn't feel that link, too. Refusing to analyze those disturbing emotions, he focused on what he knew he could handle for the moment: their desire for one another, and quenching the need burning him up like flame.

"Is that all you feel?" he asked, moving his hips against hers in a slow, evocative motion.

Her head fell back, her eyes closed, her answer a soft, enticing moan. Her hands slipped from his face to clutch his shoulders in wild abandon.

"Look at me, Caitlan," he ordered in a low, rough voice. "Tell me what your *body* feels."

Opening her eyes, she ran her tongue across her bottom lip, her breathing deep with the beginnings of sensual excitement. "I feel . . . strange. Tingly and warm all over."

He smiled, loving how utterly honest she was, how *innocent* despite her allure. "That's a good start. Now let me *show* you how you make me feel." Wedging a thigh between hers, he pressed his aching arousal to that natural feminine cove. He groaned as the length of him throbbed and strained against the fly of his jeans, and against her. He hated the layers of clothing separating their flesh.

"You make me hot and hard and hungry for you," he whispered darkly, his bold words made more provocative by their clandestine setting and the shocking way he moved against her. "I want you as restless as I am. I want you to feel that frenzied excitement build deep inside until you want to explode. That's exactly where I am, Caitlan, and exactly where I want you to be."

A small sound slipped past her lips, a whimper of need and eagerness tinged with the barest hesitation. "I already feel it."

"There's more." Moving slowly, giving her enough time to protest if she wanted to, he dropped his mouth over her parted lips, kissing her slow and wet and deep and lazy. Over and over again, sweeping his tongue into her mouth, touching and tangling with the sleek length of hers, until a moan of pleasure rolled up from her throat, until she clung to him, responding with a quick, fiery need.

Her body flowed into his and she rubbed against him, her hands moving over his chest and shoulders, seeking the hard contours of muscle and heat. A primitive shudder ran the length of him.

It no longer mattered that he'd sworn he wouldn't touch her. He needed her too badly. She was so sweet, her response so warm and open, she selflessly gave him the simple pleasure and wonder of feeling alive again.

Desire flared like wildfire in him, urging him onward. His blood pulsed in hot, heavy beats, and even as he denied the softening emotions stirring within him for Caitlan, he admitted to the desperate need to know more of her.

Flattening a palm over her collarbone just inside her shirt, he savored the velvet texture of her soft skin. His hand brushed against the chain around her neck. The heated gold singed his fingertips. While his other hand deftly unfastened the buttons down the front of her shirt, he hooked the chain around his index finger, slowly sliding down to where the medallion nestled between her breasts.

Ravishing her mouth with his, apprehensive but intrigued by the lure of the medallion and what had happened that day at the creek when he'd touched it, he defiantly grasped the pendant in his palm.

Caitlan gasped audibly and jerked back, but J.T. determinedly pressed closer and deepened the wet, silken kiss until, with a whimper, her resistance melted away and she surrendered to him. The medallion scorched his hand, but he ruthlessly clutched the gold. Seconds later, his efforts were rewarded. A shimmering heat radiated up his arm and flowed through his veins to every nerve ending. A charge of energy jolted him, electrifying him to the core of his soul. His body shuddered, wracked with mind-blowing sensations. He moaned as in the next instant the impression of being in perfect harmony with Caitlan cascaded through him, a blending of spirits, hearts, and bodies so unequivocally woven he never wanted to release her. He grew incredibly hard, painfully so, the mystifying experience inflaming his ardor.

He tore his mouth from hers, needing to know if she'd experienced the strange coupling too, or if he was slowly going crazy. One look in her eyes, bright with awareness, confirmed that she'd been with him all the way, and that she was as aroused as he by the encounter. They both panted for air, and when he pressed his free hand over her left breast her heart beat wildly beneath his palm.

"You're mine," he said fiercely, shaken by the depth of emotion accompanying the statement. Where had the possessive words come from?

"Yes," she whispered in return, her voice husky and needy.

Letting go of the medallion, J.T. tugged on the knot of her shirt, desperate to explore every inch of her with his eyes and hands, desperate to make Caitlan his in every way. Fumbling with the front clasp of her bra, he dipped his head to string a line of wet, hot, openmouthed kisses down the side of her throat.

J.T. thought he heard Caitlan murmur, "please," but couldn't be sure for the blood rushing through his head and every other vital part of his body. He lifted his mouth from the warm, fragrant hallow of her neck and shoulder just as the clasp on her bra gave way. Her full, perfect breasts spilled into his waiting hands, her pale skin gleaming in the moonlight. Her nipples drew into tight buds, from his gaze or the cold air, he couldn't be sure. Grazing his thumbs over the stiff crests, he illicited a moan of pleasure from her that echoed his own enjoyment in just watching her uninhibited response. He glanced up into her face. Her gaze was heavy-lidded with passion, any uncertainty she might have harbored minutes ago replaced by encouragement.

Her approval was all the inducement he needed. Lowering his head, he dragged his tongue across her collarbone and leisurely downward, toward the bountiful offering he held in his hands. She started at the first sweep of his tongue around the bottom swell of her breast; she moaned and slid her fingers into his hair when he opened his mouth wide over a nipple and suckled deeply, strongly, his fingers kneading the soft flesh.

A shudder passed through her and she arched toward him. Holding his mouth to her breast, she showed him in that one daring move that she needed him, this wondrous contact, as much as he needed her.

Lifting his head, he guided her slender hands to the buttons on his shirt. He braced his palms on the wall on either side of her head, looking at her flushed face. "Open my shirt, Caitie," he told her. "I want to feel your breasts against me."

She attempted the task but couldn't coordinate her trembling fingers to slip the buttons through the holes. After a moment that seemed more like an eternity to J.T., he laughed abruptly and impatiently brushed her hands aside to do the deed himself. An ever-widening V quickly appeared with each button, all the way down to his belly.

The sudden cool touch of her hands on his

heated flesh excited him beyond what he believed to be possible. Her palms smoothed over his chest in a timid exploration, the muscles in his belly rippling. Reining in his control and once again bracing his palms on the wall behind her, he curled his fingers into tight fists against the rough, cool wood. He granted her license to touch and explore, knowing it would cost him dearly but uncaring because her light caresses had him blazing like a match to dry kindling.

She looked up at him, her gaze shining with awe and sensual enjoyment. "You feel so good, like silk and steel . . ." She plucked a nipple and he drew in a quick breath, a shy, but wholly seductive smile curving her mouth. Her tongue bathed her bottom lip with moisture, and she slowly leaned forward, tentatively touching her tongue to the flat brown disc, tasting him.

Everything in J.T. coiled up tight, and he hissed at the exquisite sensations darting through him. Desire pooled heavily in his groin, pulsing, throbbing. Tangling his fingers in her hair, he pulled her mouth back under his. "Enough," he said gruffly, pleasure and pain meshing. "I'm going to die if I don't feel you against me now." He captured her mouth at the same time that he crushed his chest against her breasts. Their mutual moans of satisfaction filled the dim barn.

Releasing her hair, he slowly slid his hands down the slope of her back and over the curve of her bottom. He lifted her tighter against him, reveling in the soft sounds she made, the way her hands went wild on him, on his chest, in his hair. He bunched her skirt in his fist and drew up the material, exposing her thighs to the cool night air. Softening their kisses, he whispered against her mouth, "Hold your skirt for me, sweetheart." Having Caitlan's hands immobile and off him gave J.T. time to shore up his control again. There was too much he wanted to do to her, with her, and she already had him on the edge.

Mindless with want, Caitlan ignored the little voice inside her head warning her of the consequences that could result from her actions. After the arousing, soul-blending incident with the medallion she was burning up inside, aching to be filled, aching to experience everything J.T. had to offer. Doing as he'd ordered, she curled her fingers around the chambray and petticoat, holding the ruffles up for him.

"Good girl," he murmured. Running his hands up her thigh, he slipped his long, callused fingers beneath the band of her panties to cup her bottom. She let out a soft sigh, and he smiled.

"You have the warmest, softest skin," he said, dragging his fingers around so his thumbs brushed the soft curls between her legs in a butterfly caress.

She drew in a deep quivering breath at the husky tone of his voice and his light, teasing touch. When she looked into his eyes she saw that his desire matched her own. No matter how wrong this was, she knew she wanted this intimacy, and more. She didn't know what tomorrow would bring, but for tonight she was his.

Slowly, he knelt before her. Caitlan sensed his determination to take things slow, for her sake and pleasure as well as his own. He hooked his thumbs beneath the elastic band of her panties and slowly pulled them down, and her passion grew with every inch he exposed. His gaze devoured her like hot, licking flames of fire.

She felt no shame, only a soul-shattering longing to give him whatever he wanted from her. Her emotions were so riveting, the yearning to be with him so devestatingly powerful, she experienced a moment of panic and tried to move away. "J.T.—"

"Shhh, he said, pressing his palms on her thighs, preventing her escape. "Please let me."

Caitlan heard the ragged need in his voice, the throaty plea that bordered on sheer urgency, because it mirrored her own swirling emotions. Unable to deny what her body and soul craved, she allowed him to draw her panties down, over her boots. He helped her step out of them; then he absently stuffed the scrap of silk in his back pocket.

He sat back on his heels, not touching her when she wished he would, his gaze charting a slow, heated path up the length of her, lingering in places that craved his caress. Warmth stung her cheeks, and she closed her eyes to hide her embarrassment, knowing she must look like a shameless hussy, half clothed, breasts pouting, skirt clutched in her fists to reveal the part of her that wanted his touch so badly. Everything was bared to him, and she idly wondered if he could see or sense the deep, abiding love blooming inside her heart for him.

Love. Oh, dear Lord, she couldn't be falling in love with him!

"Look at me, Caitie." The restraint in his voice belied his heavy, aroused breathing.

Her lashes fluttered open and she glanced down at him, blushing all over again when she saw the carnal heat in his gaze. She started to lower the skirt to hide from his hungry eyes.

"No, don't," he said abruptly, stopping her. He moved closer, adoring her with his gaze. "You're so beautiful."

With him, she *felt* beautiful, euphoric.

The unexpected sigh of his hot, damp breath on her inner thigh sent a bolt of liquid heat surging through her, nearly short-circuiting her nerves. His strong hands held her quivering thighs apart and supported her when her knees would have buckled. She realized his brazen, erotic intent in the way his tongue caressed her flesh—long, soft strokes that teased and tantalized in an attempt to coax her thighs farther apart for him.

"J.T.," she gasped, hating how her voice trembled with uncertainty and the desire for him to continue with his sensual invasion. The tug-of-

Janelle Denison

war of emotions raging inside her confused her,
wanting J.T. to continue, but knowing how
wrong it would be to let him take her any higher.

But the sensations didn't feel wrong, not with
J.T.

"Open for me, Caitie," he murmured huskily,
and when she finally did he groaned deep in his
throat and pressed his mouth against the apex of
her thighs, tracing the soft, alluring folds with his
tongue, probing delicately.

Caitlan moaned at the exquisite feelings J.T.
evoked in her, soaring her out of control, past the
stars and the heavens. He pushed her closer to a
place she knew would be nothing short of
paradise.

J.T. reveled in Caitlan's open response, loving
the breathless catch in her throat and the lush,
petal softness of her desire. He nuzzled her
softly, wanting to savor the sweetness of her,
wanting to fill himself with every secret, silken
part of her. He tasted her sensual melting just as
her panting filled his head. Knowing she neared
the crest, he splayed his hands on her quivering
thighs, lending whatever support he could.

Then it came, the tiny spasms rippling through
her. He listened to her breathless moan of pleasure; then his name slipped past her lips as the
tremors subsided.

In a fluid movement he stood, ignoring the
stiffness in his knees for the beautiful expression
on Caitlan's face. Before she had a chance to float

back to earth, before the edge of her climax ebbed away, he pulled her leg around his hips, pressing denim against her sensitive flesh, and let her get used to the hard, thick length of him, and the idea of them joining completely.

Her eyes widened in shock, but before she could say anything he covered her lips with his and thrust his tongue into her mouth, kissing her slowly, deeply, showing her how good she tasted, like warm, silky honey and feminine satisfaction. He showed her with the deep stroking of his tongue how he wanted to make love to her body. Showing her, again and again, that he couldn't get enough of her, that tasting her, kissing her, touching her, was nothing compared to the way he wanted to fill her and make her his. Only his. He ached with a raw need so powerful it threatened the shields around his heart. The emotion frightened the hell out of him, but he refused to give up the sweet softness and solace Caitlan's body offered.

Caitlan wrapped her arms around his neck and held him close. Twisting sinuously, she rubbed against him, pleasuring herself and at the same time arousing him to the point of exploding. She went wild, arching closer, and when he heard those broken whimpers begin, signaling how close she was to climaxing yet again, he pulled away from her, letting her leg go.

She gave a cry of protest, and he palmed her breast, rubbing her nipple with his thumb. "Tell me what you want, Caitlan," he demanded. He tried to shake the vulnerability creeping up on him, the feeling of becoming so totally lost in Caitlan that he'd never be the same again.

She looked like a wanton gypsy, her disheveled hair framing her pretty face, her lips swollen from his kisses. Her eyes were limpid with passion and something deeper and more touching that J.T. didn't want to analyze. "I want . . ." She looked away, a timid catch to her voice.

Damn, he couldn't believe she was so flustered after everything he'd done to her, everything she'd done so uninhibitedly. With his finger beneath her chin, he brought her gaze back to his. "Tell me, Caitie," he urged.

"I want you," she pleaded in a ragged whisper. "I want this. Please."

Her confession should have brought him satisfaction. Instead, he experienced a startling wave of emotion that gripped his heart. He refused to fully acknowledge the growing feeling.

Guiding her hand to the front of his jeans, he cupped her palm over the burgeoning ridge there, leaving the ultimate decision up to her. "If you want me, then help me, Caitlan. Show me exactly what you want and I'll give it to you. I'll make it so good you'll be addicted, and I'll give you as much as you want. . . . " He let his words drift away, giving her the option of halting their lovemaking if she wanted to.

Her fingers trembled, but she didn't pull away.

A reluctant kind of acquiescence shimmered in her eyes, as if she couldn't help wanting him, any more than he could control how being one with her was becoming as essential as breathing.

"Once I'm deep inside of you they'll be no turning back," he went on. "The choice is yours, Caitie, but make your decision fast."

She did then, tugging at his zipper and freeing him. Groaning at her sweet surrender, he wrapped her fingers around his length, moving slowly, sliding against her cool palm. When the building pressure shoved him to the very edge he drew her leg around his waist once again, but this time nothing separated their flesh.

"Wrap both of your legs around me, Caitie," he said, and she did, circling her arms around his neck at the same time. Her nipples grazed his chest; their bellies rubbed erotically. Bracing her against the wall, he tilted her hips for his entrance. She was wet, very wet, and slick from spent passion, but as he pushed inside her, she stiffened and whimpered, burying her face into his shoulder.

J.T.'s body shook. She was tight, so tight he suspected this was her first time, or very close to it. But he was at a point where he couldn't stop, not even if someone put a gun to his head. Ignoring the instinctive urge to thrust deeply, he murmured soft words to her, entering her slowly. He pulled her legs as high and tight as he could around him, and with a sweet little cry she arched and he slid into that satin sheath to the hilt. He groaned as liquid heat engulfed him, fusing them as one. They fit perfectly together, he thought, as if they had been made for one another.

Wanting to lose himself in the magic of her, he moved slowly, then thrust harder, sliding deeper, over and over, until her moans of pleasure mingled with his.

Still, he didn't let go, found he couldn't release that knot winding tighter and tighter within him. With each silken stroke, the flame of desire burned hotter, incinerating his original carnal hunger into deeper, more intense emotions. He'd told her he couldn't care, but he was feeling and needing and she was the reason.

And somehow he'd known it would come to this. From the first moment in the line shack when he'd woken to find her beneath him, he'd *known* he'd have her. Then it had been pure lust. Now the white-hot need ribboned around his soul, tugging him beyond the realm of reality.

She whimpered his name, a throaty plea to end the madness he created. Her fingers dug into the muscles in his back, her legs gripped him tight, and she rubbed her breasts against his chest, begging him for the pleasure waiting on the horizon.

But she was the one who held the key to their fulfillment, he thought in a desire-filled haze. He didn't want to spiral over that crest without her, and vaguely wondered when he'd become so chivalrous, putting a woman's needs before his own. With Caitlan, it mattered.

"C'mon, Caitie," he whispered huskily in her ear, tempering his strokes to slow, deep thrusts that filled her up, then retreating until she cried for him. "Be greedy, sweetheart. Take it all and let it happen."

And then it did. Her lashes fell to sultry half slits and she moaned softly, tossing her head back. She looked beautiful, tousled and incredibly sexy while she took her pleasure. The medallion grew hot where it was crushed between his chest and hers, a tingly heat that showered through his veins like sparks of wild lightning, giving him the sensation of being one with Caitlan, she the other half of him he'd been waiting a lifetime for.

Ecstasy swelled up and through him like an explosion, and he surged one final time, surrendering himself to her without any barriers. Endless pulses of release wracked his body, the rapture piercing and overwhelming. He groaned, low and deep and animal-like, luxuriating in the exquisite awareness of being alive again, of feeling so deeply, so intimately joined with Caitlan. She erased the loneliness and absolute despair he'd been living with for sixteen long years.

Emotionally and physically satiated, J.T. sank to his knees on the cool earth floor, taking Caitlan with him so she straddled his lap and their bodies remained joined. Uncaring of his jeans bunched beneath him and the uncomfortable position, his only thought was that he didn't want to let her go, didn't want the emptiness and coldness that was sure to pour back into him once she left him.

He wondered if he was the one who'd become addicted.

In the quiet aftermath he held her close, reveling in the erratic beating of her heart against his, savoring the way she clung to him, body trembling, face buried in his neck, her breath warm on his damp skin. That damnable medallion had cooled some, but the impression of gold seared his flesh. He soothingly skimmed his hands down her back, over the swell of her hip, then up under her skirt to caress the soft, warm flesh of her inner thighs. He grew hard again, impossibly hard, wanting her with a sudden raw need that should have surprised him but didn't. Not anymore.

Leaving the temptation to touch her where they joined, to start another raging fire with a gentle stroke over her petal-soft folds, he lifted his hands to her hair, tangling the strands between his fingers. Gently, he lifted her head from his shoulder, wanting to reassure himself that she was okay.

The dazed expression on her face he understood; he felt the same way. However, the confusion shimmering in her violet eyes grabbed at him. "Are you okay?" His voice was a hushed whisper in the dark confines of the barn.

Caitlan nodded jerkily, not trusting herself to speak. She was still reeling from the flare of sensations that had burgeoned through her body the moment she'd splintered apart with pleasure. She tried sorting through the multitude of emotions, and the way the medallion had heated against her flesh, the molten fire of it nearly making her breathless.

And then she'd been drawn into J.T., physically and emotionally, sapped of every living force she possessed. The connection to him had been powerful, an undeniable pull. In the distance a wisp of a promise had beckoned to her, luring her closer and closer, until she'd been swept into the vortex, her heart blending with J.T.'s, her soul meshing with his in a complete oneness.

She wanted to explore what had happened, but the crazy things J.T. was doing to her body, the lazy, arousing slide of his hands down her back, under her skirt, cupping her breast, prevented coherent thought. She ignored the uncomfortable bite of the dirt floor digging into her knees, and the cold night air caressing her bare flesh, in favor of J.T.'s warm, reviving touch.

"I want you again, Caitlan," he said, his mouth open and hot and wet against her throat. Pulling her hips closer, he buried the thick, hard length of him deeper inside her. It occured to him then that she deserved better than to be taken in a barn, with the smell of horses, hay, and tack filling the air. "Come to my bed with me."

"Yes," she sighed. Letting her mind drift, the increasing tingling heat from the medallion began to spread throughout her body and downward, where they melded together. Curling her fingers into his shoulders, she clamped her thighs tightly against his hips.

"Ah, hell," he growled against her neck, rocking her urgently against him. "I don't think I can wait that long."

Neither did she. Basking in his caresses, her body hummed. A delicious pressure blossomed in her belly, electrifying her, causing her to move on J.T. in a shameless rhythm. He watched her, his eyes growing dark with desire, his hands on her strong and sure as they cupped her hips. Softer sensations wove through her, a longing to blend her heart with J.T.'s. Those strange sensations sizzled along her nerves again, and she closed her eyes, trying to grasp an elusive something teasing the edges of her mind.

Then it came. The name filtered through her mind, then slipped naturally from her lips, without thought or conscious provocation. "Johnny," she murmured softly.

J.T. stiffened, his blood turning to ice in his veins. A bucket of cold water couldn't have been more effective in dousing his arousal. Caitlan blinked her eyes open, looking just as surprised by the name she'd spoken.

"What did you say?" he said very calmly, wanting to believe he'd only misheard her. But he knew in his gut she'd called him by a name he'd hadn't heard for sixteen years. Since the night Amanda died.

Her gaze turned wary, snuffing out the desire. "Johnny," she repeated cautiously, as if she knew she'd said something wrong but wasn't quite sure what the ramifications were.

A sensation of being suffocated cloaked J.T. He had to get away from Caitlan, who'd suddenly, alarmingly, reminded him too much of Amanda. Those violet eyes of hers seem to lure him in, mesmerizing him, taunting him. A heavy pressure clamped around his chest, anxiety mixing with panic.

He shook his head, trying to keep his composure intact. Damn, between that medallion that always heated up whenever he touched it, and now with Caitlan calling him Johnny when he hadn't even told her his full name, he was beginning to feel like he was living in the Twilight Zone, lost between the past and the present. Ever since she'd come to the Circle R—hell, ever since she'd saved him—weird, unexplainable things had been happening between them.

Irritated by incidents he didn't understand, needing to put distance between himself and Caitlan, he lifted her from his lap. As soon as her body left his, a black, chilling emptiness consumed his soul.

She straightened up on shaky legs and smoothed her hand down her skirt, but that one act of modesty did nothing to reform the tousled, thoroughly loved woman who had been in his arms only minutes before. She still looked entirely too tempting, with her breasts still bared, and he kept from reaching for her again by thinking about what she'd called him.

Standing, he hitched up his jeans and zipped his fly, then started on the buttons on his shirt. She turned away from him and began straightening her own clothes. After everything they'd just shared the vulnerability in her movements slammed into him like a fist. Tender, forgiving emotions crept up on him, but he shoved them aside for more pressing matters.

"Why did you call me that?" he asked, his unexpectedly harsh tone shattering the silence.

Caitlan closed her eyes for a moment, trying to chase away the confusion swirling in her mind. And then there was this rejection she wasn't prepared to deal with, and the ripping pain in her soul it had caused. Opening her eyes, she glanced over her shoulder at him. "I don't know why. It just slipped out."

He jammed his hands on his hips, his eyes narrowing. "How the hell did you even *know* my name?"

The question startled her, and she grasped for the most logical answer. "I heard one of the hands call you John."

He let out a grunt of disbelief. "The hands *never* call me John, Caitlan. Most of them don't even know what J.T. stands for. And nobody calls me Johnny," he said fiercely. "*Nobody.*"

Nobody but Amanda, Caitlan thought, recalling her visions and the nickname Amanda called J.T. But why had *she* called him Johnny?

"Here," he said, bringing her out of her thoughts.

She reached for the panties dangling from the tips of his fingers. Face heating at the remembered intimacy and her uninhibited response to him, she quickly pulled them on.

"Come on; let's go on back to the house," he said coolly.

They walked to the house in silence. Caitlan could practically feel J.T. emotionally withdrawing from her. He was cool and remote, like the man she'd first met at the line shack. Gone was the tender lover and the gentle man she'd discovered over the past few days. She had the uncharacteristic urge to cry out at the loss. So many feelings and sensations clamored within her, all of them directly linked to J.T., and she didn't have a clue as to why.

And, more importantly, why wasn't she able to control her emotions with J.T., as she normally could with everyone else? Her heart overflowed with an indescribable feeling, a shattering realization that frightened her, for she knew there would be heavenly repercussions.

She loved J.T.

Chapter Ten

Love. Sitting up in bed two hours later, unable to sleep, Caitlan sketched furiously, hoping to purge her heart and soul of the emotion. The word rested heavily on her heart, burdening her with despair when it should have brought her joy. In a mortal lifetime she'd probably be ecstatic, but as a spiritual being, she'd been told an emotion as intense as passionate love wasn't possible. Her Superior had been wrong; so very wrong.

She'd done the unpardonable by making love with J.T., her only defense being that with him she experienced a connection so undeniably perfect and powerful in its magnetism, she couldn't deny the fierce longing to blend hearts and souls so irrevocably they meshed into one entity. She'd done that and more. Much, much more. Her face flamed when she recalled the wicked things he'd done to her, and her sensually uninhibited response to him.

But to have actually fallen in love with J.T., a mortal, to have given him her heart and soul as she had, was a reprehensible act that would no doubt warrant severe punishments. She was already eternally matched, her spirit supposedly secured to her soulmate while she waited as a guardian angel to be joined with him. As hard as she tried, though, she couldn't recall her soulmate's face or the warmth of his soul, because the only thing filling her up inside was J.T.'s essence.

The picture she'd drawn reflected her jumbled emotions, swirling patches and broad strokes that created nothing more than confusion. With a moan of hopelessness, she drew her knees up and hugged her sketch pad to her chest. She tried to keep herself together when all she wanted to do was fall apart, or run back into J.T.'s arms, where she'd been so content, so fulfilled.

Heaven help her, what was she going to do about J.T.? When she returned from her mission and her Superior discovered she'd given her heart to another, what plausible excuse could she give? Her actions couldn't be explained as a moment of weakness, because she'd openly wanted J.T., had felt a link to him from the very beginning of her mission. She'd ached to be a part of him, but she'd never expected to fall in love with the man, the ultimate of mortal emotions.

She couldn't allow them to make love again, not that she believed J.T. would want to after she'd blurted out the special nickname Amanda had called him. She still couldn't figure out why she'd called him Johnny, why the name had slipped so naturally from her lips. Another piece of the ever-growing puzzle to tuck away. When she returned from her mission her Superior would have all the answers to the bizarre visions she'd had, to the feelings that made J.T. so much a part of her.

Resting her head on her knees, she drew in a breath to release the awful tightness constricting her chest. What hurt the most, she supposed, was the way J.T. had shut down after she'd accidentally called him Johnny. His cool remoteness had cut her to the soul like a blade. She'd wanted to cry out at the bleakness creeping back into his gaze, the loneliness churning in the depths of his eyes. But she understood his withdrawal. His heart and soul belonged to Amanda, his eternal soulmate.

Sorrow and sadness engulfed her, and she swallowed back uncharacteristic tears. There was no future for them. Ever. Once her mission was complete, she would leave J.T. behind to continue her work as a guardian angel. But the memory of the way their bodies had been joined in complete harmony would always remain a part of her, and she didn't know if she'd survive the sweet, aching memory of it all.

The sound of someone moving around in the room next to hers penetrated the walls and her thoughts. She guessed J.T. was getting ready to start the day, as she should be doing, but she couldn't drum up the energy to move. Facing him didn't hold much appeal, especially after the brusque way he'd escorted her to her bedroom and left her there to enter his.

She sighed heavily, reminding herself that no matter what happened between them, she still had a job to do. In a few minutes she'd get up, she told herself, just as soon as the crushing despair lifted from her heart.

Staring at his freshly shaven face in the bathroom mirror, J.T. berated himself for the hundredth time for being so thoughtless, so utterly careless while making love to Caitlan.

He hadn't protected her from conceiving a child. The alarming thought had hit him like a two-ton brick while he'd been taking a shower. Unbidden, memories of the tight, hot feel of Caitlan wrapped around him had taunted his mind. Deep inside she'd been silky soft and snug, exquisitely so, and with nothing separating them he'd given her every bit of himself. He'd burned with need, had forgotten everything but the taste and feel of her.

Nothing separating them. He'd never intended to make love to her when he'd followed her to the barn, but that didn't excuse his negligence. He knew better than to have unprotected sex.

Shoving away from the sink, he muttered a dark curse and strode into the adjoining bedroom to put on his boots. He jammed a foot into one boot, arranging his jeans over the top, and then the other.

He'd been careless once before, with Stacey, and the result had been less than ideal. Caitlan wasn't calculating or manipulative, like Stacey had been in her pursuit—quite the opposite, actually—but Caitlan *would* leave to go back to the city, and he didn't think she'd be too happy being burdened with a child.

His empty stomach churned with anxiety and twisting deeper was regret. He'd marry Caitlan if she turned up pregnant, but he knew she'd grow to resent him and his way of life, and worse, he'd never be able to give her the love she deserved. He just didn't have it in him. Hadn't he learned that with his attempt at marriage with Stacey?

And then there was the strange link between him and Caitlan to consider, the way she extracted need and longing from him, and a yearning for something more. That medallion of hers unnerved him, as if it held some kind of power to connect them. Twice he'd been affected by the damned thing when he'd touched the heated gold, experiencing an out-of-body sensation straight out of some sci-fi movie. And, most hauntingly, she'd called him Johnny, when *no one* had called him that since Amanda's death.

The other experiences could be written off as an active imagination, but how had she known his nickname? Standing, he shook off the niggling doubts settling over him. Maybe he didn't want to know.

Dressed and ready for the day ahead, J.T. left his bedroom, glancing toward Caitlan's closed door. A streak of light at the bottom of the door told him she was up, and he walked over and knocked lightly, wanting to get this awkward conversation about protection and pregnancy over with.

"Yes?" she answered softly.

"It's me. I need to talk to you." He grimaced at the clipped tone of his voice and deliberately softened it. "Can I come in?"

She didn't reply; not that he could blame her. He'd been anything but congenial on the walk back to the house from the barn. Guilt weighed down his conscience when he recalled how cold he'd been, and how he'd all but deserted her at her bedroom door without so much as a good night, an apology, a promise, a curse . . . nothing.

"Caitlan?"

"Go away, J.T.," she said wearily. "I'll be downstairs in a bit."

Okay, he deserved that. He almost turned

away, but a streak of stubbornness held him there. Testing the knob, he found it unlocked and slowly opened the door and looked inside.

She sat on the bed, knees pulled up under the covers, drawing on that pad of paper she coveted. Her hand stilled and she glanced up, but she didn't glare at him as he'd expected her to. Like he wished she would, so he wouldn't feel like such an ass. No, her features were delicately somber, her violet eyes wide and glossy. The bedside lamp haloed her dark tousled hair, and he detected a faint smudge of weariness beneath her bottom lashes. She looked extremely vulnerable, and achingly beautiful.

A sudden emptiness consumed him, leaving him emptier and more desolate than ever. As he held Caitlan's gaze, something elemental shifted within him, making him too susceptible to this woman who'd intrigued him from the very first. He denied his growing feelings for Caitlan, that he was coming to care for her in a way that he hadn't cared for anyone in a long time. She made him *feel*, and he couldn't afford to. Besides, she'd only get hurt.

Pushing aside the tenderness and warmth crowding their way into his heart, he stepped inside her room without an invitation and shut the door quietly, wanting privacy for their discussion.

She returned her attention back to her drawing, the tip of her pencil scratching across the paper. "What do you want, J.T.?"

You. The word came without provocation; it was the absolute truth. All he wanted at that moment was to strip off his clothes and hers, push her back on the bed, and sink deep inside her, losing himself in her damp softness and heat. He wanted to see passion and desire flare in her eyes, wanted to experience again those ripples of pleasure that clutched him when she reached that crest.

He'd been right: once with her wasn't enough. Not nearly enough. God, he hated this weakness he had for her.

Business, Rafferty, he reminded himself. Walking to the side of her bed, he braced his shoulder against the wall, silently vowing he wouldn't touch her again.

He cleared his throat of the thick need gathering there. "We need to talk about what happened earlier."

She tensed but didn't look up at him. Instead, her pencil increased in tempo—quick, short, abrupt strokes slashing across the page. "I'd rather not."

He leaned forward slightly to get a look at what she was drawing but she held the pad at such an angle that he couldn't make out the sketch. "I'm not giving you a choice, Caitlan. I didn't protect you."

Finally, she glanced at him, confusion darkening her eyes. "Protect me?"

Damn. She couldn't be that innocent! "Yeah, I didn't use a condom, so what I want to know is if you're on some kind of birth control. The last thing I want is for you to end up pregnant. I don't think you'd want that either."

She blushed at his bluntness and averted her gaze back to her pad. "Don't worry about it, J.T.," she said quietly.

A shaft of white-hot jealousy lanced through him when he thought of her on contraceptives for some other man. He should have let the subject drop, but a possessiveness he had no right to feel provoked him into pressing for more answers. "So you're on some form of birth control then?"

His tenacity earned him a sharp look from her. Then a raw pain flickered in the depth of her eyes. "No. I can't get pregnant."

Shock rippled through J.T. Her confession momentarily stunned him speechless. When he recovered he silently berated himself for being so callous. "I'm sorry, Caitlan. I didn't mean to be so insensitive. It's just that . . ." He shoved his fingers through his shower-damp hair, now wishing he'd never broached this subject with her. "It's just that after what happened with Stacey I don't care to make the same mistake twice."

"I understand," she said softly, flipping her sketch pad closed. "But there's nothing for you to worry about."

He should have been relieved by her reassurance, but the sadness lingering in her gaze touched a chord within him. She wanted children, he realized, but for some reason couldn't have them. The thought made him ache for her.

She opened the nightstand drawer and put her pencil and pad inside. "If you're done, I'd like you to leave so I can get dressed."

No, he wasn't done. He didn't like being dismissed, and he liked even less the sensation of something still unresolved between them. Unable to get a firm grasp on what that something was, he gave her a curt nod and crossed to the door, then let himself out of her bedroom.

As soon as J.T. left, Caitlan sagged against her pillow and closed her eyes, willing away the dull twinge in her chest. Her hand absently strayed to her flat abdomen. A baby. J.T.'s baby. The thought filled her with such a sweet sorrow she wanted to weep for all the things that could never be. Where had all this longing come from?

The answer eluded her.

Freshly showered and changed into a pair of jeans and a pink sweatshirt, Caitlan went downstairs to the kitchen, prepared to face J.T. again. Except he wasn't sitting at his usual spot, eating breakfast and drinking coffee. Dirty breakfast dishes were stacked by the side of the sink, along with a platter of leftover scrambled eggs, sausage, and pancakes. Paula stood by the counter next to the sink tenderizing a roast, engrossed in her task. The clock above the kitchen window read five-thirty in the morning. Where were the men?

Drawing a deep breath for calm, Caitlan pasted on her best smile. "Good morning, Paula." Stopping at the coffeepot, she reached into the cupboard and brought down a mug, then filled it with the steaming brew. This morning a double shot of caffeine would be just the ticket.

Paula glanced over her shoulder, smiling brightly. "Oh, good morning, Caitlan. I didn't hear you come in." She gave the meat a few more whacks with the mallet. "J.T. mentioned you were awake and would be down shortly. You're quite an early riser."

Caitlan shrugged, aware of the other woman's scrutiny. "Habit, I guess."

Paula nodded. "I know how that is. My body has its own natural alarm clock built in too." She placed the meat into a roasting pan and added peeled carrots and potatoes. "Sleep well?"

Startled by the question, Caitlan slopped a dollop of cream over the rim of her mug. Grabbing a paper towel, she soaked up the mess. "Uh, yes. Just fine." She hadn't slept a wink.

"Didn't seem like J.T. did," Paula commented, her lips pursed in disapproval. "That man had the temperament of a provoked bear this morning. Even his usual cup of coffee didn't help."

Smiling blandly, Caitlan leaned her hip against the counter and took a sip of coffee. *I guess I bring out the best in him,* she wanted to reply sarcastically but kept her thoughts private.

"We had a long day at Debbie's yesterday, and he was up late last night," she said as an excuse. Both accounts were true, the latter most likely being J.T.'s reason for being so grouchy. But he'd been the one to follow her into the barn, then seduce her in the early hours of the morning. . . .

And you welcomed every one of his kisses and heated caresses.

"Did you have a nice time?"

Jarred from her intimate thoughts by Paula's question, Caitlan stared at the older woman, wondering if she somehow knew what had transpired between her and J.T. "You mean at Debbie's?"

"Of course." Paula frowned at her as she rolled out a slab of dough for biscuits. "What did you think I meant? Did you go somewhere else I don't know about?"

Just paradise, Caitlan thought. Sheer, unadulterated paradise. But she wasn't about to divulge that information to Paula. "No, we didn't go anywhere else, and yes, we had a nice time." Before she could put her foot in her mouth any further, she asked, "Where's J.T.?"

Paula dusted flour on the rolling pin and continued spreading the dough. "He left about fifteen minutes ago. You just missed him."

"He left?" Caitlan echoed. A frisson of alarm shot through her. "Where did he go?"

Cutting out round discs of dough, Paula placed them on a baking sheet. "He said he had some things to take care of in town and that he wouldn't be back until this afternoon."

Caitlan silently reprimanded herself for allowing her emotions to make her remiss in her duties to J.T. While she'd been wallowing in sorrow he'd left. Without her to protect him. "Did he go by himself?" Urgency tinged her voice, but she couldn't help it.

"He took Kirk with him." Paula sent her a curious glance. "You should have told him you wanted to go with him. He probably thought you'd be bored."

More likely he left without telling me so he wouldn't have to deal with me as a tagalong. Taking a swallow of coffee, she glanced out the window above the sink. A gray dawn was just breaking, and Caitlan could see the bustle of the hands down at the barn as they prepared for the day. She searched for her nemesis but couldn't find him. "Have you seen Randal this morning?" she asked in a neutral tone.

"No. I usually don't." Finished with her biscuits, Paula washed her hands and dried them on a terry towel, giving Caitlan a shrewd look. "Just a word of advice, Caitlan: Stay away from Randal. I don't know what's gotten into that boy lately, but he's a fuse just waiting to be lit."

Caitlan nodded and rinsed her cup. "I will."

"Good." Paula dismissed the topic as quickly

as it had been brought up. Bustling to the pantry, she brought out a container of sugar and two cans of pineapple rings. "Ever made a pineapple upside-down cake?"

Caitlan smiled. "No."

"Well, you're about to learn." Paula handed her an apron from a kitchen drawer, winking at her conspiratorially. "It's J.T.'s favorite. Maybe it'll soften him up some."

Caitlan doubted it, but she was desperate enough to bridge the rift between them to try anything.

Paula left the house a little after two in the afternoon, once Caitlan had convinced her she'd be fine until Laura arrived home from school in an hour or so. The house was spotless, and dinner was ready to pop into the oven later that evening. The sweet, heady fragrance of the cake they'd made permeated the house.

Wandering through the big, quiet ranch house, Caitlan wondered what she could do to keep herself, and her mind, occupied so she wouldn't think about what had happened between her and J.T. last night, and this morning. Going to the barn to see King was out of the question; too many fresh, sensual memories lingered there. She didn't think she'd ever be able to smell the sweet scent of hay without thinking of J.T. and the way he'd made love to her.

She thought about sketching, but discarded

the idea. She wasn't in the frame of mind to deal with the confusing visions that usually plagued her when she drew. Heading toward J.T.'s office, she decided reading a book would be the best way to divert her thoughts.

The floor-to-ceiling bookcase offered a variety of reading material. Perusing her way down the shelves, she discovered books on American history, accounting, cattle ranching, and literally a dozen other subjects. A set of encyclopedias occupied the second-to-last shelf, and below that were a row of photo albums.

Interest piqued, she sat cross-legged on the carpet and withdrew the first album. Opening the tan cover, she immersed herself in what she assumed was the Rafferty family. Pictures of J.T. and Debbie as children graced the pages, and there were even a few photographs with Randal in them. She realized Randal had the same belligerent, cocky air about him then as he did now. Picking out J.T.'s parents was easy to do; J.T. resembled his father and Debbie had the fair looks of her mother. She recognized a few shots of Frank and Paula, but other than that no one looked familiar.

Whiling away the next hour, she went down the line of albums, seeing the progression in J.T.'s and Debbie's childhood, all the way up to their teen years. When she pulled out the last album she noticed a cigar box tucked into the corner of the shelf, out of sight until she removed the last volume.

Sliding the album back into its slot, she picked up the box, then laid it on the carpet in front of her, debating on whether or not to open it. No tape or locks secured it, and there was nothing to indicate the contents were of a personal nature. Assuming it held more photographs, she lifted the lid and looked inside.

Her gaze inventoried a small stack of letters and papers, photographs, a lock of blond hair tied with a pink satin ribbon, and a black velvet ring box. Each piece of memorabilia shimmered with a strange life of its own, beckoning to a deep, secluded portion of her soul. Drawn by unknown forces, she picked up one of the letters and unfolded the page, realizing as she read the flowery script that it was a love letter to J.T. from Amanda. Her medallion warmed between her breasts, a tingle of warning she knew it was best to heed, but she couldn't put the letter down. The heartfelt words wove through Caitlan, and she closed her eyes and recited the rest of the prose out loud as easily as if she'd memorized the words, or written the letter herself.

Shocked by her ability to repeat each line word for word, she quickly returned the letter to the pile. Her heart pounded in a heavy rhythm and apprehension climbed up her spine. She now realized the purpose of the medallion's warming was to caution her, and possibly to protect her from discovering something. She ignored the warning, more determined than ever to find out what that something was. All her visions and emotions for J.T. were linked to the medallion, and she wanted to know why.

Reaching into the box again, she grasped the loose photographs and flipped through them, recognizing Amanda from her visions. The snapshots were of J.T. and Amanda as teenagers. They looked so in love with one another, Caitlan's heart gave a sharp twist of longing. Replacing the pictures, she found sketches of J.T., the paper yellowed by years, the pencil markings smudged. Upon closer inspection, she realized these sketches were the exact ones she'd drawn from her visions a couple of nights ago. How could that be possible, when she'd never seen these sketches before? Her hand trembling and her stomach clenching in trepidation, she returned the papers to their precise spot. Unable to stop herself, she touched the lock of silky hair, then fingered the ribbon. A deep, heavy pressure settled in her breast, and she swallowed back the sudden thickness in her throat. What was happening to her?

Pulling back her hand, she stared at the black velvet box. The urge to open the lid and see what it contained overwhelmed her. She chewed on her bottom lip, telling herself to put the cigar box back where she had found it and leave J.T.'s office. Without a doubt he'd be furious to know she'd gone through his personal momentos of Amanda, but stronger elements she didn't understand guided her.

The moment she touched the velvet box her medallion singed her skin. Gasping, she quickly brought the gold pendant out from her sweatshirt, but the heat was so intense it burned through the heavy cotton material. Ignoring the increasing heat, she defiantly opened the lid. A solitaire diamond engagement ring sparkled up at her, the gold band smooth and shiny. Impulsively, she removed the solitaire from the folds of velvet and slipped it on her left-hand ring finger. Instantly, a maelstrom of sensations invaded her body and mind, pulling her into a vortex of emotions so powerful she couldn't escape. The medallion burned like fire through her sweatshirt; then the startling heat slipped under her skin, spreading an unnerving tingle throughout her entire body. Her temples throbbed, and she squeezed her eyes shut to block the confusing fragmented visions swirling inside her mind.

"Will you marry me, Amanda Hamilton?"

"Are you sure?" Amanda whispered in a voice mingled with happiness and insecurity.

"Absolutely." J.T.'s. eyes shone with love and adoration. "You've always been mine, Amanda. . . . "

J.T.'s love poured over Caitlan, warm and sweet and pure. The emotion grabbed at her heart—a deep, abiding love that echoed her own devotion for him.

Janelle Denison

"Yes, John Thomas Rafferty, I'll marry you. I've loved you forever. . . . "

The buried words escaped Caitlan's memory like a well-preserved keepsake. Heaven help her, she felt as though she *had* loved him forever.

"I want to feel you inside me. Please, Johnny . . ."

Caitlan gasped when the sensation of her and J.T.'s body meshing as one cascaded over her, their souls twining in an eternal devotion that superseded a mortal lifetime. Their union coalesced love and need and longing into a glorious completion.

She blinked her eyes open, her heart pounding in her chest. Shaken by the visions and feelings provoked by the engagement ring, she started to remove the solitaire. As the band slid down her finger, tragedy rushed in on her. A sharp jolt pierced her temples.

Screams echoed in her head, her screams and Amanda's. Or were they the same? The screech of tires, the grinding crush of metal, shattering glass, then the awful, wrenching feeling of being physically, spiritually torn from J.T. . . .

"Where is she, Dad?" J.T. demanded from his hospital bed. A bandage swathed his forehead and a plaster cast encased his left arm. His eyes were glassy, but determination fired from his gaze. *"I want to see Amanda. Now."*

Jared touched J.T.'s shoulder. *"I'm sorry, son, but Amanda didn't make it. She died instantly."*

"No!" J.T. raged, the one word overflowing with hurt and grief.

A sob caught in Caitlan's throat as J.T.'s loss and sorrow became her own. Excruciating pain wrenched at her heart. Before another vision could cripple her ability to remove the ring, she pulled it off her finger and put it back in the velvet lining. She shoved the cigar box back onto the bottom shelf, hoping to dam the flood of images and emotions swamping her.

An emptiness enveloped her, and she buried her face in her hands, the wetness of tears dampening her fingers. "Oh, no," she choked, unable to bear any more of this craziness. She had to contact her Superior before she went insane, if that hadn't already happened. The visions, the identical drawings, the link to J.T., the mortal emotions, all needed explanations. And what about her falling in love with J.T.? Oh, what a mess of things she'd made!

Spurred by an urgency to find answers, she rushed from the office, swiping away the tears on her cheeks with the back of her hand. She opened the front door and nearly knocked down Laura in her haste to get somewhere private and secluded. She stopped short, her mind whirling in a hundred different directions.

"Oh, Caitlan, you scared me!" Laura exclaimed, her eyes wide. "I was just about to open the door and I didn't expect . . ." She frowned, her brow furrowing in concern. "Caitlan, are you okay?"

Caitlan mentally shook herself and forced a smile for Laura's benefit. "Yes, I'm just fine."

Laura looked unconvinced. "You've been crying. Did something happen while I was at school?"

"No, really, I . . . I just need to get some fresh air. I think I'll take a walk near the pasture." Caitlan took a few steps across the porch, anxious to be gone.

Laura started toward her, a hopeful spark in her eyes. "How about if I come with you? We can talk—"

"No!" The hurt look on Laura's face stabbed at Caitlan, and she immediately softened her voice. "I'm sorry, sweetie, but I need to be alone for a little while. How about we play a game of checkers or cards when I get back?" *If my Superior allows me to come back after I divulge all my transgressions.*

"Okay," Laura said reluctantly, her worry obvious.

Caitlan walked down the path until she was out of Laura's sight, then she broke into a run, needing to work off the anxiety nearly smothering her. She jogged alongside the fenced-in pasture, then up and over a knoll covered with wildflowers. Exhausted, she fell to her knees, gasping for breath, wondering when her heart and soul had become so tangled up with J.T.'s life. And if she'd ever be the same again.

"Anybody home?" J.T. called as he entered the house.

No answer.

"Caitlan? Laura?" Still, no reply. He glanced at his wristwatch. Three-thirty. Paula would be gone, but where were Caitlan and his daughter? After checking the kitchen and the den and finding them empty, he started up the stairs. He glanced in Laura's room first, then moved to Caitlan's, hesitating on the threshold when he saw it too was unoccupied.

He stared at her impeccably made bed, a sudden streak of guilt assailing him for the way he'd handled things with Caitlan this morning. He'd been anything but a gentleman in her bedroom when he'd asked her about birth control, and like a coward he'd left the house before she'd had a chance to come downstairs. But, dammit, whenever he was around her she brought out feelings in him he didn't want to deal with. He *refused* to deal with them, or label them, when she'd be gone in a few days. Yet he couldn't quite fully convince himself that keeping his distance until she left was for the best. He couldn't convince his body that he'd had Caitlan and she was out of his system, because she wasn't. The soft, silky feel of her skin and the feminine scent of her would haunt him for a long, long time. Not to mention those uncanny violet eyes, her dimple, and how incredibly perfect and fulfilled he'd been with her.

Frustrated, he stepped into the room, wishing he knew more about Caitlan besides the vague tidbits she'd shared. He found himself walking toward the nightstand, where he'd seen her put her pad of paper. Amanda had loved to draw. He remembered many lazy Sunday afternoons down by the creek when she'd made him lay there while she sketched him. Afterward he'd have to sweet-talk her into showing him the drawings; she'd been that modest about her ability. Just like Caitlan.

Why had he even thought that? Shaking off the apprehension climbing his spine, he opened the drawer and withdrew the pad. His conscience argued with him to put it back unopened, but he wanted more insight into Caitlan, wanted to know who or what occupied her mind in the late hours of the night while she sketched by moonlight.

Before he changed his mind, he opened the cover. He stared in stunned disbelief at a sketch of himself as a young boy, the sensation of being punched in the stomach rendering him breathless. She'd reproduced him in precise detail, right down to the stubborn tilt to his chin and the faint lines around his eyes when he smiled. He flipped through the pages, seeing that she'd drawn him in different stages of youth and as a grown man. All the pictures were meticulously detailed—eerily so—as if she'd known him fifteen or twenty years ago.

He turned to the next page and thought the clamping pressure in his chest was a sure sign of a heart attack. His blood roared in his ears and prickles of heat skimmed along his nerve endings.

In remarkable exactness Caitlan had drawn Amanda, every delicate feature of her face finely etched, along with her beautiful, beguiling smile and her dimple. Amanda's head was tilted back, her long hair streaming over her shoulders, that mischievous twinkle he'd loved sparkling in her eyes. The pose was a likeness that only could have been captured in a candid moment—how in the hell had Caitlan managed that?

"Christ," he muttered, thumbing through the rest of the pages. Caitlan had drawn a few pictures of Laura and King, and even one of Randal, but the majority of the sketches were of him and Amanda.

Once J.T.'s initial shock wore off anger settled in, prompting him into action. He wanted explanations for these bizarre reproductions. And he wanted them now.

Taking the pad, he bounded down the stairs. The kitchen screen door slammed shut, and he headed in that direction. "Caitlan?" he called, unable to contain the fury lacing his voice.

"It's me, Dad."

He ignored the curious look Laura gave him when he walked into the kitchen. "Where have you been?" he asked, glancing out the window to see if Caitlan was outside.

She went to the sink and washed her hands. "Down in the barn. I wanted to check on Missy."

Paternal instincts kicked in. "Alone?"

She nodded. "Yes."

"After what happened with Missy's kittens I prefer you don't go down there unless someone is with you." His fingers curled tight around the sketch pad, renewing his anger. "Where's Caitlan?"

"She went for a walk." Grabbing the terry towel, she dried her hands, slanting a speculative glance J.T.'s way. "What's going on? Everyone's acting weird today. First Caitlan, then you—"

"What's wrong with Caitlan?" he interrupted.

Laura shrugged. "I don't know, exactly. I came home from school today and just as I was about to come inside the house she came running out. She nearly crashed into me. It looked like she'd been crying, but she said she was fine, that she just wanted to be alone for a bit." Her fingers twisted in the towel. "I'm kind of worried about her, Dad. Maybe you should go find her, just to be sure she's okay."

Oh, he planned to. And just as soon as he reassured himself of her well being he'd get some answers. "Which way did she go?"

"Alongside the north pasture fence."

"I'll find her," he promised, striding toward the front door. "And we'll be back before supper."

Caitlan didn't know how long she knelt there in the pasture, afraid to contact her Superior but knowing she no longer had a choice. Her Superiors had no idea what she'd experienced with J.T., didn't know about the haunting visions that touched her soul, or that she'd done the unthinkable and fallen in love with J.T. Unless summoned for help or guidance, Superiors never monitored an angel while on a mission, and for that she was grateful.

A crisp breeze blew, tangling in her hair and chilling her to the bone with icy fingers of dread. The cold, damp earth beneath her knees seeped through her jeans and stole into her joints. Her tears of confusion had flowed freely, and even after they'd dried a chasm of bleakness echoed in her soul. She wished she had the ability to freeze into a statue, an emotionless slab of stone with no real worries or cares. When had being a guardian angel become so emotionally and physically draining? Never had she experienced such mental exhaustion. Not until J.T.

Not wanting to put the inevitable off any longer, she wiped the moisture from her cheeks and grabbed her medallion, silently transmitting a summons to her Superior.

"Yes? Is everything all right?"

Mary's voice drifted clearly through Caitlan's

mind. Glancing toward the heavens, a glimmer of despair swept over her. "No . . . I mean yes." Taking a deep, calming breath, she started again. "J.T. is fine," she assured her Superior, knowing that would be Mary's first concern.

"Then what is it? You look upset."

Devastated was more like it. "I . . ." She swallowed to ease the anxiety congealing in her throat. "I'm having these . . . visions that I don't understand. And at times, when I'm with J.T., I feel . . . strange things."

Silence.

Frowning, Caitlan grasped the pendant tighter. "Mary?"

"What kind of visions?" This from Christopher.

"J.T. when he was a boy, and a young girl. Her name is Amanda. From what I've learned from J.T., I believe she's his soulmate. Why am I so connected to these two people that I feel and see things they've experienced in the past?"

"Oh, dear," Mary said, her tone distressed.

"What kind of strange things do you feel?" Christopher asked in a tight voice.

Heat tinged Caitlan's cheeks when she remembered all the wonderful sensations J.T. evoked inside her. In the barn last night she'd been drawn into him, her heart and soul reaching for his as if they belonged together. She erased those thoughts quickly, before Christopher or Mary could latch onto them. She couldn't very well tell them about the *sensual* feelings she experienced for J.T., or that she'd fallen in love with him. Eventually she'd have to tell her Superiors, but not now, not until she understood more about the link she shared with J.T.

"Sometimes I feel like I'm a part of J.T., but I know that's impossible, considering I have a soulmate . . . right?" she asked tentatively, hoping they'd divulge *who* her soulmate was.

Silence.

Sighing, Caitlan rubbed her brow wearily. Why couldn't she remember certain things about her own past? "I feel like a guardian angel with amnesia," she mumbled.

Christopher chuckled.

"This is not a laughing matter, Christopher. In fact, it's all your fault," Mary said sternly.

"We need to tell her the truth," Christopher argued.

"The truth about what?" Caitlan managed to get in.

"Absolutely not," Mary said emphatically. "The mission is nearly over and we can't jeopardize J.T.'s life like that."

"Like what?"

"We can always send down another guardian to take over for Caitlan," Christopher suggested.

Panic had Caitlan blurting out, "No!"

Deafening silence.

She definitely had their attention now. She could feel them staring at her, waiting for an explanation. But how could she reveal that she wanted to stay with J.T. as long as possible, for selfish reasons they'd surely disapprove of?

Pasting on a smile, Caitlan shrugged indifferently. "I mean, I've already come this far in the mission. J.T. believes my reasons for being here, so why start with someone new that he'll have to come to trust? You just said the mission is nearly over."

"Caitlan is right," Christopher conceded. "From what we have on the schedule, in another day or two the mission should be over. Three days tops."

"What about her memory?" Mary asked.

Caitlan frowned. "What about my memory?"

"For some reason her memory wasn't completely suppressed," Christopher supplied.

"Will it hold out for another few days?"

"Possibly. If she takes care with the medallion."

"I don't like this, Christopher. I warned you how risky it would be to do this. . . . "

Frustration coiled in Caitlan as she listened to her Superiors argue about her, stretching her nerves taut. *"What* are you talking about?" she grated out.

Silence.

She closed her eyes, fighting back the urge to scream. All she wanted were answers, a clue as to why her soul seemed entwined with J.T.'s past. So far her Superiors hadn't helped her solve anything. In fact, they were arguing about her memory, and keeping J.T. safe. Maybe, if she opted for the truth, if she told them she'd fallen in love with J.T., they'd listen to her and give her the answers she sought. Maybe they'd tell her what was going on.

Dismissing the sudden prickles of awareness radiating from behind her, she clutched her medallion for courage. "There's something I need to tell you."

"Go ahead," Mary said.

The words jammed in her throat. Heaven help her, she couldn't do it! *I'm in love with, J.T. Just say it, Caitlan, and get it over with!* "I'm in lo—"

"Who the hell are you talking to, Caitlan?"

Chapter Eleven

Caitlan started at the sound of J.T.'s deep voice, the declaration she'd been about to announce caught in her throat. Whipping her head around, she glanced over her shoulder, meeting his dark gaze, smoldering with annoyance. And anger. The gold in his green eyes sparked like fire, and his mouth compressed into a harsh line. From her vantage point, he looked tall and lean and intimidating. She shivered.

Letting go of the medallion and severing her connection with her Superiors, she willed her heart to stop galloping. She hadn't heard J.T. approach. She was losing her edge, that finely honed instinct that usually kept her so alert. All because she'd fallen in love with him and couldn't keep her emotions under control.

Slowly, she came to her feet, tucking a tousled strand of hair behind her ear. "How long have you been standing there?" she demanded.

He shifted on his feet, his powerful body seemingly rippling with the movement. "Long enough to hear you babbling to yourself."

She knew he couldn't hear her Superiors, but how much of her side of the conversation had he eavesdropped on? And she'd been about to make the ultimate of confessions! Opting for the offensive, she thrust up her chin and gave him what she hoped would pass for a haughty look. "Aren't I allowed some privacy around here?"

He pinned her with a shrewd look. "Sure, as long as its near the main house. With all the strange things that have happened around the ranch, you of all people should know better than to run off on your own." His voice held a heavy dose of censure.

"I wanted some time alone to think. Out loud." Anxious to change the subject, she brushed past him, heading back toward the house. "What did you want, J.T.?"

He grabbed her arm before she could pass, bringing her up short. "An explanation."

So did she, for so many things, but it looked as though her answers would have to wait until tonight, when she'd have some privacy in which to contact her Superiors again.

The heat of J.T.'s fingers filtered through her

sweatshirt, wreaking havoc on her senses and flowing through her blood like a narcotic. The clean, masculine scent of him drifted on the breeze, curling around her. His touch aroused her in a primitive, shameless way. When she looked into his gaze she saw an answering hunger there, a need to take possession and never let go. Had making love bonded them more spiritually than before?

She tugged on her arm and he let it go. The sensations receded and she took a safe step back. "An explanation for what?" If she could only clear the husky need from her voice, she'd be fine.

He looked disoriented for a moment; then the smoky desire faded from his eyes. He straightened, a determined cast to his features. "To this."

Horror ripped through her when he lifted her sketch pad for her to see. Head spinning, the wildflowers around them became a blur of colors as she focused on the one object that betrayed her most private thoughts and visions. She'd been so caught up in everything else, she hadn't noticed the sketch pad in his hand.

She recovered from her shock. Barely. "You went through my things?" she choked, shaking off the panic creeping up on her. "You had no right!" She tried to grab the sketch pad, but he jerked it out of her reach.

A ruthless light came into his eyes, made more chilling by the outright anger in his voice. "You came to my ranch with nothing more than the clothes on your back. This is *my* pad of paper and you're living under *my* roof for the time being. Considering the strange things that have happened since your arrival, I had *every* right to see what you've been drawing." He flipped the pad open to the sketch of him as a youth. "Somehow, I hadn't expected this. I'd like an explanation, Caitlan. Now."

Caitlan trembled from the inside out, and it had nothing to do with the sudden disappearance of the sun behind a cloud. She wrapped her arms around her waist in an effort to ward off the tremors invading her body. How could she tell him she didn't know what possessed her to draw those pictures, that the images had been so clear in her mind that she'd reproduced them without any real effort. "I . . . I was just drawing how I thought you'd look as a young boy." The excuse sounded lame even to her own ears.

His eyes narrowed, skepticism mingling with blatant disbelief. "And you hit it right on the bull's-eye. It's impossible you could be this accurate when you didn't know me at that age." He thumbed to another page, his expression grim. "And how in the hell do you know what Amanda looked like?"

I have visions of her. Oh, God, what explanation could she give him that wouldn't make her sound like a psychiatric patient? She grasped the first logical answer that came to mind. "I saw pictures."

"Where?"

"In your office. The bottom shelf in your book-case."

He thought for a second, then fury blazed in his eyes. "So, you went snooping through *my* personal things?"

She bristled at his accusation. "Unlike yourself, I wasn't snooping. I was looking for a good book to read to pass some time and I saw the photo albums and looked through them. What crime is there in that?"

"You went through the cigar box." His voice was flat, his words more a statement than a question.

"Yes," she said very faintly. A shiver passed through her when she remembered all the momentos in that box, and her reaction to each of them.

He stared at her for a long moment. She could see him struggling to accept her tale for the truth. She prayed he wouldn't realize the sketches she'd drawn of him as a boy were exact duplicates of the ones he had stashed in the cigar box. Oh, what a tangled web she'd woven! And she couldn't even explain how or why.

"I don't like strangers going through my personal things," he finally said in a terse tone. "Stay out of my office unless I'm in there, Caitlan." Turning, he walked away, retaining her sketch pad.

Strangers. The word made her feel so lonely, so

solitary. After everything they'd shared he still thought of her as an intruder in his life. But what had she expected from a man whose heart had been battered and bruised? A declaration of love? No, he'd warned her up-front that he didn't have a heart to give, and she had no right asking for it. The thought brought on an avalanche of feelings she didn't want to acknowledge.

Panicked at the thought of him having free access to study her drawings, she quickly caught up to him, breathless. "Can I have my sketch pad back, please?"

"No."

"It's mine," she argued heatedly.

He slanted her an uncompromising look. "It's *mine*."

Caitlan drew a deep breath, not knowing what to say. She walked silently beside him, watching him brood and think.

Minutes later the barn came into view, along with Frank, Randal, and Mike, standing in a semicircle in front of the structure. Loud, angry voices carried their way, and J.T. frowned, glancing at his watch. The hands weren't due back in for another hour. "I wonder what's going on now," he muttered, picking up his pace.

J.T. watched as Randal shoved at Mike. The other man automatically bounded back, fists raised, face contorted in rage.

"Come on," Mike challenged. "Give me a reason to plant my fist in that face of yours!"

A taunting smile curled Randal's lips. "You're nothing but a washed-up Marine," he retorted, puffing out his chest like a peacock.

"Both of you, cool it," Frank said, doing his best to stop the two men from brawling by insinuating himself between them. Randal and Mike yelled accusations and insults at each other until their language became descriptive and crude, and they shoved at Frank to get to one another.

J.T. swore, then glanced at Caitlan beside him. "Go on up to the house," he ordered.

"I'll be fine—"

"Now!" His tone brooked no argument. He gave her a gentle shove toward the walkway and strode purposefully to the group of men.

Knowing J.T. wouldn't appreciate her verbally refuting him at a time like this, she headed toward the house but stopped after a few yards. There was no way she'd leave J.T. unprotected when Randal had murder in his eyes. She stood off to the side, out of the way, but within hearing and viewing range, so she could monitor the situation.

J.T. reached the trio, tossed the sketch pad on a clump of grass a few feet away, and assessed the situation as best he could without knowing any details. Randal looked like hell, his face unshaven, his eyes bloodshot. The faint scent of stale whiskey reached J.T.'s nostrils, enough to confirm that Randal had been tipping the bottle while working. Mike looked like a formidable opponent, jaw clenched, the muscles across his shoulders bunched as he affected a boxing stance.

Who had provoked whom? J.T. wondered. "What's the problem here?"

Randal and Mike glared at one another, each declining to comment, both too intent on waiting for the other to make the first move.

J.T. looked at his foreman. "Frank?"

Frank shrugged and stepped to the side. "You'll have to hear it from these two, J.T. The details I have are secondhand."

"Either of you care to explain?"

Mike kept his fists raised and his gaze trained on Randal, ready for any sudden moves. "You've got a drunk working for you, and he's gonna end up hurtin' someone."

Randal tossed his head, malice darting from his gaze like sharpened daggers. "And Mike's looking for a piece of that woman you dragged home with you," he goaded with a sneer. "But I already told Mike you don't share."

Like an enraged bulldog, Mike emitted a low-throated growl and charged Randal, knocking him down into the dirt. Mike threw a punch, clipping Randal hard beneath the jaw, snapping his head back. Randal howled in pain, and Mike raised his fist for another blow.

Even though J.T. had the urge to do the same thing to his cousin, he grabbed Mike by the collar and hauled him off Randal before the other man could mutilate Randal's face.

With Frank's assistance, Randal stood, stumbling slightly to regain his balance. Touching his jaw gingerly, Randal winced, then shot Mike a menacing glare.

J.T. glanced from Mike to Randal. "I'll ask one more time for an explanation," he said in a succinct tone. "Mike?" he offered, allowing the hand a chance to go first.

Mike flexed the fist he'd just used to punch Randal. "I found Randal sitting beneath a shade tree drinking from a flask—"

"That's an outright lie!" Randal burst in, charging toward the other man.

J.T. pressed a hand to Randal's heaving chest, and his cousin backed down. "Let him finish, Randal, and then you'll have your say." J.T. felt like he was dealing with two small children. "Go on, Mike."

"I don't want some drunk watching my back during a roundup. When I told him to put the flask away he started getting abusive, insulting my work, and when that wasn't enough, he started saying some things about your lady friend I didn't care for."

"Such as?" J.T. prompted, a slow burn traveling through his veins.

"He thought maybe the two of us could show Caitlan a good time." He transferred his gaze to Randal, and J.T. somehow knew more had transpired between the two men than Mike was revealing.

Randal's eyes narrowed to slits. "More like the other way around. You were the one talking about how long it's been since you've had a woman and the things you'd like to do to the *little lady.*" A sadistic smile transformed Randal's features. "Better watch Caitlan real careful J.T.—"

"Enough!" J.T. roared, enraged at Randal's insinuation.

Looking at both men, J.T. didn't know whom to believe. Their behavior was juvenile, but there was no doubt one had goaded the other. Why would Mike defend Caitlan when he didn't even know her? J.T. wondered. A code of honor left over from his Marine Corps days? Or *had* Mike been the one to make the slurs, as Randal had suggested? He didn't know, but there was no mistaking the fact that Randal had been drinking, or that problems had started arising since Mike's arrival a few months back. Both men were suspect.

J.T. decided a joint reprimand was in order. "I won't tolerate this kind of behavior from any of my men. Both of you are suspended without pay until next Monday."

Randal's face flushed bright red. "You can't do that!"

"I can, and I did. I've given you plenty of warnings to sober up. Maybe this will do the trick."

"Go to hell," Randal hissed, eyes glittering.

Spinning on his heels, he strode down the dirt drive toward his cabin.

J.T. released a long breath. He'd already been to hell and back today, without Randal's good wishes. Between his morning talk with Caitlan, finding her sketch pad, their confrontation, and now this, he was pretty well wiped out.

"I didn't do anything wrong," Mike said in a low voice.

J.T. looked from Randal's retreating back to Mike. Sincerity etched his features, but not knowing much about the man, J.T. couldn't give Mike his complete trust. "You're the newest hand here, Mike. This is the first time I've had a problem between my men."

Mike's jaw clenched, but he refrained from further comment. With a slight nod of acceptance, made more mocking by the rage of injustice burning in his gaze, he turned and walked away.

"You did the right thing," Frank said, placing a reassuring hand on J.T.'s shoulder. "Kirk found them having it out, but we can't be sure who started the fight." Frank's gaze slid beyond J.T., his eyes widening in sudden surprise. "Uh, afternoon, Caitlan."

"Good afternoon, Frank."

J.T. jerked around upon hearing Caitlan's soft voice. Seeing her standing conspicuously off to the side, hands clasped behind her back, he realized she'd never gone up to the house as he'd ordered. The sweet, angelic smile curving her

306

mouth did nothing to soften his sudden irritation. He was gonna wring her neck for not listening to him!

"I'll talk to you later, Frank," J.T. said, dismissing his foreman.

Casting a speculative glance from J.T. to Caitlan, Frank nodded, then headed toward the barn.

Grabbing the sketch pad he'd tossed to the ground earlier, J.T. strode purposefully toward Caitlan, scowling at her. "Dammit, I told you to go on up to the house."

Her chin lifted a fraction, and stubbornness sparked from her violet eyes. "I was worried about you."

He stopped in front of her, his large build shading the sun from her eyes when she looked up to meet his gaze. *I was worried about you.* Her caring words took up residence in that isolated portion of his heart, making him ache for a more physical kind of connection, a touch, a caress, a kiss, anything to ease the fierce need dominating his emotions.

Shoving those tender feelings aside, he focused on his annoyance, which was quickly becoming as thin and wispy as the clouds above. "I'm a big boy, Caitlan. I can take care of myself and my workers."

"I never said you couldn't." Chewing on her bottom lip, she shifted on her feet, suddenly anxious. "I didn't mean to become a problem with your men. I know there aren't any unmarried women on this ranch, and I never meant to . . ." A pink blush swept her cheeks. "I mean, I'd never . . ."

"You, personally, didn't do anything to provoke them, Caitlan," he interrupted. "You're a novelty to the men and it's only natural they talk about you, but I won't condone this kind of crude talk and behavior. If any one of my men so much as touches you, he'll be off the Circle R so fast his head will spin." His tone was possessive, but he couldn't help himself.

"And what about you, J.T.?" she asked very softly. Her gaze probed his, searching past the barriers he'd erected around his heart to the man who'd branded her his the night before.

Will you touch me again? He could almost see the question reflected in her eyes. His chest tightened painfully, and he resisted the urge to show her how many different ways he could touch her, make her burn for him. A gentle caress. A slow slide of his hand. Bolder, more intimate stroking.

He swallowed back the thick need gathering in his throat and lower, swirling in his belly. "I won't touch you either, so you don't need to worry about it."

She glanced away, but not before he'd caught a glimpse of hurt and hopelessness shimmering in her gaze. "It's for the best."

"Yeah," he agreed, wondering who he was trying to convince.

* * *

After supper J.T. retired to his office, leaving Laura to finish up her homework and Caitlan to watch TV in the den. He wrote up individual reports on Mike and Randal, noting their suspension, then filed the slips of papers in each of their employee files. Impulsively, J.T. withdrew Mike's file from the cabinet and brought it back to his desk to peruse.

Shuffling through the contents, he pulled out Mike's employment application. A few lines had been left blank, mainly in the family-and-relative emergency information section, but that kind of vagueness wasn't unusual when hiring a seasonal hand. Most were drifters and had no family to call their own.

Mike's reference sheet listed the four previous ranches where he'd been employed. J.T. had called two of the spreads for references, and both told him Mike was quiet but a good hand. The first ranch laid him off due to lack of work, and the other ranch claimed there had been a personality conflict between Mike and the foreman, and Mike had opted to move on. A conflict in personalities was hardly a crime, J.T. thought, unless it interfered with work, as it had today.

Randal wasn't guiltless, J.T. knew. He had a volatile temper, more so these past months since his father's death and the debts that had been heaped on him. His flare-ups and bouts of drunkenness were increasing in frequency. J.T. hoped this suspension would force Randal to get his priorities together.

As for Mike's suspension, J.T. hadn't decided whether or not it would be permanent. He didn't know much about the man, not even if he was capable of setting up the sabotage attempt on his life. But what reason would Mike have for harming him? Mike had nothing to gain, unless he'd been hired by someone, which didn't make sense. J.T. didn't have any real enemies that he knew of. The "accident" down by the creek still confounded him.

Mike had the perfect motivation for tossing the kittens into King's stall—retaliation for J.T. reprimanding him for smoking in the barn—but J.T. had no concrete evidence that Mike had actually done the deed.

Maybe he ought to cut his losses and let Mike go with a week's severance pay. J.T. had no proof the man was guilty of anything, but he couldn't afford to keep Mike on and possibly risk a potentially dangerous incident that might involve his family. Tomorrow, he decided, would be soon enough to let the hand go.

J.T. scrubbed a hand over his jaw. Hell, when had his life become so complicated? Ever since a violet-eyed woman had drifted into his life and saved him from a certain death. Even *her* sudden appearance he still found hard to believe, although he had no reason to distrust her.

Tossing Mike's file aside, J.T. reached for the

sketch pad on the corner of his desk. Leaning back in his chair, he opened the cover. The shock of seeing Caitlan's portrait of him as a young boy had worn off, but he was still baffled as to how she'd accomplished the detailed and oddly accurate sketch.

The longer he studied the picture, the more it seemed familiar, as if he'd seen this particular drawing before. Putting the pad down on his desk, he sighed heavily. His gaze strayed to the bottom shelf of his bookcase, and he thought of the cigar box he'd stashed there, and Amanda's sketches of him tucked inside.

"Amanda," he murmured, waiting for the familiar piercing pain to lance through him at the thought of her. The sorrow was dull and distant, overshadowed by his feelings for another woman. Caitlan. Despite his resolve to keep her at arm's length, he cared for her. Deeply. More than he wanted to admit. Making love to her had changed him in intense, unsettling ways.

Shrugging off the thought, J.T. stood, wanting to compare Amanda's sketches to Caitlan's. Just as he reached the bookshelf, the phone rang, detering his quest.

He picked up the receiver. "Hello?"

"J.T., I've got an emergency on my hands," Kirk said urgently. "A waterline in my basement busted, and I know you have some spare pipe—"

"I'll be there in five minutes."

"Great. Thanks."

J.T. hung up the phone, the cigar box and sketches forgotten. He strode toward the den to tell Caitlan he'd be gone for a while, and paused in the doorway. Laura sat cross-legged on the floor, her schoolbooks and homework spread out on the coffee table in front of her. Caitlan sat on the couch watching TV, legs tucked beneath her, arms wrapped around a throw pillow.

Caitlan's soft violet eyes slowly lifted to meet his, and everything in the world receded from his mind but her. The quiet longing in her gaze reached past his heart and into his soul, nestling there like a warm ray of sunshine. The powerful, unexplainable link between them tugged at his heart, wrenching it open, ultimately allowing her warmth and gentleness to breach the emptiness he'd lived with for sixteen years.

His breath hitched in his lungs. Lord. *He loved her.*

"What's up, Dad?"

Snapped from his startling revelation, he jerked his gaze to his daughter, trying to remember his original purpose for seeking out Caitlan. Certainly not to come to the conclusion that he loved her! When had he fallen in love with her? Or had it been happening all along, and he'd been too blind to see it?

"Dad?" Laura tilted her head to the side, gaze curious. "Who was on the phone?"

J.T. gave himself a firm mental shake. "Kirk.

He needs my help to repair a broken waterline in his basement. If I don't get going, he'll be up to his knees in water by the time I get there."

He looked at Caitlan and his pulse pounded, reverberating throughout his body. *He loved her.* The rusty words scratched his throat like barbed wire, yet he refused to give them release. His feelings changed nothing between them. She'd be gone in a few days, and he'd be smart to let her go now, unburdened with such a declaration, instead of a year down the road, when she decided ranch life wasn't enough for her. He had no right to shackle her here, and she'd given him no indication that she wanted to stay. She'd leave and he'd forget about her before the month was out. *Not likely*, his heart taunted.

He glanced at his watch. Eight o'clock. "I'll be back in an hour or so." Caitlan nodded, and he transferred his gaze back to Laura. "And if I'm not, I want you in bed by nine, Smidget. It's a school night."

"Okay," Laura said on a reluctant sigh.

His gaze flickered to Caitlan once more, and he struggled with the chaos raging inside him. Abruptly he turned and left the den before he said or did something that would make him look like a fool.

Caitlan watched J.T. go, hating the hollowness swallowing her up with his departure. For a fleeting moment she'd seen something soften in his eyes; then those barriers of his slid carefully into place, shutting her out. She shivered from the chill of loneliness and gathered the pillow tighter to her chest.

For the next half hour she tried to concentrate on the sit-com on TV, but her mind refused to cooperate. J.T. filled her thoughts, and all that had transpired between them in the last twenty-four hours.

A gradual uneasiness crept up on her, an awareness she couldn't shake. As if something evil was going to happen, but she wasn't quite sure what. After J.T.'s confrontation with Randal today she knew Randal was close to exploding in a mad rage. She'd seen the hatred in his eyes and sensed his building fury. She should have gone with J.T. to Kirk's, but she didn't believe the danger was with him, but lurked nearby instead, sharpening her senses to full alert.

Leaving the comfort of the couch, she padded to the kitchen for a drink of water, searching for the source of her unease. Filling a glass with the tap from the sink, she stared out the window, seeing nothing but the murky darkness of night. Black, like an impending doom. An electrical current of anxiety raced along her nerves.

King's Ransom.

The stallion's name whispered through her mind without provocation. A chill eddied down her spine. A strong, niggling intuition propelled her into action. Setting the glass on the counter, she started for the front door, stopping for a second at the den.

She stuck her head in the doorway. "I'll be right back, Laura."

Frowning at Caitlan's brusqueness, Laura stood and followed Caitlan down the hall. "Where are you going?"

"To the barn," she said over her shoulder, jogging down the porch steps. "Stay here."

Laura dogged her steps. "Dad said we shouldn't go anywhere alone."

"Stay in the house!" Caitlan ordered, her boots crunching on the gravel.

Laura ignored her. "I'm not letting you go to the barn alone. Dad's gonna freak when he finds out we went down there."

Something was wrong. Horribly wrong. Caitlan could feel it in her bones; her intuition so strong, so overwhelming, it nearly smothered her. Out of the corner of her eye she saw a large silhouette slink around the side of the barn, then disappear behind the structure.

"Hey!" Caitlan yelled to get the person's attention. A blur of shadowy movement took off toward the bunkhouse. Knowing she'd never be able to catch up to the person, she let him go.

"Who was that?" Laura asked, her voice full of bewilderment.

"I don't know." A horse's high-pitched cry, full of terror, rent the night. *King.* Caitlan broke into a run toward the barn, apprehension rippling through her. Flinging the door open, a cloud of smoke billowed out. The biting, acrid scent of burning wood slipped up her nostrils.

"Oh, God, Laura. The barn is on fire!" Caitlan's heart pumped furiously and she automatically pushed Laura in the opposite direction, out of harm's way. "Go back to the house and call Frank, and then your father."

Laura's eyes widened, her expression frightened. She clutched at Caitlan's sleeve, tears of fright filling her eyes. "Don't go in there—"

Caitlan stole a precious moment to smooth a reassuring hand over Laura's cheek. "I'll be fine, I promise, but I need you to call for help."

Bottom lip trembling, Laura nodded. "Please be careful." Whirling around, she ran back toward the house, her long hair flying out behind her.

Once Caitlan assured herself of Laura's safety, she rushed into the barn. The crackle of fire devouring wood reached her ears. Unable to see more than three feet in front of her for all the smoke hazing the area, she guessed the blaze to be at the far end of the barn.

Swallowing back the alarm crowding her throat, she started unlatching stalls and quickly guided the terrified horses, one at a time, out the side door leading to the open pasture. With each horse she released, the heat, smoke, and snapping fire intensified.

King's scream shattered Caitlan's concentration. His fear and panic squeezed her heart like a tight fist. *Please let him be okay*, she silently prayed, her only request for divine intervention.

Smacking the last mare on the rump, sending her into the pasture with the other horses, Caitlan headed toward the echo of King's terrified screams. Searching frantically through the cloud of churning, pungent smoke, she finally located King's stall and found the true source of the fire.

The empty stall next to King's was an inferno of hungry flames, the bright orange flares eating their way into the stallion's pen, lapping the walls of King's stall and sparking the hay covering the ground. King thrashed wildly, trying to escape the blaze consuming his stall.

She moved forward, grabbing an old towel someone had draped over a wooden bench. The smoke made it difficult to find the coiled lead rope hanging near King's stall, but her searching fingers finally found the nubbly cord. Eyes stinging, she threw open the stall door. Tossing the towel over King's head to shield his eyes, she quickly clipped the hook to his halter and guided the screaming and terrified horse from his burning stall.

Struggling against King's urge to flee, she blindly found her way through the barn. Smoke choked her. Every breath she took burned her lungs.

Her grip on the lead rope slipped, and King took advantage of the slack and shied away, his high-pitched neigh of fright piercing the air. A battle of wills ensued. Caitlan jerked him forward, but he was a powerful animal, driven by fear. He tugged on the rope and danced about, neighing. Thick smoke curled around them, making it difficult to see King, or the entrance.

The crackle of wood splintering sent chills up Caitlan's spine; then a deafening crash shook the ground beneath her, sending King into another fit of panic and throwing her off balance. She knew King's stall had collapsed and the fire was rapidly spreading. In the distance she heard urgent shouts for help from the hands, and tried to focus on the sound, to use it as a guide to lead them out of the barn.

Disoriented from King's thrashing, she started forward. The roar of raging fire filled her head. Scorching heat seemed to surround her from every angle, closing in like a monstrous shark feeding frenzy. She stopped short, trying to find a familiar landmark, but was unable to see anything through the murky smoke. King jerked wildly against the rope and she stumbled.

A helpless sound escaped her raw throat. The structure seemed to close in on her, snatching the breath from her lungs. Head spinning and stomach rolling, she groped for the medallion beneath her sweatshirt.

Heaven help her, she'd lost all sense of direction.

* * *

Bringing his truck to a skidding halt in front of the house, J.T. jumped out of the driver's side before the dust and gravel had a chance to settle. His feet hit the ground running, too anxious to wait for Kirk, who'd pulled up in his truck behind J.T.'s.

When Laura had called him, sobbing, and told him the barn was on fire and Caitlan was in it trying to save the animals, his heart had stopped beating. All he could remember thinking was that if he lost Caitlan in that fire he'd never be the same again.

Laura's plea of, "Hurry, Dad, I'm scared" propelled him to hang up the phone and yell the message to Kirk before bolting out of the house to his truck. The drive had taken him less than three minutes.

Now, adrenaline and gut-wrenching fear for Caitlan's life ruled him. Shoving aside his worry, he ran to the barn, his gaze scanning the area for Caitlan. His men were just arriving on the scene. Frank shouted orders as he opened the storage shed off to the side, flipped on a flood light to illuminate the area, and began tossing out buckets for the troughs, extinguishers, and water hoses.

Oh, God, where was Caitlan? Stark terror twisted in his heart as he neared the barn. Smoke spewed out the doors, the windows, and even slithered through minuscule cracks in the structure. The sinister sound of flames enveloping wood, and anything else in their path, breached the night. More adrenaline surged through his body at the thought of Caitlan being trapped in there.

"Dad!"

J.T. whipped around. Laura stood away from the activity, all alone, her arms wrapped around her stomach. The floodlight shone off her tear-streaked face. Relief poured over him at seeing her unharmed, only to be replaced by dread. "Where's Caitlan?" he asked, already knowing the answer.

A sob broke from Laura. "She's still in the barn!"

J.T. swore profanely, hating the fear that made his blood run cold. He despised even more the horrifying memories of another woman's tragic death. And that he'd been helpless to save her.

Not this time, he vowed, racing toward the barn. He wouldn't lose Caitlan. Not without a fight. Not after she'd insinuated herself in his life and made him fall in love with her. Especially not after she'd made him feel and need and care so deeply again.

Thinking only of Caitlan, he pushed aside his men and entered the barn first. The darkness of night, mingled with the hazy smoke, momentarily blinded him. He swallowed to ease the rasp in his throat, unsure if the bitter taste in his mouth was fear or smoke.

"Caitlan!" he bellowed, charging into the thick of it.

He heard her cough weakly, and King's sharp cry of alarm, just yards away from him. Breathing shallowly, he moved forward and nearly ran into her. He found her clutching that damnable medallion of hers like a lifeline in one hand and the rope secured to King in the other.

She looked up at him, gratitude touching her features. "J.T.," she rasped, then coughed.

Torn between throttling her and hugging her, he took the rope from her fingers and grabbed her arm, navigating her and King around his men rushing to put out the blaze.

Once outside, J.T. didn't give King a chance to put up a fight or turn wild on him. Keeping up a steady, fast-paced stride, with Caitlan jogging to keep up, he dragged the skittish stallion to an empty corral. Letting go of Caitlan long enough to unlatch the gate, he removed the towel from King's head, then led the horse inside and set him free.

Then he turned toward Caitlan.

Now that the crises was over his blood ran hot in his veins and his pulse beat erratically. Knowing Frank and his men could handle things without his assistance, J.T. focused on the more important matters pressing in on him.

Needing to affirm that Caitlan was truly alive and unharmed, he dropped the towel and took her face in his hands. He cupped her warm, smooth flesh, his thumbs caressing her cheeks, her nose, her lips. Reassured by her presence, giant shudders of relief rippled through his body.

Her thighs pressed against his and her fingers curled desperately into his shirt. She drew in a deep, cleansing breath; then her lashes fluttered closed and her lips parted on a sigh.

"J.T.," she whispered, leaning into him, lifting her mouth to his.

Sensing the same urgent need in Caitlan that flowed through his own body after such a harrowing experience, he crushed his mouth to hers without coaxing preliminaries or gentleness. No, this kiss was meant to possess and brand her as his own.

God, he could have lost her, he thought desperately, wrapping his arms around her back and hauling her body flush to his. He could have been thrust back into the same kind of nightmare that had shattered his life sixteen years ago. If he lost Caitlan, he'd die inside. She'd become a part of his heart and soul and he couldn't imagine living without her. He refused to think of living the same lonely, desolate existence he had before she'd arrived on the Circle R.

With a groan of surrender, he opened his mouth wider over hers, kissing her deeply, thoroughly. Her mouth was warm and sweet and generous. The gates imprisoning his emotions broke, and he poured every worry, every need, every feeling he had for her into the hungry kiss.

She tasted like smoke and woman, like life itself. He saturated his senses in her, took greedily and gave openly.

When he finally lifted his mouth from hers they were both breathing hard. Shimmering moonlight enabled him to see the exhaustion painting her features and the desire brightening her eyes. As he looked at her, drinking in her disheveled appearance and dirt-smudged face, an incredible protective feeling drenched his heart. This time he accepted the emotion willingly, treasured and cherished it like a rare jewel.

Sweeping a hand down her spine, he molded her to him. He held her so close they were practically one, so intimately he was certain she felt the hard, aroused length of him straining the confines of his jeans.

"Don't *ever* do anything so foolish as that again!" he said fiercely, burying his face in her neck, skimming his lips along her soft, warm flesh. He couldn't get enough of her. Touching her, tasting her, confirmed that she wasn't just an illusion.

She pulled back so she could look into his eyes. "I had to save King." Her resolute tone clearly stated that she would have risked her life for the horse again if faced with the need.

Her goodness and loyalty should have surprised him but didn't. Not anymore. "You could have been killed trying to save him." His arms tightened around her. "Don't you understand? I could have lost you!" *I love you!* his heart shouted, but the actual words snagged in his throat.

She smiled and touched her warm fingertips to his jaw. "I'm fine, really."

An abrupt laugh escaped him, releasing the last of the tension coiling his body. He shook his head, unable to believe how unflappable she was about the incident. "Only you would shrug this off as an everyday event. Until I find out what happened in the barn I don't want you around here. Take Laura and go on up to the house."

Her gaze flickered to the stallion in the corral. "But King—"

"I don't want you near him right now, Caitlan. He doesn't look in the mood for company." She opened her mouth, but he covered it with his hand. "If you don't stop putting yourself in danger with that horse, you're going to make me crazy," he growled. "And if you don't stop arguing with me, I'm going to throw you over my shoulder and haul you up to the house myself." His voice lowered huskily. "And I won't be responsible for what happens after that."

His sexy threat registered in her eyes.

"What's your decision, Caitie?"

She hesitated a moment, something warm and inviting glistening in her eyes; then she backed away. "I'm going." She gave him one last, lingering glance that filled him with warmth. "Be careful," she said softly, then turned and headed toward Laura.

J.T. stood there, watching Caitlan take Laura under her arm and comfort the girl as they walked up to the house. Once they were inside J.T. strode into the barn. The fire had been extinguished; now his men were busy sopping up water and piling the debris. The pungent scent of burnt wood and wet ash surrounded him.

Glancing around the immediate area, he found no fire damage. He moved with purpose down the row of stalls toward the back of the barn and froze when he saw King's burnt and blackened stall, and the stall directly next to his, the only area seemingly devastated by the fire. The beams overhead had collapsed into the stalls and would have crushed King if Caitlan hadn't saved him. Hell, those beams could have been *her* coffin!

Impotent anger tangled with new emotions swirling inside him. Who was behind this latest incident? he wondered.

Frank walked into the barn from the south end, followed by Jack, a lanky hand of twenty-two. "Once we get this mess cleaned up let's start moving the animals back into their stalls," Frank ordered.

"What should we do about the stallion?" Jack asked.

Frank picked up a water hose and began coiling it. "Hitch one of the other mares at the far end of the barn and give him his own stall for the night so he doesn't hurt anyone."

"Who's gonna bring him in?" Jack asked, hands placed defiantly on his hips. "Andy's the only one crazy enough to drag King into the barn, and he isn't here. You can't pay me to get within five feet of the beast."

"Then leave King in the corral for the night," J.T. ordered. "Andy can bring him in the morning."

Both men glanced his way. Jack's expression turned sheepish and his hands dropped back to his sides.

"Here, Jack." Frank passed the other man the water hose. "Take this back to the shed."

Jack took his cue and left.

"How's Caitlan?" Frank asked, his tone softening.

"Fine. I sent her up to the house with Laura. I think I'm more shaken by what happened than she is." J.T. rubbed at the tense muscles in his neck, still baffled at how calm Caitlan had been. No tears over the ordeal, no hysterics, just a hot, needy kiss that reached to his soul and beyond.

Glancing back at King's incinerated stall, a fresh batch of fury coursed through him. "What, exactly, happened here?"

Grabbing a rag from his back pocket, Frank wiped his dirty hands. "Seems like a fire started in the empty stall next to King's. All the animals are fine and the damage minimal, thanks to Caitlan's foresight."

A prickle of awareness skittered over J.T.'s skin. "Foresight? What do you mean?"

Bewilderment creased Frank's bushy brow. "It's the damnedest thing. From what Laura says, Caitlan ran out of the house earlier like something was wrong. She got to the barn just as the fire started and began releasing the horses from their stalls."

J.T. dragged a hand down his face, somehow not surprised that Caitlan had sensed the fire. Strange. Strange like her drawings. Strange like her medallion. Strange like the link that made her seem so much a part of him, even when she wasn't around. Who could explain any of that?

Kicking that nonsense out of his head, he re-routed his thoughts back to business. "What do you think about the fire? Was it set deliberately?" *Did he even need to ask?*

"Most likely." The tone of Frank's voice bordered on resignation as he concentrated on rubbing soot off his palm. "There was nothing in either stall that could have started the fire."

J.T.'s jaw hardened as his first two prime suspects entered his mind without any prompting. "Where were Randal and Mike?"

Frank shook his head, already ahead of the game. "I checked them out first thing. Mike had a solid alibi and Randal said he was watching TV in his cabin when he heard the hands yelling for help. Both men helped to put out the fire."

Uneasiness crept over J.T. "I want the fire marshall out here tomorrow to conduct an investigation." And maybe he'd mention the strange occurrences that had happened over the past week, just to get them recorded for future reference.

Frank nodded. "Will do."

Nearly an hour later, after the animals had been secured in the undamaged section of the barn, J.T. slipped into the quiet, dark house. The guest bathroom shower was running, and J.T. assumed Caitlan was in there, scrubbing the smoke and soot from her body. He found Laura fast asleep in her bed. Placing a loving kiss on her cheek, he smoothed the covers, then left her room and headed back down the hall.

J.T. restlessly paced the guest room while waiting for Caitlan. He tried not to imagine her in the shower, the warm water and slick soap sluicing over her silken skin, and failed. He wanted her too badly not to respond to the merest thought of her.

She was well and truly in his blood, a growing fever that made him burn from the inside out. He thought of having a wife, a mother for Laura, and how he wanted all that with Caitlan, a woman who would risk her life to save a horse. A woman who gave him so much without realizing it. Love. Laughter. Anger. Passion.

He didn't know how he'd been fortunate enough to have found her—or the other way around, as the case might be—but he was willing to fight for her, to prove that she belonged here on the Circle R with him and Laura.

Before he could talk himself out of joining her in the shower, he began stripping off his clothes. With every article hastily shed, his body grew achingly hard for her, his heart opening to receive her in the purest sense. Seconds later he stepped into the steamy bathroom and smiled when he saw her misty outline through the frosted glass shower stall door.

The time had come for him and Caitlan to settle a few things.

Chapter Twelve

Caitlan sensed J.T. before she actually heard or saw him. Eyes closed, the hot shower spray rinsed away the last of the soap from her body and hair and pounded the tense muscles across her back. An incredible awareness swelled within her, as if J.T. had reached out and physically caressed her. The shower stall door opened on a soft click and she shivered, not from the cool air rushing in but from the sensual anticipation racing along her spine.

Her lashes fluttered open and she looked at J.T., standing just outside the shower. He was naked and aroused, all sleek strength and firm, hard muscle. Liquid heat fluttered in her belly when his dark gaze slowly, reverently, glided the length of her body, and then back up again. Desire had clouded his eyes by the time he'd finished his visual exploration.

Touched by live flame, she fought the urge to cover herself. She knew what he wanted, knew she should tell him to leave, but her need and love for him eclipsed any semblance of reason or modesty she might have had.

He stepped inside the one-person stall and shut the door. Water droplets bounced off her and clung to his skin. He stood so close she had to tilt her head to meet his gaze. So close, his erection brushed her belly like a velvet caress and the tips of her breasts grazed the sprinkling of hair on his chest. Her nipples puckered into exquisitely tight buds, and she resisted the impulse to move even closer and rub against him.

The intense need blazing in his eyes kicked her heart into a heavy beat, reminding her of the desperate way he'd kissed her and held her after pulling her from the barn, as if he never wanted to let her go. Indeed, she hadn't wanted him to release her. At the time she'd rationalized his reaction as an outpouring of adrenaline and fear, but now she sensed his longing ran much, much deeper.

Tentatively, she reached up and touched a streak of soot on his cheek, wiping it away with her wet fingers. He'd put himself in danger by rescuing her from the fire, when it was her job to protect him. A tender ache wove through her.

"You could have died for me," she whispered thickly, her fingers playing over his stubbled jaw.

Catching her wrist, he dragged her hand to his mouth. He placed a kiss in her palm, then nipped at the flesh just below her thumb. "I would have, if it meant saving you." His voice vibrated with emotion.

The love in his gaze was unmistakable, echoing her own feelings for him. In that moment she knew she'd take whatever he would give her. Tonight she didn't want to think . . . she wanted to feel everything J.T. had to offer.

Curling her hand around the back of his head, she pulled his mouth to hers and kissed him without restraint. Water sluiced over them and she pressed her body to his, sliding her slick, naked breasts against his chest.

He growled deep in his throat. Wrapping his arms around her back, he pulled her closer, returning the deep, tongue-tangling kiss with fervor.

And then it wasn't enough for Caitlan. She trembled. She ached. She burned for his touch. Her medallion tingled hot against her skin, but she ignored the radiant sensation for the excitement surging the length of her body.

His lips left hers and trailed down the side of her throat to her collarbone, his tongue lapping the water from her skin. When the wet heat of his mouth closed over a turgid nipple, suckling her deeply, her need mounted. He paid homage to both breasts, then nipped his way lower, exploring with mouth and tongue and the light graze of his teeth every sensitive hollow and curve. By the time he found his way back up, he was as soaked as she. He wiped the water from his face, his gaze so passionately intense she shivered.

"J.T., please," she whimpered, plowing her fingers through his wet hair. She strained into him, yearning for the ultimate union with him, the wonderful ecstasy of being a complete part of him.

"Not here," he rasped, then groaned when she curled a leg around his hip, trapping his thick arousal between their bodies. "Oh, God, Caitlan. I want you in my bed."

Caitlan didn't think she could wait that long.

Two minutes later, their bodies still damp from the quick rubdown he'd given them, J.T. laid her on the soft quilt covering his bed. Leaving the nightstand light on low, he slid on top of her, bracing himself above her on his elbows. Her legs parted eagerly for him, but he didn't take possession of her.

The friction of his hard, muscular body pressing into her soft contours aroused her. The gleam in his eyes blazed savagely and his heart pounded fiercely beneath the hand she'd planted on his chest. Heaven help her, she wanted him like this, wild and primitive and hungry for her.

"I love you, Caitlan," he said, the words sounding rusty and unused. "I *love* you." Before she could respond his mouth swooped down on hers, open, hot, and wet, ruthless in its demands, a kiss meant to claim. The tip of his arousal touched silky warmth, teasing and tormenting her with the promise of being filled.

He tore his mouth from hers with a low groan. His gaze grew dark and smoky, his breathing harsh. "You're mine, Caitlan," he said, staking the same claim he had in the barn. "Say it," he demanded huskily.

She thrilled to the truth burning in his eyes, the same truth that seared her heart and made her wholly his. Her medallion danced like fire between her breasts, but not hot enough to dissuade her from following her heart. "I'm yours," she said, hooking her legs around his thighs, luring him toward the promise of ecstasy. "Take me."

Caitlan cried out as he drove into her, her body so primed that she accepted him in one silken stroke. He came down on her with an anguished moan, crushing his lips to hers, plundering her mouth with his tongue. His hips moved rhythmically against hers, long, fluid thrusts that escalated into something far more powerful and compelling.

And then it wasn't enough—for either of them. Unbridled passion erupted between them, white hot and untamed. Their bodies strained toward one another, both desperate to bind more than just flesh. Caitlan gloried in his sleek power, at the pleasure he so easily wove in her. Her hands touched him everywhere, imprinting everything about him to memory, knowing that was all she'd ever have from him. She poured her love into their kiss, although her heart faltered at the knowledge that she would ultimately lose him.

J.T. lifted his mouth from hers, his body rigid with control. He gazed down at her, his eyes glittering with hunger, desperate with greed. "Wrap your legs around me."

She did, hugging him tight. Holding her, he rolled to his back and pushed her to an upright position so she straddled his hips. A startled gasp escaped her as he embedded himself to the hilt. He stared up at her for a long moment, his gaze scanning her face, taking in her tousled hair and kiss-swollen lips. The large hands spanning her waist moved slowly, sensuously upward, splaying over her stomach, then tracing the outline of each rib. A hot flood of desire spiraled through her, and she moaned and arched shamelessly on him, pushing her breasts into his palms.

He touched the medallion with the tip of his finger, and the gold immediately increased in temperature, scalding her skin. Sucking in a quick breath, she reached up to push his hand away. Rebellion flared in his eyes and he grasped the pendant in his palm.

An electrifying surge of energy jolted her, traveling the length of her body like a never-ending shock wave. Sparks of heat showered within her, shimmering just below the surface of her skin and radiating downward to where she joined intimately with J.T. She melted around him, an incredible feeling of oneness meshing her spirit with J.T.'s, leaving her breathless.

J.T. moaned, his body shuddering. She looked into his eyes and knew by the bewilderment there that he'd experienced the same startling sensation. The intensity of the spiritual encounter, and the channel of energy still humming between them, frightened and aroused her.

"Take the medallion off," he said, his voice husky with sexually charged awareness.

Panic gripped her and she grasped his wrist. Allowing him to touch the medallion was one thing, but to take it off . . . She *never* took off the medallion during a mission. "J.T., no—"

"Yes," he said adamantly. "I don't want anything between us."

She hesitated for a brief moment, torn between love and duty. Then, with an acceptance that came from her heart, she let go of his hand. She, too, wanted the last barrier between them removed.

He lifted the chain over her head and dropped it off the side of the bed. The pendant hit the wooden floor with a soft *clink*. "Now ride me, Caitie," he demanded thickly, pulling her hips down at the same time he bucked upward. "Ride me hard."

His bluntness should have shocked her, but it thrilled her instead. "Show me," she said, wanting to please him.

He guided her with his hands and rolled his hips. "Do whatever feels good."

She did, giving free rein to her awakening sensuality.

He groaned, low and rough. "That's it," he murmured, driving deeper, more urgently into her. "So good."

Closing her eyes, Caitlan focused on the tension winding within her. Without the medallion, her response to J.T. was sharper, more searing than ever. Their union went past the physical joining to the emotional link that seemed to make him such an intricate part of her. Tiny shivers of awareness sparkled over her, whispering to her senses, pulling at her soul. She arched wildly on him, reaching for the brilliance glittering on the edge, the promise of fulfillment that sat just beyond her grasp. And something else: elusive thoughts and images that teased her mind.

"C'mon, Caitie," he growled, drawing in choppy breaths in an effort to hold back for her. His fingers caressed the sensitive flesh of her inner thigh, skimming higher. "Let it go."

Caitlan wanted to, but the closer she came to reaching that crest, something within her pulled back. Her heart slammed in her chest and every breath labored her lungs. A jumble of emotions raged in her, all tied to J.T. Rich, profound feelings of love and desire . . . and devastation and loss.

She blinked her eyes open and started to withdraw, afraid of what lay beyond the peak. But then J.T.'s fingers touched her where they became one, stroking silken folds with gentle determination. He murmured encouraging words to her, then more explicit demands.

Keen emotions swelled in her, clamoring for release. Moaning softly, Caitlan arched desperately against J.T. An uprush of sensations burst free, an explosion of the sweetest kind overtaking her body and mind. Sobbing J.T.'s name, she convulsed violently around him, feeling reborn, her soul renewed. From another plateau she heard J.T. call her name, heard him groan deeply, then felt the wet warmth of him fill her.

I love you, J.T., she thought, collapsing on his chest.

"I love you, Caitlan," he whispered, his body shuddering from the force of his climax. "Don't leave me."

Familiar feelings and images spiraled in Caitlan, tugging on her senses, like a powerful, inescapable riptide. She closed her eyes, and a wispy vision materialized of a dismal, gray day in a cemetery.

Dressed in a black suit, J.T. stood beside a polished coffin, pain and sorrow lining his features. He placed a bouquet of handpicked primroses and daisies on the smooth lid, his eyes bleak and empty.

"Don't leave me, Amanda, please," he said, his voice hoarse with desperation.

Amanda, now a spiritual form, looked on at the scene, at peace with herself, but still so much a part of this man she had to leave behind. I'll never leave you, Johnny. I'll always be with you. Always. *And then she reached out and touched him one last time, projecting to him all the love in her heart.*

"Amanda, it's time to go," her Superior, Mary, called to her. "You have much work to accomplish before you are rejoined with your soulmate."

Amanda. The name hit Caitlan with the force of a bolt of lightning. Mary had been talking to her, Caitlan. She remembered the conversation with clarity, recalled going to see J.T. that final time . . . *she* had been there!

A heavy, suffocating pressure compressed Caitlan's chest. She frantically searched the outermost reaches of her subconscious, digging for facts and clues to substantiate what she'd stumbled upon. A sharp pain pierced her temples, and she gasped, momentarily paralyzed by the onslaught. Snippets of her life as Amanda rushed through her mind like a movie on fast-forward: her parents, her childhood, her love for J.T., her death, her years of service as a guardian angel. And finally the memory of her Superiors suppressing her memory for this mission, then giving her the medallion to protect the past. The medallion J.T. had removed. Now, she understood the connection to J.T., the visions that had plagued her on this mission.

J.T. was her soulmate.

With a moan of utter despair, Caitlan absorbed J.T.'s body heat, overwhelmed by her discovery. Her body trembled and her head whirled. An abundance of realizations and memories poured over her, replenishing all the empty areas in her mind, her heart, and her soul. And when the torrent ended she knew with absolute certainty her true identity. Cuddled close to J.T., she began to cry, deep, wracking sobs that shook her entire body.

J.T., still languorous and awed by the power of their joining, basked in the warm, soft feeling of Caitlan curling up to him, and the sense of completion weaving around his heart. He stroked her back and threaded his fingers through her damp hair, wondering how he'd lived for so long without this woman in his life.

The sensual fog cleared from his head and he frowned, suddenly aware of the tremors shaking her body. She clung to him, her face buried in his neck, a hot wetness dampening his skin. Caitlan's tears. His body tensed with alarm. God, had he hurt her somehow?

He rolled so she was beneath him, but she wouldn't let go of the hold she had around his neck. Gently, he pried her arms away so he could look into her face. Tears pooled her violet eyes and total devastation marked her expression. J.T. panicked. "Caitlan? Baby, what is it?"

She shut her eyes, releasing another trail of tears down the side of her face. Her breath caught on a ragged sob. "Amanda," she choked out.

His entire body coiled into a tense knot at the mention of Amanda's name. Remembering the last time they'd made love and she'd called him Johnny, irritation flowed like molten lava through his veins. "What the hell are you talking about?" he demanded.

Her eyes, glossy with tears, brimmed with a peculiar mixture of awe and torment. Slowly lifting her hand, she skimmed her fingertips over his jaw, her gaze searching his features as if seeing him for the first time. She swallowed thickly, a tentative smile working up the corner of her mouth. "I'm Amanda."

He jerked away from her cool touch as if burned by flame. Fury shot through him. "Stop it," he roared, brows drawn fiercely over his eyes.

She withdrew physically, the bedside lamp illuminating her startled expression. An eerie familiarity swirled around J.T., barraging his senses. He gazed down into beautiful violet eyes so like his Amanda's, had glimpsed the dimple both women possessed, and thought the crushing pressure in his chest would be his undoing. The need and connection he'd experienced with

Caitlan had felt so damn real. . . . He squeezed his eyes shut, his stomach churning with terror.

Oh, God, Amanda. But how could that be? He shook his head, wondering if he was going slowly insane. *No!* he raged inwardly. Amanda was dead, gone from this lifetime.

A spike of anger renewed his fortitude, and he moved away from Caitlan. Rolling off the bed to his feet, he snatched his jeans from the floor and yanked them on, one leg at a time.

"Dammit, Caitlan, what are you trying to pull?" He glared at her, grasping his ire with both hands, welcoming the heated fury in favor of the softening emotions threatening to engulf him. "If this is some kind of sick joke . . ."

Her eyes widened, and she shook her head wildly. "No." Sitting up, she reached for the bunched-up quilt and covered her naked body. Her eyes filled with hurt and confusion. "Johnny, I swear—"

"Don't call me that!" His jaw clenched so hard, his teeth hurt.

She shrank back at his harsh tone. The pain and vulnerability etched on her face nearly disarmed him, but he refused to fall for the act. What else could this whole farce be? Christ, he'd fallen in love with . . . an imposter. A fraud.

Cursing himself for a fool, he grabbed his shirt at the end of the bed and shrugged into it. His fingers worked the buttons quickly as he paced the floor in agitation. He zipped up his pants, sparing Caitlan a sharp glance. "Who put you up to this? Huh?" He was going to kill the bastard responsible for this sadistic prank.

Pushing the tangle of damp hair from her face, she drew a steady breath that did nothing to clear the uncertainty from her gaze. "My . . . my Superiors."

He came to an abrupt stop, staring at her incredulously. "Your *what?*"

She pressed shaky fingers to her temples and closed her eyes, a low groan of despair echoing in the room. "This is all so confusing," she whispered.

"Well, sort it out and fast," he snapped, jamming his hands on his hips. "I'm losing my patience real quick, Caitlan."

"Amanda," she corrected in a whisper.

Dropping his hands back to his sides, he curled his fingers into tight fists. "Explain yourself before I toss you out on your pretty little ass," he said in a slow, precise tone of voice.

She looked up at him, indecision in her gaze. Swirling deeper, he glimpsed a hopelessness that brushed the edge of his heart and made him want to give into the plea for understanding shining in her eyes.

Turning away, he walked to the window and glanced outside, seeing nothing but the murky darkness of night. Propping his shoulder against the wall, he faced her again. "I'm waiting."

Her fingers pleated the sheet in her lap. "I'm a . . . guardian angel."

He gave a short bark of laughter. "Oh, that's a good one. I suppose you're going to tell me the next time I hear a bell ring, a friend of yours is getting his wings."

Her spine straightened in indignation, her eyes flashing violet fire. "Are you going to listen to me or not?"

"Go ahead." A humorless smile curved his mouth. "This tale should be as entertaining as the one you told me of how you got lost on Rafferty property." He was suddenly struck with the timely manner of her arrival on the Circle R. She'd claimed to save his life—just in the nick of time, from what she'd told him. There had been many inconsistencies in her story, but he'd had no proof other than to believe her. Could she truly be a guardian angel? His Amanda?

He studied her warily from across the room as she worried on her lower lip. He searched for something otherworldly to substantiate her claim, a soft heavenly glow about her, a shimmering halo—albeit crooked after her erotic interlude with him. Something. Anything. But all he saw were her huge violet eyes drenched with a vulnerable weariness.

He shook his head, hard. *Oh, you're losing it, Rafferty. You're finally sailing over the edge. An angel, for chrissakes!*

"Well?" he prompted.

"Can I get dressed before we discuss this?"

He wasn't letting her out of his sight. Considering her clothes were in the guest room, he grabbed a long-sleeved flannel shirt from his closet and tossed it next to her on the bed. She stared at the garment dumbly.

"Put it on," he said in a crisp tone. "It's as generous as I feel at the moment."

A slight blush rose on her cheeks, and she reached for the shirt. The quilt dropped to her waist, and he sucked in a breath at the creamy perfection of her breasts. His body leapt eagerly, responding swiftly to her beauty. The only thought in his mind was to tumble her back on the bed and forget this crazy conversation. Cursing his lack of willpower, he looked away while she dressed.

"My Superiors aren't going to be happy about this," she said so quietly he almost didn't hear her.

Perplexed by her comment, he glanced back, relieved to see her clothed from neck to thigh. "What are you talking about?"

She bent down and retrieved her medallion from the floor. The shiny gold glittered with life and energy in her hand. She closed her fingers over the pendant and looked at him. "My angel Superiors. Chris and Mary. They're the ones who assigned me to this mission."

Drained from the events of the past couple of hours, J.T. sat down on the far corner of the bed, sighing heavily. He didn't know what to believe anymore, but one thing he did know for certain—Caitlan, or Amanda, or whoever the hell she was, *did* feel like a part of him, heart and soul. Still, Amanda as his guardian angel . . . ?

He clasped his hands between his widespread legs, doing his best to keep an open mind for the explanation to come. "From the beginning, Caitlan."

Placing the medallion on the nightstand, she sat an arm's length away from him and began her tale. Her Superiors, he learned, were high-ranking angels who assigned missions and kept tabs on the activities down on earth. He listened to Caitlan as she explained how she'd seen him get hit in the head, how her Superiors didn't have anyone to send to earth to save him on such a last-minute crisis, and reluctantly agreed to send her to protect him. They'd suppressed her memory of her past with him and given her a new background and identity.

"I was never supposed to remember my past as Amanda," she concluded softly.

"Then, how . . ." He followed her gaze to the glimmering gold on the nightstand, recalling all the strange, unexplainable things he'd experienced in connection with that pendant, and with her.

"The medallion," she said, confirming his thoughts. "It links me to my Superiors. Without it on, the medallion could no longer protect my memory." She glanced back at him, her gaze overflowing with love. "My feelings for you are too strong to be suppressed without the medallion."

His anger ebbed away, replaced by a reluctant curiosity. "Changing your name and identity is understandable under the circumstances, but why would your . . . Superiors suppress your memory of your past with me?"

"Conflict of interest. We're eternal soulmates. They felt if they sent me on the mission without suppressing my memory, my feelings for you would cloud my judgment." She gave him a small, bittersweet smile. "I'm afraid they were right. My love for you is so powerful, it's distracted me from the very beginning of the mission. I've been acting more like a mortal than a guardian angel."

J.T. scrubbed a hand over his jaw, absorbing everything she'd told him. He, too, had experienced that powerful link to her, the awesome need to make her his in every elemental way possible. He could no longer chalk it up to lust; the connection had gone beyond sex, to the very core of him.

"So," he said on an exhalation of breath, "you really aren't a guest at Parson's, are you?"

"Yes . . . I mean no," she amended, shaking her head.

"Which is it?" he asked, irritation creeping back in.

"It's all part of the mission."

"How convenient." His dry tone held a heavy dose of sarcasm.

Caitlan twisted toward him, anger flaring in her eyes. "You were going to die out in the middle of nowhere! You should be grateful that I was able to reach you in time."

He could have died. Someone had *meant* for him to die. And Caitlan had undoubtedly saved him. Springing from the bed, he paced to the other end of the room, a deluge of questions overwhelming him. "How did you *really* get me to the line shack?"

As if remembering the outrageous tale she'd told him of dragging him to the shack, she lowered her eyes to her lap. "My Superiors helped."

A derisive smile quirked his mouth. "Heavenly intervention?"

"Yes." She shrugged, her hand absently smoothing over the quilt, tracing the intricate pattern his mother had created over three decades before. "Once we got you to the shack, Chris mended your head wound and I worked to get your fever under control." She looked back up, her gaze intense on his face. "I wasn't sure if you were going to make it."

J.T. rubbed at the tense muscles across his shoulders. "I don't understand. Why all the trouble to save me?"

"It wasn't your time to pass on to the next plateau." Standing, she padded soundlessly across the floor to him, her brow creased in concern.

"You don't believe me, do you?"

He stared down at Caitlan, drowning in those incredible violet eyes. He breathed deeply, dragging the warm, feminine scent of her into his lungs. God, he wanted her. Again. Regardless of the turmoil between them. That familiar tug pulled on his soul. He stubbornly blocked the feeling. "Come on, Caitlan. You have to admit, this whole scenario is a little bizarre. Even if I *did* believe in guardian angels, I think you're stretching the story a bit by claiming to be Amanda."

Her lips pursed. "I *am* Amanda."

"Okay," he relented, crossing his arms over his chest. "Tell me about Amanda."

Holding his gaze steadily, she proceeded to tell him about the pictures she'd sketched on her mission, and how they matched exactly the drawings he kept in the cigar box in the office, the ones Amanda had drawn of him when she was alive.

A shiver snaked down J.T.'s spine when he realized how close he'd been to discovering that particular truth when Kirk had interrupted him with his call for help. Then again, he rationalized, Caitlan could have reproduced the drawings as she'd originally claimed when he'd confronted her out in the meadow with the pictures she'd created in her sketch pad.

He couldn't shake his doubts, maybe because it was the only anchor he had left to reality. "Not good enough. Tell me something no one else but Amanda and I would know."

She looked thoughtful for a moment, as if sifting through memories. Then she smiled widely, a dimple appearing in her cheek. "The pie," she said.

"The pie?" he echoed, frowning.

She grasped his hand, her eyes sparkling brightly. "Johnny, don't you remember? We were just kids. Your mother made three apple pies and set them on the kitchen counter to cool. We stole one of them, along with a half gallon of ice cream and—"

"Ate all of it down by the creek," he finished, stunned by the recollection of the ancient memory.

She laughed, the sound sweet and pure to his ears. "We got so sick! We were both afraid of getting in trouble, so we buried the pie tin and the empty ice cream carton. . . . " Suddenly she grew serious, the humor fading from her eyes. "I remember everything. I remember the day you rescued me from drowning in the creek, the first time you kissed me, the night of my eighteenth birthday." She reached up and placed her palm on his cheek, her voice softening perceptively. "We made love for the first time and you asked me to marry you. It's all I ever wanted in this lifetime, to be your wife and have your babies."

As if he'd just been delivered a punch to the solar plexus, J.T. lost his breath. He stared at

Caitlan, seeing her in a different light. He saw Amanda in her soft smile, her violet eyes, and knew without further interrogation that Caitlan was telling the truth.

A maelstrom of emotions welled in him. Afraid to believe in something he'd fantasized about numerous times, he backed away from her. He had to get away, to think and sort everything out.

Spinning around, he strode to the end of the bed and jammed on his boots.

"Where are you going?" Her voice wavered with concern.

"Out." He didn't look at her, knowing if he did he'd never make it out the bedroom door. "I need time to think."

Caitlan watched J.T. leave, her heart sinking to the floor. She understood his need to be alone— he'd been dealt quite a shock—but she hated the loneliness that enveloped her on his departure. That same emptiness echoed in her heart.

"Oh, Johnny," she sighed dismally. The nickname came so naturally to her, she couldn't imagine having called him anything else. "What are we going to do?" But she knew the answer to her question. Regardless of who she was, and despite her love for J.T., she had a mission to complete. She ached with the knowledge that she would have to leave him. Again.

She slipped her medallion back on. Now that her memory had been restored, the pendant no longer shimmered with that strange energy. The vibrant life it had possessed had transferred itself to her, leaving the medallion as a device solely for use in contacting her Superiors.

Running a shaking hand through her disheveled hair, she left J.T.'s room, needing the comfort she knew King could offer her. She changed into warm clothes and a jacket and left the house heading for the corral, praying her Superiors would have a cure for her lovesick heart once she arrived back in heaven.

An hour later, calmer now from his fast-paced walk to burn off the chaos raging inside him, J.T. followed the pasture fence back to the barn. The night air chilled his skin, and he shrugged deeper into the warmth of his jacket.

Rounding the final curve from the pasture to the corral, he saw Caitlan with King and stopped, silently watching the two of them from a distance. Moonlight spilled over them, giving them both an ethereal appearance. Caitlan slowly stroked a curry comb over King's gleaming coat, her soft murmurs soothing the stallion. He found himself fascinated with the gentle way King responded to Caitlan. Now that he knew she was an angel, he understood the uncanny bond she shared with the horse.

Amanda. Caitlan. One and the same. His instincts wanted to deny her claim, but she'd given him too much proof not to believe her. The whole situation boggled his mind. He'd fallen in love with Caitlan, and never in his wildest dreams would he have imagined he'd actually fallen in love with Amanda . . . again.

Although he'd resolved that Caitlan was Amanda's spirit in different packaging, he couldn't help but think of her as *Caitlan*, the woman he'd fallen in love with. This feeling of love he harbored for Caitlan was different from the one he'd shared with Amanda. Stronger somehow, full of rich passion. An adult love. Mature and lush with promise. Powerful and everlasting, like the love for Amanda would have grown to be if had she lived.

He no longer cared *who* she was, only that she made him feel truly alive after being dead inside for so long. He'd been given a second chance, and he wasn't about to give her up.

Quietly unlatching the corral gate, he stepped inside. Caitlan glanced over her shoulder, acknowledging his presence, then resumed grooming King.

Slowly, he approached the pair so as not to frighten the stallion. The smell of damp, burnt wood still hung in the air, and he was suddenly struck with a question he should have asked Caitlan earlier, but had been too swamped by other feelings to think past the fact that Caitlan was Amanda.

Three feet away, he stopped. King eyeballed him warily but stood still for Caitlan's praise and loving ministrations. "Do you know who's behind all the incidents at the ranch?" he asked in a quiet tone.

She hesitated so long, J.T. didn't think she planned to answer him. Finally, she said, "Yes."

"Who?"

"I can't say."

"Why not? You've told me everything else." His voice rose with a touch of irritation, and King shied away.

Caitlan consoled the horse, then glanced over her shoulder at him. Even in the darkness he could see the reluctance in her gaze. "It's Randal."

"Randal? That's ridic—" He stopped abruptly, unable to deny that his cousin had been acting strange lately. Combine Randal's surly attitude and financial obligations with his drinking habit and you'd get a man on the verge of sliding off the edge. But to go as far as to commit murder . . . ? "Randal wouldn't gain anything by killing me."

"I don't believe he's after material possessions," she stated. "Please don't ask me anything else, Johnny. I've already risked fate to tell you this much. Just let me do my job and protect you." Her voice was a shade away from a plea.

Anger passed through J.T. How could he have been so blind to his cousin? Maybe because he didn't want to admit Randal, his own kin, could be so devious. "I'll get Randal help."

"No one can help Randal but himself. He

doesn't want to change. That's why I'm here."

J.T. didn't argue, though he wanted to. He didn't excuse Randal's behavior the past couple of weeks, but Randal was family, and he'd do whatever was necessary to put him back on the straight and narrow—starting with checking him into a rehab center for his drinking. Tomorrow, he decided, he'd approach Randal and tell him he's suspended with pay if he agrees to get help.

Satisfied with his plan, he pushed it out of his mind for the time being. All he wanted right now was Caitlan, except she was giving her total attention to King, stroking him and praising him. He was actually jealous of a horse.

"Can I touch him?" he asked, wanting to be a part of the bond between Caitlan and the stallion.

Caitlan framed the side of King's head gently in her hands, her thumbs caressing his muzzle, and looked into his eyes in silent communication. She glanced back at J.T., moonlight brushing her features in pale silver. "You're not a threat to him. I can see it in his eyes. Move slowly and he might let you." Grasping his halter lightly, she moved to make room for J.T.

J.T. approached King cautiously, and the horse whinnied and shied away. Caitlan reassured the stallion with soft words and a gentle caress, until J.T. stood close enough to touch him. He raised his hand and King sidestepped anxiously. Remembering Caitlan telling him

King had been abused, he suspected Randal was the culprit.

After a few minutes of sweet-talking the horse J.T. finally touched King, his fingers stroking down the strong muscles in the stallion's neck. That was all King allowed before he jerked away, neighing uneasily. Caitlan let go of King and he galloped to the far end of the corral, tossing his sleek black head, watching J.T.

"That was incredible," J.T. said, a sense of awe filling him. "I can't believe he let me get that close."

"It's a start. He's been through a lot lately." She placed the curry comb on the fence post, a smile of satisfaction gracing her mouth. "Take care with him, Johnny. He's a beautiful horse."

J.T. nodded. Holding Caitlan's gaze, an awareness swirled in the cold night air between them. Heart pounding in his chest, he slowly approached her, suddenly needing to reaffirm that she was truly alive, and not some wispy figment of his imagination.

Sliding his cool fingers into her silky hair, he absorbed her warmth and softness, gradually moving closer until his thighs pressed against hers. Staring into the face of the woman he loved, something magical and promising sparkled between them. Love—pure, sweet, and crystal clear.

With a groan of joy, he folded her into his arms, reveling in the accepting way she came to him. She worked the zipper on his coat down and slipped her hands inside, snuggling into him. Her cheek rested on his chest, and her arms circled him in the sweetest way.

Closing his eyes, he buried his face in her hair, saturating his senses in the unique, feminine scent of her. "Oh, God, Caitlan ... I mean, Amanda ...." He swore, his eyes snapping open in annoyance. "What in the hell am I supposed to call you?"

Against his chest he felt her lips lift in a smile. "For now, call me Caitlan."

Caitlan ... but her spirit belonged to Amanda. Would he ever get used to such a novelty? "I've missed you so much," he breathed against her temple.

She looked up at him, her eyes shining with adoration. "I know. I've felt your love all along."

His hands slid down her back to her hips. "How?"

"Our souls are matched eternally."

He liked the sound of that. He'd gladly be bound to her forever. "What happens now?"

She knew what he was asking. Sorrow clouded her eyes, and her smile faded away. Withdrawing from him, she stepped away and focused on King, prancing at the opposite end of the corral. "Nothing has changed," she said quietly, pain in her tone. "Once my mission is over I'll be leaving."

His body went as taut as a bow. "No."

Her gaze found his again. "Johnny, it's all so complicated. I . . . can't stay." Her voice was thick with the unshed tears pooling in her eyes.

"I'm not letting you go." He heard the desperation in his voice but didn't care. "It'll kill me to lose you again."

"No, it won't." Caitlan's heart ached for him, for everything that could never be. "The memory of me being here will fade with time."

Disbelief flared in his eyes. "You're a part of me, Caitlan." Grabbing her hand, he pressed her palm over his heart. "Can you feel that? How could I ever forget you?"

The heavy beat beneath her hand reverberated through her, flowing to her soul in a river of longing. "Oh, Johnny . . ." A sob of despair caught in her throat.

"I won't let you go twice. Not without a fight."

"You have no choice," she argued.

"I do." His hand curled around the back of her head and pulled her to him, his mouth covering hers before she realized his intent.

Caitlan gasped at the surprise attack, and he took advantage of her parted lips to sink his tongue inside her mouth. She moaned . . . in pleasure, and at the pain that would haunt her once she left him. Wrapping her arms around his neck, she clung to him, matching the silken glide of his tongue, stroke for intimate stroke.

Breathless, they broke apart. J.T. buried his face in her neck, his lips brushing her flesh, his teeth grazing her soft skin up to her ear. Caitlan shivered and hugged him closer.

"Come back to bed with me." J.T.'s voice was rough and dark with passion.

Selfishly wanting the time she had left with him to be special, she took his hand, silently leading him back to the house and up the stairs to his bedroom. In the dark hours of night and into the early hours of morning, they made love, their hunger for one another insatiable. Soft moans and whispered words blended with the sensual sliding of damp bodies and warm tangled sheets. Caitlan's love fused with J.T.'s, making the link between them stronger, more intense, more binding. She stored up every feeling, every scent and sensation for when she returned to heaven.

And if she had to suffer consequences for her transgression once she left earth and her only love, she'd gladly pay the price.

Chapter Thirteen

Caitlan gradually woke the next morning, a smile pulling at her lips. Recollections of the way J.T. had found the birthmark in the back of her knee during a very thorough exploration of her body brought a flush to her skin. Stretching languorously, she reached toward J.T.'s side of the bed and met cool, empty sheets. Blinking her eyes open, she leaned up on her elbow and pushed the tousled hair from her face.

J.T. was gone. Sunlight streamed through the window, indicating the start of a new day. The digital clock on the nightstand glowed eight fifteen.

"Eight fifteen!" she said, alarm threading through her voice. Throwing back the covers, she scrambled out of bed, unable to believe she'd slept so late, and so soundly she hadn't heard J.T. leave her. She was becoming lax in her duties.

Berating herself for letting her heart rule her head, she slipped on the medallion J.T. had insisted she remove while they made love. Pulling on the shirt he'd given her the night before, she left his room and went to the guest room to change.

After everything that had happened last night, and her confession that Randal was the person responsible for the incidents, Caitlan didn't want J.T. going anywhere without her. Randal was a bomb waiting to detonate, and nothing J.T. could say or do would change that, except maybe make Randal explode sooner. She knew that for certain, had seen the banked rage in Randal's eyes numerous times. He was on the brink.

An uneasy feeling settled within her, a sudden, dark intuition that made Caitlan anxious. Throwing on her sweatshirt, she left the medallion on the outside, where it would be easily accessible, then pulled on her jeans and boots and raced to the kitchen. Her panic increased when she didn't find J.T. there.

"Good morning," Paula greeted her cheerfully over her shoulder. Putting aside the vegetable she was peeling, she turned around, wiping her hands on her apron. "How about breakfast? I've got some leftover pancake batter and sausage."

The thought of food made Caitlan's stomach

turn. The same awful premonition that had filled her last night, before she'd located the fire, had her senses under siege again. A shiver of apprehension skipped down her spine, yet she had no idea why she was receiving such a warning, or where the danger lay. Trusting her instincts completely, she knew she had to find J.T. "Where's John—" she caught her slip—"J.T.?"

"Down at the barn, coordinating the cleanup from the fire." Taking down a mug from the cupboard, Paula smiled approvingly at Caitlan. "He said not to disturb you; thought you'd be exhausted after last night's ordeal."

Which ordeal was Paula referring to? Caitlan wondered idly, a warmth creeping up her neck. The barn fire or the first time she and J.T. had made love? Or the second, third, or fourth time he'd taken her to paradise? All had exhausted her, physically and emotionally.

"Sit down and have a cup of coffee and I'll make you a few pancakes," Paula offered, carrying the mug filled with coffee to the table.

Another ominous warning tugged on Caitlan senses, stretching her nerves to the snapping point. "I need to find J.T." She kept her tone calm so as not to rouse the other woman's suspicions of her sudden fear. "I'll be back up in a bit."

"Bring J.T. with you. He hasn't eaten yet either." A twinkle entered Paula's pale blue eyes. "A man's gotta keep up his energy."

Caitlan couldn't misinterpret Paula's insinuation and blushed. With a promise to bring J.T. back, Caitlan headed out the kitchen door, walking at a fast clip to the barn. With every step, her unease magnified, adding to the anxiety gathering in her chest.

J.T. Her eternal soulmate. The very life of her. Heaven help her, if anything happened to him, she'd never, ever forgive herself.

As she neared the barn, she could hear the men working in and around the structure. She searched for J.T. but didn't see him. In the distance the sky turned dark, carrying the promise of an abrupt storm. Black clouds rolled toward the Circle R, blocking the sun. A slight chilly breeze picked up, ruffling through Caitlan's hair and sending icy fingers of dread skimming over her nerves.

Oh, Lord, she thought. The menacing sky looked exactly like it had the day she'd seen J.T. through the portal, before she'd rescued him.

King, still in the corral, whinnied frantically, capturing Caitlan's attention. Glancing in that direction, she froze, her heart jumping to her throat. Randal, staggering along the corral fence in a drunken haze, bent and retrieved a small rock. He nearly toppled over in his task but managed to straighten up and steady himself.

Muttering a curse, he cocked his arm back and pitched the rock at King, striking his target with an accuracy that astounded Caitlan, considering Randal's intoxication. King shrieked and bolted to the other end of the corral. Whinnying distraughtly, he pranced anxiously back and forth like a duck in a shooting arcade.

Stumbling forward, Randal swooped up another rock.

Caitlan moved forward, her only thought to save King from any more inflicted pain. "Randal, no!" she yelled.

Randal whirled around. Faltering from the quick move, he came up against the fence and saved himself from falling on his butt in the dirt. Hooking an arm around a post, his back straightened. Bloodshot eyes narrowed on her, his cold, cruel smile curling his lips. "Well . . . if it isn't the *heroine* of the Circle R." His words dripped with hostility and hatred.

Behind her, Caitlan heard one of the hands say, "Better go tell J.T. there's a problem out here."

She wanted to tell the man no—she didn't want J.T. anywhere near Randal right now—but she lost the opportunity when Randal threw another rock at King, hitting the horse in the neck. King cried out and fled. Eyes wide with terror, the panicked stallion searched for some means of escape.

Randal laughed, an evil sound that slithered down Caitlan's spine. His eyes glittered with sinister pleasure. He picked up another rock, his expression daring her to stop him.

He drew his arm back, and Caitlan charged toward him, grasping his wrist before he could hurl the rock. "Leave King alone, Randal."

He shoved her back, hard. She stumbled backwards but managed to regain her footing. At least she'd saved King from further abuse, she thought.

"Bitch," Randal hissed, forgetting King and stalking her with deceptively steady steps.

Caitlan firmly held her ground, concealing the trepidation coiling in her. "Leave him alone," she said again, her voice calm. "You've terrorized him enough."

Randal waved a belligerent hand in the air, stopping a mere foot away from Caitlan. He swayed slightly, but his anger gave him a powerful fortitude. "That stupid horse of J.T.'s doesn't deserve to live."

The liquor on Randal's breath was unmistakable. Caitlan refrained from the natural urge to turn her face away from the fetid odor. As she met his gaze, something in his eyes changed. Hatred and bitterness swelled into a darkening rage . . . directed solely at her. The air around them turned icy cold.

Before she could move, he grasped her arms, his fingers biting painfully into her flesh. She winced and struggled to break away, but he tightened his grip.

"I'd have everything right now if you hadn't come along," he said in a low, menacing voice. "You had to ruin everything, didn't you? You conveniently saved J.T. and that wretched horse, but who's gonna save you?"

Mike, one of the hands witnessing the exchange, grabbed Randal's shoulder, trying to prevent the confrontation. "Back off, Randal," he said in warning.

Randal glared at Mike and slid his hand down Caitlan's arm so his fingers encircled her delicate wrist. "Get your goddamn hand off me or I'll break her wrist!"

When Mike didn't do as he ordered Randal applied pressure to Caitlan's palm, bending her hand back. Excruciating pain shot up her arm and she sucked in a breath.

Randal grinned sadistically. "Go ahead," he sneered at Mike, "give me a reason to give this bitch what she deserves."

Mike stepped back, indecision warring in his gaze. Caitlan reassured him with her eyes that he'd done the right thing.

Thunder clapped in the distance, rumbling the heavens. She looked up at the dark clouds churning in the sky and shivered, intuitively knowing the end was near. Her time with J.T. was almost over, and she hadn't even told him how much she loved him, in this lifetime and into the next. Surely after last night he had to know her heart was eternally his.

Out of the corner of her eye Caitlan saw J.T. walk out of the barn. The expression on his face turned to pure fury when he saw the way Randal handled her. *Oh, Johnny, please don't do anything foolish,* she prayed. Yet she was in no position to escape Randal, or to summon her Superiors for help.

J.T. started toward Randal, a white-hot rage consuming him. He was going to pulverize his cousin for touching Caitlan. His fist itched to connect with Randal's jaw, to pull him out of the bitterness he'd been wallowing in since Boyd's death. He'd be damned if he let anyone hurt his family, and Randal's was pushing things too far.

No one can help Randal but himself. Caitlan's words echoed through his mind, gelling the blood in his veins. Was his cousin *really* beyond helping?

J.T. stopped a few feet away, not wanting to provoke Randal into doing something that might harm Caitlan. He reminded himself that she was an angel, a spiritual form that couldn't possibly experience tragedy in its rawest sense, yet he couldn't curb the natural instinct to protect her. She was *his*, and he wasn't about to let Randal's hatred jeopardize the love he'd rediscovered with her.

Meeting Caitlan's gaze, he detected the desperation in her eyes and, deeper, fear . . . fear for him.

His fists clenched at his sides, and he battled with all the conflicting emotions clamoring within him "Get your hands off her, Randal. *Now.*"

Randal laughed condescendingly. "The high-and-mighty J.T. Rafferty speaks. Well, let me tell *you* something, cousin. This isn't the first time I've had the upper hand."

J.T. frowned fiercely at Randal, hating the trepidation crawling over his nerves. "What the hell are you talking about?"

"Last night I was going to kill that friggin' horse you prize so much, would have succeeded if *she* hadn't interfered," he said, slanting Caitlan a spiteful look. Then his mouth twisted with a touch of gratification. "And those poor kittens, such a shame they found their way into King's stall, isn't it?"

J.T. didn't want to believe his cousin could be so deranged, yet Randal was openly admitting his guilt. Worse, he showed no remorse over any of his malicious deeds. "Randal, you're a sick bastard—"

"Oh, and let's not forget Stacey," he interrupted. "I screwed her every way I could, and she still wanted more." He leered at Caitlan. "Maybe I'll screw this bitch and let you know how they compare."

Fury exploded in J.T. Rage shook every vital part of him. He stepped forward, ready to tear his cousin apart limb by limb. He came to an abrupt halt when Caitlan cried out from the pain Randal inflicted on her. A sadistic pleasure brightened Randal's eyes. One more application of pressure and the bones in Caitlan's wrist would shatter.

Adrenaline pumped through J.T.'s body, and he resisted the instinctive urge to charge at Randal, even though watching his cousin torture Caitlan ripped him apart inside. Caitlan clearly experienced human emotions and pain, and he refused to run the risk of Randal seriously injuring her.

God, he felt so helpless. Randal held the advantage, and J.T. was at a loss as to what to do. His men stood to the side, but they, too, knew they couldn't do anything to help without risking Caitlan's safety. If he could get Caitlan out of the way, J.T. knew he could take Randal down.

"What do you want, Randal?" he asked, trying to reason with him when all he wanted to do was kill him for hurting Caitlan.

"I want to bring you down, J.T., as low as I've been. I wonder," Randal said, enjoying being in control, "would you get down on your knees and beg for this slut's life?" A slow smile of satisfaction curled his mouth. "Yeah, I think I'd like that. Beg, J.T., and maybe I'll let her go." Randal twisted her hand back.

Gasping at the burning agony streaking up her arm, Caitlan frantically searched her mind for a way out of this mess. She had to find a way to reach her medallion and summon her Superiors' help. Drawing her foot back, she kicked Randal in the shin. He grunted at the unexpected painful

Janelle Denison

attack, his eyes widening. She started to repeat
the procedure. Realizing her intent, he shoved
her roughly away.

Staggering to the side, J.T. caught her before
she fell and thrust her behind him, out of the
way. He moved to tackle Randal but stopped
short when his cousin pulled a .38 from his
waistband beneath his jacket. Randal backed
himself up against the barn, pointing the small
handgun at J.T.'s chest, a crazed look in his eyes.
He was trapped and knew it. The only way out
would be by killing J.T.

"Randal, goddammit, put the gun away!" J.T.
ordered gruffly.

Randal's finger curled around the trigger. "Not
until I finish what I started down by the creek."
Slowly, he guided the barrel of the gun to Caitlan,
aiming at her heart. "Or maybe I'll put a bullet
through her and make you suffer the way I've
suffered."

J.T.'s jaw clenched, anger and apprehension
blazing through him at Randal's threat to shoot
Caitlan. If he had any hope at all of keeping her
with him after this whole ordeal, he couldn't allow Randal to harm her in any way.

"Leave Caitlan out of this," J.T. said tightly, his
body tensing to spring at any moment. "Your
grudge is with me, not her."

"As always, you're right," Randal said mock-
ingly, training the barrel of the gun back to J.T.
"You always were the golden boy around here,

weren't you? You could do no wrong. Even my own father would ask me why I couldn't be more like you. Funny thing is, I wanted to be like you. I wanted to *be* you." He waved the gun in the air, his eyes glittering with madness. "You've always had everything handed to you."

"I've worked for everything I've got." J.T. shifted on his feet, the subtle move inching him closer to Randal and the barrel of his gun. "Your father should have been more careful with his inheritance."

"Half of this ranch should have been mine, J.T.," he roared, his face turning bright red in his fury. "Mine!"

Randal continued to rave at his cousin for all the injustices done to him, his gun never wavering far from his target of J.T.'s chest. A few of the hands moved cautiously in to help, but Randal went wild-eyed and warned them back, threatening J.T.'s life. The men obeyed.

A fierce wind blew, whipping through the trees, scattering the scent of danger and peril. The black clouds in the sky churned, and thunder boomed ominously. Keeping a keen eye on Randal's movements, Caitlan slowly reached up and grasped her medallion, rubbing the warm gold with her thumb for comfort as much as as a summons.

"Help!" Caitlan projected.

"Yes, it's time," Mary answered.

Her worst fear confirmed, that her mission was

nearly over, a sob of despair caught in Caitlan's throat. She held back the impulse to beg for more time with her only love. Oh, God, how could she leave Johnny again? How could she go on without him after giving him her heart and soul—everything that she was?

"Get your emotions under control, Caitlan!" Mary ordered. *"Now, before it's too late.* You *must be the one to save J.T."*

Mentally shaking herself, Caitlan dropped her hand back to her side and concentrated on the situation, trying to anticipate Randal's next move.

Randal's tirade continued, his rage mounting without any provocation from J.T. "I hate you, J.T.," he seethed, his fingers tightening on the gun. "If I can't have the ranch, neither will you!"

In what seemed like slow motion to Caitlan, she watched in horror as J.T. lunged toward Randal, his intention to dislodge the gun from his cousin's hands. Fear tore through Caitlan and she bolted forward to intercept J.T.

Randal's eyes widened in surprise at the unexpected commotion. He jerked out of the way and leveled the barrel on J.T. again, his finger squeezing the trigger. A maniacal expression contorted Randal's face.

"Johnny, no!" Caitlan shoved J.T. aside with the force of her propelled body just as a loud crack exploded in the air. An excruciating, ripping pain pierced her chest like a lance of fire.

The impact of the bullet threw her back, and she stumbled into J.T., knocking them both to the dirt.

J.T. rolled to his knees on the ground and shook his head as all hell broke lose around him. He was vaguely aware that it was Mike who rushed at Randal, unarmed him, then threw him on the ground and pinned him there. The other men swarmed around, assisting Mike in any way they could. One of the men shouted to call the sheriff.

J.T.'s head cleared and his gaze landed on Caitlan's limp form laying feet away from him. He scrambled over to her, a deafening roar filling his ears and a sense of dread seizing his insides. He stared in horror at the blood soaking Caitlan's sweatshirt near the vicinity of her heart. She'd taken a bullet for him!

"Caitlan! Oh, God, Caitlan, no!" He scooped her gently into his arms and cradled her close, desperation ruling him. Touching his fingers to her neck, he felt a faint pulse, reaffirming that she still lived. *She can't die,* he tried to reassure himself, but the panic within him wouldn't subside.

Gingerly, he touched the bright red spot on her sweatshirt. His fingers came away wet and stained, and he moaned like a wounded animal. "Shit, you're bleeding!" he said in disbelief. "You can't be bleeding. . . ."

Her lashes fluttered open and she attempted a

smile. A *smile*, for chrissakes! Pain bracketed her mouth. Her eyes were glassy but more brilliantly violet than he'd ever seen them before.

"I'm not . . . invincible, Johnny," she said in a wispy voice. She gasped for breath, then an anguished groan slipped past her lips.

Despair clutched at J.T. "Call Dr. Henson!" he bellowed as Frank came running up to the scene. "And have him get an ambulance here immediately! Caitlan's been shot!"

Frank bolted toward the house, and J.T. glanced back at Caitlan, whose face had gone deathly pale. The pain and tears he'd never shed for Amanda gathered in his throat. "Please don't leave me, Caitlan. Please!" he rasped. "Hold on just a little longer."

"It hurts," she said, her breath catching. "I didn't think it would hurt so much."

"Shh," he soothed, brushing her hair away from her face. A tear seeped from the corner of her eye, and he tenderly wiped it away with his thumb. "Baby, hang in there. You've got to hang on!" *I won't let you leave me, not without a fight!*

Caitlan lifted her hand to his face and touched her fingers to his lips, wincing at the effort it cost her. "Johnny, I have to leave. My mission is over." She drew a breath that trembled the length of her body. "I was sent to protect you. Johnny . . . I told you I couldn't stay."

A broken sound of torment passed his lips and he shook his head in denial. "No!" Grabbing her hand, he pressed her fingers to his mouth, absorbing her warmth, her softness, everything about her.

She gave him another shaky smile, enough of an attempt to crease the dimple in her cheek. "I never thought it would hurt so much to leave you again," she whispered. "Let me go, Johnny." Her voice was barely audible. "We'll be together eternally . . . I promise."

"You can't leave me!" Holding her close, he rocked her in his arms. A sob caught in his throat and tears burned his eyes. He lifted his gaze to heaven, ready to bargain away his soul if he had to. "Please don't take her from me again," he pleaded, his voice rough with emotion. Surely if there was a God in heaven he would spare him this loss. "I can't live without her."

He placed her palm over his beating heart, willing to sacrifice the very life of him for her. In the distance he could hear the scream of an ambulance's siren and knew she'd be leaving him soon. Knew, too, that he was powerless to stop her inevitable departure from earth. Again.

The tears he'd held at bay for so many years broke free, filling his eyes so that his vision blurred. In desperation, he grabbed the medallion that had linked them so many times and pulled it off her, clutching the warm gold in his palm.

"God, Caitlan, I love you!"

"I love you, Johnny," she whispered.

A strange, shimmering warmth invaded J.T.'s heart and soul upon their simultaneous declaration. Then she was being lifted from his arms by two paramedics, and it was like they were tearing his heart from his chest. J.T. knelt there, too paralyzed by the loss to move as the two men gently placed Caitlan on a stretcher and hurriedly carried her toward the waiting ambulance.

I'll love you forever, Johnny, he heard whispered on the breeze.

And minutes later, as the ambulance pulled away from the drive, J.T. knew this was the end. Caitlan was gone, and she wouldn't be coming back. Slowly, defeatedly, he stood. An absolute emptiness enveloped him, as dark and black as the sky above, and he knew he'd never be the same again.

"No!" he raged to the heavens, his anguish echoing on and on. He choked on a deep sob, his heart and soul twisting with such agony, he wanted to die. Indeed, a part of him *had* died with her departure.

The medallion in his palm retained its warmth, and he defiantly slipped the chain over his head. It was the only connection he had left to his one true love, and he refused to give it up. He refused to let the memory of her being at the Circle R fade.

Thunder rumbled and lightning streaked across the sky, signaling the arrival of the storm. Bloated clouds floated overhead, and the temperature dropped to an icy chill.

With an odd kind of detachment J.T. watched the sheriff take Randal into custody and take statements from the men who'd witnessed the ordeal.

Mike approached J.T., his gaze going over him with concern. He shoved his fingers through his hair, still shaken by the incident. "Are you okay, J.T.?"

No. I'll never be the same again. J.T. looked at Mike, wondering if his eyes reflected the bleak despair eating away at him. He knew he owed Mike his gratitude for helping to apprehend Randal, and an apology for suspecting him of the incidents that had happened around the ranch, but at the moment he couldn't summon the words for all the anguish swirling in him.

"Caitlan's gone," he said instead, his voice sounding oddly distant even to his own ears.

Mike gave him a perplexed look. "They're taking her to County hospital. The paramedics said it looked like the bullet went clean through her shoulder and she should be fine. Heck, she'll probably be able to come back in a week or so—"

"She won't be coming back," J.T. said, his tone harsher than he'd intended.

Mike nodded in understanding. "Yeah, I guess she'd want to go back home to be with her family."

J.T. glanced up at the heavens. Caitlan's home.

Scrubbing a hand down his face, he cursed all the lonely years he'd have to endure before they were joined again.

Mike touched J.T.'s shoulder, his brow creased in concern. "Hey, man, you okay?"

"I'm fine," J.T. replied gruffly, already feeling bitter resentment settling in where his heart had been ripped out. He touched the medallion, the warmth comforting him. He wouldn't allow the sweet memories of Caitlan to fade. Ever. Not as long as he wore the medallion that kept her a part of him.

With a loud boom that reverberated beneath J.T.'s feet, the sky split open and huge drops of rain and sleet fell from the heavens. Everyone headed inside the barn to stay warm and dry. Not J.T. He stood out in the storm, waiting for the numbness of the cold, icy rain to make the sorrow and heartache go away.

Amanda sat silently in the Superior's summons room, watching as Mary paced back and forth, her gauzy white gown swirling around her legs. A week had passed since she'd left Johnny, and Amanda still couldn't shake the sorrow insulating her soul. The Superiors had given her the week off to recuperate from the emotional trauma she'd sustained because of the return of her memory, but Amanda knew she wouldn't recover from this particular heartache until Johnny joined her eternally.

She hoped she could survive that long without him.

"We *really* botched this mission up," Mary said on a heavy sigh, looking from Amanda to Christopher. "The memory of Amanda being on earth is supposed to fade. As long as he wears the medallion it will keep him vividly connected to all the memories of *Caitlan* being on Earth." Exasperation laced Mary's voice.

"He won't take the medallion off so we can confiscate it," Christopher told her. "He wears it night and day."

"Send Jay to fetch it."

"No!" Amanda said, springing from her seat.

Both Superiors stared at her.

Desperation clutched Amanda's heart. How could she explain that no matter how selfish it might be, she didn't want the memory of her time on Earth to subside from Johnny's mind. They'd shared so much, had forged a new love that superseded the old feelings they'd harbored for one another as children. In a short span of time she'd matured as a woman, had experienced a passionate love so beautiful and rare, she wanted it to flourish to its fullest capacity. That dream, she knew, was an impossible one.

"You know he cannot keep the medallion," Mary said firmly after a few tense moments had passed. "It's bad enough he knew who you were, Amanda, but he cannot continue on like this."

"I know," she whispered past the tight ache in

her throat. "But I don't want him to forget me."

Mary smiled gently. "He won't ever forget you. His love for you is too strong. You will always be a part of his heart, even without the medallion."

That wasn't what Amanda meant. She wanted to live in his memory with vivid clarity—Heaven help her, she wanted to be with him on Earth, feel his touch, experience the joy of his love. A chasm of loneliness echoed in her soul, and Amanda turned away, sure her misery reflected in her gaze.

The intensity of her emotions confused her. Why hadn't she felt this same anguish when she'd left Johnny the night of her eighteenth birthday?

"Amanda, what is it?" Mary asked, seemingly sensing her distress.

Amanda looked back at both Superiors, hoping they could help her understand the turmoil swirling in her. "When I first passed on to this plateau sixteen years ago I felt whole and complete and at peace with myself. Now, I hurt way deep down inside, this incredible sadness that won't recede."

Mary and Christopher exchanged worried looks.

"Why do I feel so different?" Amanda persisted. "Why do I miss him so much?"

"Your heart and J.T.'s blended before you left Earth," Mary finally admitted.

Amanda frowned. "My heart already belonged to Johnny. What do you mean?"

Mary grasped Amanda's hand, her touch comforting. "Just before you died, you both declared your love for one another at the exact moment, binding your hearts and souls more intricately than before."

Bewilderment assailed Amanda. "I don't understand. What will happen to Johnny?"

"He will be unable to love another for the rest of his mortal years," Mary replied sadly.

Christopher nodded his agreement. "Before we sent you on the mission we had designs to send him a sweet woman who would bear him two more children and see him through the rest of his years. Now, it will be useless."

"I'm so sorry," she said, ashamed for having caused so much havoc with Johnny's destiny. "I know He must be disappointed in me."

"No, child," Mary began, understanding and compassion threading her voice. "Once in a great while these things happen. He is very forgiving."

"Surely there is *something* we can do for her," Christopher said.

Mary shrugged. "Short of sending her back to Earth, there is nothing we can do for her heartache."

A slow smile curved Christopher's mouth. "We could petition to send her back as a mortal."

Amanda sat up, anticipation speeding up her pulse.

"Christopher," Mary admonished, squashing Amanda's hope. "That is a highly unorthodox suggestion! It's impossible."

He lifted a brow. "*Nothing* is impossible."

"It's an outrageous request." Mary dismissed the idea with the wave of a hand. "The board of Superiors will never approve of such an appeal."

"A love as strong as Amanda and J.T.'s is meant to be together," Christopher argued.

"I don't know about this," Mary persisted, her lips pursed. "You and your wild ideas," she mumbled, then offered Amanda an encouraging smile.

"J.T. is being extremely stubborn about letting go of the medallion and the memory of *Caitlan's* time on Earth," Christopher went on, championing Amanda's cause. He came up behind her and placed his hands on her shoulders, radiating reassurance to Amanda while he spoke to his equal. "They've both been through so much, Mary, in their previous life and with this mission. Now that their hearts are intricately blended, both of them will be miserable until they are once again joined."

After a long minute Mary let out a defeated sigh. "You always were a softy, Christopher." Her rebuke held a note of fondness.

Christopher beamed at the compliment and squeezed Amanda's shoulders for that one small victory. "I only believe it would be in everyone's best interest if we released Amanda to spend the rest of a mortal life with her eternal love."

Mary smiled, a sudden soft, dreamy quality entering her eyes. "It is kind of romantic, isn't it?"

"Indeed it is." Christopher's grin held triumph. "Who could deny these two the love that brought them together not once, but twice?"

Mary looked thoughtful as she considered Christopher's plea. Amanda held her breath for Mary's response until her lungs began to burn.

"Oh, I suppose you're right," Mary finally relented. "It would be difficult to deny two people so deeply in love and committed to one another. Not to mention that J.T. isn't being very cooperative with the medallion."

"Precisely," Christopher stated.

"Oh, Mary, Christopher, thank you!" Amanda breathed, smiling for the first time since her mission had ended. She embraced both Superiors. Happiness chased away the gloom of despair that had hung over her since her departure from Earth.

"Don't thank us yet," Mary warned gently. "Considering the delicacy of the situation, the board of Angel Superiors must vote on releasing you. Then *He* must give us his blessing. This is a very rare request, one that will change the course of fate, and must be thoroughly considered before a decision is made."

"I understand," she replied solemnly, trying not to get her hopes raised. Silently, she sent Him her own heartfelt appeal, praying he'd grant her and Johnny's love the opportunity to flourish in a mortal lifetime.

"We'll give you the board's final verdict by the end of the week," Christopher promised.

Five heavenly days never seemed so long to Amanda.

J.T. stood inside the corral, holding the end of the long lead rope clipped to King's halter. With softly spoken words, he coaxed the horse into in a wide circle, allowing the spirited stallion a minimal amount of control before he started the tedious breaking process. King's blue-black coat gleamed in the sun, and he tossed his head rebelliously. J.T. knew his display was more an arrogant act than any real sign of a threat.

Every day J.T. worked with King, usually in the mornings after the hands rode out and Laura left for school. Spending time with the horse made him feel closer to Caitlan's spirit. She'd left him with the special gift of King's fragile trust. Now, it was up to him to hone that bond into something more. J.T. was determined to one day saddle and ride the stallion that had shown so much promise before Randal started abusing him.

Randal. Anger welled in J.T. He still found it difficult to believe his own cousin had tried to kill him. Randal had admitted to everything. Open murder threats, even after Randal had been apprehended, combined with his murder attempt and arson, would land him years in prison. Even though it pained J.T. to see his cousin in such a position, he refused to compromise the safety of his family or his men. Pressing charges had been difficult, but his only choice. Randal had shown no remorse for his evil deeds, or for shooting Caitlan.

Familiar grief and anguish twisted J.T.'s insides. Two weeks had passed since Caitlan had left the Circle R never to return. Two weeks since he'd become nothing more than flesh and bones, his heart merely an instrument to pump blood. He was empty inside, more lonely and desolate than he could ever remember being.

Everyone believed she'd gone to County hospital, then flown back home to be with her family. J.T. knew better, but there were times when he caught himself believing the same thing . . . hoping and wishing that she was a mortal and would return to the Circle R to live with him forever.

She was gone from this lifetime, and some days he didn't think he'd survive the endless years until they were joined.

She'd told him the memory of her being on Earth and the pain of losing her would ease in time. With the medallion, everything remained sharp and clear, reassuring him that he hadn't dreamed Caitlan's brief existence—reassured him he wasn't slowly going crazy.

Some days, he truly wondered.

King's canter slowed and he whinnied soulfully, bringing J.T. out of his thoughts. Coming to a stop, the stallion's ears pricked forward and he stared off into the distance. A gentle breeze blew around them, rustling the leaves in a nearby tree and scattering a warm, spring scent.

"What is it, boy?" J.T. slowly approached the horse. King glanced at him and whinnied again but didn't shy away. Reaching up, J.T. stroked his hand down King's sleek neck. "Good boy," he murmured.

"You handle him well."

J.T.'s hand froze in midstroke and his insides twisted into a huge knot of trepidation. Caitlan . . . Amanda. Oh, God, now he was hearing her voice. J.T. clenched his jaw and squeezed his eyes shut to ward off the sweet voice filtering through his mind.

The corral gate unlatched, and King started forward, neighing softly. The lead rope tugged in J.T.'s hand, and he dropped it, allowing the horse to roam freely.

"Hello, King," came the feminine voice again, then light laughter that ribboned around J.T.'s soul. "I missed you too, boy," she said.

Drawing in a deep breath to release the tension coiling his body, J.T. opened his eyes and turned, finding Caitlan—Amanda, he corrected himself—rubbing King's muzzle just five short feet away from him. The horse nudged her hand affectionately, his eyes shining with devotion. J.T. stared at the two of them, the pressure in his chest increasing with each passing second. She looked so . . . real.

She glanced his way, her violet eyes dancing mischievously. "Is something the matter, Johnny?" The laughter in her voice belied the concern creasing her brow. "You look as though you've seen a . . . ghost."

"Oh, God," he choked, scrubbing a hand over his jaw. "I *am* going insane!"

A beautiful smile wreathed her face. "No, you're not," she said softly. Leaving King, she approached him. The breeze sifted through her silky brown hair, ruffling the strands like caressing fingers. Like *his* fingers itched to do. She stood in front of him, love and promises sparkling in the depth of her gaze.

He swallowed back the thickness in his throat, unable to believe she stood within touching distance. Curling his fingers into fists, he curbed the impulse to reach for her and haul her into his arms—to reaffirm that she wasn't just a figment of his imagination.

"Amanda?" he asked tentatively, afraid if he spoke too hopefully she'd disappear like a wispy curl of smoke.

She shook her head. The bright sun shot gold threads through her hair and added a slight flush to her cheeks. "Caitlan," she corrected. "Amanda died over sixteen years ago. You know that. She can never come back."

"You left me, too, and you said you weren't

coming back," he replied, unable to contain his bitterness over what had happened to her. To them. "So what are *you* doing here?"

She stepped closer. With a gentle smile, she lifted her hand and smoothed her palm inside the collar of his shirt. He sucked in a breath and flinched at the unexpected sensation of her fingers sliding over his collarbone.

"Caitlan," he said on a low groan infused with all the anguish filling his soul. "Why are you here?" he asked again, his voice brimming with misery. "To torment me even more than I already am?"

"No." Her fingers curled around the gold chain just inside his shirt and withdrew it and the medallion. Holding the pendant in her palm, she met his gaze steadily. "My Superiors are quite upset that you won't relinquish the medallion."

She'd come to sever the only link he had to her. The thought sent a shaft of anger through him. "I don't want to give you up, or the memories of our time together," he said fiercely, grabbing her hand and dislodging the medallion from her grasp. "I *won't* give you up, or let those memories fade, even if it means keeping the medallion. I love you, Caitlan."

Pleasure brightened her eyes and a warm, sensual smile curved her mouth. "I love you, too, John Thomas Rafferty. Even more than I thought possible." She gave him an upswept look that heated his blood. "They say the second time around is always better than the first."

Her subtle insinuation teased him, made him wish for things that could never be. His fingers circled her delicate wrist, and the pulse beneath his thumb leapt rhythmically, throbbing with vitality. His own heart thudded in unison with hers.

Damn. She felt so real, so warm. *So alive.*

He pushed her hand away, irritated with himself for hoping and believing in the impossible. "Dammit, go away!" he growled, spinning from her. He plowed both hands through his hair, nearly pulling out the strands in frustration. "I can't take this anymore. Just go away," he said, his voice a desperate plea.

When I turn around she'll be gone. Poof. Back to heaven where she belongs. He did, and she wasn't. Fury built in him until he wanted to explode. Why was she tormenting him this way?

"Go away!" he yelled, the words booming like thunder. Then he glanced around surreptitiously, grateful to find the area still deserted. King whinnied uncertainly at J.T.'s tone and cantered to the far side of the corral. When J.T. looked back at Caitlan, she was smiling—*smiling*, for chrissakes!

"I can't go away," she said, shrugging negligently. "Unless you want me to take your truck and find a motel room in town—"

"What the hell are you talking about?" he cut

in. He jammed his hands on his hips, his stance rigid with tension.

She tucked an errant wisp of hair behind her ear, secrets sparkling in her violet eyes. "Well, it seems you and I are stuck with one another for at least fifty-two years."

"Quit foolin' with me, Caitlan." He glared at her, annoyed with her nonchalance. "You're not making any sense, unless I'm due to die sometime soon."

"No, you're quite healthy," she said, strolling toward him with a sultry look in her eyes. "And the Superiors don't anticipate anything fatal befalling you for some time yet." Stopping in front of him, she reached out and toyed with a button on his flannel shirt, driving him to distraction with the innocent gesture.

Arousal hummed in his veins. "Caitlan," he warned. His low voice vibrated with longing and need, but he kept his control tightly leashed.

She sighed, as if put out by his insistence. "According to heavenly plan, you'll live to be eighty-six, and you'll have three more children and sixteen grandchildren." Leaning close, she walked her fingers up the front of his shirt, her expression playful. "You'll grow old with one woman. A very special woman."

His lips tightened. "Stop it, Caitlan. That won't happen." How could she think he'd marry another woman when his heart was nonexistent without her?

"It will," she vowed, sliding her palm back inside his shirt, this time to seek out warm, firm flesh, then his nipple. She rolled the nub gently between her fingers, and he drew in a quick breath, his eyes flaring. A siren smile lifted her lips. "Do you think you can put up with me for another fifty-two years?"

"Oh, God," he groaned. He stepped back, stunned at what she was suggesting. His spine bumped against the fence railing, preventing him from escaping her.

She laughed lightly. "There you go again, Johnny, looking as though you've seen a ghost."

Realization slowly dawned, and he stared at her incredulously. He found it difficult to believe Caitlan could truly be his in this lifetime. "How . . ." He couldn't even find the words to ask the hundreds of questions whirling in his mind.

The look in her eyes told him she understood his confusion. "Between you keeping the medallion and me moping around heaven, Christopher and Mary decided to put us both out of our misery." Caitlan went on to explain how their hearts had entwined so intricately when they'd both declared their love at the same moment. "However, the board of Angel Superiors had to vote on my release, and they almost didn't discharge me from my guardian duties because of the drastic changes it would cause in destiny." She glanced heavenward, smiling appreciatively. "But then He made the final decision and blessed us with a full, rich life together." She transferred her gaze to J.T., her expression impish. "And here I am."

J.T. glanced down the length of her, then back up, frowning. It couldn't be as easy as that. "You took a bullet for me. Everyone thinks you went back home, to Chicago. What will they think when they see you?"

"I'm sure they'll think I recovered from my injury quite nicely." She pulled back the collar of her shirt, showing him the puckered flesh she'd acquired as a result of being shot. "And then they'll think I came to my senses and realized I couldn't live without you."

He glanced at the stitched wound, realizing she'd saved his life not once but twice. This whole angel business still boggled J.T.'s mind, and he knew it would take him a while to understand it all.

"Are you really real?" he whispered, disbelief still holding him captive.

"Flesh and blood." Holding his gaze, she moved closer, until the tips of her boots pressed to his. "Touch me, Johnny."

Tentatively, he raised his hand and cupped her cheek, his fingers caressing silky soft skin. The muscles in his stomach tightened. She closed her eyes and sighed, nuzzling into his palm. A frisson of heat spread up his arm and throughout his body, awakening senses that had shut down when she'd left him. Caitlan felt real, alive; but then, he'd thought that while she'd been a guardian angel.

Then touching her wasn't enough. Sliding his fingers into her hair to cradle the back of her head, he slipped an arm around her, bringing her body flush to his. She flowed into him, becoming a part of him. Reveling in the way her soft contours matched his harder ones, he stared into her bright violet eyes, seeing every feeling in his heart reflected there.

She linked her arms around his neck. Lashes fluttering closed, she pulled his head down to her. "Kiss me, Johnny," she breathed. "I need you."

With a groan of complete surrender, he dropped his mouth over hers, drinking in the honeyed taste of her. The silken glide of his tongue stroked over hers, then deeper, demanding her acquiescence. She yielded, body and soul.

He broke the kiss, breathless and aroused. Hugging her to him, he absorbed her warmth, wishing they were in the privacy of his bedroom, instead of standing out in the corral with King watching them.

Then he decided he didn't really care, because he wanted everyone to know the depth of his love for Caitlan. Holding her left hand, he knelt in the dirt on one knee before her. She glanced down at him, surprise and a touch of delight entering her eyes.

"Johnny?"

"Caitlan, will you marry me?" he asked, his voice strong and sure.

She smiled, her dimple creasing her cheek. "Seems I've heard those words before."

"Except this time I'm never letting you go," he said, twining their fingers together. "You're mine, Caitlan. Now and forever."

"Yes, Johnny," she whispered, love and eternal loyalty glistening in her eyes.

"You'll marry me?"

"Try and stop me."

Joy poured through him, and his body shuddered in relief. Standing in a fluid motion, he kissed her again to seal their vow—a slow, lazy kiss that held the promise of so much more. Her love wrapped his heart and soul in contentment, filling every aching, lonely part of him.

Minutes later, they came up for air, lightly pressing their foreheads together. Caitlan's finger followed the gold chain around his neck to the medallion between them. Holding the golden pendant, she pulled back to look into his eyes.

"I don't think we'll be needing this anymore."

"Not even for a keepsake?"

She shook her head, her mouth lifting in humor. "No."

He sighed, reluctant to give up something that held so much significance. Taking off the medallion, he held it in his palm, a sudden knowledge filling him. Looking deeply into Caitlan's eyes, he smiled. "You're right. I have everything I could ever want right here in my arms. And I don't want your Superiors looking over our shoulders for the rest of our lives."

"Then let's give it back."

J.T. stepped back and looked up at the stretch of clear blue sky above them, holding the medallion tightly in his palm. Gratitude wove through him, and he whispered, "Thank you for giving me Caitlan back."

"Take care of yourself and Caitlan. You won't be given another chance."

Stunned by the voice he heard out of nowhere, J.T. glanced sharply at Caitlan.

She laughed lightly, seemingly having heard the advice, too. "No, you're not going crazy," she confirmed.

"Thank God," he murmured. Looking at the medallion one last time, he took a deep breath, then drew back his arm and pitched the gold pendant straight up into the air.

He grabbed Caitlan's hand, and together they watched sparks of sun dance off the gold disk as it soared higher and higher into the sky. A second later, a flash of light burst the medallion into glittering stardust that shimmered like tiny angels up into the heavens, showering love and peace all around them.

An Angel's Touch

Time Heals
SUSAN COLLIER

Tired of her nagging relatives, Maeve Fredrickson asks for the impossible: to be a thousand miles and a hundred years away from them. Then a heavenly being grants her wish, and she awakes in frontier Montana.

Saved from the wilderness by a handsome widower, Maeve loses her heart to her rescuer—and her temper over the antics of his three less-than-angelic children. As her angel prods her to fight for Seth, Maeve can only pray for the strength to claim a love made in paradise.

_52030-3 $4.99 US/$5.99 CAN

An Angel's Touch

Where angels go, love is sure to follow.

Don't miss these unforgettable romances that combine the magic of angels and the joy of love.

Daemon's Angel by Sherrilyn Kenyon. Cast to the mortal realm by an evil sorceress, Arina has more than her share of problems. She is trapped in a temptress's body and doomed to lose any man she desires. Yet even as Arina yearns for the safety of the pearly gates, she finds paradise in the arms of a Norman mercenary. But to savor the joys of life with Daemon, she will have to battle demons and risk her very soul for love.

_52026-5 $4.99 US/$5.99 CAN

Forever Angels by Trana Mae Simmons. Thoroughly modern Tess Foster has everything, but when her boyfriend demands she sign a prenuptial agreement Tess thinks she's lost her happiness forever. Then her guardian angel sneezes and sends the woman of the nineties back to the 1890s—and into the arms of an unbelievably handsome cowboy. But before she will surrender to a marriage made in heaven, Tess has to make sure that her guardian angel won't sneeze again—and ruin her second chance at love.

_52021-4 $4.99 US/$5.99 CAN

Dorchester Publishing Co., Inc.
65 Commerce Road
Stamford, CT 06902

Please add $1.75 for shipping and handling for the first book and $.50 for each book thereafter. NY, NYC, PA and CT residents, please add appropriate sales tax. No cash, stamps, or C.O.D.s. All orders shipped within 6 weeks via postal service book rate. Canadian orders require $2.00 extra postage and must be paid in U.S. dollars through a U.S. banking facility.

Name_____

Address_____

City _____ State_____ Zip_____

I have enclosed $_____in payment for the checked book(s). Payment <u>must</u> accompany all orders.□ Please send a free catalog.

An artist with no palate for business, Margaret Masterson can create a world of excitement on canvas, but her love life is as dull as flat paint. Then a carriage ride on a foggy night sweeps her back to Regency London and the picture-perfect nobleman she's always yearned for.

Preoccupied with marrying off his rebellious sister, Adam Coleridge has no leisure to find a wife of his own. Yet when fate drops Maggie at his feet, the handsome earl is powerless to resist the desire she rouses in him. But with time fighting against them, Adam fears that not even a masterpiece of love can keep Maggie from becoming nothing more than a passionate memory.

___52060-5 $4.99 US/$6.99 CAN